PIAZZA
CAROUSEL

JULE SELBO

Dakota, Inc.

Grazie to Anthony Fellow for bringing me to Florence, to Mark, Lilliana, Sally, Marie and Mary for solidarity, to John Paine for his insight, to my Big Boy Posse and At Rise. And to the Mud Angels and all Florentines for loving their city and its art with an inspired passion.

Prologue

From my mother's journal. Written fifty years ago.

My day 3, Florence

Cimbabue's Crucifix. Rescuers wade through the flood waters inside Cathedral Santa Croce now to get to it, lift it down. Maybe 600 years old. They say water up to Christ's halo, wood saturated with sludge, the paint and gold leaf washed off. Rescuers collect gold flecks from muck. Water receding. Some. Saw Zeffirelli with camera and crew, filming. Famous people sending money. Drawing attention. It can only help. Cold. Wet. Fingers raw, skin cracking. Tired but no time to rest. News of the Crucifix brings thirst for more. Such hope here, if you don't have faith it is too sad. But all around me. I see hope. 'Grazie' is the word I hear the most.

Jenny
November, 1966

Chapter 1

I celebrated my thirty-fifth birthday alone last night.

At the last minute—actually just hours before our flight—my husband announced he couldn't join me in Florence this year.

"Big deal at the office, sorry, but can't get away…" Stan's voice on the phone sounded rushed.

"But we're all packed…" I remember looking at the carry-ons at the door; they were like anxious kids wanting to get to a birthday party.

"All my stuff's in the TravelPro bag—lucky I said we should pack separate."

"I slipped one of my sweaters into your…"

"Just take it out. It's a drag I know, Lyn. But being junior partner now and…" I could hear in his voice that he was multi-tasking. Going through files. Motioning to his para-legal for coffee. "I was only going to stay for a few days anyway. You'll be busy."

"Stan, you always join me."

"Come on—'always'? Three years isn't even a tradition yet."

"It is to me."

Stan jokes that I ritualize everything—from our Sunday morning coffee, bearclaws and hard copy of the *New York Times* to our monthly hot-mud-soaks at the very retro-hippie Manhattan spa hidden in the village streets close to the Hudson River.

"Stan, we booked the cooking class with the butcher in Panzano and…"

"Damn. I'm coming." I thought he had changed his mind, but it became evident he was talking to someone in his office. The next words were to me. "Lyn, sorry, gotta go. Meeting. Big client—big deal. This is a good one for me—prove my stripes. Have a good flight."

"It won't be the same."

"Don't make me feel guilty. Babe. Gotta go."

"Okay, I'll call when I get there. I love…"

He had rung off. I growled in frustration.

Susie, my best friend since junior high, stuck a hand out from behind the closet door.

"Found it." She waved my silver-gray airplane-sleep-pillow in the air. "It was behind those silly beach hats we bought on the Cape. Remember, I tied the ribbons on them?" Susie stepped out of the closet wearing an oversized sun hat, its brim draped with a striped grosgrain that hung down her back to her waist. She reacted to my slumped shoulders, my less-than-excited face. "What's wrong?"

"Stan's not coming to Florence." I pulled my sweater from Stan's TravelPro.

"Really? What did he say?"

"Work."

"Oh." She disappeared from view as she put the beach hat back in the closet. "You'll be okay, you've got so much to do. You have a deadline on your book. You have teaching. Now he won't get in the way. Won't distract you."

I was sarcastic. "Thanks for being pissed with me."

"Are you pissed?" She moved to me and slipped the sleep-pillow onto my computer case.

"I feel like I should be. But he always makes me feel like he's right."

My cell phone buzzed.

Susie looked at the message on the phone's screen. "Your Uber's here. You're cutting it close." She grabbed the handle of my bag and was quickly out the door. She called over her shoulder. "I can come back in and lock up. Your emergenc-key's in my pocket."

We headed into the street, the warm New York City afternoon. She nodded to the waiting driver. "She's your ride. Lyn Bennett. Airport." She saw her reflection in the car's window. Smoothed her blonde hair so it fell perfectly over her cheek.

"I should remind Stan to cancel the wine tour in Chianti." I searched for my phone. "Maybe he'll find a way to get away."

Susie put her hand on my arm. "You love Florence. You're amazingly happy there. You're excited, right?"

"Of course I am, but…"

"Concentrate on what your mom said."

I was off to spend a month 4000 miles away to honor her request: 'Find me in Florence'.

Susie hugged me, really close. "And you know I love you."

She was squeezing me so tightly my neck ached. I was suddenly worried. "Why do you sound super serious? Are you sick?"

She laughed and pulled back. "No, I am not sick! I just wanted to tell you. To remind you."

"In case my plane goes down."

She screeched. "Don't even say that. Bad luck!"

"It's because you feel sorry for me because Stan bailed. I mean, I guess he's right. Our schedules aren't always going to match. Work-wise."

Susie kissed both my cheeks. "It'll be for the best. Don't miss your plane."

I could smell her perfume. She closed the door. I am not sure if she heard me, but I knew she could read my lips. "Love you too."

She waved as my Uber sped away.

So here I am, at the Caffe Gilli in the heart of Florence. Alone. Ordering my morning caffé americano. My mother's journal, the leather-bound pages that I climbed into the attic to retrieve after her funeral, is in my bag. Its weight is a reminder of my promise to myself. Follow her memories. Rebuild her moments. *Find me in Florence.*

And while I'm here, I'll work with a group of aspiring writers. Not teach, really, just help them explore their unique voices in a city renowned for its art, innovation and inventiveness. No rules. Give them an opportunity to dismiss the 'should' from their creative psyches and just let their work be what it is going to be.

I should try to take my own advice. I have been struggling to find the shape of my next book: my mother's story. Find what it will be.

The tuxedo-jacketed waiter delivers my caffé americano in a beautiful silver pot along with a cornetto semplice on delicate china. Most people here call the cornetto semplice a croissant—they are shaped the same but I know not to expect the French flaky buttery crunch and lightness. The consistency of the Italian cornetto is closer to a brioche—doughier and yeast-ier—and most are topped with a slightly-sticky orange-scented glaze and some are filled with custard or Nutella or jam. Best to hold it with the paper napkin it's served on—or commit to sucking on fingers the rest of the day.

And I don't want to do that in Florence. It's a sophisticated city. Not a walk-around-suck-on-your-sticky-fingers city.

There's a man sitting at a table on the far side of the open-air patio, an espresso near his resting hand. Sharply dressed in a pressed Egyptian cotton shirt, cut in the form-hugging Italian style, a silk tie, pleated dress pants and shined Italian leather shoes. The left side of his face droops from cheekbone to chin; I wonder if this is a result of a stroke. Some nefarious clot that delayed blood reaching the brain for a dangerous period of time. This man's half-handsome, half-fascinating face is in repose; his eyes closed, an appreciation of the early morning sun on his face. I wonder if I will have a stroke—today or tomorrow, in a year, in thirty years?

Like my mother.

I remind myself to have red wine with my mid-day meal. Harvard Women's Health Watch recommends red wine because it contains resveratrol and suggests it is a possible stroke deterrent. The article also mentions regular exercise as a deterrent. I prefer the wine regimen. Susie would say "Alla vita al vino! To life and wine!" Susie is a force, she's fabulously sure of everything.

I am waiting to feel that. Someday. To feel like I'm in the right place at the right time doing the right thing with the right person. It's not the "grass is always greener" syndrome, it's different than that. My mother would say to me over and over, "Lyn, my heart, you will feel settled when you live—with everything in you—even down to your toes. You can't always 'watch'."

"Mi scusi, signorina. Perdone."

Startled, I look up.

The early sun obscures his face. He looks tall. He holds a scarf in his hands. My scarf.

"Signorina, e suo?" Is this yours?

Yes, it's the inexpensive, bright red scarf I bought at a kiosk yesterday for 5 euro on a rare it's-my-birthday-live-a-little-dare-to-shine whim. Thought I'd brighten my nearly-everyday black shirt, gray pants and black boots ensemble. I like color, sometimes I just feel I appear ridiculous in it. In black and gray I am just one of many. I had wrapped the scarf around my purse handle because it was too warm on my neck this morning. It must have slipped off my bag and fallen to the ground. I take the scarf. "Grazie, grazie."

He walks to another table. Sits. "Un espresso, per favore," he says to the passing waiter. Because no one tips in Italy—unless it is an extra special experience—waiters rarely put forth any effort to please the customer. A person's lucky if service is attentive in any way. However, this waiter nods at the tall, dark-haired man in a white shirt and tie, they exchange a friendly greeting. He might be a regular patron.

Sport coat and dark jeans. Polished leather shoes. A leather brief-case. There is so much leather in Florence—on people's backs, on their feet, in shops, in kiosks, some expensive and buttery soft, some rough and stiff and inexpensive. The city smells of leather.

Across the piazza, street vendors push their carts into place, be-gin to set out their wares. I sigh, think of last year. Stan and I sat at this table. Stan ordered the American breakfast at the Gilli: eggs and toast. Italians use eggs to bind their frittatas or they hard-boil them and slice them onto sandwiches—they don't torture and sear eggs and then pile them in a pale-yellow mound on a plate for a morning meal.

Stan laughed. "It's my Nikes and the scrambled eggs. Screams USA."

I told him it was also the way he took up space; the American 'importance glow'.

"And what's wrong with it? Americans like to have space around them. And everyone thinks they're important. It's part of survival." He winked at me. "But maybe my halo's a bit bigger than average."

I teased and told him that he was as far from a 'saint' as anyone could get.

"Last night took you out of that category too, blue eyes." His eyes traversed my neck and breasts—I knew he was re-savoring the hours we'd spent in bed. He went back to chewing. "Anyway, who wants to be a martyr?"

"Or kind." I laughed.

"Or good."

"Or generous."

"Not in a lawyer's nature." He winked again.

"At least you don't wear a baseball hat, Bermuda shorts and knee high tube socks. Someone has to see you eating breakfast to get the first American hint."

"You hold these Italians up too high, Lyn. Things take too long to get done here."

"I appreciate that they know how beautiful 'the old' is…"

"You just don't like things to change. And you're always ana-lyzing too much and observing. And making up stories." He leaned over and kissed me. "But that's what writers do, right? That's why you get invited here to teach. 'Cause you know how to observe and get it all down on paper." In the last two years, Stan had carved out a week from his work schedule to visit me in Florence during the month-long Writers Now Retreat seminar. This visit will be entirely different. Seeing Florence through my alone lens. Not clouded by how Stan sees it.

Caffe Gilli is in the Piazza Carousel. That's not its real name, it's what I call it because with the multitude of piazzas around every cor-ner, it's hard for a relative newbie to Florence to keep them straight. I like to imagine the site as it once was, an old Roman forum with a temple dedicated to Mars—the city's patron god before Christianity was adopted. Then in subsequent centuries, it was home to the Flor-ence ghetto and a maze of shops called the Mercato Vecchio. Then it changed. Its official name is the Piazza della Repubblica, it was gutted in a movement in the late 1800s called *Risanamento*. Risana-mento, in Italian, means rehabilitation. Now, I look at the high-end cafes, hotels and shops that frame the square, the bustle of the well-heeled. I've taken tours with historians who put on very sad, 'how could they have done such a thing' faces, and claim the risanamento of this historic piazza was not rehabilitation but ruination. Change. Unavoidable, perhaps.

From here, it's a five-minute walk to Florence's most famous bridge, the Ponte Vecchio, and a five-minute walk in another direc-tion to the Il Duomo de Firenze, the city's most famous cathedral. In the center of the Piazza della Repubblica is the beautifully antique carousel filled with brightly painted wooden horses. So, it's easy to say, "Let's meet at the Carousel." Everyone knows it—its golden frame studded with sparkly oversized faux gems, its gilded kings' carriages, fresh flowers in pots and the lilting accordion recordings of Neapolitan ballads. If Paris is officially the city for lovers, Flor-ence has to be a close second. I did read an article recently that named Las Vegas as a top city for lovers and that made me wonder about the very notion of romance.

The voices of two stylish Italian matrons taking seats at the table next to me invade my thoughts. Their dialogue is piercing. A simple conversation in Italy can sound like a murderous argument; these two may be talking about a lunch menu or how to get red wine out of an heirloom rug yet they continue to top each other in volume and pacing, making loud and staccato declarations, always using their hands to punctuate strident opinions. They order cappuccinos like the waiter should have read their minds and go back to blaring their conversation as if they were the last two women in a deaf world.

"Matteo, come stai." A thin woman in a Prada dress and Ferragamo Vara pumps—I saw them both yesterday in the shop windows on Via Tornabuoni—approaches the tall man who rescued my inexpensive (okay, let's call cheap) bright-red scarf.

So. His name is Matteo.

He stands, pressing his tie to his abdomen so it doesn't swing into his espresso. I can see his profile; strong brow, Roman nose, a smile that creases his cheek. The stunning woman kisses him on both sides of his face. He signals to the waiter to bring her an espresso. She takes a stack of brochures from her shoulder bag and places them on the table. They divide the brochures and confer. Now they are both checking their iPhones. I can't hear their voices over the Italian matrons but they seem to have a rhythm and a quiet ease with each other.

I finish my pastry and my caffè americano. Check my watch.

Almost time to work, writers will be arriving.

I head towards the Ponte Vecchio and turn left and walk along the Arno, the river that runs through Florence. It's moving fast today, the result of the sudden rain last night. It's early, the start of the day, but lovers are already taking selfies—kissing and canoodling on the stone walls between water and city. The mediocre violinist I remember from last year and the year before, his instrument case open at his feet to attract tourists' coins, plays *The Godfather* love theme. This is the only tune he seems to know. Professors, students, shop workers, dog walkers, businessmen and women hurry to their destinations. A tour bus pulls up and a gaggle of Chinese tourists descend onto the street to march behind a guide waving a bright green flag through the air.

I lift my bag onto the river wall, feel the shape of my mother's journal within it. I gaze into the Arno, think of the time my mother spent here, fifty some years ago. Her stories of how the Arno catastrophically flooded Florence in 1966—priceless Roman and Renaissance artwork and irreplaceable ancient books and maps and prints and centuries-old letters housed in the city's museums and churches and libraries were in danger. One day, when she was helping me streak my dark curly hair with orange highlights for a junior high Halloween party and we were waiting for the sprayed-on color to dry, she took a large book off the shelf in the hallway. We sat on the edge of the bathroom's tub and looked at a map of the Tuscan region and she explained how the LaPenna and Levane dams in Valdarno, 34 miles away, ruptured during heavy rains and sent over 70,000 cubic feet of water per second towards Florence, traveling at almost 40 miles per hour. "Think about it, Lyn," she said later as we drove onto the Cross Island Parkway in Queens so she could drop me off at the party. "Water was coming into the city as fast as we are driving right now—as fast as the cars on the other side of the highway are going past us." She told me how most of the electrical power was out in Florence. "It was incredibly dark at night, dots of yellow light from candles danced in the air." I was barely listening—I remember I was worried that the orange streaks in my hair were too scary-stupid for my Halloween party and that my dance moves would suck.

I twist the two thin silver bracelets on my right wrist. These were my mother's favorites; she wore them every day. She would move them up and down her arm as she planned trips for the family to visit Florence. But my father always found some excuse—and those trips never happened. "But you must go someday, Lyn," she said. "Florence inspires." She showed me photographs she kept in a small wooden box in her closet. Photos of herself as one of the

Angels of the Mud—'Gli Angeli del Fango'. As the river water rose
and fell, volunteers arrived from around the world to wade through
the detritus in attempts to rescue Florence's rich history. My mother
was in the photographs; part of the Mud Angel rescue teams. This
was before she married my father and settled in New York. "At least
3 million books, Lyn—and probably more—and over 1500 works
of art—probably more—were damaged or destroyed in that flood. I
wanted to save everything, we all wanted to save everything. But we
couldn't." She sighed. "So many lost treasures."

After her first stroke, when I sat next to her on our comfy living room couch near the warmth of the fire my father had built in
the fireplace, we thumbed through her picture books on the flood.
She spoke slower and slurred a bit, forgot some words, but I could
tell memories were dancing in her head. She told me that when she
arrived in Florence, workers were clearing up the landslides on the
roads. I looked at the old black and white photos of the aggressive
waters that tore open oil tanks and caused slippery naphthalene to
gush into the melee. "600,000 tons of mud, Lyn, and oil and trash and
so much, so much water. So many homeless, over 10,000 families."
She told me how hospitals were evacuated and needed medicines
were lost. We paged through to look at Donatello's 1454 wooden
statue of *Magdalene Penitent*. "She was in the Baptistery of San
Giovanni. This…" She traced the concave lines of the emaciated
body of Mary Magdalene, the long, pained, distraught, disturbing
face in the photograph. "She is starved, see? From living in the des-
ert where she meditated—hating the world, hating herself, trying
to forgive—after the crucifixion of Christ. She was almost buried
in muddy water—but she withstood. The water rose to her large
hands—see—they're awfully big—see how they're pressed to her
chest, always praying."

She said it was sad because the flood could have been avoided; the Arno, Florence's life-blood, had flooded to devastation levels before, the first one recorded was in the 12th century and then
again in the 13th and 16th centuries. We studied reproductions of
Leonardo da Vinci's drawings. "In the early 1500s, he drew up these

plans for river control. But no one paid attention, he wasn't popular with the rulers. The Medicis. Da Vinci was very flamboyant, Lyn, and even though Florence was relatively open, seems there was a 'don't ask, don't tell' sort of policy. Da Vinci may have flaunted too much." She sighed, told me how even Michelangelo, decades later, designed dams, but no projects were ever brought to fruition. Change did not happen.

And so, in 1966, Florence experienced great devastation.

And now I am here, fifty years after the fact, feeling the outline of her journal in my bag. It holds clues to stories she never told me, that I missed the telling of. Photos she had never shared with me. I look down into the river, fight the wave of sadness mixed with guilt. I see myself sitting next to her hospital bed, her thin, dry, beautiful hand writing on the pad of paper we used to communicate. She wrote: "Honeymoon suitcase. Attic. Bring?" I told her of course I would. She continued her effort: "Find me in Florence."

But I didn't get to the attic, I didn't bring the suitcase—or those memories—to her in time.

Chapter 2

I press the buzzer and hear the heavy, oak doors unlock. They're at least twelve feet high and four inches thick. The wood in the door's center panel is carved, an artist's vision of St. Daniel of Padua, a martyr known as the patron saint of prisoners. Hundreds of years ago, this building was used as a jail; it now houses artist lofts and Zumba classrooms and a floor dedicated to the Writers Now Retreat, the brainchild of ex-pat Mildred Evan who writes and illustrates children's books.

It takes a strong push to gain entrance. Ahead of me, the worn, stone stairs that the incarcerated once climbed, lead to the third floor. I enter a spacious room; the ceiling is fifteen feet high and features a faded fresco of frolicking cherubs playing harps and reed pipes. I hear, "Hi there, I'm Beth Ann, I recognize you from the picture on the back cover of your book. You're Lyn." She waves her soft fleshy arms to take in the other four writers in the room. "We all been gettin' to know each other."

Beth Ann's drawl drips with Southern sweetness. I know, from her application to the seminar, that she's in her forties and from Atlanta Georgia. Today she favors a sequined t-shirt and jeans that accentuate the weight on her lower hips. Her unnatural blonde hair is teased and dowsed with hair-spray. Her brown eyes are friendly but I see a wariness too, as if she knows her affability can make her a target.

"Fantastico—as they say in Italy," I joke. I pull off my scarf and tuck it into my bag.

"We just all love your books, we were just sayin' that, that we just love your books." Beth Ann is talking fast, excited.

"'Course they're not like best sellers, but—ya know—ya gotta have more plot for that. I like action, just to let everyone know right off." This comes from the stocky lounger in the only cushioned chair in the room. He wears a Seattle Mariners baseball cap, and I surmise this is Vic. After reading his application, I had predicted a mix of testosterone and ADHD and I realize now I may not have been far off. His bravado is palpable, like a slap in the face.

"But she won awards for her two books." Beth Ann decides to be my champion. She turns back to me. "I can't wait for your next one. It's been awhile."

I had written two books in three years. Then it took me four years to complete this last one. "I've got a new book on my publisher's desk now. Waiting to hear what they think"

"Oh that's scary." Beth Ann looks me up and down. "You look taller on your book jacket."

"I'm 5 foot 8." I laugh. "Is that tall enough?"

Vic guffaws. "Not for the NBA."

"Taller than me." Beth Ann smiles.

I look to the slim, multi-ethnic woman in her late twenties, with deep honey-colored skin and moss-green eyes, standing alone, near a tall shuttered window. "You must be Rivenchy—from Aix Au Provence." I move to shake her hand. From the self-story she provided on the application, I knew she grew up in Paris, Casablanca, Miami and Vienna and lives now in the south of France, in the penthouse of a high-rise building that overlooks the Mediterranean Sea, paid for with trust fund money. Her father is an American business-man; her mother is a Moroccan psychotherapist. Rivenchy holds her model-proportioned body with tight control; her spine straight, chin high, nose flared as if ready to smell danger. She touches my hand and pulls away. I wonder, in a quick flash of judgement, if danger—to Rivenchy—is anyone getting too close.

Beth Ann is still seeing herself in the hostess role. "And this is George. I thought he looked like the youngest here, but then Rivenchy is only 27 and George is 30. So, he's second youngest."

George's hair is thick and unruly; he's picking at indiscernible lint on his khakis. I know he attended Johns Hopkins University and studied mathematics. And then an event changed his life. As I take my notebook and pens out, put them on a small table near one of the chairs, I venture—testing his desire to share. "It's interesting how you happened to be living in Florence, George."

George swallows and reveals a quiet voice. "Ahh, well, I won the lottery when I was 20. I was living in Baltimore, Maryland. But…" He pauses, as if re-living the thought process he experienced years ago. "It was busy there, and a lot of concrete, and there was a cafeteria below my dorm room and I could smell the old grease they used. Since I could, I decided to move to Europe. Eventually I liked it here, in Florence, the best."

Vic is curious. "So, it was like a big lottery? Tons of money? You have to pay taxes on that right?"

I want to keep on track. "We'll get to questions later, over wine maybe—if George doesn't mind the interrogation."

"Wasn't interrogating." Vic defends himself. "But sure, hey no offense." He nods towards a portly man in his 50s, wearing a sweat-er vest and short sleeved shirt. "His name's Charlie."

"Yes. I'm Charles, a Brit. You can tell by my accent. Live here with my wife, in Florence, outside the old city, where the tourists don't go much."

I recall Charles' short biography: As a young man with high hopes, he didn't score well enough on his exams to go to a top university in Great Britain, so he took a job in the distribution arm of an important but snooty publishing house and submitted articles on fly fishing and foxhunting to sporting magazines under a pseudonym, Richard Hindquarters. The articles became popular and were collected into a book; the book was eventually distributed by the snooty publishing house. Charles was contacted—as Richard Hindquarters—to meet with Prince Philip at Buckingham Palace and share sporting tips. He never did tell the royal personage his real name. The next day he quit his job in distribution to concentrate on a novel about a fox.

Charles is sharing with the rest of the writers. "My wife was transferred to Florence a few years ago. Then the textile company was sold to a Chinese businessman—you'll find that is happening more and more in Italy—but my wife speaks Italian, Chinese, German and, of course, her native English, therefore she retained her job."

Beth Ann coos. "Lord, how can people be so smart?"

Charles continues, "Well, we appreciate the opportunity because this place is magical."

"Yes, every stone has a story." I laugh but I know it is true. Every ancient stone has witnessed passion or joy or love or lust. Loss. The old streets frame centuries of tales. "Let's get our chairs in a circle."

Beth Ann picks her computer bag off a chair, moves next to George. "I got a new laptop for this trip. My little baby I call it, kinda holds my life." Beth Ann laughs. "I know it sounds silly but this little three-pounder knows the most about me."

Vic interrupts. "The computer knows nothin' that you don't tell it."

Beth Ann giggles. "Well, hon, I suppose that's true. But it's where I share my most innermost thoughts and worries and dreams. Maybe that's why I feel emotional about it."

Charles moves a chair into the circle. "It's actually quite common, isn't it? Because much of the capabilities of our brains remain a mystery and we're not able to store and retrieve thoughts and information in a reliable way, our electronic devices have become our surrogate memory banks. You are right." He nods to Beth Ann. "Everyone loves a friend who remembers everything we think or say or do."

"Thank you for your understanding, even though I don't understand much of what you said." Beth Ann grins.

"Is that why you write, big guy?" Vic eyes Charles' rotund belly.

Charles considers, "Are you asking if I write in order to feel as if I have a friend who will listen to me?"

Vic says, "Sounds ridiculous even as ya say it, right? Come on, let's get real. It's just about telling a story from here." He taps his forehead. "About knowing how to grab someone by the balls or tits or nose or ear and seizin' on them so hard they decide not to sleep or eat till they get to the end of the story. Not about telling a friend what you're feeling, that's for blogs." He looks to me. "What do ya think?"

I sidestep, "I think there are lots of reasons."

"Now that you finished your latest novel, what are you going to write next?" Beth Ann leans towards me, her mascara is thick on her heavily shadowed eyes.

"About my mother. Her time here in Florence. Fifty years ago. During a disastrous flood."

Beth Ann's brow furrows. "What happened to her?"

"She helped out, retrieving damaged art. I have notes on some of the stories she told me over the years. I've read a lot, talked to people. Now I am trying to find someone who may have worked alongside her. Knew her in those weeks. If I get lucky. After she died I discovered some attic finds—a few more clues." The journal in my bag is full of my mother's quick notes. Torn tickets. Drawings. Worn photographs she had never shown me. "Actually, first thing tomorrow I meet someone at the British Institute. So cross your fingers." My heart beats a bit faster with anticipation. But I push on. "Let's concentrate on all of you. I hope you'll embrace a purpose for this time—to be writers. Not tourists. Not fitting your writing in between searching for the best pizza or pasta or Florentine steak." I hand out sheets of paper—my restaurant picks. "I've made a list of some of my favorites so you can start with these if you like—they're all in different neighborhoods. Finisterrae or La Menagere for early morning coffee, Il Pizzaiuola for pizza, Il Caminetto for fish, Cinghiale Bianco for wild boar pasta, Angiolino's for risotto, Osteria Santo Spirito for mussels and there are more listed."

Beth Ann's eyes light up. "Oh, wonderful."

I continue, "It doesn't matter what support or discouragement you may have come across before. It now matters that you will be writers here—today—with stories to explore."

"Ya mean we have to start something new?" Vic asks.

"Old or new, my hope is that you'll work from where you are now, in Florence. What being here brings up." I pass a stack of notebooks and bag of writing utensils to Beth Ann. She takes a cranberry-red notebook and a ballpoint and passes the options to Charles. "Within a five-minute walk of this classroom is the Piazza Santa Croce. There are cafes there, there are places to sit and people-watch, there are kiosks filled with all sorts of things. The church—called Basilica di Santa Croce—is magnificent. Michelangelo and Galileo and Rossini and Machiavelli are buried there. There are smaller side streets behind the basilica filled with artists' shops. I want you to people-watch. Construct a character piece inspired by the most interesting face you see. Don't overthink it. I'll see you back here in forty-five minutes."

George clears his throat. "I'd like to use my own pad of paper. My legal pad here."

"That's fine." I wave to them as they disperse. "Ciao."

I walk across the hallway to check in with Mildred. Her gray hair hides her face as she bends over her desk; she's brushing a wash on a piece of artist's paper. She has a sketch of a princess sitting atop a huge pea propped up beside her; must be for her latest book. Her watercolor and pastel sets are open. Her colored pencils and markers stand in an old chipped coffee mug that is stenciled: "Home is where the heart is. Got one?" I hate to disturb her when she is working. I back out of the doorway.

"How are they?" she says, not looking up.

"I'll tell you later. I can see you're working."

"Tell me now in case I have to deal with any personalities."

I give her a rundown of the temperaments and other character traits I picked up in the short initial meeting. "I surmise it's going to be interesting."

"Always is. Wasn't it your birthday yesterday?"

"Yes. Thanks for remembering."

"Stan sent something here."

"He did?" I suddenly feel better.

"In the mail. Or Fed Ex. I guess that's still mail. Over there in the corner."

I see a thick mailer with my name on it. It feels soft, nothing hard inside.

"I'll treat you to a birthday hot chocolate at Café La Posta one of these mornings. Soon as the weather breaks."

We both like to get up early. And Café La Posta's hot chocolate is thick and perfect on a cold morning. "Supposed to cool down next week."

"Next week then. You pick the day. Where are the students by the way?"

"Sent them on a 45-minute write—get them looking at Florence as a fresh canvas. Hopefully."

"Glad you're back, Lyn." She looks up from her design and her light gray eyes smile at me.

I give a little push, "Stop taking time off from your work to chat. Get back to it."

She groans and concentrates on choosing a particular colored pencil.

I move back to the seminar room with the Fed Ex mailer. I'll open it later, when I'm alone in my apartment. I hold the soft, squishable mailer and head to the window, open the shutters to feel the warm sun. My body tingles in appreciation. In my mind's eye, I see Stan, the first time I saw him, walking through the front door of the house in Queens with my brother. I was twenty-six and working as an assistant in a literary agency in New York City. My brother Rick, who is two years older than I am, started asking a group of buddies over to my parents' home to watch football with my father on Sundays. The gatherings would start in early September and go all the way through playoffs and the Super Bowl. I visited my mother most Sundays, she was having more and more trouble remembering where things were: the forks, the plates, her coat, gloves, pictures of her sisters who had perished in a car accident in their teens. She'd sit at the kitchen table while I cooked a week's worth of meals and put them in Tupperware containers—labeling them M for Monday, T for Tuesday, W for Wednesday, TH for Thursday, F for Friday and S for Saturday. Sunday, I would show up to cook again.

My brother introduced me to Stan as the "wanna-be writer who makes great pasta and answers phones for a living." I referred to him as the bartender with dreams of being a senator. Rick did go into local politics five years ago and made the right connections and got backing from the right businessmen and is now running for State Senator.

I was a wanna-be writer. Every morning before work and every late night after work, I occupied booths—some lumpy, some comfortable—in various all-day, all-night coffee shops around Manhattan and worked on my first novel. With great anxiety, I finally submitted it to Starrk Publishing through an editor friend of Susie's-then-boyfriend who wanted Susie not to break up with him. Susie and I danced like mad-women the day his favor paid off, my novel was accepted and slated for publication.

Susie broke up with her then-boyfriend a week later. She toasted me. "I only stuck with him for you, Lyn. Don't forget that."

One Sunday, after the Saturday Susie and I spent celebrating till closing at a chain bookstore that stocked my book on the 'New Fiction' shelf—sneaking gulps of champagne from the split bottles in our purses, Stan came into my parents' kitchen carrying a copy of the neighborhood paper that had done a small story on my small success. He re-introduced himself to me as a lawyer who planned to marry me within the year. I asked him if he'd had one too many beers. His eyes were too bright and he agreed that his fifth beer could be giving him too much swagger. He laughed, like this was going to be a moment we would remember forever. There was a crumb of pizza crust on his sweatshirt. His wiry body seemed to fill the kitchen and I was aware of his sturdy legs in the worn jeans that rested on his hip bones and of his Nikes—the ones designed for runners. I avoided taking in his incredibly square jawline and his persuasive grin. I know he felt his effect on me and enjoyed the fact that I was uncomfortable. He waved the weekly paper in the air as he exited the room. "Congratulations."

I quickly ducked out the back door. But Stan got my phone number from my brother. Rick would give away anything for a potential vote. Months passed before I agreed to go out with Stan. I didn't want him to feel like he could assume I'd just capitulate to his will. But he was persistent and that impressed me. Reminded me of stories my mother told me of how my dad had pursued her, convinced her to move from Kansas to New York to start a life with him. True love. Something I wanted.

All these thoughts as I drop the Fed Ex mailer into my bag.

I hear the seminar writers coming up the stone stairs.

Chapter 3

Beth Ann's most interesting face:

She's a pretty ordinary-looking woman and she sure hugs a quiet spot on the old wall by the big Italian church. Her freckly nose is buried in a map. She looks 45 or so, and nothing is going right for her and she hopes that something on the map will give her a boost. But she sure doesn't hold much hope because her ex-husband has just won the custody battle and now she can only see her two kids once a month and on every other holiday. She used to take drugs because she was unhappy and she was a pharmacist so the pills, they were just there and she didn't resist and so she lost her license. But now she's clean and wants to distract herself from how much she hates herself. The map she is looking at is only lines and colors and names of streets to her because she can't decide on any destination.

It's after class and I'm still thinking of Beth Ann's 'face' as I walk towards the river and the Ponte Alle Grazie. I gaze at the personalities displayed on the faces of people I pass—the complacent, the smug, the anxious, the unsettled. I stop on the bridge and watch the rowers, in colorful sculls, glide by on the brown water. An elderly woman in a long, well-worn black coat stops near me and looks down into the slow-moving river. A soft, warm breeze bathes our faces.

"Questo ponte e stato fatto saltare in aria," she says, raising her eyes to me. She's telling me that this bridge had been blown up. She points to the quiet Oltrarno neighborhood, "I lived there." She points in the other direction to the crowded, loud, café-rich and leather-shop studded Santa Croce area. "Couldn't get there. War."

I knew, in August 1944, the Germans, in a futile attempt to stall the Allied forces in World War II, blew up the seven-arched Ponte Alle Grazie along with three other bridges in Florence; the Ponte Vecchio was the only one spared. Deliberate ruination, not only of history but of a city's conduit to families, to sources of food, income and jobs. I've seen pictures of mothers trying to cross the river over the huge broken hunks of the bridge that filled the river, moving around destroyed boats and military vehicles, trying to reach a child, or a grandmother or a husband and the disbelief and despair on their faces. I look at the silver-haired woman, realize she would have been a young girl in 1944. She nods at me, picks up her nylon shopping bag and moves off.

The unsettled feeling continues to nag at me. I push it away.

I've stayed in the same apartment in the San Niccolo neighborhood every September for the last three years and it feels, to me, like a cozy nest. The bedroom is large; out its window there is the sliver of sky between adjacent buildings and a view of the hills that shelter the exquisite, historic town of Fiesole. In the late afternoon, the same black cat with one white paw pads across a nearby tile roof and settles in to gaze at the bedroom window and mew loudly—as if he is the solo performer in an outdoor theatre. Stan named him Frankie Firenze.

The apartment can be rented short-term and Mildred knows the owner, a Florentine named Antonio Franco who always wears a brightly colored tracksuit. The apartment building is on a small narrow street leading to a small piazzetta (a mini-piazza) with an enoteca (a regional wine shop with a small food menu), an osteria (local food is served at communal tables) and trattoria (casual, seasonal food and usually open noon to midnight) and a ristorante (white tablecloths, open for lunch and dinner hours only) and a small vegetable market, a tabbachia, coffee bar and fermenteria—a small shop stocking everything from dishwashing liquid to shoe pads to diapers to Halloween masks and toys. It's a quiet neighborhood and when I am there, I always feel as if I've lucked into a special place.

Signor Franco also owns the Hotel Cascini, a romantic boutique hotel of 15 rooms, next door to my apartment building. Vines hug its ancient exterior walls and large pots of fragrant flowers stand guard at the entry doors. The receptionist, Lucia, embraces retro fashion, wears her hair in a new style every week and has the extra key to my place—in case I ever need it. Lucia is twenty-four and very sure her boyfriend is going to propose marriage on her twenty-fifth birthday, which is just over a month away. Today Lucia's hair is aqua-colored and piled rakishly but perfectly on top of her head. She waves at me, bright and cheery, as I pass by.

I use my key to enter my apartment building.

I make myself a coffee and take the seminar writers' pages from my bag. Vic's most interesting face catches my eye:

A really hot woman took her tit out—brought the baby boy's hungry maw to it. Kid was really happy. And yeah, I was happy watching. And then I saw him. The guy with the hat. Hands in his pockets. I sat and watched this guy with the birthmark on his left cheek—shape of a lizard, its tail a gash—right under his eye. I wondered. About murder.

Makes me laugh. A man determined to see what he wants to see. Rivenchy's page—her most interesting face—slips from my grasp, I pick it up off the floor:

He undressed her with his eyes, layer by layer, her silk blouse flew away in the breeze, her rose-colored camisole barely containing her bosom separated in slow motion, the skirt that hugged her buttocks like a glove slipped off and puddled around her six-inch alligator heels and revealed her thong that was only a wisp of lace not even attempting to cover her finest temptation. He is mesmerized and the small table cannot hide his attraction. He placed a stack of a hundred Euro bills on the table. She set a slim hand on the bills and her bracelet sparkled. She demanded high payment for her services. He followed her.

I wonder who the woman was that Rivenchy saw and decided to write about. What prompted this flight of imagination. I wonder if this reflected a truth or if this is how Rivenchy sees the world?

I take the Fed Ex mailer from Stan out to my small balcony that overlooks the ancient wall framing the Bardini Gardens. The Bardini connects to the famous Boboli Gardens behind the Pitti Palace but, on its own, it is small and tourists rarely find it. I sip my coffee. Open the mailer. It's my New York Giants sleep-shirt, well-worn and incredibly soft due to years of washing and drying in our apartment's machines. I can't believe it; why is Stan sending me this? Disappointed and a little irritated, I read the note: "Noticed you forgot to pack this. Know you like to sleep in it. I'll call you, we need to talk."

We need to talk.

What does that mean?

Not exactly the "Happy Birthday" sentiment I was expecting.

Maybe he's being sentimental. Wants to remind me that this Giants jersey had once been wrapped around my diamond engagement ring. I smooth the white letters on the blue shirt. The edges are frayed, the stitching now thin. Before the official proposal, Stan had become a regular addition to the family. He helped rebuild the back porch, putting in the wheelchair ramp for my mother when her ambulatory skills diminished. He helped re-wire Dad's 1969 Mustang convertible. Dad figured he should sell the car to settle the hospital bills—but Stan made a deal with him; he'd give Dad a down payment on the car and then pay $200 a month until it was paid off, as long as my Dad drove the car and kept it in top shape. This allowed my Dad to get ahead of the medical costs and still tinker with and drive his 'Stang. It turned out Stan had asked my Dad's approval to officially float the marriage question—so Dad knew what was planned for the beach walk Stan asked me to go on after the Super Bowl game. Susie had wanted to join us but Stan grabbed our jackets and pulled me quickly out of the house while she was distracted pouring celebratory beers for my brother and his friends.

Stan and I walked Rockaway Beach. It was deserted—and the air was cold. Stan put a hand on my arm and stopped me, took out the jersey that was stuffed in his pocket. "Lyn Bennett, you made me wait. You made me prove myself. And that was okay 'cause I want to marry you. Can we do this?" He looked enormously sincere and long-suffering and sweet. He pulled me in so tight and kissed me so long I couldn't breathe. He extricated the jewelry box from the jersey fabric and slipped the simple diamond engagement ring on my finger and gazed at me, wanting me to officially agree. "You gonna wear this? Show it to everyone and let them know you're off the market?" I stared at the ring and nodded. His serious face broke into a smile. And then we were both so excited that we broke into a run and chased each other along the edge of the water as the breeze grew stronger and the last leaves of the season flew off the trees and swirled across the sand.

When Starrk wanted to publish my second novel, Stan insisted I needed to shop the manuscript to a more prominent house. He used his connections to arrange for it to be read at one of the major publishers. They were interested. Stan insisted on looking over the contract. He negotiated a more advantageous royalty fee for me if the novel sold well. His firm represented some heavy-hitter fiction writers and he gave the book to a few of them and three agreed to review the book. When it was released, Stan went on Amazon and bought multiple copies every week to boost the sales numbers.

So, within a year of the post-Super Bowl beach walk, and my acceptance of the simple diamond engagement ring and Stan's suggestion that we pick a date in the near future so that my mother would be able to be a part of the event, I was cooking M, T, W, Th, F dinners for Stan.

It was a beautiful ceremony. Susie was my maid of honor. My mother sat next to me at the reception and squeezed my hand tightly while the toasts were made. Her eyes bore into mine—it was like she wanted to share something with me but her faulty brain-to-speech capabilities denied her. Her eyes filled with tears of frustration and she squeezed my hand harder.

I look at Stan's scrawled note again: We need to talk.

Chapter 4

Later. The sun is about to set.

I walk back across the Ponte Alle Grazie and head down one of the narrowest streets in Florence, the Borgo Santa Croce. I arrive at the 13th century building; the stone street is dug up, stone pavers piled to the side. Orange safety cones and yellow caution tape alert pedestrians to avoid a deep hole that's been dug to allow the doctoring of water pipes well past their prime. It is a constant struggle to keep Florence's services in working order. I hug the walls of the buildings to avoid the dirt and broken pavers and make my way to #4. This is where I take Italian lessons.

Valentina is my teacher and she does not appreciate tardiness. I check my watch again. Two minutes to spare.

I pull the buzzer for Parola, the language school, and am buzzed in. I climb the wide stone stairway—three flights. I hear footsteps coming towards me and I look up.

Matteo walks down the stairs; the tall and broad-shouldered man from the cafe this morning who retrieved my scarf. I feel my face light up, "Ahhh Matteo, buonasera," comes out of my mouth before I even think that this man, of course, would not recognize me—I am just another foreign interloper in his city, invisible to its permanent population. I can't believe I just called him by his name. So intrusive. So assumptive. So weird. Not like me at all. I want to disappear.

Matteo stops. Clearly wondering how I know him.

I stutter, my face feels hot. "My scarf, la mia sciarpa. Questa mattina. This morning." I feel ridiculous.

A faint recognition.

"Si. Si. Your scarf. Caffe Gilli."

There's sudden sweat in my armpits. "Mi dispiace." I'm sorry, I mumble.

His brow furrows, wondering if I intend to say something else. I have nothing. He turns and moves on, waving, "Ciao." He takes the last two steps and disappears around the corner. I can hear the heavy door closing behind him as he leaves the building.

I feel like the awkward, nerdy character in a teen movie that has been caught stalking a crush. I try to shrug it off but I can't ignore how my heart is racing. And then I giggle, shocked at my reaction. I hurry up the stairs.

Valentina is twenty-eight years old and teaches the complex, complicated, captivating and frustrating Italian language. She has beautiful Mediterranean features: dark hair and eyes with arched brows, a wide forehead and olive skin. She is very strict and extremely opinionated. She continually tells me that the pronunciation of her native tongue is not my strong suit. She looks appalled when I put the accent on the wrong syllable and lectures that, for example, if I put the accent on the first syllable of **an**cora, I am saying 'anchor', if I put it on the second syllable, an**co**ra, I am saying 'again'. And when I do not lovingly roll the 'double L' of words like 'bella', 'bellissima', 'pennello' and 'ombrello' on the roof of my mouth, she glares as if I am maligning all things Italian. But she does not give up and continues to put me through drills, assuming that multiple repetitions will eventually take effect. She does comment on my quickness of understanding the basic rules of the language—like proper singular and plural conjugations and gender specific words. Gender specificity with nouns is a crazy idea to most Americans because we use 'the' so universally and happily. Valentina reminds me that my strength—my cognition, my knowing the right word and article—and my verbal usage are far apart.

la casa—house (feminine singular)
le case—houses (feminine plural)
una casa—one house (feminine)

il caffé—coffee (masculine singular)
i caffé—coffee (masculine plural)
un caffé—one coffee (masculine)

I wonder aloud often, during class, who decided a flower (il fiore, un fiore) was a masculine word and an automobile (l'automobile, un'automobile) was a feminine word. Valentina shrugs and says that is the way it is and that is how it will be forever and even wondering about it is a waste of time. Just memorize.

25 euro later.

Armed with a few more words and phrases, I pull open the huge door that leads to the street. Florence, at sunset, stirs something in me. The soft lights from the small shops flow onto the aged stone streets, there is no hawking or harsh come-ons from the shopkeepers; they are proud and patient. The outdoor tables at the bars and cafes are topped with candles and appear as friendly stops on life's road, they welcome and promise a break from planning and doing. Perhaps the adjective is 'infectious'. I feel light and homey and happy as the glow of the dropping sun blends into the night.

The cafe at the end of the block, Moyo, is filling up for its popular early evening apertivo. For the price of a glass of wine or beer and one or two more euros, a customer can graze buffets of pasta, sandwiches, roasted and pickled vegetables, prosciutto, olives and cheeses. Italians meet friends and sit for hours, nibbling and talking and then, finally, go off to dinner. Many tourists and students-studying-abroad pile their plates high and return to the trough too many times and consider it a cheap evening meal. Stan would stack his plate with focaccia, cheese, salami and potatoes and I would pick a few olives and peppers and savor the camaraderie of the tradition.

I see him.

Matteo sits at a corner table on the outdoor patio, gazing in my direction. He stands when he notices me. The patio's string lights sparkle behind him. He waves and motions to the empty chair across from him. "Prego. If you would like."

Excuses do come to mind. Jet lag. An imaginary appointment with my writing seminar administrator. Plans to see a movie. A waiting husband. An explanation that I have a book contract that needs to be fulfilled and I should be back at my apartment, that I should be writing.

That word that keeps popping into my brain. Bothering me. 'Should'.

I realize Matteo is watching me, waiting for my answer. There's something about his body that takes up just enough space. He has a nose that has a jag in it, I wonder if it had been broken when he was a child. The feeling I felt on the stairs of the language school building returns; I'm the teenager with raging hormones determined to make her look ludicrous. Speech escapes me.

"You know my name. And I do not know yours." He looks at me as if challenging me to be spontaneous. Italian men are famous for looks like these.

But he has rescued my scarf and I have embarrassed myself on the language school's stairway. In a way, there is a connection. And this is casual, happenstance. And a glass of wine and apertivo, being part of an easy Italian tradition, is suddenly appealing.

"I want to know how you knew my name. And I enjoy practicing my English." His hair is thick and a little long, it hangs to the top of his crisply ironed shirt collar. He uses his hand to sweep the falling lock of hair off his forehead. "Prego."

I surprise myself and accept the chair. I explain: "I heard—the woman you met for breakfast after you saved my scarf—she called you Matteo."

"Ahhh. You listen to others talk at their private tables." He pours me a glass of wine. "Try the vermentino."

I confess, "Maybe I do listen a bit. My friend calls me 'the ultimate observer.' But the woman did say it pretty loud. It is your name—Matteo—right?"

"Yes. And yours?"

"Lyn."

"One of the short American names."

"We do tend to get to the point."

"With a 'y'."

Yes.

"We don't use the letter 'y' in the Italian language. Here it might be Liniana. Or perhaps Linia. Unless you have a middle name—"

"Katherine."

"With a 'k'?"

Yes.

"We don't use 'k' in Italian. It will have to be Caterina. With a 'c'. Linia Catrina."

"That makes me sound like an incredibly sturdy princess chosen to marry some bearded Polish prince and live in a snow-covered remote castle outside Krakow."

He laughs. "Si, it does. Liniana is softer on the tongue."

"My mother did call me that when I was young…Liniana."

His English is excellent. And he appreciates my attempts at Italian. He tells me his younger sister, Valentina, works at Parola, the language school.

We are amazed she is my teacher.

There is a bit of family resemblance. In the eyes. Deep brown. And his hair, it's thick and wavy. And attention to the details of the Italian language must run in the family.

"So you know my sister."

"I do."

"She can be a pain in the ass."

I laugh. He is incredibly easy. And, in addition, we totally agree.

"But she believes the Italian language is the most romantic. Because of Dante."

I speak slowly, trying to get the line of one of Dante's poems right, "Ho incontrato te e…and…I write…qui inzia una nuova vita…"

"I first met you and now, in 'scrivo', I write how I…begin a new life." He smiles. "Your accent is…not bad."

"There's no reason to be dishonestly kind." I laugh, enjoying myself. Even with my terrible pronunciation.

"Did you learn that poem with Valentina?"

"No, my mother taught me that phrase, she loved everything Italian."

I tell him about my mother joining the Mud Angels in 1966, after the flood.

"Ahhh, one of our rescuers. Was she assigned a specific place?"

"She volunteered—or was assigned—mostly at the Biblioteca Nazionale."

I tell him how she told me stories about standing in lines with her peers at the National Library to pass soaked and sodden ancient books to higher, safer ground where restoration experts logged in every item.

"I have seen many of the experts' records, covered in dirt and stains. Meticulous as they could be, but the conditions were very bad. Very wet."

I find myself just talking, sharing my mother's memories. I tell him I am here to explore her story, gather more research and seek out specific information. I do know that during the intense weeks, there was very little heat or ready food—but wine was a constant.

"As always." He smiles and I see a slight dimple in his cheek.

I tell him of her tales about taking quick naps in a sleeping bag in a cold and damp hostel, squeezed in with Germans, Brits, Aussies,

Americans, Japanese, Greeks and Italians and how they all huddled together for warmth and begged each other not to eat too much garlic or too many beans.

"And now you will write this story of your mother—of times when closeness was maybe too close."

"She stayed for two months to help." I said. And then suddenly I remembered how, after a specific recollection one Christmas, my mother had looked out at the snowy and cramped streets of Queens and said softly, that she would've stayed forever, maybe, but she had promised my father she would be back in time for their wedding. This memory takes me back. Tears nearly spring to my eyes and I quickly ask him about his work. "Now, tell me about you."

Matteo is one of the acquisition directors at the Uffizi Museum. He works on a team that authenticates Renaissance art. He also pursues clients who may be willing to deed their important holdings to the museum—if and when they find themselves feeling burdened by the responsibility of taking care of an artistic treasure. Or if they are feeling their mortality and want to deed their holdings—with proper plaques to ensure their largesse will not be forgotten—to the museum.

"I would like to thank your mother for her service as a Mud Angel."

"She's passed on."

"I am sorry to hear that."

"She never came back?"

"No. It never worked out."

"That's too bad."

"I have her journal with me—I just recently found it. From that time. I'm going to try to match her notes to places."

"I would like to see it. And I am sure others would like to see it too. Florentines like history."

"It's a lot of disjointed entries. Need to connect the dots."

"There is a man in charge of the Restoration Center at the library who was a Mud Angel, full of stories if he is in the mood. A family friend. Perhaps their paths crossed. He is difficult to convince to make time for anything but work. But maybe there would be a chance."

"I would like to meet him. If I could."

Matteo nods, as if tucking the possibility away. "That flood is a time we commemorate and those personal items—the memorabilia—can add much to a gallery showing on the topic."

"My mother would have loved to be part of anything like that."

"Then that is why, perhaps, we have been put in each other's path." He suggests, if I have no plans—and if I would like—that we continue our talk over dinner at his friend's restaurant. He leads me westerly on Via dei Neri to a small street, Via Magalotti, and towards the family-run restaurant l' Che Ce' Ce'. Matteo tells me it is run by Gino and his nephew, Alberto. "Gino is over 70, he has prepared food in the small kitchen for 45 years and Alberto wants him to retire. But Gino, he likes the rhythm of the kitchen, cooking the primo—the pasta—and the secondi—the meats and fishes—and the sharing of limoncello with customers."

Via Magalotti is a narrow street and the restaurant's windows shed the only light into the darkness. Crisp white curtains frame the window. Matteo tells me Gino's wife died last year and now Gino rarely leaves the restaurant before midnight and he is there again mid-morning to prepare the mid-day meal for customers. He naps during the afternoon break in the small office off the kitchen. And then he mans the stove again for the dinner hour.

Gino kisses Matteo on both cheeks. I am introduced as "…an American, a writer and a daughter of a Mud Angel." Gino looks overly pleased and pumps Matteo's hand, "Va bene, va bene, va bene." Alberto stands back, watching. His face looks set in a smile, but his eyes are not friendly.

"She is married. She is only here for four weeks, working as a teacher. La maestra. She is letting me practice my English with her," Matteo tells them.

Gino nods. "American women are very independent."

Alberto grimaces. "Like all women now. Not just Americans."

Matteo slaps Alberto on the back. "You are right, amico. And ultimately, si, that is lucky for us."

Alberto's scowl makes it clear he does not agree.

Gino announces he will serve us his specialties. He mentions the recipes were born in his grandfather's hands, they have been in the family for generations. And then more customers arrive; Gino and Alberto leave us to greet them.

Matteo fills my wine glass with a pinot grigio from the Castello Banfi winery near Siena. He tells me it's a relatively young winery, by Italian standards. "I can trace my family back 400 years. We have been Florentines for at least that long."

"I have no idea who my relatives were 400 years ago, 300 years ago or even 200 years ago," I admit, feeling remiss.

"You must."

"The roots—and branches—of my family tree are pretty unexamined."

"We Italians cherish the past. It is still alive with us. Americans are always busy with the present." He shrugs, as if to say this is simply an interesting observation. Not a judgment. "What can you put together?"

I set out what I know. "All right. My family: my father's father's father—my great-grandfather—emigrated from Ireland and was a fireman in Queens—that's just outside Manhattan. My father's father—my grandfather—choose plumbing as a profession because he didn't like fireman's hours and figured installing toilets didn't come with too many death-defying risks. My dad, when he was about twenty-two and ready to join the plumber's union, saw an ad in some car magazine about a 1956 Chevy Corvette Muscle Car for sale in Wyoming. He hitchhiked across country; the plan was to buy the car and drive it back to Queens and be a very cool single guy with a super fabulous car. He met a girl mid-way in middle America, in Kansas…"

"And that was your mother, who became one of our Mud Angels."

"Yes. Si."

"What was her name?"

"Jennie. Jennifer."

"Mmmm. Not an Italian name. Was she called 'Ginerva' while in Italy?"

I don't know. "She never told me."

"It's not quite Jennifer. But, as close as we might get." He folds back the cuffs of his shirt, his hands are strong and veined, his lower arms are lean and muscular.

Gino brings perfectly shaped vegetable flans to our table. "Buon appetito." He smiles and moves back to the kitchen. Matteo nods for me to take a bite; I do. I nearly groan with pleasure at its intense flavor of creamy asparagus and parmesan. "Oh my."

"Si. Very good." He takes a bite and looks at me expectantly. "Tell me, how did your parents meet in Kansas?"

"They happened to be standing next to each other, waiting in line to see the newest James Bond movie, *From Russia With Love*. My mom's father owned a Hop and Burger franchise—it's all about beer and burgers in Kansas. After my dad met my mom, he stayed there—in the Midwest—he told me he worked making fries and burgers at the franchise until he could get my mom to agree to marry him."

"The Corvette? Did he forget about it?"

"Oh no, my father never forgot about his cars. She finally agreed to marry him, with a few caveats. She wanted to finish her art history degree first but she would transfer to Queens College. When there was a plan in place, my Dad got on a bus to Wyoming, picked up the Corvette, drove back to Kansas and picked her up and they headed back East. She lived in the dorms on campus. With her father's help, my dad opened a franchise of Hop and Burger in Bayside, Queens. He had to pay a bit of protection to the Sicilians…"

Matteo laughs. "Yes, it is amazing how American movies love to tell us all about the Sicilians controlling things in New York."

Alberto arrives with small plates—two grilled shrimp resting on creamy polenta infused with caramelized onion, tomato and olive oil. The scent of the dish is exhilarating, the flavors concentrated and heady.

"*The Godfather* is one of my personal favorites," I tell Matteo as I sip the wine that was poured to compliment the wonderful bite of food.

"But there is also *Goodfellas, A Bronx Tale, The Professional…*"

"You like American movies."

"Very much."

I ask, "Have you seen *Married to the Mob?*"

"If it's going to be about the mafia in America, I prefer it a bit realistic, not a romantic thing—or a comedy. I like *Brooklyn Rules*, also *King of New York, Find Me Guilty,* and of course *Donnie Brasco*. Italians fascinate everyone." He raises his eyebrows; his eyes twinkle.

"We do make a lot of films about Italians."

"But *Gomorrah*, we Italians made that movie."

"I don't know it."

"I saw it on my 27th birthday, that I remember for some reason. Almost ten years ago. It takes place in Naples. Where the mafia—well—is 'alive and well' even today. At least 'well' for them. Or not. It is a very difficult film about the state of young people caught in the crime world. You might find it interesting. So now, get back to your family."

I continue, "Well, one Hop and Burger turned into eight—mostly in Queens and Brooklyn. When Hooters opened around 2002 in the New York area, it dug into my dad's business a bit—and when he realized my brother and I weren't going to take over, he sold out. He was ready to retire."

"America is built on the idea that anyone can become anybody. That is one reason your country is very appealing."

"A plumber's son can open a burger joint, yes. Precisely possible."

Gino delivers the salmon. It is coral pink, set on a streak of basil pesto cream. He refills our wine glasses. "And so far?"

"Magnifico, sono molto soddisfatto," I say and they laugh, enjoying my lame and slow pronunciation combined with my effort to express myself in Italian. "Magnificent, I am very happy and satisfied."

Gino pats me on the shoulder and heads back to his kitchen.

I cut into the salmon, it flakes into succulent bites, "You studied American history?"

"I had a teacher at the University. He loved everything American. Cowboys, oil men, the Wild West, the freedom to be someone new—to shape one's own destiny perhaps."

"We like to believe that if you get an education, it's pretty open."

"And is that true?"

"For some. But there are other factors. Like life. Sometimes life can get in the way of opportunities."

Matteo pours more wine for us. "Tradition. The family. As you know, very important here. I followed in my father's footsteps."

"Did you want to do something different?"

"No, I like knowing my father's work will continue. It makes sense to me because I know of his passion. In fact, today was a good day. There is a specific acquisition for the museum that he had in play when he died. One that I may be able to bring to completion. It would be a coup. For Florence. For Italy. For my family name."

"Really. A painting? A statue? Map? A book? What is it?"

"I cannot say more. I'm sorry. I should not have mentioned it. But you are easy to talk to and I hope it will come to be. The acquisition. I plan. To make it closer to the possible."

Gino brings over a bottle of limoncello and a bottle of grappa. We opt for the grappa. It's technically a brandy, made from stems and seeds of harvested grapes and it's supposed to aid digestion, but its 50% alcohol level can go straight to my head—so I have no idea if it ever affected the workings of my stomach. Gino tells me the best way to drink grappa is to fill the glass one-quarter full and wait for 10 minutes so the liquor can rest. Then take a tender whiff of it and let the aroma touch your senses; don't bury your nose in the glass too long, the vapors of the alcohol will tire out the sense of smell. Take a sip, wash it around your mouth and then swallow to experience the full taste.

This we do.

After we say goodnight to Gino and Alberto, Matteo walks me across the Ponte Alle Grazie towards San Niccolo and to the door of my building. We pass the hotel and Lucia, just about to finish her shift, waves to me from behind the desk. She is always peppy.

Matteo smiles. "Grazie mille, Liniana."

"No. Thank you. Really. Grazie mille." I open my door with my key and step inside. I take a glimpse over my shoulder, and he is already walking away, down the quiet street, past the bust of the Madonna that was carved in the 15th century and mounted into an alcove in the stone wall. Matteo turns and waves and then continues on.

I mutter to myself, "Buona notte."

What a surprising night.

Chapter 5

Early morning.

My cell phone is ringing; the identification reads 'Stan'.

"Lyn, how's it going?"

"Fine. Is everything alright?" I blink—long blinks—and my eyes finally focus on the view out the window; the clouds are thick. It looks like it will rain. "Thanks for my Giants' shirt. I'm wearing it now."

"I was thinking of coming over."

"Here?" I'm surprised. My morning wits are not yet sharpened. "Did plans change? What about your meetings?"

"I'll get to Florence on Friday. I can do my work virtual for a bit. My plane lands Friday, just after four. Through Paris."

"I have students in the afternoon, I don't know if I can meet you at the airport."

"I'll see you at the bar at the Hotel Bernini. Get there when you can."

My mind is clearing; I sit up in bed. "This is a surprise, this is great…"

"Need to see you."

"Need? I got your note. 'Need' seems to be the word of the…"

"Gotta go. Getting the high sign here, meeting about to start." Stan's voice quickens.

I want to talk more. "Why 'need'?" I tease. "Is this because you missed me on my birthday?"

"Sorry, gotta go be impressive. See you soon. Bye."

He has hung up.

He'll be here in two days.

The cheery Italian doorman at the building that houses the British Institute has a round, pink face. "Brits are on the second. The door is at the end of the hallway, it is painted the color of a pink rose. You have to ring bell."

"Thank you. I'm here to meet someone and I don't want to be late. I'll take the stairs."

"Ahh, you are American."

"My accent?"

"Si. But too, Americans do not dawdle. They take the stairs. The Brits can wait, they take the elevator. But it is very small and very slow so—si—you make the right choice."

I charge up the stairs, my energy high, looking forward to meeting Mrs. Marybelle Price, a former Mud Angel from Manchester, England who has spent the last fifty years in Florence.

I ring the bell and I am buzzed in. A woman with thinning orange-tinted hair sits behind the reception counter. She wears bifocals with baby blue frames that rest low on her nose and are accented with a sparkly strap that drapes over the neckline of her pale blue cashmere cardigan. London newspapers are piled on top of the counter. The walls behind the woman who is paying no attention to me are covered with weeping shelves, weighed down by heavy hardback travel books by British authors. She peers up at me and frowns. "Are you a member? I don't recognize you."

"I'm here to meet Mrs. Marybelle Price."

She sniffs, grabs at a tissue box and dabs her narrow nose. "We put her in the ground yesterday. She is no longer available for any meetings, I'm afraid."

The excitement that had propelled me up the stairs peters out like air from a pricked balloon. I lie because I want to believe my lie. "I'm sorry, I am not quite following."

"Mrs. Price has breathed her last, dear. It was very sudden. But she was in her nineties. The gin and tonics were last night. Right here."

I look at the reception area, the worn chintz-covered couches, the properly tired and mismatched low lamps, the collection of porcelain teapots and bottles of gin on a table. I see the poster-sized picture of Marybelle Price topped with a garland of braided lilies. Mrs. Price's sturdy face is a study in dewy wrinkles; deep crinkles frame large gray eyes, she favored penciled-on eyebrows and bright magenta lipstick painted on thin lips. A red headband secures her permed hair from dropping onto her face and large pearl studs gild her earlobes. Her eyes gaze right at me, as if welcoming me, as if promising conversations. It's disconcerting; her letter had been cheery and bright, she wanted to take a close look at my mother's photos, wanted to share her memories. "Oh my dear, I'll tell you everything, every peep that lingers in the corners of my old brain. I was a mod rocker from Tottenham Court Road, arrived in a miniskirt and a red velvet bomber jacket, absolutely unprepared. But diva went out the window when I saw all that muck and water and I got new ugly duds and went to work. We'll have tea and speak of your mother."

My disappointment overwhelms. I feel absolutely selfish.

The receptionist blows her nose. "Her husband, he was Italian, he passed on five years ago. She never did have any children. Her niece was here but she flew back to England this morning. She was a hoot, Marybelle Price."

"We were going to talk about her experience as a Mud Angel." My voice is flat.

"Oh. Bad timing."

Her lack of empathy feels cruel but I remind myself that Mrs. Price's demise has taken a toll on her and my frustration means nothing to her. "I'm sorry about your friend."

"Well, when people get old, it's best to make time sooner rather than later. We do wear out."

I know she's not scolding me personally, but a familiar guilt sparks.

"Let's salute her." The woman with the orange hair pours two shots of gin from the bottle on her desk. Hands me one and raises her shot glass towards the full color poster. "Saluto!"

We down our gin.

Chapter 6

The writers in the seminar room seem apprehensive. Charles moves the chairs across the stone floor and into a circle. I open the shutters on the tall windows and notice that the sun has burned off the clouds.

Everyone is a bit cautious. Reluctant to read their fresh material. They pour themselves coffee from the thermos Mildred has set on the table. Finally, Beth Ann throws her hands up in the air and says she'll dive in. She reads:

Some people would not consider one day a long time, not even two days when you know tests are being done and the medical people are looking at the war of tiny cells you can only see in a microscope. It's a war cause those cells are using Billy Jo's body as the host and she wanted them out, to slide down a toilet or be in the spit she was always hocking up. So Billy Jo thought about time and how she used to think: "I guess I'll take that stuff to the Good Will next Tuesday or I'll give myself another hour before I stand outside the house I used to live in, hoping to get a glimpse of my kids." She wondered if the kids and he—the man who, on the altar, said he would be there for her always—answered the phone every time she called or just once in a while because she tried not to call every hour but she did sometimes and no one answered a lot of the time. She was glad for her dog, Billy Jo really loved her dog. He only had three legs but he was strong and she was glad he stayed by her side.

Vic growls. "Your sentences are too long."

I remind Vic that his sentences may be shorter and others might write longer sentences—and like handwriting or fingerprints or a swab from the inner cheek, individuality is to be celebrated.

"You wouldn't say that if you were a criminal." Vic points at me. "Excuse me?"

"It's like this, if a criminal could not be identified by individual markings—if there wasn't DNA or fingerprints or iris identification—and if a criminal wasn't caught in the act, he could get away with a lot more crime."

Charles notes, "That would be reverse science fiction, I believe. That none of those things exist today."

Vic challenges, "And you know how much money writers make writing crime and sci-fi?"

Rivenchy slips her sweater off, the room is beginning to warm. She tells Beth Ann she knows she would like to read Beth Ann's stories because there's a sadness there she hopes can be fixed. Beth Ann beams and calls her 'Sweetie, honey' and thanks her. Rivenchy doesn't meet Beth Ann's eyes, but her nose doesn't flare.

Charles wants to know if it's autobiographical. I interrupt, protective. I remind them we, as writers, must let the work stand alone. That's what our job is, and it doesn't matter ultimately if it springs from somewhere in our minds or if it's a catalog of actual details or a mix of fiction and real events. As long as it is still true to us—the writer.

"Lyn, he just wants to know if I am sick," Beth Ann says quietly.

"I don't mean to pry." Charles' eyes are kind.

"They tell me I'm cancer-free now. So, everyone—all right?—everyone can just relax."

"Okay. Good for you." Vic leans back in his chair, testing its tipping point. He wants to move on.

I hand Beth Ann one of the simple street maps Mildred provides in the office and tell her I will be sending her, when we take our break, to work at the Biblioteca delle Oblate.

"To where?"

"It's a small library a few blocks from here. Has a café on the rooftop terrace. An inspiring place. It was originally a convent for the Oblate order, they were the first nurses of the city who concentrated on taking care of the poor. A rich banker, Folco Pontinari paid for most of it, in the mid-13th century. He was also the father of the beautiful and virtuous Beatrice, the great unrequited love of the poet Dante. Beatrice was Dante's inspiration for *La Vita Nuova*—that means *A New Life*—and also for his guide in Paradise in his *Comedia*."

"*The Divine Comedy*," Charles says. "Dante didn't call it divine. Someone added it."

George adds, "Three hundred years after he wrote it. An editor who wanted to sell more books."

I laugh. "Sounds like a publishing ploy."

Rivenchy nods. "I like that it's about his travels through the Inferno hell, Purgatorio and then Paradiso. And who ended up where. And why."

Beth Ann goes to fill her coffee cup. "Even I've heard of Dante but I didn't know he lived here in Florence."

I tell them that during our first stay in Florence, I took my husband to as many works of art I could find that depicted Dante Alighieri; I was fascinated with him because he was one of the first to move away from composing poems in Latin—the language of the privileged and educated—and write in the language of the Tuscan people. And he wrote about ordinary mortals, not gods or mythical heroes. I head to the bookshelf resting against the thick plaster walls and pull out an art book. I place it on the table in the center of our circle and open it to show them di Michelino's painting of Dante. "This is in the Cathedral Santa Maria del Fiore—di Michelino painted it in 1465—it's his version of the hell Dante describes in *Comedia*. See—Dante stands in front of his hell with Florence's Duomo on his right."

Vic leans in. "What's it mean? He's protected from hell by the church?"

Charles gives his opinion. "Or by God, if you choose to take it in a spiritual way as opposed to the transitory power of a church."

"But the Dante guy's standing in the middle so maybe he could go either way." Vic goes right for the conflict. A natural storyteller.

I laugh. "In the Bargello, there's a fresco by Giotto that shows Dante standing in Paradise, a woman at his side. I like to think it's Beatrice."

I remember Stan and I gazing at the fresco. Stan commented that Paradise looked like a lot more fun than hell and I told him that Giotto was making it simple. That where Beatrice was—that was heaven for Dante. Stan called me a romantic and pulled me into a secluded street and kissed me.

I tell the writers that Dante was a rock star of his time because he elevated the idea of love above duty or carnal desire. Rivenchy questions, "Why is it always the love story we want to know about?"

Vic growls, "Not me."

"Love stories are good, honey." Beth Ann pats Vic's arm. "Just as good as stories about murder and bad things."

Vic digs in. "Can't convince me of that."

Beth Ann is interested. "Who is this Beatrice he loved so much? She musta been special."

I fill in details of the personal story of Dante and Beatrice: The Pontinari and the Alighieri families lived near each other. The Pontinari's fortunes were thriving; the fortunes of the Alighieri family were not. When Dante was nine, he was invited to a party at the Pontinari home and experienced love-at-first-sight when he set eyes on eight-year-old Beatrice. Her father, like all Italian patriarchs, had charge of his children's lives and when Beatrice was young, he entered into a contract for her marriage to Simone dei Bardi, a son in a wealthy family. She was married to Bardi when she was in her early teens.

Beth Ann sighs. "It's a sad story of love-you-never-got."

"Exactly. Unrequited. A few years later, Dante married a woman named Gemma—he had been contracted to her since the age of 13. They had seven children."

"Seven. Oh my. How lucky!" Beth Ann giggles.

Charles adds, "But Beatrice remained Dante's idea of perfection. When she died in her early twenties, Dante concentrated on writing poems to her memory. *La Vita Nuova;* most famous one."

Vic snorts. "Bet his wife liked that."

I add that as far as I know, no one has ever found a poem that Dante created for Gemma.

Beth Ann frowns. "That's sad. Her husband always loved someone else."

Vic yawns. "Ahhh, she got seven kids off him, she did okay."

I can't help but think that perhaps Vic's romantic side is underdeveloped.

Rivenchy shakes her head at Vic. "You have never been in love?"

"Hey, that's kinda personal."

I remember that Stan found the history of Dante and Beatrice interesting—to a point. The day before he left to go back to New York that first year, Stan opted to watch a soccer match on television at The Red Garter Sports Bar while I made a visit to Dante's death mask at the Palazzo Vecchio. I inspected Dante's weary and wise mask. I imagined that on his death bed, he dreamed of reuniting with Beatrice. His great love whose death seemed to open, for Dante, new paths, new vistas, new ideas. La nuova vita. The new life.

"I'll go now," Vic says. He reads:

This morning, the model's body was found, the rope wrapped around her ankles and her dried blood a deep maroon col-

or—looking ugly as shit—sticky and thick. No beauty there. She swung in the air off the bridge, her head only a foot above the rat-infested river water. Another murder in the ancient city.

Vic clears his throat. "That was just setting stuff up, to grab the reader by the cojones. Now I switch to my main character." He reads:

I watch him watch her, smoking his cigarette. This is what he is watching: A really hot woman in the square in front of the church pushing a baby carriage. It's Martenella—the wife of Franco, the illegitimate son of mob boss Casoni. Her dress is short and loose, making men think of easy access. The watcher enjoys the view.

A short fat nun in a brown habit joins Martenella. The watcher knows her name; it's Sister Benedict. He notices the white sports socks and scuffed leather boots under her rough habit. The two women—one hot and one not—kiss on the cheeks. The watcher knows they grew up together in a rancid home for kids.

The watcher's name is Finn—he also grew up in that home, full of kids whose parents were in prison because of crimes they committed against the state. The kids were raised by ZeroGO founder Joseph Parn. He told them he would be their guide. Their punisher. Their surrogate mommy and daddy.

I watch the watcher named Finn watching them.

Vic, puffed and proud, is sure he's impressed. "Pretty good shit, huh? Grab 'em by the throat."

"Who is the watcher who is watchin' the watcher?" Beth Ann is confused.

Charles adds, "It's a lot of watching, isn't it?"

Vic points as if to tell Charles he's hit the target. "We all watch. We're all watched. There's danger in that." Vic looks at me. "Where do I get sent?"

"Santo Spirito. Other side of the river. It's an old section of Florence. Story goes that the powerful Caponi and Ricci and Frescobaldi families built homes there 700 some years ago—families who ran money-changing businesses and wool shops. Important industries."

Vic's already writing down ideas. "And they controlled the city through controlling the money and the jobs. Old time gangsters in tights and skirts. Using violence when necessary. How it always goes, am I right?"

"Back then there were two factions, the Guelphs—they represented the working poor who wanted the rich to pay more taxes—and the Ghibellines—the rich nobles who wanted to hold onto their money. Power kept shifting. An assassination of one of the leaders of the Ricci faction took place on the steps of the church in Santa Spirito right after a mass."

Vic likes these scenarios. "Always someone trying to kill someone else."

Charles adds, "Human nature. There is an innate belligerence in us all."

"Damn straight." Vic puts a 'thumbs up' in agreement.

A sudden memory of my mother sweeps over me when I see Vic give the 'thumbs up'. When she lost her ability to speak and we were settled in to watch a movie, I'd hold up DVDs until she gave me the "thumbs up". Invariably, she'd choose an Italian movie starring Sophia Loren and Marcello Mastroianni. Or looking into the chocolate box, when I'd finally find the salted caramels she loved—she'd give me a "thumbs up". Or when we would both notice my father napping over his car magazine. She'd wink at me and give me a "thumbs up" and pat her heart, a signal she was feeling a wave of love. A rush of missing my mother sweeps over me and, surprisingly, my regret at missing Marybelle Price, of not searching her out last year or the year before, plagues me. Timing. Not putting things off. Priorities. I breathe out my angst and bring myself back to the writers.

Vic is writing in his notebook. "Santo Spirito. Everything's 'saint' something around here." Vic stuffs his notes into his pocket. He gives a deep burp.

Beth Ann sighs. "Honey, how old are you?"

Vic winks and snorts, enjoying his role as bad boy of the group. Charles reads:

The red fox was not an ordinary fox. Most definitely not ordinary. He wasn't a hunter or roamer in the Maremma woods, not far from Florence. He was more of a thinker. No one thought much of him. Pynon, the fox, often wondered about grand things, such as stars and wondered if he could find a way to leave the ground, the dirt, the woods where he did not feel like he belonged. Pynon wondered, could he reach a star?

George offers his help. "I like stars. If you choose a star or a galaxy, I could do some research for you."

"Excellent, that's an offer I will accept and I will reward you with an apertivo at my favorite spot."

I suggest Charles spend time at the Parco Della Cascine on the western end of Florence. "I know it well," he says. "Used to be the royal hunting ground and now it is a slightly tamed, a-bit-of-bucolic wilderness in the city." He tips his head. "I now defer to the woman from France."

Rivenchy's expensive perfume wafts towards me as she opens her notebook. She reads:

The purse was of supple leather, it was achingly soft, like warm skin. Lavanna has touched it. Her fingertips felt it and it was like traversing a very smooth and chiseled chest, skin warm from sex. The pads of her fingers travel over the ribs, the taut muscular wall protecting the cavity below the abdomen and down to his pelvic bones.

She looks up. "That's it."

"What? That's it? Are you kidding me?" Beth Ann giggles, frustrated.

Rivenchy shrugs. Smiles.

"Erotica." Vic declares. "That's what they call that."

Rivenchy shrugs again, her secret pleasure of sharing her work is not so secret anymore. I can tell she enjoys it.

George clears his throat, his eyes glance over towards Rivenchy and then away quickly. "It is evocative."

Vic barks, "I said erotica."

George nods. "Yes. But then I said evocative."

I suggest Rivenchy check out the shops in the Piazza Carousel. She could walk through Prada, Louis Vuitton, maybe through La Rinascente, the department store that reminds me of Bloomingdale's in New York City. Find some interesting faces.

"Write more about a leather handbag?" Rivenchy asks.

"All right." I hadn't said that at all. But it's what she heard. I didn't want to lead her.

"About a handbag," she repeated, her mind making connections. "Or about the woman who chose it. Or who inspired her to choose it. "

We all look towards George. He goes to the white board and uses the marker. He writes:

I, as ALOM,
$X1 = vl+ax$ *so* $X1+X2$ *r*
$f+a=+l$ *so 0 and r/f*
therefore aahhh or nahhhhh.

Vic leans forward. "What is this? We have to be math whizzes to get it or what?"

"I'll prepare a decoding." George's voice is soft. "But I'd just like to get further with it now. While it's still in my head."

"That's fine," I say. "Whenever you would like to share, let me know."

Vic's ready to go. "Okay, I say we go to our spots. When do we come back?"

I stand. "We'll meet again after lunch."

The others head off, George lingers. "I do want my story to become clear." He uses the board again. "Love—the 'vl'—and anxiety—the 'ax', I see as two conflicting but necessary emotional elements. And fear. The 'r/f' is an antigen that, when introduced into the vl+ax equation, can cause increased instability. X1 is my main character and X2 is the person he desires. Perhaps I should mention that all women are even numbers and the men are odd numbers."

I'm fascinated—and trying to keep up. "Okay."

"Both feel trapped."

"Trapped?"

"Though they don't know it. Their unhappiness has become a habit. Because they can't see the importance of how every action increases or decreases the percentage of fear and anxiety and ultimate stasis. Standing in the way of joy. Well—perhaps I am thinking that balance is everything."

I study his concentrated face as he looks at his equation—his story—on the white board. He says, "ALOM, if you want to know, stands for 'alone male'."

Chapter 7

I head to the grocery store. Stan will want salami, prosciutto, capers, crackers, honey for his morning oatmeal; he'll also want grapes and apples. We'll eat the grapes in bed.

As I shop I go through a list in my head; take out the extra pillows in the apartment's closet—Stan likes to sleep on two pillows and prefers them soft, check to see if the television is working—Stan likes the noise in the morning and we did get CNN on the apartment television last year, move my things into two drawers in the dresser so that Stan can unpack his socks—he always packs too many—and boxers. Check that there are enough hangers, Stan likes to hang his shirts.

Carrying my groceries, I pass the Hotel Cascini. Lucia, behind the receptionist desk, calls out to me. "Buona giornata Lyn! Buona giornata, vieni qui!"

Lucia's now-platinum-colored hair is done in a pageboy today, a tiny bow sits on top of the teased crown, right above heavy bangs.

Her bright pink shift and purple stockings nearly blind me as she hands me a slim linen envelope with my name written on it. She tells me that her boyfriend's mother gave her a teapot that had belonged to her boyfriend's great grandmother. She is glowing; it has taken her two years to feel his mother did not hate her. This is a great sign. She wiggles the fingers of her left hand. "Soon." She points to her fourth finger, imagining the ring she wants to wear on it.

"Lucia, do you think you are too 'in love' with love?"

"Can it be too much?" Lucia dances happily behind her desk. She points to the small envelope. I can tell she's curious. "This came for you."

I take the envelope and can't help giving her advice. "Life still has to stay real. Love is just one part of it."

"Oh no. No. You are wrong. Love is everything. Makes everything better. I know. I know it."

The phone rings and she answers, "Pronto." Someone wants to make a reservation and she takes down the information.

I climb the stairs to my apartment, take out the thick note card that rests inside the envelope.

Liniana,

St. Mark's English Church. Ivan Yanakov, a Czech, in piano concert tonight. Wednesday. Music of Franz Liszt. 20:30. I invite you. If you would like. Matteo.

I am traveling for business today but I will stop at the Odeon Bistro for apertivo at 19:00. Join me before concert. If you like.

Matteo

I imagine the building of Matteo's invitation. Maybe there was brief thought about last night and the benefits of practicing his English as he checked his calendar for his plans for the evening. Maybe he realized he has no big plans, really. So why not a small concert at the small church on Via Maggio? Why not invite the American and continue to practice English? I imagine his next thought: Why not share apertivo and a glass of wine with the American before the performance? Third thought. Did he like the idea? Why not. He sends the invitation. He thinks perhaps the American will like the idea.

No. I should not like.

I cannot like this idea.

I move my clothes to one side of the closet to make room for Stan's shirts. Susie always kidded Stan about his blue and white striped cotton shirts. Some had wide stripes. Some had thin stripes. She would bait him, tell Stan that if he wasn't wearing a Giants jersey, he was wearing a blue and white striped shirt and perhaps it was time for a change. I always imagined a beautiful salesgirl had once mentioned to Stan that stripes were a good look and that the blue brought out the color of his eyes. When Susie teased him, he would tell her fashion didn't pay his bills and his choice in shirts kept life simpler. Lay off.

About a year ago Stan did change it up a bit; he added a few options to the preferred black and gray suits he would wear for work. He added a pinstripe and even a few tailored sports jackets. It was after he made junior partner and his boss started dating one of the Victoria Secret models. The firm was now getting third row seats to fashion shows—good seats behind the celebrities and magazine editors. Susie usually used Stan's tickets; she'd chat up the buyers from online stores and tell them about her new line of swimsuits and beachwear.

When Stan began to take a greater interest in his 'look', it gave Susie and my casual window-shopping days a purpose. We'd end up looking at ties for him; she would pick out the brighter Tom Ford silks—the plaids and the polka-dots—and tell me I had to throw out all his tried and true boring choices from Brooks Brothers.

I glance at the clock—wonder if Susie is still sleeping. It's five hours earlier in New York City. Is it too early to call? She's my touchstone, I rely on her to put things in perspective, to encourage, to be there to talk through stories, to tell me about her latest romantic and sexual adventures. We love to joke that we're kindred spirits because we both hate broccoli and love cauliflower, we like to try out new cocktails and wonder how each is affecting our brain cells and we both get frustrated with the snippy baristas who ignore women and google-eye male customers. She knows I am struggling with my mother's Mud Angel story. We've talked so many times about the dreamy, sometimes mischievous gleam that snuck into my mother's eyes when she told us about how, even in the crisis, her boots sticking in the thick mud, she could look up and see the towers of Florence and know it was one of the most romantic cities on earth. We would wonder about how hard it was to picture a parent—my mother in this case—young and free and not caught up in the lives of her children.

After my mom's ischemic stroke, my Dad and I and Susie moved her into an assisted living residence. Susie thought of my mother almost as her own, she relied on our warm kitchen and my mother's soft advice and gentle prods to follow whatever Susie's latest dream might be. My Dad, Susie and I would play cards with my mother and pretend that my mother could still make cogent decisions in games of '21' or 'Baseball'. Finally, 'Go Fish' was the game of choice. Most Saturdays, my Dad would head off to his favorite sports bar and Susie and I would bring in mom's favorite fettucine alfredo from Columbo's and keep her company. Because my mother's access to speech was impaired, conversations were now limited. As she savored the creamy noodles, her eyes would follow me around the room as I folded laundry and Susie would make her laugh by telling crazy accounts of us as renegade girl scouts; tie-dyeing everything in sight including my brother Rick's white jockeys and taking subways to historical sites when we were supposed to be logging in actual hiking miles around Manhattan. Susie loved earning her Girl Scout badges and had her vest filled long before me. I can't remember how she supported some of her claims—like milking a goat—but she did get a badge for things way beyond what she really accomplished. It was a game to her. She ironed the badges on her vest in amazing patterns; this was her first fashion statement. My mother would look at me and shake her head, amazed and amused at Susie's adolescent disregard for playing by the rules.

I remember one day, Susie embellished a school dance disaster story for my mother's enjoyment—she explained the details of how every boy, excited by his heterosexuality, lined up to land a wet one on my lips at the Charity Kissing Booth. Sol Kirsch with his braces packed with gummy white bread from the bologna sandwich he'd eaten at the buffet, Gregory O'Brien who sweated so much because he didn't know what to do with his hands and how Billy Benson cried because he was too emotional about this benchmark moment. My mom couldn't form many words—but she could chortle with glee. She reached for my hand and kissed it with a big "smack". We all hooted with laughter. Then Susie took a romance novel out of her purse and read the most turgid passages. I tried to take the book away but my mom pointed her finger at me with that 'don't you dare' stare I knew so well. Her eyes twinkled as Susie dramatically read about breasts caressed by rough calloused hands and large members protruding under thin jodhpurs. I retreated to my mother's older scrapbooks, enjoyed only half listening; my favorite photo was of my mother as a dedicated Mud Angel in Florence—sitting on the shoulders of a curly-headed, tall fellow worker in muddy jeans and tall rubber boots; she was holding up a 12th century solid silver candlestick that she had retrieved from the muck, surrounded by other Mud Angels raising their hands in victory. Her grin spreading from ear-to-ear.

I punch Susie's number into my cell. She's between guys right now—chances are she's half asleep, knowing she should get up and head to the gym.

The connection goes through and I can hear her phone ring. After five rings, it goes to her voicemail. "Hi, it's Susie. Crazy sorry to miss your call. Really. I'm probably signing another big contract for my beachwear line, 'Susie on the Beach'. But you're more important than any multi-million-dollar contract. Really. Want to talk to you. Leave me a message and I'll get back to you real soon."

I leave a message. "It's me. Wish I could talk to you. All's beautiful, calm, amazing here, hasn't changed. Stan's coming for a visit, gets here tomorrow. That'll be nice. Students are an interesting bunch. Miss you. Love you."

I click off.

I check my email. One from my agent. She lets me know she hasn't heard from Harledge Publishing yet. That she's not worried; they know I have a fan base.

"Not a big one," I mutter to myself.

As if anticipating my reaction, there is a follow-up email from my agent letting me know she's already submitted the book for the Mauree B. Award, the Peller Award and the Roner Seal Award. She thinks that since the Peller recognized me four years ago, that might be an efficacious bet. And she reminds me again she's not worried a bit about the slow response from the publisher. That they are not holding it against me that I missed my deadline. Ah, there it is. The guilt she's trying to instill.

I nibble on the grapes, remembering how the third book took me four years to finish. I was as frustrated as my editor at Harledge. But settling in after the wedding, it took me awhile to get back into my writer's rhythm. Then my mother died and my dad got sick and was buried next to her. And when the money for the Peller Award came in, Stan wanted to take my small inheritance, my small award money, the sale of my Dad's Mustang—Stan had paid it off and now owned the title outright—and his promotion bonus and dive into the condo market.

It took me six months with a real estate agent to find the right Manhattan address. I love it; it's a few blocks south and east of Union Square. Part of the block is protected by the Landmarks Preservation Commission and even though our building is not designated historic, we are surrounded by buildings often referred to as the 'Victorian gentlemen who refuse to die.' We had to re-do the kitchen and Stan thought he was doing me a favor by letting me make all the decisions regarding our home. I got frustrated. Susie would insist we go on long walks to clear my head. She'd listen to me lament that I had lost momentum with my book. She told Stan to stop the 'hon-ey-do' lists he gave me. He told her to 'lay off'. I finally started us-ing her apartment to write. She'd be out working with designers and investors and I would make coffee in her small kitchen and write at the table near the window.

Susie will call me back. I know. As soon as she can. But it would've been great to hear her voice.

Time to get back to the seminar room. And then to the library for research. I grab my bag. The note from Matteo is there, next to my bag. I have no way to contact him, no way to let him know I won't be joining him.

If you like.

Obviously—a last minute thought to include me in his plans. I didn't want to be rude but…nothing to be done about it.

It's nearing sunset and I head towards the river and to the Biblioteca Nazionale Central Library. It's only a few blocks from our seminar room. The mini-journeys of the writers in the seminar—to the var-ious places I assigned them—added fuel to their ideas and Vic had brought a few bottles of wine that went well with our discussion. Now it's my time to work.

The Biblioteca Nazionale is open until 10 pm and I am de-termined to be disciplined. Stan's visit will cut into writing time, there's no way around it. I enter and show my pass to the security team. This library is not open to the public, you have to show research credentials, provide a passport and sign, practically in blood, that you mean no harm to the library or its vast collection. It had its birth in 1714 when Cosimo III de' Medici, the Grand Duke of Tuscany hired Antonion Magliabechi, a goldsmith, to organize the Medici artwork, books and antiques. Magliabechi was an ec-centric, he ate only eggs and bread and avoided social interactions. On his deathbed, he bequeathed over 30,000 books to the city and suggested the decree that a copy of every book and manuscript written in Tuscany—and eventually in Italy—had to be given to the Medici library. The book collection soon became so massive that the Biblioteca Nazionale was built near the river. It holds original works by Galileo, de'Grassi, DaVinci, Dante, Petrarch, Machiavelli, Umberto Eco, Cesare Blabo and others—more than six million volumes, three million pamphlets, over 25,000 manuscripts and over a million autographs of people who have made a difference in the world. In 1966, when the Arno flooded, its treasures were desperately vulnerable. These were among the things the Mud Angels—my mother standing in the midst of them—were trying to save.

The library established the Art and Artifacts Restoration Center after the 1966 flood. My mother hoped to visit it, maybe even volunteer there, but she kept putting her plans aside. I remember once she had her bags packed and was ready to go. I was eight years old. My Dad was sitting at the kitchen table, staring at the clock on the wall. I was upset because she was going to miss my spelling contest at school. Rick was saying he guessed he could figure out how to work the washing machine to get his football jersey clean. But he didn't want to touch my underwear so he wasn't going to do any other laundry when she was gone. My mother stood next to her suitcase, her eyes were heavy that day; I remember being surprised because she looked like she had been crying and my mother did not cry. My Dad looked out the window and mumbled that her taxi had arrived. Rick and I stomped off to school.

Later that day, after cardboard-tasting pizza in the cafeteria, I stood backstage for the beginning of the spelling contest. I saw my mother entering the school auditorium and taking a seat in the front row. She hadn't gotten on that plane. She put her family first.

I show my ID and my library access card, I put my sweater and bag into a locker and take my laptop to the cavernous reading room. I pull out the chair at one of the communal tables, it squeals against the stone floor. Professors, researchers and historians—bending over their books or intent on their laptops—curse me under their breaths. The Biblioteca delle Oblate, where I sent Beth Ann, is always abuzz with noise and students. In stark contrast—this library is like a tomb.

I check the time. Take out my notebook.

I get distracted by an older man sitting at a desk in the far corner, surrounded by books. His massive head of curly gray hair gives him an absent-minded professorial look; he almost blends into the shelves around him, as if he is a fixture in the place.

My stomach growls.

I envision the cafes filling up with tourists and locals about to enjoy apertivo. I think of Matteo arriving at the Odeon Bistro and looking to see if I am there.

If you like.

I open my mother's journal. Look at the timetable she jotted down for herself—departure from New York City and arrival in Pisa, a list of times of expected busses from Pisa to Florence. These are scratched out, her note next the bus schedule: *never came*. Joined the hitchhikers. I glance at a page of my notes, remembering a story she had once told me that took place only days before she found her way to Florence. A group of German study-abroad theology students were out dancing late on the night of November 4, left a nightclub near Palazzo Pitti just after midnight. On the street, they faced torrential rain and realized the powerful river water was rising higher and higher at an amazing pace. The gas lamplights were already dysfunctional and no longer provided light. The uneven stones that made up the streets were quickly buried deep below water—invisible and hazardous. No one wanted to trip and fall; terrified, they held onto others' hands and chanting prayers, strode against the assaulting weight of the water which was soon up to their knees. Getting to their apartment on Boboli Hill was their only thought. Finally, with the rain pounding on their bodies, they reached the apartment and raced up the narrow stone interior stairs and tumbled inside. Opening the window, they could only stare down at the increasing devastation. Not a wink of sleep that night as they tried to warm the room with candles, fearful the end of time—doomsday—may be upon them. My mother arrived in the aftermath of the shock and panic, when blame was not being put on God but on faulty dam oversight. I think of my father, always careful, never wanting to travel beyond where his cars could take him. And of my mother, traveling alone into a disaster area, to a world where she knew no one, did not know the language, did not know if she would have a roof over her head. Hoping to help save incredible history and beauty. I try to imagine the scene. She did not capitulate to my father's fears for her. I can imagine his entreaties, wanting her with him, safe. But she knew where she needed to be.

I check the clock on the wall.

Across the room, I see an especially thin woman with a scarf tied around her head, part of her hairless pate visible. I guess she's in her twenties. She wears thick glasses and writes furiously in a sky-blue 5x7 moleskin. I imagine she has decided that whatever she is writing about is very important and this helps her ignore the ticking clock inside her.

I turn the page in the journal and notice, again, the date at the top of the page. November 14, 1966. My mother had used a ballpoint pen to sketch a scene: a table with a lit candle on its center, seen from a bird's-eye view and six people—all with heads bowed and hands outstretched to hold onto each other—sitting around it. A warm gathering. Under the sketch, she had written: *R told us "And even God rested on the seventh day"*. To the side of the picture was a list:

> *roasted on fire carrots*
> *charred fennel on fire*
> *tomatoes from canning jars heated in fire*
> *3-day old bread soaked in olive oil*
> *wine wine wine wine more wine*
> *Dessert: salty chips. How much I MISS SALT!*

I have wondered where this dinner took place. What is the story behind it? Where was the fire? A fireplace? A campfire? Much of the city had been without gas and electricity for days. I notice, for the first time, a tiny corner of the journal page—folded over. I unfold it.

There, in wet-smeared ballpoint is: *Poggi. Sister. Fire. Food.* Who is Poggi? Is it even a name?

I gaze up at the large clock on the far wall.

I imagine Stan arriving in a day and a half and tossing his bag into the apartment and wanting to dine at Ristorazione Donnini, in its shiny, modern interior.

I think of Matteo's invitation and how it was worded. Generous. Thoughtful. I recall his eyes, curious. His questions about my family and how enjoyable it was to talk with him. And now he's sitting at apertivo at the Odeon Bistro, perhaps by himself, casting his eyes into the surroundings wondering if his invitation has been accepted.

If you like.

I check my watch. I contemplate the clock on the wall.

Shit.

I stop at the non-descript entrance to St. Mark's English Church, the small church that was built in the 1500s; it was once part of the old Medici Palace and where Machiavelli lived for a time. The double doors are closed. Am I too late? I press on them and one creaks open.

The director of the church is there; he is placing a sign in the middle of the lobby.

No one allowed inside after the concert begins

"You just made it." He sniffs in his English accent, thinking less of me because of my tardiness.

I slip in the doors that lead to the nave, where the parishioners sit during services. There are no pews, just rows of wooden chairs covered with thick red cushions. The church leaders seem to have embraced the idea that being comfortable—while contemplating sins or life-after-death or the mysteries of God—is perfectly acceptable.

There is a buzz of anticipation. Many people are speaking English. This is an Anglican church, very close to the British Institute where Marybelle Price and friends drank tea or gin and listened to lectures on art or science or philosophy or other topics of interest to ex-pats who find that Florence is more 'them' than their native lands.

The director closes the doors to the nave behind me and he dims the lights. There is a strong illumination on a highly-polished Yamaha concert piano standing a few feet in front of the altar. It glows, like a halo of patent leather.

I see Matteo. He's in the last row of chairs on top of risers placed against the back wall. His briefcase is on the chair next to him. He waves me over.

I step over a few audience members and sit next to him, sliding my computer bag under the chair. He hands me a program. I say, "I'm sorry, I…"

"You made it. I had to assure many people I had a guest arriving and that I must keep the chair free. I wasn't popular but now you have not made me a liar." He looks at a couple across the aisle and grins. "You see, she did come. Lucky I keep the seat." He leans into me, "They were not pleasant with me."

"Mi dispiace, I…" I keep saying I'm sorry.

"You do not have to worry," Matteo says.

At this moment Ivan Yanakov, the pianist enters. He is dressed in black, looks my age. I know—because I Googled him—he's won major competitions and played at Carnegie Hall and with the London Philharmonic. He also conducts at the Czech National Symphony Orchestra and gives master classes all over the world.

The enthusiastic audience applauds. He nods his pale face and looks out at all of us. His thin, long fingers are cupped together. "Florence I love. I travel the world and I appreciate Hong Kong and Frankfurt and Berlin and Paris and America, but Florence, and this church, it is very special. My friend…" Ivan gestures to the church's director, "…has agreed that the proceeds from this concert will be used to support the church's missions in Africa. Let us begin."

Matteo looks at me, whispers nearly soundlessly, "You like music?"

I nod. I do like.

Yanakov sits at the piano and the room is absolutely silent. It's more than politeness. It's expectation. Yanakov does not disappoint. The music transports me. I don't know much about Franz Liszt other than he was Hungarian and composed over 150 years ago. But I can attest to the fervor in the composition, its urgency and its insistence and how it seizes my complete attention. I watch Yanakov's fingers caress and fly over the keyboard. I feel myself lose all connection to my day-to-day thoughts, my worries, my lists, my rituals and my 'shoulds'. The music is not a background to my situation, it is a language that I listen to and feel and interpret in my own way.

An hour later—and it seems like a much shorter time—we are on our feet, cheering Yanakov's performance.

Matteo leans into me. "Yes, it spoke to me too."

"What do you mean?" I ask.

"I was watching your face."

Yanakov stands in the small lobby next to a table where the church's 'Contribute to our Mission in Africa' basket rests and receives compliments from his departing audience. Matteo adds euros to the basket and shakes Yanakov's hand. I am so aware that Yanakov's hands are his most precious appendages, I don't want to overwork them. I keep my hands behind my back and thank him. And thank him. And thank him. "No. Really. It was really—wonderful." I am aware that I sound like an inarticulate American.

We step out into the street. There's been a light rain; the air smells clean and fresh. Matteo tells me we must have gelato—it will help us digest the music. I laugh, happy to anticipate the coolness of the icy treat.

We cross the street and walk up the narrow alley towards the Piazza di Passera. "Thank you for the invitation to the apertivo, I'm sorry I couldn't join you."

"It was a last minute idea." Matteo takes off his jacket, the night is still warm.

"I had work to do at the library."

"I saw friends there, at Caffe Odeon. We talked of futbol and politics." He laughs. "As always."

"I'm sorry I didn't know how to get in touch with you. The invitation said you would be out of town until…"

"I should give you my cell number," he says.

"Oh. Sure."

"Then you can text me if we make other plans sometime—if you will be able to join me or not."

It makes sense, of course, but it feels like I am opening a door that I am not supposed to open.

"Earlier today I was in the vineyards near Panzano." He walks leisurely; the Florentine pace.

"For work?" We are walking down a narrow alley, home to many art studios that are closed for the night but still entice passersby with the displays of their work in dimly-lit windows.

"It always takes me to different places." He takes my computer bag from me, carries it as if it weighs nothing.

I notice again how tall he is, how his shirt covers his broad shoulders and looks crisp even after a day in the country. I wish I had added earrings this morning, wish I had the casual elegance of so many Italian women. "Was this for the special project you told me about—the part of keeping your father's Uffizi project going?"

"You remember."

"Yes, that you search out missing works, authenticate things. Find treasures hidden in attics and cellars and hidden passages."

"You make it sound as if I am a detective. Maybe I am." He changes the subject. "Did you have Italian lesson today?"

"No. Tomorrow. I met with my students and then went to the library…"

"Yes, you told me about the library."

A motorcycle speeds towards us. Matteo grabs my elbow and pulls me close to the ancient stone building. I am pressed against his shoulder for a moment, he smells like fresh sandalwood, it must be his aftershave. His fingers stay on my arm. And then, the motorcyclist, waving his thanks for giving him room, is gone. We separate.

We reach the piazza and head into the very small, very white, very organized Gelateria della Passera. The woman behind the counter, with a fleshy neck, heavy breasts and sad eyes, has a harried look. Matteo tells her he has brought his American friend here because it is the best gelato in Florence. She beams for a moment—

then goes back to an impatient, melancholic scrutiny that seems to say, "Decide. I have people waiting." And it's true. People are lining up behind us. I peg the choices: raspberry, fig, clementine, banana, pear, lemon, pistachio, chocolate-orange, hazelnut, vanilla, mint, almond, crema, chili pepper, blackberry, strawberry and mango. I can't choose.

Matteo tries to help. "The pistachio has a touch of sea salt in it. Americans like salt."

"We do?"

"Do you deny?"

My mother's 'I miss salt!' flashes in my mind. It's true, American food is saltier. And I am a fan of sea salted caramels and dark chocolate with sea salt. Salted popcorn. Salted pretzels. Salted peanuts. Italians do use salt more sparingly, perhaps more judiciously.

"I'll have pistachio and sea salt," I tell the sad-eyed woman behind the counter.

There are benches in the center of the piazza. People gather here to enjoy the gelato and the wine they take out from the small bistro nearby. An accordion player and guitarist walk through the piazza, adding music to the lovely night. Matteo digs into his double scoop—one of fig and one of clementine. "My parents wanted a musician in the family, they arranged piano lessons for me when I was six. I took lessons every week until I was twelve. After six years, they realized I was not going to have a breakthrough and be able to play anything of complexity."

"Was that a huge disappointment?"

"Doesn't every parent want a genius?" He smiles, savors a spoonful of fig gelato.

"My mother wanted me to be an archeologist. We watched the *Indiana Jones* movies once a month. We went to the King Tut exhibit at least ten times in the first month it was in New York."

"But she liked that you eventually decided to be a writer?"

"I think so. But she was worried too. Made me get a double degree at the University—English *and* accounting. I barely passed accounting. This gelato is amazing. I can taste the salt crystals."

The musicians notice us and move in our direction. They nod and wink to let us know they are playing now just for us. I need to put a boundary on this lovely evening, even though I know the invitation was simply a friendly gesture on his part. "My husband is arriving tomorrow."

"How nice for you."

"I know. It was my birthday a few days ago and I think he's coming to celebrate. A little late but he had to stay in New York for work."

"You must bring him here."

I glance around. Stan likes hotel bars, where he will find other Americans. This would not be his taste.

"You don't like?"

"I like it very much. But he has his favorite places already. I am sure of one thing—he will get his favorite pork and salami sandwich at All'Antico Vinaio. He is willing to stand in line for that."

He laughs. "Ah, even I will stand in line for their porchetta panini. How many years are you married?"

"Five."

"Congratulations. My parents, they were married forty-four years, until my father expired, and my grandparents for fifty-one years, until my grandfather was taken. The women, they last longer. Today, things are different."

"What do you mean?"

"Divorce rate rises. But still, in Italy, it is under fifteen percent. In Rome, more cosmopolitan, the big crazy city, it is higher. Almost thirty percent."

"That's double. Urban romance must be in danger."

He joins in my faux dismay. "Yes, to love in Rome is not a sure thing. However, in Paris, over fifty per cent of marriages end in divorce."

"And you know this why?"

"Valentina knows it. She reads magazines. She likes to tell me marriage in Italy is the safest."

"What do you think that means in the long run?"

"Italians like to suffer?" He grins. The musicians are ready to move on. Matteo hands them a few euros.

"Lyn?"

I turn around; it's Mildred. I feel a blush spring to my cheeks, not sure why her finding me here, sitting here with Matteo, makes me feel like a kid caught with her hand in the cookie jar. She carries a good-sized canvas stretched on a frame under her arm; she is just coming from her painting group. They meet once a week to paint together at a friend's studio in Santo Spirito.

"I hope you tried the hazelnut." She eyes my gelato.

"I went for the pistachio and sea salt. To support the idea that Americans are addicted to salt."

Mildred contemplates Matteo. "Hello."

"This is Matteo Marcioni. He is the brother of Valentina."

"Not our Italian teacher Valentina?"

"Si, I am afraid so." Matteo admits.

Mildred is amused, "Your sister, she is a monster."

"Yes, very true. I know. I had to grow up with her."

It's all in fun but I am thinking Valentina is definitely an experience not to be missed. Mildred started taking lessons from her years ago when she moved to Florence full-time. She told me that Valentina was one of the best instructors, but if I wanted to have fun and feel no pressure while learning Italian, I should ask for another instructor. I signed up with an Italian named Ignacio, but he quit the day before I began, and Valentina took over his classes. I guess it was meant to be.

"Out for a stroll?" I know Mildred is wondering how Matteo and I happen to be out together.

"We went to St. Mark's to hear a piano concert," I tell her.

"Ahhh. I didn't know you knew each other."

"We've just met." I feel the color sting my cheeks again. "At Valentina's school."

Mildred accepts the connective tissues. "Well, the churches have the best concerts. Now to get my hazelnut gelato. Watch this for me, will you?"

Mildred rests her canvas against the bench. We inspect the painting in progress, the half-formed faces of some of the most revered saints of Italy and scenes of their tribulations: St. Agnes—choosing death by fire rather than lose her virginity, St. Barbara—beheaded by her father for following the Christian faith, St. Lucia—covered with pitch and oil and lit with fire when she refused to give up her Christian faith (but her body refused to burn), St. Catherine and St. Agatha and others—their breasts and tongues cut off because of their beliefs.

"This is a serious subject," Matteo says, deadpan. But I hear a humorous consternation.

"During the day, she illustrates children's books. Maybe this is an outlet." I'm surprised too. I didn't know Mildred was interested in saints or torture or earlier centuries when fathers and emperors and officials came up with bizarre torments to force women to bend to their will.

Mildred comes back with her gelato. She sees us studying her unfinished work. "It's a commission. I'm pretty sure he's into domination and sadomasochism. A very old Italian wrinkled gentleman from a prominent family who has a secret room in his palazzo. He insists on remaining nameless."

Matteo finds the positive. "Well, it's very artistically done."

Mildred shrugs. "I have a few more martyrs to add. It will be a conversation piece."

Matteo nods. "Absolutely."

Mildred sucks the gelato off her mini-plastic spoon, "It has me wondering why the virginity issue was so major back in the day. Kids now just 'hook up' and consider sex exercise. 120 calories for every half hour."

"Really?" News to me.

"Some study put that out. Others put it up to 300 calories. I guess it depends on the lovers." She turns to Matteo, "You're Catholic?"

"Si. My family is Catholic, si."

"Can you tell me why it is so important that Mary, the mother of God, never had sex? That Jesus was not born of a love between a man and a woman but through God's idea carefully placed into her womb."

"I will introduce you to my parish priest. He likes to talk about these things."

"Virginity and purity and female torture?"

"Oh yes, perfect topics for him." Matteo smiles.

Mildred laughs and shrugs. "Maybe I shouldn't be painting things like this. Just makes me mad." She swallows the last of her gelato. She looks at me and suggests, since we are neighbors, we walk back to San Niccolo together. It makes sense. Matteo lives east of Piazza Santa Trinita, the other side of the river and in the opposite direction of my apartment.

I didn't realize it was late. I thank Matteo for inviting me to the concert. He says he hopes my husband arrives safely and that we have a most pleasant time in Florence together.

Chapter 8

I wake up in my Giants t-shirt, not feeling rested at all. I roll over and feel like I am getting up on the 'wrong side of the bed.' The sky looks dark. Rain is in the forecast.

I smooth the covers and, almost out of habit, place Stan's pillows in the right spots. I put out wine glasses, a corkscrew and a bottle of Valpolicella. I put on the white silk shirt Stan likes; Susie helped me pick it out for the law firm's summer party out in the Hamptons. I wrap the red scarf around my neck to brighten the look, hoping it will chase my unsettled feeling away.

I head across the river to my morning lesson with Valentina. She glares at me when I arrive. "Mio fratello?"

"Your brother."

"Si. My brother."

"I met him."

"I know. He tells me. Of course he tells me. I am his sister. You do not tell me."

"I have not seen you since I met him…"

"It's no good."

"What is not good?"

"He is too good for you."

"Huh?" What's her problem?

"He is good."

"We are friends. Solo amici."

"This is not good."

"Valentina, why are you being so rude?" I grab my raincoat, scarf and bag. "Maybe it's not a good day for a lesson." I head to the door, angry.

Valentina gets there before me, truly concerned. "Where are you going?"

"Someplace I won't be insulted."

"What are you talking? How do I insult you?"

"You do not think I'm good enough to be friends with your brother. I'm insulted."

"My brother is too good."

I don't have the patience for this; my unsettled feeling is turning into a headache. Valentina touches my arm. "Please sit. We misunderstand each other. It is just my brother is good. Do not be angry with me. He will be angry with me if you do not like me."

"What do you mean your brother is too good?"

"He has a woman who wants to marry him and he is too good not to be married."

"Matteo didn't tell me about a girlfriend."

"That the woman wants him to marry now, very soon. And she is the right woman for him."

I don't really follow but I say, "Fine."

"She is the right woman."

"Fine."

"And you—you are married."

"My husband is coming today."

"Good. You and your husband are still good."

"Why wouldn't we be?"

"America has many divorces. I read about them. Italy—we do better. Florence, of course, does better than Rome." I do not tell her Matteo has already told me the percentages. "Now, we do the lesson? You have to pay no matter and I just had to be honest. You like honesty."

"I suppose I do. Yes."

"So there. We'll have our lesson now."

I sigh. "Fine."

For the next hour, Valentina is particularly strict and unappreciative of my attempts at correct conjugation and verb usage. She reminds me I will never truly understand Italy, for only Italians can really understand what it means to be a citizen of one of the most amazing countries in the world. She grills me on vocabulary and circles a list of words I am to study for the next class.

Her timer goes off. End of class. As I pack up my notebook, I finally ask, "Why does Matteo not want to marry this woman who wants to marry him?"

Valentina goes off again, "Of course he does. But he is stupido, he is out of his mind, she is perfect. Matteo is stubborn. Idiot. Maybe, since you say you are friends, you talk to him. Tell him he is idiot and he should have babies with Bernadette. She is ready for babies. I too, I am ready for babies but no man except for the ugly macellaio—that means butcher if you have been studying your vocabulary—only the ugly macellaio asks me and I am vegetarian so, it is evident, I cannot marry a butcher and added to that, he is too short and has no hair. I like hair on the head. Italian men with hair on the head I like. You talk to Matteo. He is an idiot. Tell him that in English. Don't try to speak Italian, he will never understand you."

I pick up a caffè americano on the way to Writers Now Retreat. I arrive and Rivenchy is ready to read:

Lavanna interviewed at La Rinascente, because she decided she would like to get a job. And this was a job where she could be around tres belle, nouvelle choses—new things.

Silks. Leathers. Shiny glass cases. Lace-edged lingerie. She was hired straight away and put in the intimates section. She was wearing her black jersey pencil skirt and tangerine silk blouse and was naked underneath. She considered what would feel most stimulating, insistent against her skin. She chose black and fine lace and slipped into a dressing room and took off everything and then she pulled on and strapped the items over her most sensitive parts. She caressed the items that now engaged with her body heat. A moment later, shirt and skirt in place again, she marched out, the new bra and panties her secret to keep secret for the day. She saw a salesman in the men's section. He was folding shirts and even from a distance she knew he smelled like sharp soap and expensive hair gel that would feel wonderfully sticky in her fingers. Incredible.

Rivenchy's French pronunciation of "incredible" hangs in the air. She's caressed the word. In-cred-ahb-la. She looks up, her face flushed.

Vic speaks first. "I see what's going on. Like this stuff in the store makes your Lavanna chick think about sex."

Rivenchy considers, "A woman like this—she dresses to feel who she is, n'cest pas? And a man dresses how?"

Vic shrugs. "I don't put on my boxers and think about sex."

Rivenchy touches her long neck; explains, "I slip on my panties and camisole and dress and stockings and imagine them being slipped off by a man who enjoys how delicate the fabrics are and how they feel on his rugged hands. And he feels how fortunate he is to hold something so precious."

"What's so precious?" Vic asks.

"Me. Of course." Rivenchy looks surprised, as if his question is naive.

I admire Rivenchy's confidence. That she feels she is a precious thing. I think of Stan, slipping into our New York apartment's shower with me, pressing me against the tile wall, our bodies slick and soapy. Frisky, mischievous—the early days of our marriage.

Beth Ann wants to know if Rivenchy bought anything at the La Rinascente. Rivenchy points to the coat rack. Below her soft cashmere shawl is a shiny shopping bag. Rivenchy gives a sidelong wink at Beth Ann.

Beth Ann giggles, loving the titillation and she and Rivenchy high-five. Rivenchy is opening up.

Vic wants to know if something will happen in Rivenchy's story.

I point out that something has already happened—that we are all engaged and questioning and thinking and wondering.

Vic presses. "I mean, maybe she's a klepto. Does she pay for this stuff?"

"Oh, I fancy she does." Rivenchy thinks about it. "It's not about stealing."

Vic pushes, "I mean is something gonna happen? Is there a hidden code inside one of the pockets of one of those purses? If this Lavanna chick buys this lace stuff, does the tag have a code on it that puts her into the middle of an espionage plot of like maybe an international crime?"

"It's just about her fantasies," Beth Ann reasons. "Not the outside world, but the inside world."

"So a book for frustrated women who sit around and want to touch themselves."

"You like women, Vic?" Rivenchy eyes narrow as she pronounces his name 'Veec'. She swings one of her long legs over the other and leans towards him.

"Sure. I'm a heterosexual guy." Vic's defensive.

"But you do not care to know how a woman's mind works?"

"Like pushing a slick, round, really heavy boulder up a slippery hill while wearing greased-up shoes. Guys can't understand women. But I get what you're doing with this Lavanna. She's like a nympho."

Rivenchy's lilting laugh sparkles in the room, it's light and effervescent and her usually controlled demeanor evaporates. She is suddenly softer, younger. "If you want to make yourself irresistible to women, you could clue in maybe un petit, Veec."

Vic shakes his head, can't figure out why his ideas are being dismissed.

Charles makes a comment that his wife seems to like cotton undergarments. Beth Ann giggles and suggests he consider—for his wife's next birthday—a consultation and shopping spree with Rivenchy. "Women like beautiful underwear, but sometimes don't buy it for themselves." She sighs. "The lover, appreciating it—now that's a nice moment."

Charles leans into George. "Maybe we'll both go and learn a thing or two."

I am enjoying the feedback and point out to Rivenchy that her work is responsible for us "getting to the personal". Exactly what a writer wants to happen. Stan would marvel at the letters I got from readers of my books. "It's like they won't just let you just have it be over, story done. They want to keep talking about it."

I check my watch. Stan's plane will be landing in a few hours.

Beth Ann's eyes fill with tears and she hands me her notebook, "Here, you can read this later when you got time. It's about my dog."

"Is your dog with you?" I ask. "In Florence?"

"He's in quarantine until Monday. Three more days."

Charles rests his hands on his Buddha-sized belly. "I would like to meet Jackson. I could go with you to the animal center and translate if you need any help."

"Oh, that would be nice." Beth Ann beams at him.

Charles says he's not ready to read today. "George has told me the make-up of the Milky Way—and I expect it will work quite well for Pynon, my fox. I gazed at the stars from my balcony last night. And came up with some ideas. Tonight, I will sit down and write."

Vic reads:

The watcher…

Charles says, "You have two watchers—a watcher of the watcher and…".

"Right now I'm writing about Finn, the watcher of the fat nun."

Martenella di Casoni, the hot mother with the great legs, takes out a small box wrapped like a present. Hands it over to the fat nun like it's just someone's birthday. Finn stands, surprised, realizes it's going down right now. He's here to get that box. The gun is a Parn 5-60, he has hidden it in his jacket and Finn takes perfect aim. Just a pop is heard. Martenella, hit in the back and through the heart, drops to the ground. The wrapped box hits the stones, skids away from the body. The fat nun thinks fast, grabs the box and scurries off as tourists shriek and run for cover. Finn is quick but the nun surprises him, she's pushing through the crowd like a rat through garbage. He's lost her.

Rivenchy leans forward. "What is in the box?"

Vic points at Rivenchy. "That's what I want you to want to know."

Beth Ann wants to know who is taking care of the baby in the baby carriage and Vic lets her know that the puzzle will be filled in. "No worries."

George goes to the white board hanging on the wall of the room and writes:

X1 (Man) + X2 (Woman)
@ JPL 2+00 r/f ~ =[],<> oi, oi ?/

George translates, "Man and Woman who work at the Jet Propulsion Laboratory—full of fear and truncated senses of self—the '~' represents a decision to marry. It's a marriage of convenience so that children can be had. The '<>' represents that they never regard each other close enough to know any other underlying reasons each of them might have." His grimaces, disappointed in himself. "It's not totally clear yet, I know I have to make it clearer."

"Do you want us to ask questions?" I ask.

He gazes at the whiteboard. "Let me work on it. Maybe tomorrow."

"I get the dilemma." Charles goes to stand next to George, studies the letters and symbols. "Yes, it's quite hard to open up sometimes."

George nods. "Yes."

"I do like the shape of the situation these two people are in. I wish to hear more." Rivenchy's soft voice is clear.

George takes a deep breath; his back seems to broaden a bit as a sense of pride wells up. But he doesn't turn to meet Rivenchy's eyes.

I hand out an assignment, and they pack up their papers. I hear them discussing where they might settle for a glass of wine.

I check my watch again.

Stan's plane should have landed.

Chapter 9

I head towards Piazza di San Firenze to meet Stan at the elegant lobby bar of the Hotel Bernini.

He sits in a high-backed velvet bar chair, deep into his martini. I surmise it is his second or possibly third because his eyes are heavy and his lips stretch into a tense smile—he puts on this smile when he wants to cover a dark inebriation with faux good cheer. I realize I'm disappointed, but I give him room—it's a long flight and he's been working overtime at the firm. And his hair is dipping across his forehead in the way I find endearing, like it does in the morning when we wake up beside each other.

He stands as I approach. "You couldn't cut your class short? I've been waiting. I told them to bring a white wine when you got here—pinot grigio they say is their best by the glass." He raises his hand to get the bartender's attention. "Let's eat at Donnini, okay? You look good. Silky shirt." He kisses me quickly. "That runway at the airport is too short. My stomach was in the seat ahead of me. Why they can't dig out a few hundred more feet of tarmac, I don't get. There's unemployment in Italy. There are able backs and shoulders—they could do it by hand."

"You didn't say how long you'll be able to stay." I drape my raincoat over the back of the chair. "I made a list of things that are happening in the city." I lean in and whisper, "And I put extra pillows on the bed." My lips linger on his; I can taste the gin.

"Maybe get a pair of shoes ordered—do the fitting and they can be shipped. Not much more on my to-do list really."

I sit on the bar chair next to him. "Are you wearing a gray shirt?"

"What?"

I tease, "It's a solid gray shirt—where're the blue and white stripes?"

"It's kind of a gray blue—still good with my eyes." He's defensive. "Right?"

I laugh and buss his cheek. "It's nice." He smells of American Crew shampoo and aftershave. "When did you have time to shave?"

"Did a touch-up before we landed."

"You missed a spot." I touch his jawline. Stan has a strong jaw. Since he runs and works out and is lean, the bones of his jaw stand out. He has a great profile.

My wine appears.

"So—having fun?" He glances at me sideways.

"I like my students." I put my hand on his. For the connection.

"Getting your own work done?" He sounds abrupt. Like a taskmaster.

"I'm putting aside time." I think about leaving the Biblioteca Nazionale to attend the piano concert with Matteo. A bit of guilt. I take a sip of my wine.

"You have a deadline, don't you?"

"You know I do. Let's not talk about work."

He stays on point. "Going straight to e-book maybe with this one."

Surprise is clear in my voice. "What? That's not my contract."

"It's how people are reading. Harledge called me. It's the way things are now. They want you to re-consider."

"But Stan, my contract is for hardcover, paperback three to six months later depending on sales and the e-book in that order. You helped me get that." I rub the gold band on his left hand, put my head on his shoulder. "My lawyer husband took care of it all."

"Publishing is trying to keep afloat, Lyn. You can't be a dinosaur."

I pull back, look him in the eye because his voice has an edge to it. "There are still people out there who like to hold books and I am one of them. It's great there are other options but—having it in book form—it's just something that is important to me. You know that."

"And you are one that believes in contracts." Why does he sound so angry? He must be tired.

"Sure. Legally binding agreements. It helps keep everyone on the same page. You're supposed to support my interests."

"I just don't want you to piss off Harledge."

"Are you being snarky because you've had too many martinis or are you going to use jet lag as an excuse?"

"It's just that you get a little prissy about things being done a certain way."

"Just contracts." I can't help it. Annoyance creeps in. Why is he being so aggressive? "What's wrong?"

"Nothing. I'll let Harledge know. Hungry?"

"I haven't finished my wine." I survey the floor near us. "Where's your bag?"

"Oh. With Wyatt—from work."

"Do I know him?"

"I don't know. He came to hand-hold a client here. Left my bag at his hotel—you know, the Grand Cavour where the Donnini restaurant is. I'm his boss, so I can take advantage. Didn't want to schlep it."

"You said you needed to see me."

"Is that how I put it?"

I laugh. "Yes. 'Need' is a potent word."

Stan seems nervous. He always gets bossy when he's nervous. "Let's go eat."

We proceed to Ristorazione Donnini on Via del Proconsolo. Street vendors are closing their kiosks, wheeling them away for the night. The streets seem strangely empty; a splattering of rain finally fulfills the forecaster's promise. I pull up the hood of my raincoat.

Stan takes the collapsible umbrella out of his suit jacket pocket. It's small but it covers him as we walk.

I want to get a sense of home on the other side of the ocean. "Did you see my brother on football Sunday?"

"The big politician? Sure. He's feeling his oats. Says he and the Mayor are best buds now."

"Marlene wants to get pregnant."

"Yeah, your brother told me. Says she's driving him crazy."

"Maybe we'll all have our kids around the same time." I take his arm. "The little munchkins could be really close cousins."

His steps quicken. "Let's get out of this rain."

A lot of Americans and Brits eat at D.O.C. Donnini; the waiters all speak English. The décor is sleek, glass doors and glass panels face the street, lots of oversized lighting fixtures, white chairs, white tablecloths, high food prices. Only the painted frescoes on the ceiling remind the diners they are in an ancient building. Stan orders another Tanqueray martini.

The restaurant is connected to the elegant and expensive Grand Hotel Cavour. The building was built in the late 1200s, across from the Bargello, an impressive building that was originally a palace, then the headquarters for the city's police, then a prison and now a museum that cares for works by Donatello, Ghiberti, Bruneschelli, Luca della Robbia. It's one of the most beautiful museums in Florence.

Stan selects a primo (prosciutto and figs), secondo (Florentine steak). I'm still full from the lunch at the seminar room.

"Let's get a bottle of wine." Stan signals the waiter. "Castello 2008 if you got it."

The waiter nods and heads off.

And then, over Stan's shoulder, I see her in the hotel lobby; it's divided from the restaurant by glass doors. "Stan, look—is that—?" I can't believe it. "It's Susie!"

He doesn't turn around. He concentrates on the breadsticks on the table and mutters he wants olive oil for dipping purposes. He knows better, bread before the meal—and especially soaking bread in a pool of olive oil—is an American habit. Not done in Italy.

I stand and wave. "Susie!"

She hears my voice and turns. She excuses herself from her conversation with a thin, gangly, bespectacled man in a light raincoat who has his head bent over his cell phone. She joins us and I hug her.

"I thought you couldn't come!"

"I worked it out." She is always beautiful, tonight her hair is pulled back in a ponytail and her skin is flawless.

"This is a great birthday surprise." I am really touched. "Is that a new raincoat?"

Susie smooths it over her hips. "Big sale at Barney's."

I turned to Stan. "This is so fantastic." I include Susie. "Both of you. Thanks."

"She wanted to surprise you." He nods towards Susie.

"So fun. Did you come together?"

Susie affirms, "And with Wyatt."

"Good ol' Wyatt." Stan's tone is derisive. "Sit down so we can order."

"You want me to join you now?" Susie asks.

I pull out the chair. "Why not? What are you talking about? Sit, sit—should we have Prosecco? To celebrate my birthday and your coming all this way." I turn to Stan. "Let's have a wonderful Prosecco."

"We already have a great wine."

The waiter has arrived with the wine and the maître is already sliding a table over next to our two-top. Susie slips into the chair next to Stan. "Well, then. Wyatt should join us too. Do you know Wyatt?" Susie looks around and motions to the lanky man.

He approaches. "Hey boss."

Wyatt Nostron is a few years younger than Stan. He wears heavy rimmed glasses. His sandy hair is combed straight back but there's a cowlick on his hairline—just above his right eye—that forces a few hairs along the scalp to stand straight up.

Stan motions to the waiter to pour the wine. "Drink up, everyone. It's good stuff."

Wyatt doesn't give the impression that he wants to stay but Susie points to the seat next to me. He sits.

"Nice to meet you, boss's wife," he says as he tastes the wine.

"How long can you stay?" I ask Susie as I clink her glass with mine.

"Oh just a few days." She takes a deep sip. "I want to do Cavalli and Ferragamo first, just to dream. The weather's about to change at home and it's time for a fantastic winter coat. And I want to go to Mannini's and order a pair of shoes…"

"So does Stan," I say.

"Well why not, right?" She empties her glass, Stan fills it. His is empty too, they're drinking it like water. Susie glances at Wyatt. "I'll point you to all the great shoe shops. Mannini still has my measurements, I'm sure, and I want to get that "butter" leather this time. Wyatt, did you decide if you want a pair of handmade shoes?"

Wyatt adjusts his glasses and picks up the menu. "Haven't really thought about it."

Susie continues, "Stan, you need to pick out your leather too." She digs into her purse, pulls out a lipstick and quickly applies it. "Don't need to do museums this time, only here for a few days. Wyatt, you'll probably want to…"

Stan waves for another bottle of wine, interrupts. "Wyatt probably has some ideas of his own. And he is supposed to be working."

I ask, "You haven't been here before?"

"No." Wyatt licks his lips before he talks. "No". That was two licks.

"Do you know what you want to see?"

"Any gladiator forums around?" Another lick.

Stan is concentrating on gulping his wine and ignoring Wyatt. I want to be helpful. "Florence didn't preserve theirs—you could take the train to Rome. See the Coliseum."

"*Ben Hur*—the one with Charlton Heston—it's one of my favorite movies."

"Shot in Rome," I tell Wyatt as Susie breaks a breadstick in half.

"Yeah? Maybe I'll take a day to go down there. What do you think, boss?" Wyatt is trying to be deferential.

Stan waves him off. "Put on a tunic and helmet with a feather. Why not?"

Wyatt laughs, as if it is the required response.

Susie pushes back from the table. "You know, I'm not hungry. Wyatt, you ate on the plane too. I'll show you the piazza where the David copy is—it's got some other great statues too." She puts a hand up to me, a signal to stay put. "Sure you two have a lot to catch up on. Stan kept saying the whole way over that you two haven't had time alone for a while."

Stan's eyes are on the chandelier hanging low over the restaurant's center glass table. A large vase of fresh flowers is surrounded by silver bowls filled with figs and porcini mushrooms.

Wyatt licks his lips, dips his head at me. "Well, nice meeting you finally."

"We'll see each other tomorrow, maybe."

Wyatt does not confirm the possibility. He and Susie walk out of the restaurant into the rain. They both hold umbrellas; Susie's bright pink and his black. They pop open in unison. And then I watch them head off in opposite directions. Odd.

"Anything with Wyatt and Susie? He doesn't seem to be her type."

"I don't think he's her type."

"I thought she was going to show him the Piazza della Signoria and she went one way and he went the other. Seems they don't like each other."

"They don't even know each other. As far as I know."

"You two are sweet to come here. It's sweet."

"She planned all this."

I wonder why his mood is so dark. I joke, "That's not romantic; I know Susie's my best friend but you could've lied and said you planned all this to surprise me."

"Sorry."

His Florentine steak arrives. He pushes it aside. "Guess I'm not hungry either."

"Should we get your bag and head towards San Niccolo? I picked up a few things at the grocery. You know the apartment's cozy—especially on a rainy night."

"Let's go to that wine tasting place near the Ponte Vecchio."

"I have class tomorrow, and I have some reading to do. If I keep drinking I won't be able to do it. And you must be tired."

"You can get a soda. I gotta visit my favorite spots, right?"

"Well, okay. Let's get your bag."

He's insistent. "It's a ten-minute walk. I'll come back for it."

"But the Ponte Vecchio is on the way to the apartment…"

"I'll come back for it. Stop controlling."

"What's wrong? How come you're so—snappy?"

"Snappy."

"Like that."

"Kind of an old word."

"Just came to mind."

"Pissy. Jerky. Ass-holey."

"Those words are crossing my mind too."

"I didn't sleep on the plane."

"Let's go to the apartment—you can sleep."

"I'm going to that wine tasting place." He gets up. "Coming?"

A bullheaded stubbornness can accelerate in Stan with every cocktail. He grabs his jacket. "I'm going."

I sit back. He's the one who decided to visit me in Florence. Why is he determined to ruin the night?

He's muttering. "Anyway. Probably easier if I just not worry about the bag at all."

"What?"

"Yeah, no need to take it to your apartment."

"I'm not following."

He dips his head. "It's already in a room. Here. I have a room. With Susie. We decided—it's time to let you know what's been going on."

A piercing pain strikes behind my eyes. "What's been going on?"

"I have a room here already. We have a room. Susie and me. And we came here to tell you."

My gut wrenches, I almost gasp with the ache. Out of the corner of my eye I see a bright pink umbrella walk in front of the glass entrance to the restaurant. The umbrella stalls, turns and moves back the other way. It's clear Susie is pacing up and down the street. The umbrella appears, now right in front of the heavy glass entrance and stalls again. I stare. Susie sees us. Her eyes land on Stan's. And then she looks at me.

She can read my face. She moves off quickly.

I notice the whiteness of the tablecloth. At the one fig Stan didn't eat off his primo plate. My head starts to spin. "Why?"

Stan sits back down at the table. But it's not to answer me—it's to grab his umbrella from the floor.

"Why?"

"Well, I'm sorry, it's not like it was a plan. Just evolved. I guess."

"Evolved." My voice is a strained whisper. "Over how long?"

"Lyn, this isn't easy for me either. But this is how things go—it's not like we have kids or…"

That was on the agenda. Now that the latest book is finished.

Stan rubs his neck, it's as if he resents the need for more explanation. "Lyn, you always think things should not change. Last forever. But you know—I handle my clients' divorces—and things do change."

"I thought we were—we were committed to loving each other."

"Look, I regret this happened, it's not like I'm not repentant. But love is selfish. You know that. You fall in love. It's about seizing it. It's just—you know you gotta seize it. No one wants to hurt anyone." Stan digs in; he has to be right. When I first got to know him,

I thought it was strength—his ability to adhere to the black or the white, his ability to argue and sway. I knew I saw the world as more gray, but I still invest in promises made, promises kept.

"You and Susie?" The person I told all my secrets to, the person I shared a pact with the first day of junior high—no matter what we would sit together at lunch so we never appeared like losers. The person who sat and asked my mother for advice, the person who approved my choice of wedding dress, the person who told me to stand up to Stan when he got overworked at Tander, Ron & Public and assumed his life was more important than mine.

"We just have to accept it, Lyn. Change. That's all it is—okay. Change. Things change."

The waiter arrives with the second bottle of wine; it's opened.

"Shall I pour, sir?"

"Ahhh. Well. I guess—sure." Stan always has a hard time passing up a drink.

The waiter fills Stan's glass. He's about to pour the deep red wine into my glass. I shake my head. "No. Thank you."

Stan raises his hand to the waiter, "Now that I'm thinking about it—you can bring the check and—just take the bottle away, put the cork back in it and send it up to Room 336."

"Yes, sir."

Stan gulps his wine, his eyes flit to the door, to the chandelier. He attempts to make his thoughts logical. "Look, you love it here. Florence. And you're busy here. That's why we thought it was a good place for you to settle in with the news."

Just that they had this conversation makes me nauseous.

"Room 336?" My voice is darker. Stan can hear it.

Stan's eyes dart to me. "Lyn, I said I was sorry. We'll all just adjust."

"All of us?"

"It's hard for all of us." He has the gall to chastise. To make me feel selfish.

My fingers wrap around the closest thing; it's the small glass candleholder, shaped like an open box, there's a wafer of wax floating in a viscous, iridescent liquid and the lit wick shines. I wind up and throw it at Stan's head. He senses my intent and stands to get out of the way and the candleholder thuds against his chest—his gray shirt now has a sticky blob staining it.

"God Lyn, what're you doing? Geez, my shirt—this is from Barney's—what're you doing? You want me on fire?"

"You cheat—you asshole." My world is crumbling and he's worried about his shirt.

He motions to the other people in the restaurant who are now observing us. "Okay maybe this was a bad idea talking to you in a public."

"You think I care that anyone—everyone here—knows you're fucking my best friend?"

Stan feels the room turn on him. "Shut up, Lyn. Just shut up. Don't embarrass us."

I grab the one hundred and fifty dollar cut of Florentine steak and slap his chest with it. Lots of cow fat. Grease. Good.

The maître hurries our way, two waiters behind him.

I grab the plate with one fig on it and frisbee it at Stan's head. He puts out his hand for protection—the plate hits him on the knuckles and flips over and lands on the floor with a heavy cracking thud.

"Ahhhh! Goddamnit—stop being crazy!"

"You fly over here to tell me this like you're doing me some favor?"

"Not here, Lyn! This is not where we—"

"Tear up our contract? Oh right, I'm the problem because I believe in keeping vows."

"Dial it down!"

The maître is behind Stan. "Excuse me, signor—"

Stan whips around and locks eyes with the maître. "Yeah, so yeah, I'm a guest at the hotel and I am going to my room and she…"—he waves in my direction, "…is not a guest here and I am a lawyer and I did not throw anything here—for the record—but any damage—I will pay for it. You can escort her out of here now—we're done." He circles so everyone in the restaurant can hear him.

"And you all are witnesses that I did not initiate this attack—and did not participate." He strides out.

"Go to hell!" I yell after him.

He's already crossing the lobby of the hotel. "Shut up, Lyn!"

Chapter 10

My hands shake as I grab my coat and bag. I'm breathing like there's no air in the room or at least none available to me. It's been sucked out by the someone who has already moved on to Room 336. God, my chest hurts. My throat and lungs are burning.

I head out. The maître is at my heels, I have forgotten my scarf. "Signora, la sciarpia, per favore. Would you like me to arrange a taxi?" His voice is concerned and I barely hear it. I cannot look at the diners staring at me. Pity or anger or disgust, I don't want to see their eyes.

I step out into the rain.

I pull on my hood.

No sign of a pink umbrella.

I feel like my fist could go through the three-foot thick walls of the Bargello.

Only a gaggle of Chinese tourists on the street—all men—they wear white shirts tucked into belted brown pants and thin neon-green rain ponchos available at kiosks for 4 euros for the unprepared.

On the Via del Proconsolo, I head south. Then west. Then north. The rain is coming straight down, steady and hard. I don't know if I'm on a warpath to find a pink umbrella or if I want to get lost. Want the disorientation. Want the blankness. The disarray in the mind. But I have created too many landmarks for myself in the city: La Rinascente, the Church of Santa Trinita, the street filled with tiny Korean restaurants near the train station whose windows are fogged up now because the hot pots are inside and the cool rain is outside, the Central Mercado, where Stan and I binged on anchovy and butter sandwiches—I push away the image of Stan, butter on his lips, racing back to the food counter to order three more. The Piazza San Lorenzo where we sat and watched a parade of Florentine musicians playing Renaissance instruments and my thoughts of sometime doing this with our children. The Piazza San Marco where the obsessed monk Savonarola plotted against the city and destroyed countless works of art all in the name of the Church. Plots. Betrayals. Stan and I were dismayed at the people who fell under Savonarola's spell, the people who trusted him and destroyed great paintings and great books and many lives. I groan, so aware—in this moment—of the irony of Stan being dismayed at betrayal. I want to pound on the church's doors. Insist Savonarola's hell be open to Stan.

I step under the shelter of a bus stop. Gaze at the rain.

No pink umbrella in sight.

Destruction. Disposal. I realize that, to Stan, I am absolutely disposable. So easily replaced. How can it be so easy—all over in just a few words. A statement of his desires. My desires, my investment means nothing. Just words in a restaurant, over wine and food, end it all. Rivers did not part, there was no explosion, no beat of impending danger. Just words. Just matter of fact. "We will all have to adjust." I continue on, breathing hard again. I try for deep breaths, try to stop the rage from surging up and out into wails of anger.

When I pass the carousel, closed for the night, its canvas cover tied tightly over the shiny and colorful wooden horses—I know I've done a long loop. Hours have passed but this immense, pent-up physical and mental distress continues to fill every corner of my being. My heart is still pounding. My mind is still racing. I move towards the Ponte Vecchio. Maybe the river and the misted lights reflected in the moving water will appease in some way.

The bridge is people-less, the jewelry shops that line its edges closed hours ago. The drenching downpour has urged all to enjoy the interior warmth of bistros or bars or apartments or hotel rooms.

What are Stan and Susie doing together right now?

I stop by the Cellini fountain. It stands in the center of the bridge. I think of Room 336.

Do I storm it? Do I stand wild-eyed and wet in the doorway and see crumpled sheets and tossed clothes and a bottle of Castello 2008 that has been huddled over as they discuss my reaction, my tossing of food and their future?

I glare at the bust of Benvenuto Cellini. Asshole. I never liked that he was given this prominent place and tonight the unbalanced, venal Florentine who lived more than 500 years ago especially offends me. He took what he wanted when he wanted it and damn to all others.

"Hey. You're not gonna jump, are you?" The voice comes from the shadows on the opposite side of the bridge. Behind a canvas covered kiosk. "I feel rotten too."

I don't want to engage with a stranger. I move away.

Footsteps follow me.

"You sure you want to be alone?"

I turn, fast. My arms shoot out—fists clenched, jaw tight and teeth bared. I spit, "Get away. Get away. I'll scream—just get the hell away from me!"

He steps into the light. It's Wyatt, holding his black umbrella over his head. The Wyatt who wants to go to Rome and imagine Ben Hur's chariot in the gladiator ring.

"Does that tough talk work? Shouldn't you have mace or something?"

"I do have mace." It's in my hand. I always keep it in the side pocket of my bag. My voice is deep and gravelly and very unfriendly.

He steps back, now a little afraid of me. "Okay. Just to let you know, you don't have to activate it. I'm harmless."

"Shouldn't sneak up on people." I bring my arms down.

"Yep. Okay. Yep. My stupid."

I turn back to the river view. I know I am chewing my lip too hard, I know I could break the thin skin, but I don't care.

"I had a feeling it was coming. I didn't want to be part of it."

He got my attention, I twist my head towards him. "What do you mean you knew it was coming?"

"Stan's my boss. I mean, he's a junior partner—makes him—kind of my boss."

"And?"

"I didn't want to be part of it—didn't seem like you knew it was coming."

"I did not know it was 'coming'."

"Figured. Hey, it sucks."

"How were you part of it?"

"Just that one of our rich clients is here and wants on-the-spot legal advice—he's buying some fancy condo near the St. Regis hotel—and I was sent to give the papers a once-over, confirm the final details, oversee the signing. Stan heard I was coming and said do him a favor and come to dinner when we all got here. He said, 'I'm meeting my wife. You come with Susie'. Didn't give me a choice really."

"But you said you knew…"

"I said I had a feeling. That there was some kind of plan."

"You knew about them? Everyone in the office knew?"

A low, mean rumble of thunder. The rain falls harder now.

"Do you want to get under the umbrella?"

"No." The hood of my raincoat is soaked and heavy and feels appropriate.

"Saw her waiting for him a few times after meetings. Kind of hit me—like they stood too close together. And then I heard them talking on the plane. It's not like they just came out and said I was supposed to be a beard. But I sussed it out—what I thought was going on."

On my furious trudge through Florence in the last hours, I had gone through every look, every word I could remember in the last months. Had I been stupidly blind? I remembered thinking about how I was always defending Stan to Susie and defending Susie to Stan. They had always been at odds, as if they were jealous of each other's place in my life—but the war between them had seemed to have heated up. It was exhausting. How long have they been playing me? I lean forward over the low stone wall of the bridge. The incredibly low barrier hits me at my knees.

"Maybe it's not a good idea for you to be leaning over the side of a bridge right now."

"Go away."

"But you gonna just hang on this bridge? You're not going to jump, are you?"

I'm incredulous, his words slam me in the gut. "No. I'm not thinking about that."

"Good. That you aren't thinking about it. That means you don't crumble. I mean, I asked 'cause I don't know you and so I didn't know if you're like an emotional person."

"No, you don't know me." I scrutinize Cellini. "Maybe I ended up here 'cause I'm attracted to assholes."

"Excuse me? Are you calling me a…"

"Cellini's an asshole."

"Don't know anything about him."

I point to the dark bust. "A creepy but beloved native son of Florence." Cellini was a musician, a sculptor, a goldsmith, a poet, an unwelcome sodomite, a thief, a murderer and a planner and perpetrator of violent assaults. He even bragged about his less than stellar attributes in a book he wrote and still he received commissions from

Popes and other rich Italians to create magnificent medals, coins and statues.

"How can men act like total shits and still make it big—they move right on." I glare at the bust of this man who let his emotions lead. Maybe I should take a lesson from him. He was never politically or socially correct. He took revenge on anyone he thought did him wrong—revenge with malice and forethought. "One time he decided to plunge his dagger into the legs of someone—he didn't want to kill the guy—he just planned to cripple him for life. He wrote about that. Proud of it."

"Glad I didn't know him."

"Also wrote about conjuring devils to attack his enemies." I hear myself—angry, clutching at distraction and purpose at the same time. "Maybe I should find some of Cellini's devils."

Wyatt's voice is light but cautioning—as if my rambling is a sign I am at a breaking point. "Look, if they are devils out there to hire, as a lawyer, I advise you…"

"No, thanks." I walk to the other side of the bridge, frustrated with legal-ese, of 'should'.

He has an idea. "Look, maybe you should let me buy you a drink."

I spin around and shout at the top of my voice, "God, no!"

Wyatt steps back. "That was kind of vehement."

"I don't want to get a drink. With you. Or anyone."

"Got it. Got it." He licks his lips.

"Every time I look at you I envision Stan. So, I don't want to know you."

"I get it." Still, he doesn't move. "It's just I don't know where I am really—I don't know anything around here and I'm sick of walking around wondering if I'm gonna like this bar or that place and I don't want to go into the snotty places in the hotels and it's raining and I mean it's pretty here that's for sure—but it's raining and I want to end up in a good place since I'm not going to be here very long. Could you just ahhh—point me to a bar that's good?"

We're close to Via San Jacopo. I point and tell him to walk a hundred meters or so until he sees the Friends Pub on his left; it's a popular spot. Sports on multiple televisions. Ex-pat patrons. People he'll be able to talk to. Good wi-fi.

"Thanks. And again. It really sucks." Wyatt licks his lip and decides not to say anything else. He heads off, the black umbrella high in the air. He turns and yells, "I never thought Stan was a good guy anyway so I say you should say 'good riddance'."

I turn in the opposite direction and move towards San Niccolo.

The dark and ominous Zuma Social Club, situated at the apex of a triangular bike-park platform dividing the street along the Arno, Via di Lungarno, and the Via di San Niccolo that leads to my neighborhood, is just opening; its hours are 10 pm to 6 am. I've been told any kind of drink or drug or stimulant or depressant or desired hallucinogenic can be gotten in its dark rooms. And any less-than-socially-acceptable-desire can be made clear here and there will be something or someone to fulfill it. People are arriving, umbrellas held low over faces; they don't appear like they're entering for adventure or for fun. They look like they are being pulled into the mouth of a beast.

Umbrella-less and soaked, I pass by.

In my apartment, I let my raincoat fall to the tile floor.

The room exudes the aura I administered this morning. Of being expectant. The wine. The two glasses. The unlit candles, matches beside them, at the ready. The bread on the board. The extra pillows on the bed.

I open the refrigerator and cupboard and dump their contents into a trash bag. Salami. Cheese. Crackers. Oatmeal. Capers. I don't bother putting my coat back on; my shirt is already soaked through. The bottoms of my pants are heavy and wet. I drag the bag down the stairs, it bumps against every step, gets heavier as I muscle it through the door and outside. I slog to the garbage and recycle containers at the end of the block, lift the top of the container with a blue lid marked 'Waste'—this plastic box is for things that cannot be recycled because they mold, decay and get toxic.

I'm about to stuff the bag in here when I see a body asleep in a doorway. This person is maybe twenty—his scrawny dog is next to his worn backpack and a torn blanket is wrapped around his chest. He's stretched out half into the rain. Perhaps a traveling college student and he's run out of money and doesn't have parents to call for help. Or he's an adventurer seeking identity and the quest has gone sour. Or he's been robbed. Of money. Of friendship. Of trust. Or he paid the deposit for the expensive impossible at the nearby Zuma Social Club and when he couldn't pay his bill, he was kicked outside to sink to the sidewalk here. Sleep has pulled him into a safer place, for a few hours.

I put the bag of food next to him. The dog raises her head for a moment, sniffs the air, barely opens her thin eyelids; she's too old and too wet to even whimper. She nestles closer to her partner.

The Zuma Social Club door opens and a large man comes out, he must be the bouncer. He's three hundred pounds and his arms are thick as the pillars on the portico of the Uffizi. He looks over at the sleeping young man, the dog, and me—my hair pasted against my head, my sodden shirt dripping off my shoulders, my rain-soaked face. He pulls out his cell phone; I know he's notifying the police. Florence does not appreciate loiterers or anyone who takes away from the perfection and beauty of the city. Boy and dog will soon be drying out under the eye of the urban watch—the polizia municipal.

I trudge back to the apartment before I have to explain myself to the polizia. My legs are heavy. My ankles are cold and I know my shoes are ruined. I am fine being drenched.

The lights on either side of the entry doors of the Hotel Cascini are golden; they shed a soft, dreamy glow onto the rain-drenched stone street. The door of the hotel opens. Lucia's boyfriend has picked her up; it must be the end of her shift. She wears a 1960s plastic raincoat with yellow daisies embossed on it. They are lovers, arm in arm, moving onto the street. He holds the umbrella over them both and they press against each other under the streetlight.

I stop. Their happiness stings. I want to shout that faith in love is fleeting. Don't feel too much. Don't trust too much. But I stay in the shadows. I wait for them to walk off.

I feel lost. I have no idea what someone's supposed to do when she's told her marriage is over. When she doesn't have a best friend to call.

When change is now a force that cannot be sidestepped.

Chapter 11

The sound of my cell phone. A text coming in.

It's the next morning. I'm half asleep. My terry cloth robe is twisted around my naked body. The blankets have been kicked to the floor.

My mouth is dry. My neck hurts, the tension unreleased; it cracks as I turn to reach for my phone. I read:

We left Florence. You know I never want to hurt you but this can't be denied. Love. It's more than I can turn away from. It really is. So sorry. We have to talk. Susie.

I delete it. I turn off my phone. It seems unreal. A bad dream.

But I know it's not.

I think about going to Caffé Gilli. Stick to a routine.

But I can't get out of bed.

The cat, Frankie Firenze, is on the roof outside the window. He cleans his dark whiskers with his white paws and watches me as if he can read my thoughts—as if he can follow my mind as it slips from one recollection to another:

In high school, Susie's boyfriend, skinny Griffin who was an all-state high school shortstop and collected porn, was two-timing her with Titiana, a girl from the other side of Bayside. Tatiana wore tight jeans and tighter t-shirts with messages that told anyone looking at her plump perk-i-fied breasts to either drop dead or jerk off. Her boots had silver spikes on the toes. Her hair was colored a deep black and she chose an Addam's Family shade of lipstick. Next to her, blonde Susie was like a delicate preppy Barbie doll. Susie put up with Griffin's fascination with Tatiana for months; she claimed her love for him and her support of his dream of being a professional baseball player would win out. But Griffin eventually chose Tatiana and wouldn't take Susie's calls and avoided being within a hundred feet of her. Susie gained fifteen pounds.

Stan told me the night he proposed—after the Super Bowl—that he believed in me and believed in us. I remember thinking that I should be happy for this. I decided to follow the "should".

Stan's law firm handles high profile divorce cases. Every day he deals with people wanting out of marriages. Does he think our marriage is just like others that go rancid? Just like all the others that fall apart?

How many times did I listen to Susie bitch about love?

Susie was married once. To Gilbert Vander. She thought she was in love with her-squeeze-at-the-time Jacob when she met Gilbert. She had volunteered to help organize a Viennese Modern Collection at MOMA, a special summer event to please Jacob's family; they had fled Vienna in 1940 and became successful New York bankers after the war. Just as she was researching taking classes in the Talmud and considering converting, Jacob announced he had committed to marry a woman more pleasing to his family and the family holdings. Susie blamed his mother—'the racist money-grubbing bitch'. Susie, anger consuming her, continued on with her volunteer work at MOMA so Jacob would still see her twice a week at the meetings he now attended with a short, round, mouse-faced fiancé whose hair was pulled back in a severe bun with the help of two plastic headbands and primary-colored plastic hairclips. Susie told me 'Pellet Eyes' (her name for Jacob's wife-to-be) watched him every minute. Two weeks later, she met Gilbert at the museum; an investment manager interested in the claim of one of his clients concerning a lost Holbein (or was it a Rubens?) that had been found in a dirt-covered crate in a cave in Northern Germany—hidden there by Field Marshal Goering and earmarked during Hitler's glory years for the Fuhrermuseum. Gilbert's client was successful in proving the provenance of the painting, was given ownership, and then sold it to a museum in Boston for 10 million dollars. This gave Gilbert's client more money to invest in stocks and bonds and made Gilbert richer. Susie followed opportunity, married Gilbert a few months later on a drunken weekend in Las Vegas. A year later it became clear that Gilbert really preferred sexual romps with his male assistant. Susie and I huddled in my apartment and finished three bottles of wine cursing Gilbert and giggling about bad sex. "Your life is always together," she said. "How come no one loves me?" She fake-cried and we chortled. But Susie did get a good settlement. Enough to start her 'Susie at the Beach Wear'.

Stan, on our wedding day, waiting for me at the front of the church. My father walking me down the aisle. My mother sitting in the front pew. My mother's face. Her eyes meeting mine. I could read her 'hope' for happiness for me.

My parents' comfortable marriage. They grew to have very different interests and dreams. I could see that as I got older. But they were always there for each other.

Susie is beautiful, her delicate face and nose, porcelain skin and blue eyes seem to have an inner light behind them. Her mouth is not delicate; her lips are very defined and large for her face. In the last years, she's leaned towards darker and redder lipsticks that draw attention to those lips.

Susie laughing too hard at Stan's jokes.

Betrayal is a monster that feeds on trust.

The terry cloth robe is bunched under my ribcage. Its bulk digs into my skin. I don't re-adjust; I don't smooth it out.

I don't want to think of the conversations about me that took place after sex between Stan and Susie. Maybe it was like this:

Stan: We're not gonna tell her about this.

Susie: Of course not. It was the martinis. No one needs to know. She's my BF. I feel terrible. It was the martinis.

Stan: Yeah.

Susie: I'm drinking too much.

Stan: You got a clean towel I can use? Gotta take a shower. Lyn knows your perfume.

Susie: In the closet in the bathroom. There's an extra robe too. Gilbert left it.

Stan: So you do this…on a regular basis?

Susie: I'm not married anymore. I 'do' this when I feel the urge.

Stan: So I was just an urge.

Susie: Because of the martinis. You?

Stan: I've thought about this. Us. You. Before. I'm sure you have too. Thought about it.

Susie: Why do you say that?

Stan: Tell me if I'm wrong. I thought I saw a look.

Susie: Maybe you saw a look. But it was probably too many martinis.

Stan: Yeah.

Susie: This can't happen again.

Stan: No. I'll take a shower and…this never happened.

Or maybe it was like this.

Stan: That was the best I have ever—

Susie: You and Lyn don't…?

Stan: Not like this.

Or maybe it was like this.

Susie: I want to cry. I betrayed my best friend. I'm a terrible person.

Stan: You're too beautiful to be sad. It's my fault. I dreamed about you and god, I wanted those lips all over me.

Or this.

Susie: My therapist told me to pursue all my desires. Not hold back.

Stan: You didn't hold back.

Susie: My therapist said 'as long as your desires don't harm others, act on them.'

Stan: Didn't harm me.

Susie: What about Lyn?

Stan: Lyn who?

And they laugh.

Frankie Firenze stretches. He pads closer to the edge of the near-by roof. I imagine he's asking me if I want to continue this misery or if I plan to heave myself out of bed to go to my Italian lesson.

I turn on my phone and cancel my Italian lesson. My voice is so rough—the manager at Parola assumes I'm sick. I agree. I am. Sick to my core. I turn off my phone.

Frankie Firenze hisses, disappointed in me. He arches his back and turns away; clearly I am no longer of interest. He shakes his rear end and twists his torso to give me one last gander that asks: Is this your plan? Rot in your bed until your flesh withers and your bones break from disuse? Allow the landlord or Lucia or Mildred to find you when the stench of your distress and disenchantment with all things human wafts out and into the city? I groan. I wave the cat away; I don't need judgment. Has he no pity?

He pees on the roof tiles.

It's so calculated that I imagine he's peeing on my bed. Soiling my refuge.

Chapter 12

Hours later.

Mildred is in her office. She looks up as I pass. "Lyn, your agent called. She said you're not answering your cell or getting back to her on her emails."

"Took a day off from communication."

"Why are you wearing that hat?"

"Like it." It's a khaki-colored rain hat that droops over my face and low on my neck. Definitely not stylish. And since it isn't raining anymore, superfluous. But I don't want to show my face, I am afraid it wears my hurt.

Loser.

Is that how I feel?

It's a shock that "loser" is a word that pops into my mind.

Did I feel like I failed a competition? Failed to be compelling enough to maintain a prized position—to be the recognized, main, immutable object of passion and devotion of another person. The one put first in line above all others when faced with possibilities for romantic, hedonistic, sexual entanglements. Denial of all others. The other. An element that disrupts the normalcy of life. Susie. The other.

But in the past, she was the one standing right by my side.

Sounds like a horror scenario.

I hear a low growl, a signal of pain. Or is it danger? It's coming from deep inside a closed throat. Mine.

"Could be your agent has news about your book." Mildred is eyeing me, maybe she notices my heavy shoulders. That I'm not listening to her. My lack of being present. Her face definitely registers disapproval of the hat.

I roll my shoulders, tell myself to show some spine. "You never know. I'll check in with her. Thanks, Mildred."

I head into the seminar room. Beth Ann and Rivenchy look startled when they see me. Beth Ann comes over quickly. "You all right, honey?"

"Absolutely." I say.

Vic comments on the hat, "Looks like something a spy in the Amazon would wear to ward off monkeys. Or like a super condom on a thin pecker."

"Oh please, Veec." Rivenchy puts her hands to her ears, wanting to block out his remark.

Charles tells Vic he has a very descriptive bent.

Vic snorts, "It's just the writer in me. Sorry if I offended. But ya gotta admit, it's a weird hat."

George scrutinizes the hat. As if it is an alien on my head.

I take it off and hang it on the hooks provided for coats and bags and ugly hats.

Beth Ann puts her jacket on a nearby hook, revealing her bright turquoise t-shirt sequined with a design of pink stars. "Maybe you caught a bug."

"No. No."

"Your skin's as pale as a newborn piggy's butt, honey."

"Thank you for that image, Beth Ann. But grazie, I'm fine. Fine."

"Your forehead's got a huge wrinkle in the middle. I didn't notice you had one before. I think it's new. Mine does the same thing when someone pisses me off and I hold it all in." Beth Ann gazes at me like my mother used to when she knew I wasn't telling the truth.

I can hear the rasp in my ragged breath. Suddenly I really miss my mother. I know she would be sad about how awful I feel. When Stan and I got engaged, she held my hand and said, "Who you commit to loving is the most important decision. And maybe no one can make that decision until they have lived a lifetime." Her hands were dry, thin. She was getting weaker. I told her, "Mom, that makes no sense. I want to commit to love now so I can live within it. Not wait." She smiled and said of course—that was the dilemma. She added that if people did wait a lifetime, important things could never happen. Like me, she said. She would never want to miss out on me, her daughter. I kissed her cheek. Right now, at this moment when the what-I-thought-of-as-the-true rug has been pulled out from under me, I want to sit across the kitchen table from my mother and pour my heart out. She would make me soup. I know she would.

"Make sure you're takin' care of yourself—if it's a bug," Beth Ann is saying.

I tell her, "I'll take extra Vitamin C today."

It does amaze me that my legs, my eyes and ears, my plans for class and all everyday concerns of life are still functioning and moving forward. Things are the same but not at all the same. My personal emotional earthquake has a huge effect on me but not on others who expect things from me. I need to honor my commitments. I should keep going.

Should. That word again.

The seminar writers pull out their pages and share anecdotes about museum visits, food and their writing. I wonder about the pains that might plague each of them—pains they do not discuss because they are too raw. Or too personal to share with those who see you in only one way. The devastation inside me threatens to own the center of my mind. I make an effort: "We should get to work." I lead them to the large conference table at the far end of the room. Charles has brought bruttiboni for the group—biscuits made from hazelnuts and egg whites that look like misshapen dumplings. The name for these sweet and sturdy treats translates as "ugly but good". Charles moves the open box towards me, "They're excellent with coffee."

I appreciate the gesture. "Nice of you to think of all of us. I'll have one later."

Beth Ann says, "Oh I shouldn't." She bites into a bruttibono. "Mmmmm, yummy. Oooh, I am glad I didn't wait."

"Nuts and meringue baked slowly, superb Italian idea." Charles places the box in the center of the table.

"Let's get started." I take out my notebook.

"I want Rivenchy to go first." Beth Ann's eyes twinkle.

"C'est vrai?" Rivenchy is surprised.

George mutters agreement. "Seems now we're all very interested in shopping."

Charles laughs and slaps George on the back. George looks pleased that he has made a sort of joke.

Vic sighs. "Oh man, more fantasies about sex?"

"I hope so." Beth Ann giggles.

Vic snorts. But he peeks at Rivenchy and I discern his anticipation as she smooths her short suede skirt and swings a bare leg over the other. One of Rivenchy's low heeled, leopard-skin shoes dangles off her toes. She clears her throat, fills her lungs and begins:

Grayson was on the 4th floor, in House Goods, on a ladder, hanging a 'Special Sale' sign. Lavanna was coming up the escalator, headed for the employee's break room. She passed by and noticed the promise of his long legs and rounded ass under pressed gabardine slacks. The shiny black leather belt around his waist. "Wait." She was afraid his eyes would see the heave of her breasts. "Wait." He climbed down the ladder and took her hand and pulled her gently down the hallway. They reached the stock room, leather purses there on shelves, leather jackets on hangers, new linens stacked by color in cabinets. He closed the door and said, "I do under-

stand 'no'". She mouthed 'yes'. He dropped his head into the curve of her neck, his lips insistent as he unbuttoned her black silk shirt, his hair brushed her cheek as he unzipped her suede skirt, his hands strong on her skin, he pulled her close so she could feel his heat through the fine cloth of his clothing. She breathed in the perfume of leather and...

Rivenchy stops, "And if I write what happens next with Lavanna—and him—will people want to read it?"

Beth Ann leads the encouragement.

I glance down at my open notebook. My mind's propelled to the memory of Stan pulling me into our bedroom, kissing me as we undressed for bed. His socks. Always fresh socks. Two or three times a day. The pair I bought him for Christmas—red, with a Santa sliding down the chimney stitched on them. Stan sitting on the couch with my Dad who always wore his ugly Christmas sweater on present-opening morning. I see Stan driving in the 'Stang after my dad died and we advertised it for sale, we are delivering it to its new owner. Our leaving the 'Stang in its new driveway, Stan never gazing back at the vehicle that—for years—had felt almost like part of the family. Stan, cash in his pockets, relishing the thought of moving on and never looking back at the treasure left behind.

I pull myself out, I don't want memories to rule. Vic is waving his hand in the air like a child who thinks he has the right answer, "Okay, Riv—let me tell you some possibilities here. This guy could be about to steal from her. Use her for somethin'. Like set her up for a big fall in a big scam he's got going."

He is like a broken record. I tease, "Vic, write your own story. Not Rivenchy's."

Beth Ann adds, "Maybe he's just gonna have wonderful sex with her and…"

Vic presses, "And then what?"

Beth Ann finishes her sentence with dreamy appreciation, "…and do it again. And again. And again."

"Let's talk about this," I venture. "Not every piece of fiction needs a set-up, complications, climax and resolution. Some work just starts. And ends." Every word causes my gray matter to tumble to the rumpled sheets of Room 336. "Your fiction can look at a place. A feeling. An idea."

"But then it shouldn't be not called a story." Vic does not let up.

"Perhaps it is something else entirely. I am just saying, problems don't need to be solved—lots of problems are never solved. Right?" I view them, my heart pounding because my words hit too close to home. I try to escape my feelings, access another part of my brain. "Samuel Beckett did it—maybe we'll look at parts of his *Unnamable* next week."

"Who's that?" Beth Ann asks.

I explain, "An Irish writer…"

Charles jumps in, "Lived a lot in Paris. Wrote in English and in French."

"Lived?" Beth Ann catches the past tense.

George nods. "Pretty old when he went the way of all flesh. Great writer."

I tease Charles and George. "So, you two like to read about the despair of man."

Charles laughs. "I'm a Brit, I enjoy Irishmen suffering and questioning reasons for existence. *Godot. Unnamable.*" He recites from memory, "'For to go on means going from here, means finding me, losing me, vanishing and beginning again.'"

"I don't read books by fancy big-word writers. Nobody does anymore, right?" Vic says.

"Different audiences for different books," I say. "Can't predict." No predicting when others' choices will affect everything.

Beth Ann is being thoughtful, looking at Charles. "I like what you quoted from that Beckett writer—'cause when you do move forward sometimes you feel like you're losing yourself. And you wonder if you'll ever slow down to allow the old 'you' to catch up again."

George speaks slowly. "I don't think I care about plot. I care about how Riv—Rivenchy…" He steals a glance at her beauty and

I wonder if this is the first time he has said her name out loud. He continues, "…is reducing a relationship to an equation—two similars reacting in similar ways. The trajectory of their relationship could be predictable unless a foreign agent is introduced. There is a predictable path until modification is introduced. It's just the truth of it."

"That's what I am saying—without the ten dollar words." Vic interjects, "Introduce some conflict."

"Or not." I want to pat Vic's hand to calm him down. "Rivenchy may not be looking at change. She could be just looking at 'being'".

"Oui. It's animal magnetism." Rivenchy shrugs, it seems she doesn't want it to be complicated. She breathes out, her full lips soft. "Lavanna, my character, she is just floating. Searching—searching for a purpose. All she can do, right now, is live in her senses. I do not know if there will be a change. I wonder about it, but I do not know." Rivenchy turns to me. "I do not want to have a plan."

Beth Ann announces she'll go next. "Just to let you know, I heard I can pick up Jackson—my doggie—tomorrow." Her upper-body moves in a happy dance. She lets us know that after the seminar, she and Jackson will be traveling to Ravello on the Amalfi coast. "Jackson'll love smelling the sea." She doesn't know how long they'll stay but she wants to walk in the famous gardens there and she loves the fact that a reclusive silent movie actress—Greta Garbo—used to stay there. "So I didn't write much, except for this:

Jackson was on a leash and Billy Jo's sister, Georgina, held the leash. And when Jackson saw Billy Jo walk out of the rehab clinic, his three legs buckled and he dropped to the ground, his whimper so deep that Billy Jo could tell it came from a deep part of his heart. Georgina insisted Jackson's tears were as big as Billy Jo's—but Billy Jo reminded her sister that dogs can't cry like humans but Georgina said she was sure as hell positive Jackson did shed those croco-dile-sized tears.

Beth Ann turns to me. "Like you said, Lyn, write about where we are right now today—and where we see ourselves tomorrow." The sun streams through the open window and Beth Ann's sequin-studded t-shirt sparkles.

Her words transform into neon signs in my mind. They flash 'Today.' I resist enumerating a consideration of names for yesterday. 'Super Suck Day.' 'You're a Wuss Day.' Or 'I would like to bomb Room 336 Day.'

Charles is taking the attention, tells us he's still in the research stage, "As you know, Galileo was born in Pisa but spent a lot of his time in Florence. He was the first to develop a telescope he could use to document individual moons—like those moving around Jupiter. He got everyday people during the Renaissance excited about astronomy. I thought I would set my story about Pynon, the fox, in the time of Galileo. Maybe he even knows of Galileo. He'll choose the star he wants to travel to. I decided to name the star 'Another World'."

Vic has an opinion. "Sure, it's 'another world', but you could use a cool name that sticks, you know. Like Tatooine or Mustafar or Naboo. Like in *Star Wars*. Or Hala or Xander. Like in *Guardians of the Galaxy*. Or Solaris. Or Vulcan. Like in *Star Trek*."

"Remember," I remind Charles. "It's yours to live as you want."

"'Live' as I want or 'write' as I want?" Charles has a questioning look in his eyes.

I correct myself, "To write as you want."

My mis-speak rattles in my mind. 'Live as you want'. The bullshit of it all. I thought my 'want' was shared. I tell myself that 'want', ultimately, is a one-person thing. And life is determined according to who wants what.

George hands a piece of paper to each of us. "This is, umm, the code breaker. Since the story's in verse—and ahmmm, specifically in relatively short lines, should make it manageable. The code's not rigorous. Here is what I have today." He goes to the white board and writes in code. Charles uses the cheat sheet and decodes for us:

Two cannot be one, Newton decreed.
We're lost in cold logic, so precise and alone. I agreed
To marriage, friends. Making a pact.
Accepting the lines as drawn. We think we cannot expect more.
We tell ourselves.

George adds more. Charles decodes:

But one day, across a room,
Science from me flew to you. It was
Not computable.
You lead my gaze from project to unknowing need.
And if ignorance were bliss I'd sacrifice all I own.
All I know
For your sweet kiss.

Vic leans in, "Okay, I can see that *'vl'* means love. You got something for 'hate'?"

George looks surprised. "At this point, it does not factor into my story." He tells us his plan. "I could have the code breaker at the end of the book, then people can access it and get the story faster. Like the people who like to look at the answers of the crossword puzzle before they start." He doubts himself. "Or maybe I should have it, ahmmm, on a website and not in the book?"

Vic speaks up, "I just gotta say this, I know this is for the real smart-brains out there, but I don't see big sales, buddy."

Rivenchy interjects, "Veec, you are such a downer."

Vic is surprised, his chin pulls back and his eyes widen. "I am?"

Rivenchy nods, "Isn't that what you Americans call someone who questions everything and sees nothing positive? Or is it kill-joy?"

Vic settles back; her words have stung. "I was just trying to be honest. Helpful. Sorry."

Charles adds, "I have to disagree with Vic. George's style is for readers who like to read a particular way. I am sure George is not unique in this and there could be a strong reception."

George beams. "That's fine. As long as there's someone."

His words hang, resonate for me. "As long as there is someone." How important that is to each of us.

Chapter 13

We take the ten-minute walk to the market district, I've arranged a visit for the seminar writers at the Biblioteca Laurenziana, a beautiful and intimate library designed by Michelangelo in the early 1500s. It's part of the Basilica San Lorenzo. We move onto Via Roma and then turn onto the narrower Borgo San Lorenzo—past the mobile phone shops, modish clothing stores, small panini shops and restaurants. The sun is warm and there is a breeze, slightly cool. I am too disquieted to enjoy it, too tense. Every place reminds me of times when I walked by with Susie. Or Stan. Or the three of us.

Soon the street opens into the Piazza di San Lorenzo and there is the basilica, standing grand and venerable. Technically it is incomplete—because Michelangelo's design for a Carrara marble façade was never realized. I always marvel at how gorgeous I find it; its unfinished rawness and today, I am touched at how it can soothe me. My mother told me of how she used to come here, to the steps leading to the massive entry into the church, with other Mud Angels when the waters of the 1966 flood receded; they would climb the steps to the immense church and be grateful that is was built higher than the street and there would be no digging through refuse and sludge here to save its irreplaceable artifacts. She told me the *angeli* would enter the church and huddle in the Sagrestia Vecchia, the Old Sacristy designed by Filippo Bruneschelli, and recharge before going back to their back-breaking and soul-wrenching work near the river. For every treasure they saved, there were others beyond salvation. Some lost forever.

I pull myself out of reverie and let the writers know how pleased I am to share the Biblioteca Laurenziana with them. I tell them, that in the year 393, one of the first churches in the piazza was consecrated by the controversial theologian St. Ambrose—he had been a governor and bishop of Milan and had an enthusiastic ardor for virginity, persecution of Jews and charity for the poor and suffering.

Beth Ann raises her eyebrows. "Sounds like there's good and bad in him."

Vic adds, "Yeah, in everybody."

"Then a thousand years later, Cosimo de'Medici the Elder—he was the first in the Medici political dynasty—and a big collector of books and manuscripts, wanted to show off the city's wealth and engineering skills. It was important to impress—so Medici decided if he could impress all of Italy—that would impress all of Europe—and of course, impress God." I tell them Bruneschelli was given the commission to construct a major cathedral where the smaller church stood but he died during the process and others were tasked to finish it. So, in this one structure, important artists and engineers and craftsmen from different generations put their marks—Bruneschelli, Michelangelo, Tribolo, Donatello and others. "But Angelica, she's my friend—one of the many international scholars who focus on Florence—she'll tell you more." We enter the shaded corridor south of the wide steps of the church and pass through into the historic church and grounds. Angelica, in a deep orange shirt, rust colored slacks and strands of red glass beads around her neck, waits for us. She has worked in the preservation of the library's holdings for twenty years. I kiss her on both cheeks and, with a grin, introduce her as "the crazy Polish academic who always wears orange and pedals through Florence on her orange bicycle, her orange basket usually full of books and bread and wine."

Angelica's energy is boundless; she lives in a fifth-floor walk-up, dates an Italian construction worker; they rock climb and he can barely keep up with her. She holds up a finger and asks the seminar writers to give us a moment. She takes me aside; her excitement is palpable. "Remember, I told you about Domenico—he was eight years old when your mother was here in Florence. He is here now."

"What?"

"He was able to come with me today to meet you. Remember, I told you he would maybe. He loves to talk about how he rode in his father's truck during the flood and handed out food and blankets when some streets were cleared. He says he liked meeting the Americans the most, he tried to meet them all. There he is, talking to the padre."

I do remember asking Angelica to see if Domenico could talk with me but the request had flown from my mind. I see him standing a few feet behind Angelica, he wears heavy denim work pants and shirt, an open orange safety vest. He holds a yellow construction helmet under his arm. He is talking to an earnest young priest dressed in a long black cassock and shoulder cape, the white clerical collar bright around his neck. They are looking up at the basilica San Lorenzo, pointing, concern on their faces, at its unfinished facade. Perhaps they are discussing the constant repair needed on the roof or the gutters or the crumbling stone. Domenico's hair is salt and pepper, heavy black brows shade his eyes, his face has the ruddiness of a man who works outside. He looks sturdy—like he'd be able to lift the tree off your damaged body or help you swim to shore when your boat goes down or scare off a mugger out to cruelly break your bones. Clearly my disaster mode (or desire for a hero to make all things right again?) is working overtime.

"Angelica, is he taking a break from work? How long does he have?"

"He has to confer with the padre and will be ready to meet you in ten minutes. Then he has one half hour." She pulls a peach-colored scarf from her bag, wraps it around her neck, it compliments her orange shirt. "I told you he might come with me today. How could you forget? You were so excited."

"Sorry—just a lot has been happening and it slipped my mind."

"Lyn, this is a favor he is doing." Angelica looks frustrated with me. "I don't want to tell him you cannot now talk to him. Is that what you want?"

"No. No. Of course, I want to. Thank you, you know I am grateful." I can't blurt out that my emotions are raw from recent wounds. I don't want to explode. The option of denying the day huddling under covers is long past. I steel, determine to sublimate feelings, push them down, hope for numbness.

"The Trattoria San Lorenzo is open. Very convenient. I told him you will meet him there." She points to the café next to the basilica. "Order the cheese plate and artichokes. He tells me he likes the artichokes." She is checking out the seminar writers. "Looks like a good group."

"They are."

"You can be with us until we get to the library—then you can go meet Domenico. I will take charge of the writers from there."

Angelica leads us through the cloisters that surrounds an interior garden. This served as a place of respite for the monks that used to live on the premises. I pat my bag, feel my mother's journal inside and force myself to concentrate on the questions I want to ask Domenico. We enter the ricetto and head up the splendid, curving, three-tiered staircase designed by Michelangelo and made from one of his favorite materials—pietra serena—a blue gray sandstone. I am calmed by this staircase, maybe it's the perfect proportions, its simplicity, its endurance.

At the top of the staircase, the main room, the Sala di Lettera, is revealed. It's a massive, long library room with a center aisle and, to me, looks like a chapel—a dedicated space for thought, reflection, reading. The floors are intricately tiled, designed by Il Tribolo—an artist who is mostly known by his nickname 'trouble'. He was a prankster, a pesterer, a bravura agitator who eventually found peace through his art. But his nickname stuck.

I half-listen as Angelica tells the seminar writers that the library holds over 10,000 manuscripts, including ancient papyri from Egypt, ostraca (writings on clay surfaces like pottery or writing on broken pieces of stone) and codices (books of ancient scripture and records of statutes of various civilizations) and Greek, Asian and Italian books printed before the 16th century (incunabula). I want to sit where the religious scholars would sit on library's pew-like benches—and rest my forehead on the cool wooden slanted desks in front of the pews—designed by Michelangelo—where the monks could comfortably contemplate and write. Steal a bit of their peace. I hear Angelica tell the writers, "The authors whose works are held here, we may never know some of their names but they made it their mission to leave records of their eras. You all understand how much work that is. And they didn't even have computers."

Angelica is leading them towards an adjacent conference room. She'll show them some of the precious holdings. She tells them she can talk about how the ancient manuscripts were translated—decoded. If it would be intriguing. The writers turn to George. His eyes brighten. Charles and Rivenchy tell Angelica they are definitely interested in the decoding process.

I slip out to meet Domenico, order a caffé americano and wait for him at a table in Trattoria San Lorenzo. He arrives as my coffee does, and he reaches out a brawny hand. My hand feels tiny in his. "Buongiorno. Me, I am Domenico." Domenico opts for a beer to complement the cheese and artichokes I've ordered. He doesn't need encouragement, this is a man who likes to talk. His English is choppy—but better than my Italian. "Si, Americans—I met very many. My uncle had tabbacheria—and a pick-up truck, il suo autocarro. When we drive the truck with food and coats and scarves, we also bring cigarettes. The Americans—they want American cigarettes. The Camel cigarette and the Winston—most popular, but we run out quickly and soon everyone smokes Muratti and Fortuna. The 'morte sicura'—the death that is certain—cigarette that became famous from our Italian movies—that came years later. You like Marcello Mastroianni? He knew how to smoke a cigarette."

"Si, certo." The famous Italian actor. I nurse my caffé americano.

"You know him from *Divorce, Italian Style*. Every man wants Sophia Loren even if he tries to avoid admitting it."

Divorce. That's the word I hear.

Domenico forks another slice of artichoke. "Italian men, in the end, we appreciate the female cunning. Madonnas who know best and know how to get a man to get it."

At this moment, female cunning brings up visions of best friend subterfuge. I rally and decide I have to steer the conversation. "My mother was mostly helping at the Biblioteca Nazionale." I take my journal from my bag, pull out a picture. "This is a picture of her in 1966."

Domenico studies it. "Is this the only photo you have?"

I slip a group picture out of the catch-all folder at the back of the journal and put it on the table. On its back is written in my mother's hand, *"all of us, Nov 20"*. He looks at the shot of two dozen Mud Angels standing on the steps of the Biblioteca Nazionale, posing like a small graduating class. The photo is watermarked and smudged, slightly out of focus, many individual faces are indistinct. Shoulder to shoulder. Some are serious, some smile, all are exhausted. "This is the group that she worked with mostly, I think. Posing in front of the library."

Domenico uses the end of his fork to tap the photo next to a stout, bald, middle-aged man in a white lab coat. "That is Ciro, he was one of the head people. He is an artist-medico, some say a surgeon for art, he brings many art back to life. He much liked Fortuna cigarettes. My uncle, he save cartons to take to Ciro because he was very important in saving paintings. When Ciro die, all of Florence mourned."

I point to my mother. She stands in the back row, she looks small, but she is one of the workers that sports a grin from ear to ear. She is flanked by two tall Mud Angels, their faces both mottled by watermarks. Domenico is focused on a slight, light-haired man—maybe thirty years old in the front row. "That looks like old Signor Velicchio."

"You know him?"

"He was called Elvis because he loved to twist. See how his leg—it is kicked out like he wants to start dancing."

I look at the photo, and notice how the man's knee is bent and his lower leg is rising. How his hips are tweaked and his hands spread as if he is on stage. His face is up, chin high, his face finding the light of the day.

"I go to school with his granddaughter when I was a child and dance at her home very much."

"Do you think Signor Velicchio is still alive?"

Domenico chews an artichoke, thinks on my question. "I would have heard if he was not. He came to my uncle's funeral—mmm—one year ago and I see his granddaughter again. They live on Via Poggi. I would hear if he went to his Maker."

The word—Poggi—rings a bell. I quickly page through the journal, get to the drawing. Unfold the corner of the journal. "Poggi is the name of the street Signor Velicchio lived on—or might live on still?"

"Si. Velicchio famiglia, live on Poggi. It is north of the train station. They don't move. Everybody who fit, stay in the family home—maybe not if there is very much unhappiness but if you can get along. You stay."

"Domenico, would you be able to give me the exact address? Help me contact Signor Velicchio?"

"I will ask. This is important to you."

"Yes. It is very important to me."

"I will get in touch with Angelica when I know. Thank you for artichokes." Domenico grabs his yellow hardhat and lumbers out.

———

I sit on the steps of the basilica. The sun warms me. I imagine this is the very spot my mother sat, exhausted but exhilarated by her work. I close my eyes. I listen to tourists bargaining with the street vendors. An accordion being played—somewhere close. Bicycles passing by. The honk of a Fiat. The smell of everything Florentine. Beth Ann's hand taps my shoulder. The seminar writers are excited, enamored by the idea that thousands of years from now, someone might find their work among an odd collection and point to it as illuminations of peoples' lives and ideas.

"Anything's possible," Vic jokes.

Beth Ann tells me, "We all decided to have dinner together tonight—end of our first week—before the weekend break. One of those places on that list you gave us. We want you to come with us if you can?"

Charles adds, "If you require a more formal invitation, how is this: If you would deign to sup with students, we promise not to think less of you."

I look up. They're waiting for my reply.

"Writers are constant students, that includes me," I tell them. "And most writers are very fond of food and wine."

Beth Ann leans in and whispers. "Come with us, Lyn. Maybe it will bring some color to your cheeks."

The invitation hits a nerve; it feels kind-hearted and caring. My chest gets tight. I breathe deep, push out the tightness.

Then the real question rises to the fore. Do I want to go back to my apartment and be alone?

Chapter 14

Six bottles of Chianti later.

We're at the Osteria Santo Spirito and I know I have had more than my share. The osteria has wide wooden plank floors, mismatched chairs and tables, coral-painted stucco walls studded with framed paintings and poetry—works of Santo Spirito neighborhood artists. The waiters are tattooed and young. They share gossip as they pass each other from dining area to kitchen as if we are invaders at their private party but still serve us with precision and Italian insouciance.

Thin shavings of prosciutto and salami served on a large wooden board disappear within minutes. Vic orders another one, telling Rivenchy he does not intend to be a 'killjoy' tonight. She calls him "Veec" and teases him that all persons must stay true to themselves. They laugh. Three orders of mussels and extra bread arrive. The shells are shiny black and the meat pinkish-orange, large and plump; they've been steamed in garlic and wine. The smell is intoxicating.

I push against the memory but it resists and takes hold: Stan and Susie and me, steaming mussels in Cape Cod when we rented a house for a week with my brother Rick and his wife. Stan and Susie taking the bags of shells and other garbage out together—I remember telling them to make sure to put the brick back on the top of the trashcan so the raccoons couldn't get in and make a mess of things. Rick and I washed dishes and laughed that Stan would choose to do any other chore rather than scrape food off plates and put his hands in soapy water. I wonder: Had Stan and Susie taken this time alone to furtively grope and plan to sneak time to be together later?

Anger threatens. My jaw gets tight. My teeth clench.

Vic nudges me. "Teacher, you want that last mussel?"

"It's all yours." I swallow the rising rage. I concentrate on the arrival of the gnocchi, covered with a truffle-infused cream sauce— tempting in a large shallow copper pan. It is slipped onto the table. The parmagiano-reggiano grated on its top has been browned. The golden rustic crustiness of the cheese is perfect.

Charles breathes in the scent of the cheese. "Ahh, from the best vacche rosso—red cows of Parma. You should all go there, see the farms."

An appetite surges back. Now I am ravenous. Am I moving out of self-pity and despair? I can feel the shift—or is it just the wine igniting a belligerence in me? My body now desires strength.

I decide to bury my feelings in food. Tastes that demand attention.

Another bottle of Chianti.

I picture Stan turning up his nose at the Tuscan wine list here last year. Middle-range Sangiovese, he said. The wines served here are not complex, he said, they are made for everyday consumption, nothing special.

I pour myself another glass. I like these wines. Screw Stan and his arrogance. I like that the wines taste simple and seem proud of their peasant pedigree. I order another bottle of friendly, family-feeling wine. I stand up and holler, "This wine is on me!"

An hour later.

Did I tell them about the Zuma Social Club? I wonder because the extra-large, mean-faced Bouncer has stepped aside for us. We enter its dark door. We weave down the narrow, murky hallway, pass under a black-light lit sign that features a warning in multiple languages: "We reserve the right to refuse service to anyone who judges and does not leave their inhibitions outside." My steps are unsteady. But I am ready.

It's almost pitch black. I can't see where the walls are and I don't want to reach out, afraid of what I might touch. The smell is intense—incense, herbal tobaccos, marijuana, perfumes and man scents are powerful. And there is something else in the air. Resistance to 'should'? Finally, the hallway opens up to reveal a dimly-lit room, filled with booths, easy chairs and low tables, slouchy couches. In the corners, large pillows are scattered on the Persian carpets.

Bottles of alcohol stand on glass shelves behind the mirrored bar. George stands next to me; he immediately sees a pattern. "There's a predominance of whiskies, second being tequilas and varieties of grappa. Very surprising."

My concentration wanders, George's voice fades. Is that half-naked fat guy in the corner sucking on the hookah getting his long hair braided by three women? And getting a foot massage by a mustached man sitting at his feet? It seems so. His belly is huge and he wears large diamond earrings, I can see their sparkle from across the room.

Vic calls out in a loud voice that it is time we move onto grappa. We gather around a low table, most of us sitting on floor pillows. Vic thinks the grappa should be drunk as shots—quick, like tequila. I remember the advice from Matteo's friend, Chef Gino. I tell the writers to let the grappa rest in their glass, then take a sniff of the liquid—a gentle sniff so not to blow out their senses of smell. Vic breathes in too hard and yelps, "Holy crap!"

A young woman with white-blonde hair plastered to her head, 1920s flapper style, and wearing a skin-tight black mini-dress with carefully ripped fabric in its mid-section plops on a pillow next to George. She hands him a lighter so he can light her expertly rolled joint. She shows her tongue provocatively, proud of its triple-studded piercings. I hear George say, with a slight drunken slur, staring at her studs. "Lettuce must be problematical." She answers in English with a German accent, "Cooked spinach and onions get attached the worst. But I can't say if it's the same for everyone because I do eat a lot of spinach and onions. What do you like to eat?"

As George considers his answer, Vic suddenly pulls me up and over to the small dance floor in front of the DJ booth. Vic shakes his ass and ribcage and stays in his own space, looking down at the floor. No parallel participation. That is fine with me because I am just swaying and dipping and wondering if the lap dances in the corners are being engaged in by strangers or by very good friends.

The hammer-like music beats into my nervous system.

An inch above my eyes, under my skull, I feel a pounding. I try to expel it by stretching my neck. Nothing helps and the strident bass of the music adds to the thump, thump, thump.

Rivenchy and Beth Ann join us on the dance floor. It becomes a girls' fest. Our arms drape across each other's shoulders, we rock back and forth. A tall Swede or German or Dane (Aryan being the operative word), wearing a tight white t-shirt and black leather jacket, approaches Rivenchy. She deigns to meet his eyes for a moment. Then she moves away from us and begins to dance with the tall buff blonde—they gyrate in each other's vicinity, subtly concentrating on each other's movements but with cool detachment. At least for now. I move off, hoping for Rivenchy's sake the leather of his jacket is of high quality.

Beth Ann waves to me. I think it's her dance moves, but it's her sign for leaving the dance floor; she bops back to the table where Charles sips his grappa.

Vic is now dancing with a group of women with shaved heads.

I continue to sway and dip.

Thump thump.

The smell of the room is getting too close for me. The lights blur.

I notice a door to the side of the bar. There seems to be a steady stream of people moving in and out. I wonder what goes on behind those doors.

I slip off the dance floor and head to the Ladies Room. Two female patrons sit on the floor across its doorway, deep in conversation, nearly nose to nose. I have to step over them.

The Ladies Room is large and dark; the walls are painted dark gray. A dim pink lightbulb swings on a cord from the ceiling. The pummeling music blares, the walls cannot keep it out. Pulsing an insistent beat. The walls shake. I sit on the closed toilet seat and put my head between my legs because the room is spinning.

Susie's betrayal. Thump. Large. Thump. Looms large. Her friendship, our phone calls, our secrets, our fears. Our meet-ups over coffee, wine, pizza, our weekly walks to discuss anything that came into our heads—our families, our futures, our dreams, our neuroses, our romances. Those walks had—actually—ended. A year ago. Thump. Thump. I was on a book tour for a month and then went to teach my second seminar in Florence and she was starting her business but emails, texts continued. We still communicated long distance. We would walk by shops, thousands of thumping miles from one another and take phone-photos to send to each other if a dress or jacket or pair of shoes needed to be commented on.

I stand up. I nearly scream, "Stop thinking! Stop!" I feel dizzy. I stare into the dark mirror. I glare, hoping the attempt for control will steady me.

Bump. Thump. Since junior high. Inseparable. Susie knows me best. Once my mother was gone, she was the one who knew me best.

In the mirror. My face is pale. My lips drop at the edges. My cheeks feel heavy.

After high school—after Susie gained all that weight being sad and angry when her boyfriend chose another girl, she went on a routine that sculpted every curve to every advantage. Body perfection. The goal. Thump. How long ago was it that she'd told me she was taking a break from searching—trying—trying to add a man to her life. This time, she told me, she told me, she told me—the beat—

the beat of the music is un-escapable—she told me she wanted to be—wanted to be pursued. She didn't want to have to convince a man she was something/someone he needed. She wanted to test that old-fashioned notion that a man would recognize that his life would be meaningless without her, see her as the mother of his children and mistress of his home.

Why did Susie want what was mine?

That idea stops me. The idea of "mine."

My husband. My friend. My life.

The music gets louder—a loud Turkish pop song fills the dark Ladies Room.

I lean my head on the porcelain frame of the sink. It's cool. My fingers clench the sides; my insides are roiling. Sweat beads on my forehead.

Do I fight this? Their decision.

A crash of cymbals, a long strident sound of trumpet.

Do I confront and argue and demand the clock rewind?

But I know it can never be turned back. Nothing is ever really mine. Anyone's.

My fist hits the sink. I want the music to stop wailing. I want my head to stop pounding.

I don't know how much time passed. A loud banging on the door. My body jerks, hard. Startled. I remind myself where I am. I am sitting on the floor, my knees pulled up to my chin, neck stretched, head back. My eyes gawk at the pink lightbulb as it swings back and forth with the pulse of the music. I pull myself up and open the door. A girl with a purple scar from nose to ear waits outside. Her eyes are dark, I can't see color in them, only blackness.

It's well past midnight. I stumble to the table where Beth Ann and Charles sit. Charles is jubilant. "I know this is not an appropriate place for my wife to bring her uptight Chinese business clients. And not a normal stop on our Brit ex-pat social route. But, tonight. Perfect. I feel like I'm living on the edge."

Beth Ann grins. "Are you feeling better, Lyn?"

I lean into them, thank them for including me in the night's activities. "Time for my head to head home. See you after the weekend."

Charles suggests he walk with me but I tell him I'm only a few blocks from my apartment and that I will be walking on Via San Niccolo where the cafes are still open. There are still plenty of people enjoying the night in Florence. I tell Beth Ann to enjoy her reunion with her dog, Jackson. She assures me she will.

I teeter and lurch towards the front door.

Outside, I get my bearings. The Bouncer's attitude is clearly dismissive, his glower seems to say that I must be a lightweight, that only the weak exit the Zuma Social Club before dawn. He feels sorry for me.

Little does he know how sorry I feel for myself. And how that makes me angry.

I rub my face, hard. I shake my head and force my legs to take me to my apartment.

Chapter 15

Next morning.

 Lucia knocks on my door. I get up to answer, my head still hurts. "Mildred says you're not answering your phone." Lucia is dressed in pink today—slim 1960s cotton pants and a pink gingham double-breasted short jacket. Her hair, now-bright golden blonde, has a pink streak in it. She looks like an Easter morning. Too bright. I wish she would go away.

 I mutter, "I was sleeping."

 "She says you must come to the seminar school to get messages." Lucia leaves to head back to Hotel Cascini's reception desk. "I will let her know you'll be there soon."

 The seminar writers have three free days. To write. To travel. Venice, Torino, Rome, Pisa, Bologna, Modena…only train rides away. They have told me their destinations—but the details are, at this moment, not clear. I do remember they promised to carry their notebooks and favorite writing tools wherever they went. Always be prepared when the muse strikes. The writers' mantra.

An hour later, I slowly trudge up the worn stone stairs to Mildred's office. My legs feel heavy. My lips are dry.

There is Valentina, sipping one of Mildred's carefully-made café espressos. I almost groan.

"You are here. You feel better?" Valentina always goes right to the point.

"Mmmm?" Hung over, I'm not ready for Valentina's high-energy barrage of questions.

"You skip class yesterday because you were ill?"

Words come slowly. "Yesterday. Si. I wasn't feeling well. Si."

"I can tell by looking at you. You don't look your best. But today you will be fine."

I didn't want to tell her that her aggressive style of teaching might put me over the edge today. To lower her voice a notch. To back off a bit.

It was like she could read my mind. "I will be gentle with you," she said. "Last lesson I was not gentle perhaps. No? And today I have a surprise for you."

I am not in the mood for surprises.

"You must get all you have paid for. Do not waste your money by skipping classes. You must continue and one day you can speak to Italians. We have many interesting things to say."

She is so full of it.

"We will have an excellent class. I will see you soon. Be ready for the surprise." She moves out quickly before I can find an excuse that will suffice. I sigh and sit down in one of Mildred's office chairs.

Mildred looks at me, trying to fathom the reasons for my condition. "Your agent called again."

"Damn. I was out with the students last night. I forgot to call her."

"How could you forget? It's your latest book. You're waiting to hear." Mildred hands me an espresso, "One of Italy's hangover cures."

"I guess I need to check in and face the music."

"Why do you think it's going to be bad news?"

"Just questioning myself on every front," I tell her. "You know how it goes. Just a funk."

"Want to talk?"

I sidestep. "Let me concentrate on some positive news. Angelica found me a guy named Domenico, I talked to him yesterday about my mother's story. And I think he might have a real connection for me. Someone that she worked alongside—I think. This Domenico is going to make contact for me."

"Good. That's good." Mildred pats my hand. "Is that why you got so wasted? Celebrating?"

"The seminar writers seduced me."

"Sure." I know she doesn't believe me.

Mildred goes back to work and I go to the empty seminar room. I finally turn on my phone. Three texts. One from Susie. I delete without reading. Another from Stan. I delete without reading. And one from my agent, Verdine. I read Verdine's message, "Can you get to Rome tomorrow? Call me! I don't care what time it is."

I check the time. It's near the end of the business day in New York City. My head hurts, deep in my gullet I can still feel the alcohol from last night. I select her number in my phone. Punch it.

She answers the phone, "Literary Now."

"Verdine, it's Lyn."

She is immediately at a fever pitch. "And you have an excuse? What is going on? Why isn't your phone on? Why don't you answer my emails?"

"A lot's been going on." I imagine Verdine's glasses sliding down on her tiny-designer nose, her multi-ringed fingers pushing the frames back up impatiently. Her dark curly hair tucked behind her ears. Her white shirt from the Jones New York businesswoman collection, open at the neck and sleeves pushed up to reveal stacks of bracelets that match her oversized pendant necklace.

"And that's an excuse? We have some talking to do, Ms. Writer."

"About the book? What did Harledge say?"

She is more concentrated on reciting the rules-as-set-out-by-Verdine than answering my questions. "You can't drop off the face of the earth, my dear. I can't reach Stan either and that cannot happen."

"Verdine. Stop yelling at me."

I can hear her rustle papers on her desk; she finds the pertinent information. "Lesli Plattson, the director. She was up for an Academy Award for that movie about that time-traveling person who finds out that a hundred years in the future she is a terrible and sadistic empress of the universe who keeps people in slavery on some planet..."

"I saw it." I want to stick to the topic. "What does she have to do with my book? Just tell me what Harledge has to say."

"Paramount wants your book."

I take a moment. "What?"

"The movies. Your book for the movies, Ms. Successful Writer." I know Verdine has a smile on her face now; she knows my knees are going weak.

"Un minuto, per favore."

"What? Don't speak Italian to me..."

I didn't realize the Italian had rolled off my tongue. My mind is reeling. "My book is selling to the movies?"

"Maybe. A good maybe. And this Lesli Plattson wants to meet you. She's in Rome for just a few days. At that big studio where they do movies..."

"Cinecitta."

"And why would I know the name of it? But you see, Ms. Writer, you know. Cause you love all that is Italian. She wants to meet you. Paramount Pictures sent your book to her."

"Harledge sent the book to the studio?"

"Always, that is how it goes. Everyone wants to make big bucks. Maybe this Lesli will want to adapt it and direct it. This is what Paramount is thinking. No putting it off, you will go to Rome. Impress her. I have to talk to Stan. We have to work out the details, but he's not answering his phone either. How am I supposed to do business if..."

I come back to my senses quickly. "Don't call Stan."

"When the movies make an offer, we gotta be sitting at the negotiation table making a few demands."

"I'm sure you and I can take care of it." My hands are sweating.

"Stan'll get every penny out of this—he's a shark."

"Verdine, don't bring Stan in—it's not a good time." I have to find a way to stop her from getting him involved.

"You two are fighting? Don't fight now, love spats are a waste of time when there's money to be made."

"You're my agent, right?"

"The one who wishes you would write faster. Yes."

"And it's my book. I mean—I am in charge of who my lawyer is. "

"Stan's a shark," she repeats.

"There's that lawyer you use for your other clients."

"Calvin. He's shark-ish too."

"We'll use Calvin."

She sighs. "Okay, I won't get in between anything. I won't call Stan again. But you don't want to mess this up. I have a mortgage to pay."

"Just tell me what I need to do."

"You need to get to Rome, Ms. Can't-You-Hear-My-Voice?"

"All right. I'll go to Rome. Meet the director. When?"

"Tomorrow. Pay attention. Let no grass grow under this. I'll call Paramount. They'll do the travel itinerary for you. Keep answering your phone."

"I promise." And then I want to hear it—make it official. "So Harledge is really on board with the book?"

"They're jumping up and down. It's on the rush pile—hardback as soon as they can get it out."

It's unbelievable. One part of my life is under a dark cloud—and now a ray of light finds its way through the gloom.

"I'm heading over to Joe Allen's for black bean soup then to a new play—all singing, all dancing something about the financial crisis and how greed consumes us all. Sounds like entertainment, right?"

"Have fun, Verdine. And thanks."

"Congrats, Ms. Keep-On-With-That-Next-Book. Let's ride the success."

We disconnect. I look around. The high ceilings of the seminar room, the tall shuttered windows, the thick plaster walls—they look beautiful. In one fell swoop, they look more incredibly beautiful than ever before. I turn slowly, 360 degrees. Then open a wooden shutter. A stream of sunlight hits me. I convert, for the moment, disbelief in the benevolence of the world to a hope that there will still be stellar moments.

And then my phone buzzes. The alert flashes "Susie". I let it go to voicemail and my fingers fumble as I try to cut off the connection. I hear Susie's voice. "I am a coward." She is talking fast, her voice covered by her hand against the elements. I can hear muted sounds of bicycles and cars in the background. Maybe they are in Milan. She might be standing on the narrow Via della Spiga, her back against the sunbaked stones of a palazzo, near Hermes and Louis Vuitton, tugging at the scarf perfectly wound around her thin, white neck. "We just decided—Stan decided—no, wait, I guess we both decided—but after all it is his decision. It is his decision, Lyn. But I know. We should have all sat down together. Looked at each other with the love we all share. I didn't know you would throw things— well the shock I guess. You're just in shock." I can see the tight line of my mouth in the reflection of the antique window's glass. How my eyes have no light inside them. Susie continues. "Of course, I should have talked to you, just like we talk about everything, but you can see how hard this is and it had to be Stan's decision. I can see you shaking your head at me. Okay. I'm a coward. I'm meeting Stan at the Mandarin Oriental bar. He was very upset that you threw things at him. But we'll get over it." The sound of a Florentine ambulance—the hard, ear-splitting horn solo blasting to warn pedestrians of a driver's determination to get to an emergency—drowns her out and the phone flashes red. Call completed. Or she gave up. Or she was mowed over by ten thousand pounds of moving machinery. I couldn't get myself to care one way or the other.

For the moment, I continue to be still, inured to the violent pushes and pulls of the galloping—sometimes sullen, sometimes wrathful, sometimes self-pitying—thoughts filling my consciousness. I can't hold onto Verdine's ray of good news. I can't hold onto any emotion. Maybe I can thank the hangover. Maybe I am tired of feeling too much.

Chapter 16

I head to my Italian class. I push through the heavy door and climb the hard stone steps. I focus on imagining myself in Rome. There with a purpose.

I can hear Valentina's voice, that strident Italian tone that is always a bit louder than is comfortable to American ears. I enter the office; shelves of language books and flyers from yoga schools, sports bars and wine tours. Valentina sees me. "Lyn. Very good. You are here. Matteo is here too. More chance for you to speak l'Italiano."

I see him.

Matteo leans against a long table that holds three computers and a small copy machine. His legs are stretched out; he holds a brochure. His heavy silver-plated watch hangs loosely on his wrist and the glint of it leads my eyes to his strong hands. He looks up as I come in; he's relaxed, calm.

"Buongiorno, Liniana." Matteo's eyes crinkle at the edges when he smiles.

Suddenly I am aware that I look like shit. I move my hand through my hair, hoping it will look like I brushed it this morning. I wish I had moisture on my lips. I bite them.

A woman stands next to Matteo—the same one I saw at the Caffé Gilli—she has short-cropped thick hair styled to frame her intelligent face. She wears a silk shirt paired with perfectly creased trousers, a scarf expertly draped around her neck. "And this is our friend, Bernadette. She and Matteo stopped by together to discuss a trip we want to take—the three of us. To the sea."

"Nice to meet you, Bernadette." I curse my jeans and sneakers.

"In Italiano," Valentina insists.

Matteo holds up his hand and laughs. "Valentina. Per favore. Wait until you are in the classroom."

Bernadette smiles at me. "I have heard about you. Piacere di conoscerti."

Valentina takes charge. "And now my surprise. We are going to the opera tonight. One of my students and her husband had to go back to Germany and cannot use the tickets I planned for them. Matteo says your husband is here. I will find a man for me—and the six of us will go." She looks at me. "Your husband will like to go to the opera?"

That stabbing pain behind my eyes suddenly flares again. I try to maintain a composed face. I lift my chin, think defiance will cover. I get the words out. "No. No. Grazie. Non e possibile."

Valentina plows on, "It is sure that it is possible. You must tell your husband we will have good wine before. It is *Cosi fan tutte*, Mozart's funny opera."

Matteo puts a hand on Valentina's arm. "They must have other plans. Stop pushing."

Lies tumble out of my mouth. "He's left Florence already. For work. He had to travel. For work."

Valentina sniffs, miffed. "Well, then you can come with me and Matteo and Bernadette. That means we now have two tickets left."

"I am going to Rome tomorrow," I tell her, trying to extricate myself from her plans. "I should pack."

"Packing takes no time. This is a good event and Florence is proud of it. Do you have a student that is handsome who might like me?"

Matteo guffaws.

"Matteo says I am too strong for many men so maybe if you have a very strong handsome student."

Bernadette interrupts as she straightens Valentina's collar—obviously, they know each other well. "You are not so strong, cara. It is just your need to have your own way all the time."

Valentina says of course she wants to have her own way all the time, and why not? "Why be passive is my question for you, Bernadette."

Bernadette comes back at her, a delicate smile on her lips. "There are times to let things be and see what comes to us."

"But then you have no chance in shaping your own destiny, you are only like a leaf blowing in the wind."

"Sometimes the wind is hard, sometimes it is soft. Who controls the wind?"

Bernadette and Valentina go back and forth in Italian so quickly that I cannot make out what they are saying. Matteo shakes his head affably, clarifies for me: "This is a question that is always at the forefront of Valentina's mind. She can argue for a long time on who is in control—is it fate that is in charge or can we—just human beings—control our own destiny. She insists we can have a hand in what happens to us."

I nod. "Yes. Maybe. But it is always a question."

"Do you think so?" He looks like he wants a definitive answer.

"How can we know? Are our decisions really ours? Or is everything pre-ordained?"

"Si, now I know you understand Valentina's favorite topic." Matteo's dark eyes smile.

He is very different from his sister; he seems to be patient and accepting and open to letting things—just be. My worry about my tousled hair, my thrown-on sweater diminishes.

He checks his watch. "Valentina, basta. I cannot be late for my meeting. The opera is on, that is all I need to know."

Valentina takes a deep breath. "Si. We are all going to the opera. Now I teach. Come, Lyn, we are in room number D." She picks up her notebook and motions for me to follow her.

Bernadette takes Matteo's arm and they head out. She is talking to him—his head is bent towards her.

In the classroom, Valentina hands me a worksheet on adjectives and explains how the adjective must reflect the noun in feminine or masculine terms. The fact that the words—such as scarf, table, backpack, tree, problem and nearly every word in the Italian language—is designated feminine or masculine by their articles tires me. Now choosing the adjectives to match words that are arbitrarily (as far as I can tell) assigned to be feminine or masculine makes me doubly tired. Valentina can sense it and, for a moment, takes pity. "What will you wear to the opera?"

"I didn't bring anything—elegant—fantasia." I try to use some Italian words. "I packed for casuale, not the opera—mi dispiace."

"You'll come to my home. I have things that you can choose from." She raises her eyebrows, getting to the bigger topic. "Now what student of yours is appropriate for me?"

I tell her the writers in the seminar have a few days off. The two single men in the class are most likely traveling.

Valentina sighs, disappointed. We go back to adjectives.

After class, Valentina shows me her two-seater Vespa motorcycle. It's yellow and green, she is proud that it is a hybrid and uses electricity first and gas only when it must. She assures me of its safety and explains that Piaggio, the manufacturers of the Italian Vespa make each one with pride. They had made fighter planes in World War II but their plant was bombed. Then, because of restrictions on manufacturing military equipment post-war, the Piaggio family had to do something new. "Many people had to change. Fiorentinos managed to do it." She continues, tells me how the Piaggio family decided to re-tool to make much-needed affordable transportation for Italians. She taps her temple. "Very smart. And when Audrey Hepburn rode one in the movie *Roman Holiday* with Gregory Peck on the seat behind her, suddenly everyone wanted one." She tells me the word "vespa" can be translated as "wasp". I marvel that she can make everything an offshoot of our lessons.

She takes an extra helmet from the Vespa saddlebag and hands it to me. We rumble down the stone street and head along the Via Lungarno Vespucci, past the Museo Galileo and the Uffizi. We pass Stan's favorite wine bar, I can't help but look at it, its outdoor high tables and sparkling glassware; a flash of memory threatens, I push it away. We continue over the stone streets towards the Ponte Santa Trinita and suddenly, surprisingly and unexpectedly, shouts and shrieks fill the air and a group of football-jerseyed and white-tube-socks-wearing tourists on Segways shoot out from a side street in front of us.

Valentina swerves and brakes hard. I fall forward and slip off the seat. I try to put my foot down to save myself from toppling and my ankle buckles. A pain shoots through it and I collapse and land on my shoulder—luckily off onto the narrow sidewalk away from traffic. Valentina swears at the tourists who Segway off, waving half-hearted apologies. Valentina yells after them, calling them ridiculous two-wheeled-accidents-about-to-happen.

Shit. My ankle. My shoulder.

Someone crouches down next to me, blocking the afternoon sun from my eyes.

"You're kind of unlucky lately. That's pretty suck-y."

It's Wyatt. Florence is a small city, not even fifty miles square, and most visitors and locals walk, gaze, eat, shop and go to museums near its compact center. It is not unusual to pass the same people on the street, see the same people in the most popular trattorias and enotecas. Not unusual at all to see people you do not want to see. And now the one person who knows about Stan's dismissal of everything I thought was my marriage is in my face again.

"Don't joke." I grit my teeth. Wyatt helps me up. My ankle throbs.

Valentina is off her Vespa now. "Do you know him?" She eyes Wyatt suspiciously. He still has his hand on my elbow.

"Not really," I grumble.

Wyatt assures her, "Enough to know I'm not trying to steal her purse."

"His name is Wyatt," I tell Valentina.

"Americano."

"Yep. Sure am." He licks his lips.

"How tall are you?" Valentina takes off her helmet, her long dark hair falls down her back.

"Almost six feet."

She likes that. "Taller than me but not too tall." Valentina complains about the Segways—waving in their direction. "The almost-accident. It is their fault. Florence is best on foot."

Wyatt agrees with her.

Valentina appreciates this. "You should agree. I grew up here. I will know."

"Well, nice to meet you. I'm Wyatt."

Valentina introduces herself and turns to me. "Maybe Wyatt wants to come to the opera tonight."

What? I am too surprised to respond. Doesn't anyone care about my injuries?

"What opera?" Wyatt is curious.

I find my voice. "I am sure he doesn't."

"Mozart." Valentina looks up at Wyatt, assessing him. "I have an extra ticket. In a box."

"A box?"

"My family has a box. Una scatola."

This is news to me. The night is sounding fancier. A private box at the opera.

"I could do Mozart. It's only the Russian ones that are tough for me." Wyatt is actually considering the invitation.

"Good. Tonight. You are Lyn's student?"

"No," he clears that up. "Acquaintance from New York. Here on business and done with business and I have a few days to be a tourist."

"Hotel?"

"Grand Hotel Cavour," he tells her.

"On Via del Proconsolo."

"Yep."

"Business expense account?" Valentina always wants the details.

"Yep."

"Take a taxi. We will meet there and I will have your ticket." She shakes his hand. "It is because Lyn's husband had to leave Florence for work—we have an extra ticket."

Wyatt looks at me but doesn't comment on the untruth.

Valentina continues, "We will meet at the lobby of the opera house for apertivo at 19. That is 7 o'clock at night, in how you tell time in America. The Opera di Firenze, the opera house on Via Vittorio Gui. Your hotel will know. Tell them to tell the taxi driver."

"Okay."

Valentina nods for me to get back on the Vespa. "Torna sulla Vespa. Let's go."

I groan, not looking forward to getting on the cycle.

She chides, "Americans are supposed to be fearless."

"Not all Americans," I say. "You have to stop generalizing."

She laughs. "I say get back on and I will drive faster to take away your fear."

Wyatt looks at me, wondering whether I will pick relative safety with him or opt for Valentina's bravura.

I get back onto the Vespa, mostly to escape Wyatt's company and all that he reminds me of.

Valentina waves at Wyatt. "Until tonight. Opera di Firenze."

We speed off.

Chapter 17

Valentina pulls up in front of her family's apartment building. It's on a small street off the Piazza degli Strozzi. We slide off the Vespa and I limp after her as she pushes her scooter through the gates and into an interior courtyard. Roses and irises bloom, small delicate olives trees with silver-gray leaves shade the stone walks. There is a marble fountain, in its center is a stone figure of a small girl draped in a soft shift holding a vessel to dip into the water bubbling below her.

The stillness of the scene wafts over me. "It is peaceful here." There are tufts of thin grasses, soft yellow flowers that grow close and low—all perfectly manicured and resting against ancient sandstone boulders.

Valentina parks the Vespa in an alcove and we walk through the gardens to the large double-door entrance.

"If you are very bad hurt, you would not be able to walk on your foot at all."

I realize this is Valentina's way of deciding I have no broken bones.

Through the doors. The sounds of traffic and business interests of Florence disappear. The entryway is cool. A black and white marble floor, an iron medallion in the center; it is a coat of arms—a shield with two swords and a lion carved into it.

"That's our family crest." Valentina leads the way to the glass-walled, tiny elevator. Up we go.

We pass the first floor.

"My grandmother lives on this floor—on the left. My uncle across from her on the other side of the building."

We pass the second floor. "My two aunties, never married, live here together—on this side. They use the smaller apartment on this side for mia zia Maria's painting studio. The light is good there."

The elevator stops on the third floor. We disembark and stand on the landing. Valentina points to the stone stairway that lead upwards. "My mother lives on the top floor. She has the most sunlight and yet sometimes she prefers to keep her shutters closed to better watch her TV. I tell her it is a waste and she tells me that everyone can live as they want. She thinks I'm bossy."

"And you are bossy, Valentina."

"And why not? If I know how the world should be, why not try to make it so?" She searches in her purse for her keys.

"Sometimes you can't control everything."

"Should I not try?"

I think of how, right now, I would like to have a magic wand to refigure, re-design and re-dress my life. "I don't know."

Valentina finds her keys. "La mia famiglia lives in this building for 300 years. We try to do some kind of renovation every 50 years to try keep up with things. But many times, there is a problem—you have to remember that it was built before electricity and indoor plumbing is what it is today. The walls are almost ten inches thick, so any ristrutturazione is a major idea. But good news, I have bought a new refrigerator and washing machine this year and I celebrate that."

In the small landing there is an alcove with a coat rack and a framed photo of Matteo and Valentina. They look younger, maybe it was taken ten years ago. They stand, older brother and happy sister, their arms around each other, looking happy, in front of the fountain in the courtyard.

There are two heavy doors on either side of the alcove. Valentina pats the door on the left. "Matteo lives on this side."

The door to Matteo's apartment is made of oak; it's thick, solid, darkened with age and centuries-worth of air and polish.

"I live here." The door is painted a high-gloss chartreuse. The color makes the dark iron doorknob loom large. "Matteo laughs about my door. But it makes me smile, like I am Alice in Wonderland entering my world."

We walk into a small foyer. It connects to the living room. Valentina opens all the shutters and then the windows—light and air breathe into the apartment. The ceilings are at least 12 feet high, the walls are painted in wide stripes of soft Venetian gold and sage, a thick band of cream-colored paint runs around the top of the wall and connects with the soft golden paint of the ceiling. Overstuffed, slipcovered chairs have a colorful array of knitted throws tossed on them. Through an arched doorway, I see a small dining table and beyond that, through another archway, a galley kitchen is visible. But it is all the paintings on the walls that draw me in. Some are misty scenes of contadini fishing, some are of country folk tending tempting vegetable stands with the Florentine hills as a background. Some capture bathers on the beach, watching the calm Tyrrhenian Sea.

Valentina sees me looking at the artwork. "Those I painted for my grandmother when I was first in art school. When she comes upstairs to visit me, she likes to look at them to remind her of when she lived outside Florence as a young girl. She insists she still has much peasant in her. But if you meet her ever, don't believe her. She has an active account at Ferragamo."

I am taken aback. "Did you say you painted them?"

"Si, that is what I love. To paint. Come see what I am doing now." She leads me down a hallway, to a room with large windows. "My studio."

On an easel is a portrait of Matteo. His face—lean and angular—his loose hair blows a bit in the wind. He is standing in front of a side entrance to the Uffizi, a frieze of angels and saints behind him. The frieze is captured in a dreamy manner; the focus is on Matteo.

"Valentina, I am blown away."

The studio walls are covered, floor to ceiling, with canvasses and tacked-to-the-wall sketches. The colors are strong, there is a dreamlike quality to the work, the brushstrokes are short, dabs of color like those of the Impressionists but over smooth, finely de-tailed images.

"These are all yours?"

She shrugs, but nods her head. It's as if she is dismissing them but there is an interest in my reaction. My eyes move to sketches of Matteo—one of him as a young teen, on a beach. To me, the short brushstrokes over the image of Matteo look like wind—a strong wind right on the canvas. There is another of Matteo sleeping, age twenty maybe, a book on his chest. A cloud of mist behind the im-age, as if it is his dream. Another of Matteo and Bernadette sitting in a garden. Leaves falling around them. These are beyond the tradi-tional, finely crafted paintings in the living room. These have Valen-tina's personality; they feel uniquely representative of her.

"I didn't know you were an artist." I am not sure why, but I feel guilty. I have thought of Valentina only as my funny, pain-in-the-ass, loveable language teacher.

"I don't know if I am." Valentina's voice is very serious.

"Why would you say that?"

She shrugs again.

"Why do you not want to use that word?" I watch her thoughtful face for clues.

"Artist?"

"Yes. Why don't you want to use that word?"

Valentina sighs. "Because it means more than just a 'painter'. Or a 'sculptor'. Or a 'composer'. It is a special level of someone who—tries to create. Wants to create something special."

"You're really talented." I survey the paintings and the drawings and I am pulled in. "Because your work evokes feelings. That's what artists do."

"Ahhhh, feelings." She looks at her work again, assessing my definition of "artist". She shrugs again, does not want to be lugubrious. "We must get ready for the opera. Come into my room."

She leads me to the end of the hallway. We enter Valentina's large bedroom. Her bed is unmade; clothes are scattered on chairs and shoes are piled in the corners of the room.

"You will sit on the bed. Protect your foot." She pulls up the blanket, tucks it in.

I do as I am told. But I remind her that her bossiness is coming out again.

"Because I know what will be good for you." There is no arguing with her. "Now take those pillows and put your foot up on them and I will show you what dress you might want to wear." She opens a painted wardrobe that stands against the wall. Clothes burst out, plunge forward as if crying alleluia for the sudden breathing room. The colors of the fabrics—the blues, greens, blacks, golds, reds— are rich and lush.

"My mother, my aunties, my grandmother—they love clothes. They insist life was more stylish when they were younger." She points to a small painting above her bureau—two women sitting on antique, velvet covered chairs. "Mamma and Nonna, so proud and chic in their Gucci wrap dresses. You know Gucci started the company here in Florence." She opens the bottom drawer of the wardrobe and lifts out Gucci evening bags. She places them on the bed. "My mother was upset when one of the last Gucci heirs was murdered. Everyone found out it was one of his stupid ex-wives who paid for the murder. It was a terrible shitty mess." She holds up a dress and presses it against her body. She checks its length, shakes her head. She puts it back into the closet and surveys other choices. "Mamma and Nonna think going to the opera in pants is a sin. I would have to go to confession." She laughs. "We dress for the opera—this family."

Valentina plops on the bed, causing my leg to slide off the pillows.

"Sorry," she apologizes as she puts my leg back in place. "Time to talk turkey."

"Turkey?"

"Isn't that how you say 'truth' in America?"

I have to admit we do have such a silly phrase.

"This Wyatt. What do you know of him?" She catches a glimpse of herself in the mirror, smooths her dark hair and lifts her chin up, wanting to see herself at another angle.

"Nothing. He is a lawyer. That's all I know."

"How can you not know anything more?" She eyes me suspiciously.

"I met him two nights ago. For the first time."

"He seems to know you." She reaches for a tube of lipstick that is on the table next to the bed.

"He knows only a few things about me." I want to change the subject.

"He acts like he wants to take care of you." She applies lipstick—the dark rose color stains her lips.

"No. You misunderstand."

"Your husband is all right with that?"

"No one wants to take care of me."

"Except your husband, no? That's what husbands do."

Not necessarily true, I think.

She continues, "I just wonder about the perfect height of Wyatt. What else is perfect, or not. I wonder."

I snap. "You invited him. You can find out about him yourself."

"Text your husband about what he thinks. What he knows about this Wyatt." Insistent could be Valentina's middle name.

"No, I am not doing that."

"Why are you so stubborn?"

"My foot hurts." I make a move to get off the bed. "I'll just go to my place. I won't be able to go to the opera. Could you move so I can get my leg down?"

She doesn't move. "You have to go to the opera. You said you would, I have a ticket for you and now Wyatt is coming. Why won't you text your husband, it's not too much to ask. Why are you angry? We are friends, no?

That she wants to be friends strikes me; I feel a physical tightening in my chest. The word 'friend' feels like danger signal.

"Friends help each other, right? It's okay, you don't have to ask your husband. But it was just a favor. For a friend." She sets the lipstick tube back on the bedside table. "I should meet your husband. Is he always too busy that you can't text him?"

"I'm not going to text him."

"Why are you looking so angry?"

"Because you won't stop…"

"I am not asking very much."

"Okay. You want to know?" I realize I am furious. "I won't text him because, two nights ago, my husband told me he does not want to be married to me anymore. So, he really wouldn't want to go to the opera with me, would he."

Valentina stares, shocked for a moment.

It's silent.

Suddenly my sobs come. They heave up from my chest. I struggle to find air—the sobs are taking it all up. I try to open my mouth wider but no air can enter because the sobs are filling my lungs, my nose, all my airways. My shoulders heave; the cries are coming from deep. Deep. I feel my body double over.

Valentina grabs me and hugs me. "Calma, calma, oh sorry mi dispiace, calma calma." My head is buried in her hair; she mutters in Italian that she is a terrible cruel person and should die immediately and she is very very sorry to upset me.

The tears that refused to come for two days are finally gushing and I want to stop them from cascading down my face. But my body is not listening to my mind and I shed gallons of salty tears onto Valentina's shoulders.

"Calma, calma." Valentina pats my back. I finally catch breath in gasps. I straighten. Lean back. Wipe the wetness from my cheeks. She hands me a tissue. I blow my nose.

We sit there for a moment.

"So you cancel your Italian lesson with me because of this?"

What? I nearly scream in disbelief. Is she really turning my tragedy into a slap in her face?

"I didn't feel like taking an Italian lesson. Okay?" I glare at her.

"You let him win."

"What do you mean?"

"You have a plan, a desire, a life and when he is stupid and makes a decision that affects you, you let his stupid actions win over you."

My voice rises in pitch, I can hear I am at a near-wail. "It's sort of a big deal. Finding out your husband's dumping you and moving on."

"Yes. I know. But you cannot let yourself be a victim. And stop your life. Cancel your Italian class." Her eyes are wide, she is adamant.

What is she not understanding? I defend myself, my voice dripping with sarcasm. "It was a day when I couldn't care less about masculine and feminine articles."

"About something important."

I shoot back, "One lesson? Of a language, as you tell me over and over, that I will never be good at!"

"You will never speak as an Italian."

"Teachers are supposed to encourage. Did anyone ever tell you that, Valentina?" My voice is even higher, argumentative. She is infuriating.

"In America, maybe. In America, everyone is told they are beautiful and talented and important."

"That is a generalization! You make so many generalizations!" I can't believe she's lecturing me. Dissing me.

"American always want positive reinforcement. Very difficult for them to just accept the truth. They will never be masters of our language. But they must try. I just want to be truthful."

I want to throttle her. And a moment ago she was patting my back and telling me she was my friend. I take a deep breath and challenge, "How can you not understand?"

"I did not meet your stupid husband but I know when someone stomps on your heart it can make a person doubt. Think there is something wrong with their self. But that is not necessarily true." She puts her hand on my arm. "Maybe he will see the light and want to take away his words."

Her fairy-tale prediction hits me hard.

"He's already sleeping with my best friend." My voice is dark and then my breath catches again, silent tears pour down by cheeks.

She pulls back. Takes a moment. "Doing sex with your best friend?"

"She texted me that they are in love." Another wail comes up from my gut. I put my hands over my ears. I don't want to hear myself. Damn it.

Valentina gets up and leaves the room. I feel as if my ribcage can't contain the storm inside me. I wonder if it is possible for someone to die from betrayal?

Valentina is back quickly, with an opened bottle of wine and two glasses. "Okay. I get it now. Now I understand why you cancelled your Italian lesson."

Chapter 18

B y the time we arrive at the elegant Opera house for the apertivo, Valentina and I have finished that bottle of wine on empty stomachs. I feel lightheaded and spent.

She's dressed in a fuchsia vintage Chanel knit skirt and jacket and rose-colored Ferragamos that her mother wore on her wedding day. I wear a 1980 Roberto Cavalli; it's a vibrant blue jersey cocktail dress. Valentina also picked out low, black-lace heels for me so that my ankle would not be too stressed, and a deep purple silk evening coat that feels nearly weightless. I wonder if I am too much of a carnival of color; my black jeans and dark sweater are on the floor of Valentina's bedroom.

Wyatt stands by a small tall table in the apertivo lounge. He's in a suit and tie, his light brown hair slicked back. He has an opened bottle of Fontodi Chianti Classico and three glasses are on the table. A bowl of potato chips rests next to the glasses. I marvel again at how many places offer potato chips as a bar snack and wonder how many I would need to eat to soak up the alcohol already in my system.

Valentina smiles at up at him. "Very thoughtful, Signor Wyatt."

He's appreciative of her compliment. "I wasn't sure how many were coming."

Valentina tells him there will six in the party. "We'll need more glasses. More wine."

"I can take care of that." Wyatt pours wine into a glass. Hands it to Valentina.

"It is good to have a man who sees what needs to be done." She sips her wine. "I have never been to the United States. Is New York City the best place in the world as everyone says?"

Valentina is baiting him. I know her style: mild interrogation that moves into slightly heated disagreement that causes the blood to rise and allows her to measure someone's spark and spunk. I doubt Wyatt will stand up to her test.

"Sure it is. New York is great." Wyatt pours wine for me.

"How can it be better than Florence?" Valentina asks.

"Florence is great too." Oblivious to her process, he pops a potato chip into his mouth.

"And you have not had time, really, to make a real conclusion as to which place is better, is that not right?"

"Only been here a few days. True." He lists a few things that come to his mind. "Feels really old here. In a cool way. And it's got a lot of great art, that's for sure. In and out of the museums. Lots of narrow streets and narrower sidewalks. And dogs seem to get priority for sidewalk space. Weird. And, for sure, really good restaurants."

"And yet you think New York City restaurants are better."

"Did I say that? I mean, they're good."

"Better than our Tuscan food?"

"It's very good too." Wyatt looks to me for support, starting to suspect Valentina is setting traps.

I do not engage. I wish he wasn't here. I sip the wine. It's got a full round taste and it's comforting. I look around, the lounge is filling up with opera-lovers, many dressed in designer finery, others more casual.

Valentina focuses on Wyatt. "You think Florence and New York are both best."

"Maybe."

"How can that be?"

Wyatt eats another chip and straightens his glasses. "Nothing has to be the 'best'—for every person. Perhaps we should consider that option, Valentina."

Valentina brightens, she likes hearing him say her name. "You think that is possible?"

"Yep. I do." Wyatt leans into Valentina. I realize he finds her charming.

"But you love our Chianti." She wants to finish on a Firenze-winning statement.

"Sure."

"Si. Our Chianti is magnifico."

Wyatt looks at me. "Wine okay with you?"

"Fine." I nod.

"I asked the wine guy behind the counter for a good bottle," Wyatt explains to Valentina.

Valentina laughs. "I am sure he sold the American the most expensive one."

"I figured." Wyatt winks at me.

I ignore his overture to draw me into the conversation. I do not want to be his buddy.

"You are on expense account." Valentina moves closer to him.

"Yep."

"Good. Then, shall we have another bottle?" She touches his arm.

Wyatt laughs, clearly enjoying her. He heads off towards the bar.

Valentina calls after him, "And three more glasses. My brother and his girlfriend. And my friend will come—he is not a boyfriend—just an old friend—not a boyfriend." She wants to make sure the relationship is clear. "There will be six, enough for a nice group."

Wyatt waves his understanding and leaves us so he can get in line at the bar.

Valentina leans into me. "Does he have a regular lover in New York City?"

"I have no idea."

"There you are." It's Matteo. He joins us.

Valentina turns to her brother, sees that he is alone. "Where is Bernadette?"

Matteo is in a black tuxedo jacket, skinny black tie and polished shoes. Apparently, he also takes his mother and grandmother's instructions about dressing for the opera to heart. I notice how the tuxedo jacket hangs on his broad shoulders, it's elegant but he wears it casually, like he's used to it. I take another sip of wine and look away.

Matteo tells Valentina, "Bernadette had to leave for Paris tonight to make an early meeting tomorrow. Came up last minute."

"She is not coming?" Valentina is not pleased.

"She is on the plane now."

"Now we have un biglietto un piu. Terrible." Valentina's cell phone buzzes. She reads the text. "Two extra tickets. Luis is also not coming." She focuses on the extra tickets. "I could try to sell the tickets outside."

"Let it be, Valentina. Let's just relax. We'll have more room to breathe. Americans like to have space, they do not like tight quarters." He smiles at me.

She breathes out, hating that everything is not going as planned. "I'll go tell Wyatt." She hands Matteo her wine glass, "You can have this, it's very good. The perfectly tall American bought it. A friend of Lyn's." She's gone before I can correct her assessment of my relationship to Wyatt.

Matteo stands across the table from me. "Ciao, Liniana."

I suddenly feel conspicuous in the borrowed dress and purple evening coat. I twist my silver bracelets, something I always do when I am uncomfortable. "I must look like your sister, your mother, your grandmother all in one."

"I don't understand." His brow creases in confusion.

"Valentina picked the dress and coat out. They came from her closet."

"Bellissima." Matteo fills my glass and pours himself another glass of Chianti Classico.

"I mean I am wearing clothes that have been in your family for a generation at least."

"On you, they look good."

He finds it all normal. Just fine.

"I was at your home. The whole building is filled with your family."

"Si. Not an American thing to do. But Italians, we often stay— together. It is good. It works. If we need something. We are not alone. My grandmother is 95. My mother is almost 70. And then Valentina, across the hall, I can always encourage her to paint. It is good." He holds up his hand and grins as he makes a point, "But, it is best to have my own place within it all. There are some things we do not want everyone to know. No?" He laughs and shrugs. "Of course, eventually everyone knows everything."

I tease, curious. "You have secrets you don't want your mother to know about?"

"Does that not make sense? I am a man." He is so easy. Always relaxed.

"Valentina has done wonderful paintings. With you in them."

"Si. There is a show in a gallery one week from tonight. Her first time to be galleried. She is very nervous."

"She didn't tell me."

"Valentina is pretending it is not happening. To keep this evening tranquillo, do not tell her I told you." He challenges me with an offer of a potato chip—as if my acceptance of the bar snack will seal an agreement.

"Si. I promise." I bite into the chip and enjoy his uncomplicated company.

The Teatro Opera seats over a thousand people, it's a magnificent, modern, welcoming space. Valentina tells me that the family's large donation to the construction of the new building put them in possession of tickets. A box. We are close to the stage, raised above the orchestra level and slightly hidden from view from other audience members. I sit in my comfortable armchair in a designer dress, feeling the buzz from the wine. Valentina smiles back at me as she sits next to Wyatt. Two empty chairs separate them from Matteo and me.

The opera, composed by Mozart, is sung in German. Matteo wants to make sure I know the story before it begins, "Do you know it?" I tell him yes—I know enough to follow the story even if I can't decipher all of the Italian subtitles on the thin screen above the stage.

The performance begins. Mozart and his librettist, Da Ponte, based *Cosi fan tutte* on the idea of 'fiancée swapping', a theatrical plot that has been used for centuries—even by Shakespeare. I know it's a comedy: Don Alfonso—a man who enjoys creating havoc—makes a bet with two soldiers, Ferrando and Guglielmo, that their girlfriends, Dorabella and Fiordililgi, cannot remain faithful in the face of romantic opportunity and sexual temptation. Alfonso insists to the soldiers that there is no such thing as a faithful woman. The soldiers want to prove him wrong, they come up with a plan; they lie to their girlfriends that they have been called away for a mission and bid them farewell, asking them to remember fidelity is of utmost importance. The girlfriends pledge their undying love. The soldiers feign their departure and quickly double-back, disguised as rich, royal Albanians (in turbans and robes and moustaches). They employ heavy seduction techniques to test their girlfriends' fortitude. Dorabella and Fiordiligi are stand-offish at first—but then begin to enjoy the flirtations. The 'Albanians' are relentless, sexy, charming, royal. Inevitably, the women's emotions do become engaged and they agree to marry the Albanians. Alfonso, sure he has won the bet, is elated. He and his partner-in-manipulation, Despina, draw up bogus wedding contracts. Now, the broken promises of the females are a matter of record. Just then, Dorabella and Fiordiligi hear military music announcing the return of soldiers to the city and they panic, realize they must tell the truth about their inconstancy. The cynical schemer Alfonso takes glee in their pain because he has proven that women are not to be trusted in love. 'Cosi fan tutti' translates to 'women are like that.'

I push thoughts of Susie and Stan from my mind. I tell myself to concentrate on the music.

I know the story twist is about to happen.

Dorabella and Fiordiligi get wind of the bet—they discover the plan, the disguises and the subterfuge. Realize how they have been manipulated and expected to be weak. Incensed, they decide to teach their lovers a lesson and flaunt their sexuality in ways that cause the men to doubt the prowess of their manhood. And because the opera is a comedy, when it is revealed that the ladies know that they have been the victims of deception—everyone agrees it was a fantastic, fun dupe despite the fact that it has just been proven that hearts and love and fidelity and honesty are fallible. All's well that ends well because—in actuality—didn't the women fall in love with the 'same' men (just under another guise)? Didn't they just prove that true love actually triumphed?

It's a lively opera about cynicism, manipulation, seduction, lies and betrayal and errant human emotions. I cannot help compare the story to my life. But my life seems about as comic as a funeral procession.

I shudder, it's as if a chill has run through me.

Matteo feels it. "Are you cold, Liniana?"

"No. I'm fine. Grazie." I pull my coat tighter.

After the opera, we have another glass of wine at the theatre bar and decide to walk back to central Florence. It's a beautiful night, we move onto narrow stone streets and make our way to the Via di Santo Spirito. The antique shop windows are softly lit; reminders of centuries of fine taste and appreciation of craft and art.

Wyatt walks beside me. "That was a fine, funny opera. Thanks."

"I had nothing to do with it."

"You could've told Valentina not to invite me."

"Well, she did. And she asked me if you have a full-time lover back in the States."

"Full-time?"

"Someone serious."

"Oh. Serious." He shakes his head. "Not a big fan of time-sucking coupling at this point."

"Coupling?" I heard the disparagement in his voice.

"Being part of a committed pair." Wyatt stops to look in the window of an antique store.

"I know what coupling means." My eyes land on the centuries-old tapestries on the store's walls, the silk threads woven and stitched to reveal a bucolic picnic scene in an Italian park full of deer and rabbits. An idyllic time.

Wyatt points to a polished antique walnut desk. "That's amazing. Beats my Crate and Barrel standard issue." He goes back to our conversation, thoughtful. "I work with women who want to rule the world. And just want sex for sport. It's okay—like playing a pick-up game of basketball. You get a work out—but you know it's just—for the moment." He sounds disappointed, sad.

Valentina calls to Wyatt, she wants to point out something in another shop window. He joins her. Matteo moves up next to me.

"You are more quiet tonight, Liniana. Than our other times together. And I am not sure you enjoyed the opera."

I reassure him, "I did enjoy it. And I am glad to be invited. I am sorry if I am a bit tired."

"No apology needed. It's nice to be more quiet sometimes."

We walk. His strides are long. I am wearing heels and babying my ankle, so mine are not. He adjusts his pace to mine.

"Did your husband enjoy his sandwich at All'Antico Vinaio?" Matteo is making conversation.

My breath tightens. I lie, "He got very busy. I am not sure." I change the subject. "I am going to Rome tomorrow."

"Yes, you said that. Rome, you like it?"

"I don't know it well. I have a meeting. About a book I wrote. Someone might want to adapt the story into a film."

"Very exciting. No?"

"I think so."

"You will be back for Valentina's art opening?"

"I'm only gone for one night."

"That is good, I will send you an invitation to the gallery."

The air is fragrant with the breeze from the river, from the restaurants, from the flower boxes attached to the windows of the apartments above the shops. Matteo asks, "The train to Rome is fast. Good. You are taking it, yes?"

"Si." I check my watch. "And I should head home, I'm on the earliest train."

We are at the Ponte Santa Trinita—where Valentina and Matteo would turn off to go to their apartments. Wyatt offers to walk me the rest of the way to my place, he says he could then stroll across the Ponte Alle Grazie to the Grand Hotel Cavour. But Valentina takes my arm and insists we all continue; she declares she has not had her exercise today, that she and Matteo will even walk Wyatt to his hotel after they drop me off because Florence is compact and it is a lovely night.

Matteo goes along with her plan.

We are steps ahead of the two men, she leans into me so Wyatt and Matteo cannot hear. "For an American, he is not too pushy or too loud or too know-it-all."

I know she wants more information. "No serious girlfriend."

"Ahhh. Now he is even more on the good side of my American list."

Ten minutes later we arrive at my door. Valentina is a bit giddy with the star-filled night, the soft glow of light, the wine consumed, Wyatt's possible availability and the excitement of sharing the city she loves with Americans. She is bubbling over, wanting to make us all feel close and special to one another. "Lyn, do not think of your husband leaving you and a divorce ahead—your stupid husband and his betrayal—toss it in the garbage."

There is an awkward silence.

I can't believe she is so absolutely oblivious to her insensitivity. I don't look at anyone directly but I can see out of the corner of my eye that Matteo looks confused. Wyatt looks concerned.

Valentina continues, has no idea she has ripped open my wound again. "You have friends who are much better. A stupid cheating husband is not one to care about. Mia cara, mia amica, you are too good for such pain." She gives me a hug and kisses both of my cheeks. "Caio, bella. We will be your new friends. You have us now. Be happy with that."

I want the street to open up and swallow me.

I push open the heavy door, ready to slip inside. I glance at Matteo, his head is tipped to one side, his face serious—almost angry. He is glaring at Valentina. Then his eyes move to me, but do not stay. They move to the softly glowing lamp above the door to my building.

Valentina is still talking, "We will now walk Wyatt home and maybe we will all do something together again before the tall American flies home. Or maybe he will love Florence so much, he will stay." She takes Wyatt's arm and laughs. "You can never compare New York to Florence properly if you do not taste the best tri-color Pizza Margherita, named for one of our Queens." She turns back to me and waves. "Ciao, mia amica. Buonasera."

Matteo is still gazing at the lamp above my door.

I step inside. The door slams shut behind me.

Chapter 19

Next morning. Early.

I leave my apartment with an overnight bag and walk towards the train station, the Stazione di Santa Maria Novella. The streets are quiet. I cross the Santa Trinita bridge and move along Via de Tornabuoni past Ferragamo, past Prada, past Cavalli and turn east at the Cos store onto the narrow one-way street. Barely wide enough for a small car to maneuver. The street-cleaners and window washers are at work. A few tourists are ahead of me, pulling rolling bags or wearing backpacks. I imagine they are excited to be off on adventures.

Inside the station, I peer up at the electronic schedule that hangs high on the wall above the coffee shop and bookstore. I see the earliest Trenatalia train to Rome is on the schedule, expected to depart, on time, from Track 12. It should arrive in five minutes.

I buy a caffé americano and head towards Track 12.

A tall, lean man in jeans and a tailored jacket stands there; a small travel case in his hand.

"Matteo?" I am surprised.

Matteo turns to me, gives a slow smile. "Ahh, buongiorno, Liniana. I wondered if I would see you." He has a bottle of water in his hand. "An unexpected meeting came up. I too will be on the earliest train."

"When did you find out?"

He speaks quickly, "When I arrived home last night. There was a message." He glances at my ticket. "You have chosen the quiet car."

"I always hope."

"Italians cannot be quiet. You should know by now. To not talk—to many Italians—is to be dead."

I am aware of the fresh scent of his aftershave. I laugh. "Yes, I know. And I have to admit I'm not above pointing to the 'silenzio' placard in the quiet car and hope the cell phone talks with 'Mama'—to discuss pasta or the latest family drama—can be postponed for a few hours. But it never works. Italians look at me as if 'silenzio' has nothing to do with their lives."

Matteo puts on a serious face but his eyes glint with humor. "I am sad to say that your extra ten euro is not well spent."

"Paramount Pictures is paying so I thought I would risk it again."

"It is never bad to hope."

We stand for a moment. There is a discomfort. He seems a bit off, not as relaxed as normal.

I recall last night—Valentina blurting out my situation and the evening ending abruptly. And uncomfortably.

He is on my wavelength. "I do not mean to pry, but I thought about you last night. And the circumstances with your husband."

I look off, embarrassed. "I wish Valentina hadn't brought it up."

"She sometimes does not think about proper places in which to talk of personal things."

"It was a lovely night—the opera, the walk. And then, it ended a little...weird."

"Valentina did not mean to make you feel badly. I know that about her. And I would like to say, and then I will not say more, that I do not like to think of you as unhappy."

My voice is thick, but I try to sound sure of myself. "I'm fine. I'm fine." I feel more discomfited now because it sounds as if I am trying to convince myself.

The train arrives. We join the travelers moving towards the coaches. I ask him about his unexpected meeting in Rome.

"Si. A meeting about moving the sculpture by Salvi and Bracci to Florence—you know it as the Trevi Fountain."

I stop. "You're joking."

"Of course." He grins. "I did not imagine you as gullible."

I shake my head ruefully. "I'm not. Usually. Must be an off day."

Our conversation is superficial as we walk down the platform. He doesn't relay any details of his real purpose for his trip. Maybe it has to do with his father's work, the work he wants to complete. He says, "I would have tried to change my ticket so that we could talk together as we travel, but as is sometimes the case, the morning train to Rome is sold out. Business people traveling." He runs his hand through his hair, moves his case from one hand to the next.

My words tumble out to fill up space. "And shoppers going early enough to get a complete day in. I know. I took this train last year for the super sales in Piazza di Spagna—shopped all day, I was back in Florence by midnight." As soon as I say it I regret opening that memory. Susie and I shopping. Having pizza at Farine before collapsing on the train, shopping bags on our laps, excited about our designer bargains.

"Here is my coach." We arrive at Coach 4, the quiet coach.

Other passengers board.

"I have an idea." He is very casual. "I could take you to dinner in Rome, if you are available, at my favorite spot."

I hesitate, I don't like to feel as if someone is putting himself out because he sees me as pitiful, as an unhappy person who needs care. "Oh. Well, I'm not sure of my schedule. And really, I'm sure you're busy. You don't have to feel…"

He interrupts. "We have cell phone contacts now of each other. If you would like, I will call you and we will see if our schedules can match. Now we must board the train or be left behind."

I take my seat next to a dapper older gentleman wearing a double-breasted navy suit jacket with a pocket handkerchief and silk scarf hanging loose around his neck. His moustache is groomed and polished. His grey slacks are pressed and his shoes are shined. The two seats facing me are occupied by priests.

My first trip to Rome was three years ago—traveling on a high-speed train just like this one, at over 180 miles per hour. Stan and I had almost missed it and we tumbled into our seats across from priests heading to the Vatican for the Italian Bible Association Conference to discuss Divine Revelations. They talked about the then Pope—Pope Francis—and how he believed that God's Scriptures were nourishment for all and how the Pope wanted the Bible to be made more accessible. Stan and I were not up on the latest theological discourse and Stan changed the subject, told them we were from a suburb of New York City and he had always wondered about the differences between Irish-American priests and Italian-American priests—besides the whiskey versus the wine flowing in the rectories between masses. Stan and his charming smile and his fast jokes. We all had fun.

I push aside the recollection, tell myself to concentrate on making new memories. That don't deflate fine moments. And today will be a fine day, I tell myself. It will be a new adventure. And how nice it was to see Matteo. And this meeting with the film director is a pat on the back—it's amazing that my book is being considered by the studio. I tell myself, stay in the present.

I see that the priests across from me today are both reading *The Adventures of Tintin*. One is reading *Red Rackham's Treasure* and the other is reading *Land of Black Gold*. There is a stack of other high-gloss, brightly-colored comic books featuring Tintin between them. They are totally engaged in the do-gooder adventurer's exploits.

I remember my mother telling me how, exhausted after a week of toil in the detritus of the flooded Biblioteca Nazionale, one of the Florentine natives—a fellow Mud Angel—led a group to the San Miniato al Monte basilica, on the hill overlooking the subsiding waters of the Arno. Grateful to be above the fray for a few hours, they entered the small church and rested on the hard, wooden pews. Some of the Florentines who had fled their flooded homes were sheltered here. The priests of the church shared their blankets and slowly my mother's body warmed. The priests heated water over a fire so she could wash off cold, thick mud from her arms and face. The priests shared bean soup. And wine. The young Mud Angels, resting against each other to increase heat, slept. Only an hour or two. With renewed energy, they went back to work. And the priests continued to care for those who had lost their homes.

I look out the window. We are already speeding into the countryside.

I text Angelica, let her know that if Domenico contacts her with information on a possible meet with Signor Velicchio, that I will be back in Florence tomorrow.

The older gentleman beside me is reading a folded newspaper. His eyes closing.

The priests are intent on their reading. Amazingly, my quiet car to Rome is actually quiet today.

I slip into sleep.

The scent of Matteo's aftershave still in my nostrils.

Less than two hours later. Barely mid-morning.

We walk towards the Boscolo Exedra Roma hotel, only a ten-minute walk from Rome's Termini, the city's central train station. Matteo, who has told me he had decided to wait for me at the door of my coach because he has time before his meeting and he didn't know if I knew that the Boscolo Exedra Roma was an easy walk from the train station. "The Boscolo is convenient. For this reason, there is no need for a taxi. I have the time. I will show you."

The light is different in Rome—there are more whites and grays. Florence has a golden hue. And the traffic in Rome is more intense; the sounds on the wide streets are different, there is more honking of horns and revving of engines of cars and motorcycles. Insistent noise fills the city. Florence has wonderful pockets of quiet. Pedestrians seem to rule the streets of the old section of Florence. Moving vehicles of all sizes and shapes rule the streets of Rome. Everything is faster in Rome.

"What time is your appointment today?" I veer towards Matteo to avoid a tour guide encouraging passers-by to sign up for wine tastings. Our bodies collide for a moment and I am momentarily aware of the lean hardness of his frame.

He takes my elbow and we sidestep a gaggle of Italian grandmothers stopping to talk to one another in the middle of the sidewalk, plastic shopping bags full of fruit and vegetables over their arms. "Ahh, my meeting time is flexible. It will be a lunch, maybe long. Maybe short."

I take in the book stalls that line the Via della Terme di Dioclenziano. They hold new and used books in Italian, English, French, Turkish and Spanish—in nearly every language. Matteo follows my gaze. "They may be selling your books in there."

"That's a nice thought."

"You like to be a writer?"

My answer is like a knee-jerk reaction. Quick. I notice how sure I am. "Yes, I do. I look forward to writing every day. Putting aside the time for it. There's a writer I admire—her name is Joan Didion—she said once that the reason she writes is to find out what she thinks. Other writers have said things close to that. You know—it's a process—like painting. Start with a blank canvas." I realize I am babbling, but I forge on. "In a way, it's like that for me. A process of finding out. Whatever. My mother always teased me about it. I observe life a lot, I take it all in, I love facts, I love history, I like to listen to people. And when I write, it seems that's the time I put it together. To make sense of things. For my characters. Which means, I guess, for myself."

"So, you figure things out as you write."

I feel a bit embarrassed. "Sometimes it takes me awhile to figure things out."

"That could be good. You give people—you give life a chance. Don't make snap judgments or decisions."

"Sometimes I envy people who see the pros and the cons more quickly. Good and bad. The ramifications of a choice."

My mind takes a sudden turn and a question blares at me. Had I made the wrong choice in romance that day Stan proposed on the beach? Or was it the right choice at the time? Am I naïve to want— or expect—love to last forever?

We cross the street and approach the city's vast Piazza della Repubblica. A colossal fountain is in its center, cars race around it and then head off into multiple streets; it's like a mammoth roundabout.

Matteo points to the hotel facing the fountain. "Very elegante. Lussuoso. Many Americans, many tourists who like opulence stay here." The Boscolo Exedra is fronted with a wide curving marble veranda, its roof supported by broad stone columns. There is an open-air lounge where guests sit on couches and overstuffed chairs sipping morning coffees. I feel pampered already, knowing I will share the luxury for the day.

We enter the hotel lobby. Sunlight streams in the high windows and warms the creamy-white marble floors and walls. The chairs and couches are mushroom-colored. Brilliant orange birds of paradise are tucked into oversized thick glass vases. Silent doormen and porters and concierges adorn the space, intent on making sure guests' needs are met. I tell Matteo I feel quite special to be going to the reception desk and explaining that Paramount Pictures has reserved a room for me.

"Is that similar to announcing that the Pope has arranged for your room?"

"A bit." I laugh. "America reveres huge corporations. Microsoft. Apple. Amazon. Professional sports. You know."

Matteo's cell phone rings. "Scusami." He answers it and speaks, "Bernadette, sei ancora in Paris? Ahhh bene, uno momento." He tells me he will wait across the lobby while I check in. He leaves me to sit in a chair to continue his conversation.

I move towards the reception desk, imagining Bernadette, her lean stylish figure sitting in a Paris café, checking in with the man everyone waits for her to marry.

There is a person at the reception desk, talking to the dark-haired, dark-eyed woman standing behind the hotel computer. I notice her hair is coiffed and polished to an elegant sheen. The reception clerk next to her, talking to a stylish woman in a Chanel suit has a similar coiffure. I wonder if this hairstyle is required to work in this hotel.

The man talking to the graceful check-in woman dips his head to the side. I know that dip. My feet feel, suddenly, like cement blocks. I cannot force them to move. My coffee, so comforting on the train, turns sour in my stomach.

Stan turns and sees me. The sunlight that—a moment ago—streamed through the revolving doors and high windows of the vaulted lobby disappears. I feel a darkness—whether it's real or not—wrap around me like a boa constrictor intending to squeeze my lungs of every particle of oxygen.

Stan moves toward me, his hands up as if to advise caution. "Lyn, don't even think about throwing anything at me."

The frisbee-ing of plates I aimed at his body at the D.O.C. Donnini restaurant must have made an impression.

"I am here to talk to you. It's in your best interest." Stan's voice is measured. As if talking someone down from a ledge.

I stare at him. I don't register what he is saying. I'm like a deer caught in headlights, sensing danger but not sure which way to go. Do I stay or run—hoping to escape—but fearing nowhere promises safety.

Stan continues, "I talked to Verdine and to tell you the truth, I wasn't sure if you'd show up. You aren't answering your cell phone. I want to make sure you don't lose this movie deal."

I realize I am not blinking. Stuck in the fight or flight moment.

"Listen, I guess you're in a sort of shock. I probably didn't handle giving you the news well. But I don't want you to regret not taking care of your interests. I want to do what I do—take care of your contracts and stuff."

I find my voice. "Stuff?"

I see him scramble. This press, the rhythm of his aggression is transparent. He would brag about it at the end of the day, how his bosses told him he could spin a negotiation better than anyone.

He's still talking, "I just want to make sure you take care of business."

"I told Verdine not to call you."

"She'd left a message. I called her back. She was hedgy but I finally got her to tell me what was going on. Congratulations on the reception of the book. But what's disturbing is that Verdine told me you want to cut me out on this."

"Cut you out?" My voice is monotone. My ninja behavior at the D.O.C. Donnini was high voltage and physical. This pressure brings on a stronger sense of danger and makes me more cautious.

"I was a part of the sale to Harledge, I got you and Verdine introduced. I put together the deal."

I can't believe he's taking a kind of ownership of parts of my life.

"Look, the partners in my firm are going to see this as a sweet piece of business. They'll put their power behind it. And movie contracts can be tricky. I've already contacted an entertainment lawyer in Los Angeles to make sure everything's covered."

"No."

"What? What do you mean, 'no'?"

"I'll tell Verdine to tell Paramount you are not involved."

"Don't be reckless. I know you…"

"I won't be reckless." I feel trapped. My feet still cannot move.

"Good, 'cause Lyn, time to be smart. Not emotional. Like I said, it's not like I don't want what's best for you. We all gotta be able to put business and relationships into separate categories."

Matteo joins us. "Liniana, is your reservation in order?" He notices the distress on my face. He glances at Stan. "Ci scusi."

"Who are you?"

Matteo doesn't bother to answer Stan. He looks to me. "Is there a problem?"

Stan bullies. "Not that concerns you."

Matteo's closeness steadies me. I mumble, "This is the person who is dissolving our marriage—the one...you heard about."

Matteo gazes more closely at Stan. His eyes are hooded and he's looking down because Stan is a few inches shorter than he is.

Stan's chin goes up. "I asked, who are you?"

I wonder if Stan is staying at this hotel. It's like he reads my mind, he holds up his room card. "I found out Paramount was putting you up here. I knew we needed to talk before you went to see that director today—so you wouldn't agree to anything you shouldn't agree to."

I finally attain mobility. I turn and walk off. Matteo follows.

Stan follows. "Where are you going? Don't just walk away."

Matteo's hand moves to my back, he serves as a buffer between Stan and me.

We reach the revolving door. Susie is coming in with shopping bags. She's not smiling, not the normal Susie-shopping-spree face. She looks drawn, tired.

She stops when she sees me.

Stan doesn't see Susie; he is still concentrated on forcing my attention. "Lyn, be reasonable. I'm trying to do the right thing for you."

Susie drops her eyes and does not leave the safety of the revolving doors. She continues in a full circle and exits onto the veranda.

Swisssssh is the sound.

Swissssssh. Susie's turned right and is now out of sight.

Stan taps Matteo on the shoulder. "Excuse me, I asked who you are."

Matteo turns to Stan. Stan's chest is wider. His pecs and neck are thicker. And he's from Queens. A scrapper by nature.

"You don't need to know who I am," Matteo says. "Liniana and I have plans and we are leaving now."

"Lini-what? What the hell?" He turns to me, curiosity bursting from him. "Who's this Italian?"

Matteo takes my elbow and leads me to the side door.

Stan doesn't give up. "Come on."

The doorman opens the door for us, very polite, unaware of the intense drama that makes my chest ache. Matteo tells him that we will need a taxi immediately.

Stan follows us out. "Lyn, be prudent."

The doorman is already down the steps of the veranda. He reaches street level. He alerts a waiting taxi, opens its door. We get in.

"Lyn. This is ridiculous." Stan's voice is near—and louder, more insistent.

The taxi door closes. Matteo tells the driver, "Casa Montani, Piazzale Flaminio, per favore."

Casa Montani is tucked into a quiet street near the Spanish Steps; it does not call attention to itself. Pietro, the thin and refined manager at the small boutique hotel, welcomes Matteo; they are old friends. Matteo stays here whenever he is in Rome. Pietro assures Matteo that the room the owners keep free for family will be made available. The reception area is filled with heirloom antiques and mid-century art work. Matteo tells Pietro that a car will be arriving to take me to Cinecitta in a few hours. Pietro nods and motions for me to take a seat in the receiving room. He takes my small bag and moves up the carpeted staircase. A pot of tea is brought in by Pietro's wife, Yvette. Matteo is on his cell, letting the Boscolo Exedra know I will not be staying there for the night and arranging for them to alert Paramount Pictures. I send a text to Verdine, let her know that Paramount can now pick up the tab at the Casa Montani.

Matteo sits next to me. I sip my tea. My hand trembles. He checks his cell, probably for information on his meetings.

"I hope I didn't cause you to miss your appointment."

"Do not worry. It is still early."

I try to lighten the moment. "I usually don't need the knight in shining armor protection."

"Is that what I was?"

"You did take charge."

"My apologies."

"I needed to get out of there without a scene. That hotel's much too fancy for a knock-down, drag-out."

"Knock-down, drag-out?"

"Fist fight."

"Is that what was about to happen?"

"Not literally. I don't think so. Just—thanks for the save."

"I am sure you would have managed on your own."

"I can. Manage. But that was—finessed. And I want you to know, just because we are friends—I don't mean to assume, but we are sort of friends…?"

"Si. Friends. Si. Of course."

"I want to make sure you know I don't want to impose on that. I can handle my own dramas." I realize the lightness I am trying to infuse into the conversation is not there. I sound hollow. I hate it that Stan can disrupt my emotional balance.

Pietro comes back and tells me my room is ready. He will alert me when the car to Cinecitta arrives.

Matteo tells me not to worry. He thinks I will like staying at the Casa Montani.

Pietro waits for me to follow him.

I go to my room.

Chapter 20

Lesli Plattson is about my age and three inches taller than me. She wears a flowing long silk coat, open to reveal a leopard printed shirt, skinny jeans and tri-colored short leather boots. Her long blonde hair is pulled back into a low ponytail. Gold earrings with pressed copper lions' heads on the ends dangle from her earlobes. She stands at the coffee bar, an empty espresso cup before her. She is on her cell phone and Billy, her 25-year-old chubby assistant whose hair has been buzz cut, is at her side on another cell phone.

Lesli sees me and hands over her cell to Billy. "I'm like on hold. Tell him I'll call him back." Billy is now on double-cell-duty but seems totally used to it.

Lesli's attention is fully on me. "You must be Lyn Bennett—I'm like pumped to meet you. I'm Lesli. Your book needs to be brought to the screen—amazingly few stories about women who make the hard choices. You ever write a screenplay?" She talks with no breaks, one idea pressed against another, non-stop.

"No. I've read scripts but…" I consider my days as an assistant in the literary agency.

"Do you want to take a try at it? They're like fun, just takes getting used to for most novelists."

"I'm more comfortable writing prose, really."

Lesli's cell phone, in assistant Billy's hand, vibrates. "It's yours," he tells her. She waves for him to answer it. He does and responds to the caller in very good Italian.

"You're from New York." Lesli leads us towards the double glass doors leading to the backlot.

"Queens."

"I'm from the Valley. Southern California. Like—you know. Loved film all my life. Like it's just crazy that I am here. Like I'm in the den of the Italian cinema gods." She turns to me, readying to push the doors open with her backside. "I'll show you around. Mussolini's idea, building a big film studio in the 30s, to rival Hollywood." She grins. "He's not like my favorite Fascist, but most are way too opinionated for me anyway."

Billy, following us, has just taken another call and interrupts, "Lesli, sorry. Security at the front gates says there's a Stan McNamara here to see you, he says he represents Lyn Bennett's interests."

We stop.

They both look at me. Lesli asks, "You brought someone with you?"

"No. In fact, I told him not to come."

Lesli rubs her left earring. "I don't really think we need anyone—this is just for us to see if we can get on the same page. But if you'd feel more comfortable…"

I nearly spit out the information. "He's a lawyer—he also happens to be my husband who told me three days ago he was dumping me for my best friend."

I realize the more I say it, the more real it becomes. And the more real it becomes, the easier it is to see my new relationship status as a cold fact. Not talking about it, keeping it an inner angst, my secret—and running the whys and wheres and hows on the hamster wheel in my brain only allowed for a disbelief, something I could try to bargain away. Once Valentina made it public—it became a reality. And now I'm blurting it out too. Actually, it feels more empowering.

Lesli exhales. "That fuckin' sucks."

"And so, you can see how inaccurate that sounds—that he says he wants to protect my interests."

"Inaccurate. Diabolical. Selfish. Fuck 'im is what I say."

I nearly growl. "You can have your assistant say that to him."

Lesli turns to Billy. "Tell security to tell this guy he is not needed."

Billy moves off to relay the message. I am not sure if "fuck 'im" will be included in Billy's conversation. But I surmise the hard line will be communicated.

Lesli sees my flashing eyes. She calls after Billy, "And ask them to escort him off the lot." She turns back to me. "You okay?"

"Don't worry about me," I say. "People get screwed every day and why shouldn't I be one of them?" I make a vow to myself right then and voice it. "I plan to be a grown-up about this."

"Good luck with that." She pats me on the shoulder—her touch feels as if she knows how hard it is to be grown-up sometimes. Then Lesli gets back to business. "Hopefully you'll get the magic feel here. Forget the guy who fucked you over and now can't get in on this." We leave the café and head towards the sound stages. "Luckily Mussolini thought film was a great propaganda weapon. He had the studio built when Italians still hoped he might be the answer to their economic and social problems. If only we could re-do history with hindsight. Sometimes we can't know, when we're in the thick of it, who's the best person to trust."

Her words don't pull me into a funk. Just ring true. Words that I can keep in the go-to advice column in my grown-up brain.

"Did I hear you right? Your best friend?"

"I thought she was."

"Whoa. There's that need for hindsight again."

Cinecitta is large. Its standing outdoor sets are made of spray-painted Styrofoam and stand in for stone temples and palaces and back streets of Italian villages. Lesli tells me, "During the war, Cinecitta was used for the army. 'Course a lot of Rome was bombed and after the war—homeless sheltered here. Didn't have anywhere to go. Then in the 1950s, Rome, realized they had to attract money in a real serious way. So, they cleaned the lot up, rented it out to Hollywood for 'sandal dramas' like the *Hercules* movies—the cheesy ones starring Steve Reeves...and then *Ben Hur* was filmed here too, late 50s. The chariot race right over there." She points to a huge expanse in the back area of the lot. "Took them three months just to shoot that sequence. No CGI back then." She waves towards one of the soundstages. "*Cleopatra*—with Elizabeth Taylor—shot there. Man, I tell ya, I love to imagine the massive productions, the cameras, the extras, the logistics. Gets my blooding going." She points to an area near the large man-made lake. "See those wooden buildings there? That's what's left of the set of *Gangs of New York*—you know, the film done by Scorcese with di Caprio. You like movies, right?"

I tell her I like the film stories that make me think.

"You and me both. Dumber-than-dumb scatological frat-boy comedies—not my style." We head towards huge soundstages. "You madder at him or her? Husband or best friend?"

"You mean who is sentenced to the hotter hell?"

"Yeah. Whose flesh turns into crispy crap first?"

I know the hurt goes deeper than I have been willing to face. "I don't know how she could have done this to me."

"Yeah, I'd probably put her closer to the fire."

She stops in front of the largest rectangular soundstage. "Would like to be a permanent fly on the wall in this place. Stage 5—where Fellini shot *Satyricon* and *La Dolce Vita*." We stand for a moment; I feel she is re-playing some of his greatest filmed moments in her head. She finally shakes off her reverie. "Okay, now let's concentrate on us."

We walk through the standing sets of the television mini-series *Rome* and talk about the main character of my most recent novel, the one that interests Paramount. About an art history teacher who finds out her ex-husband, running for public office, has sold his soul to the devil—literally—in order to profit from the miseries of his town after a catastrophic hurricane. The teacher's name is Melanie, a divorcee, and she struggles to deal with the wreckage of her home and community and the treacherous, greedy bankers and contractors who prey on the pain and suffering of the neighbors she loves or hates or has complicated relationships with—but who must now all band together to face this disaster. When Melanie finds out her ex-husband has sold out, she is propelled into running against him in the upcoming election. She ends up flushing out his deep criminality and selfishness. Melanie has never put herself on the line before, she was always one to try to bring calm to every situation, sacrificing herself in order maintain peace.

Lesli tells me she responds to the awakening of a voyeur to action. Lots of people now, she says, get their lives off television or the internet and are not on-the-street involved. This has disaster, betrayal, love, crime, it's about a woman finding her strong voice. "I never paid attention to that 'glass ceiling' for women in the industry. I put a lot of action and violence into my films to like prove I could do that stuff too, just as good as male directors. I earned some cred and a shot to pick my next project. Now I want to do this. It's got what I want to say." She adds, "And a lot of visual stuff too. That just makes it's easier to get the suits to sign off. We'll start with the disaster—I'm gonna construct the biggest, baddest hurricane—put the audience feeling like they're right in the middle of it and then we'll go character all the way."

We are back at the café and order glasses of wine. As I eyeball the memorabilia in the gift store—movie posters, coffee cups, t-shirts, aprons, wine-openers and books on famous Italian filmmakers, Lesli continues with her plan. "I'll get the studio to commit.

I'll do a rough draft of the screenplay—then you can see what I am thinking about—how I see how the story might transpose to screen. Action. Locations. What happens where. Then I'll send it to you and you fill in or take out or add whatever. From that point, we'll hash it over together, talk about casting possibilities. I promise I'll try not to be too pushy about my ideas but you must be willing to fight for yours—'cause I can get pretty pushy." Her grin grows wide.

I tell her I do have a strong spine.

"Yeah, you have a quiet thing going on but you don't impress me as a pushover." She pries, searching my face for a reaction. "That lawyer husband of yours knows that, right?"

I think about it. Wondering how Stan really did see me. As the woman to whom he announced his intentions to marry within a year—the one who fell in line? As the woman who spent months finding the right home? As the woman who shopped for the right presents for his boss and his assistants? As the woman who shared her family because his was dysfunctional? As the woman who thought his energy and take-no-prisoners style would never be targeted directly at her? "He's pushy," I say. "I did let him lead—a lot. Maybe I thought of it as my part of making the relationship work."

"You had to work to make it work?"

Her question stops me. "That's what you do, right?"

Lesli shrugs. "What do I know? My relationships last a production cycle. From pre-production to a red-carpet opening night. Then I'm on to the next thing and that usually includes moving onto the next man. I figured relationships work or not. Why should I work at making them work?"

"Merging lives—it's not easy."

"Well, sure, but it shouldn't be 'work'."

Lesli's lips crease into a knowing half-smile. "I have a nose for pushover. I've learned to run from those kinds because they make me feel like I'm a my-way-or-the-highway-monster and I don't like to feel that way. I like push and pull coming from both sides. I think you and I could do this."

We toast each other.

"We'll get our agents to talk. Get the studio not to bullshit us on the contract. How does that sound?"

In the car on the way back to the hotel, I want to share my good news. I call Verdine; no answer. I have to leave a message. I call my brother. No answer. Everyone in New York is asleep.

So I text Matteo.

Dinner works for me. I would like. Liniana

The car lets me off at the Casa Montani.

There is a small dress shop across the street. A simple black dress is in the window.

Inside the store, I see vintage jewelry in the case by the register. Cashmere pashminas on a center table.

A shoe store is only a block away.

I return to the hotel and my cozy room. I take a hot shower. I pull on the fluffy robe that hangs in the small marble bathroom and stretch out on the chaise in front of glass doors. They open to a small ivy-covered balcony. I am tucked away, feel as if no one can find me except for those I want to find me. For this moment, this lovely cocoon is a most wonderful place.

Matteo, in a dark gray jacket, white shirt and soft gray and white striped tie, sits in the comfortable chair in the reception area, reading a newspaper. A glass of wine is on the table next to him. I take a moment, liking the way his upper body fills the back of the chair, how his long legs stretch out in front of him. The way he is intent on his reading. His calmness.

He looks up as I enter. I see him notice my dress. My dark hair pulled up in a twist. The vintage earrings and Italian flats.

He stands and asks Pietro to call a taxi for us.

The restaurant is bustling. The maître leads us past a credenza piled high with desserts: panna cotta, torta della nonna, tiramisu, dense flourless chocolate cake, eclairs, cheesecakes, fruit and biscotti. Past a table of cheeses: a huge wheel of parmigiano, bowls of fresh mozzarella, mounds of oozing burrata. Copper bowls and giant whisks hang on the walls. Waiters rush piping-hot bowls of pasta from the kitchen to the diners. The smells are amazing. We are seated in a center table. The din in the restaurant is lively, it is a place to be cheerful and laugh, to appreciate the constant motion. Behind us is a party of businessmen, to the side is a gaggle of sisters fawning over the one who is very pregnant, to the other side is a chicly dressed, elderly foursome, on their third bottle of wine.

Matteo takes off his jacket and hangs it on the back of the chair. He unbuttons his cuffs and rolls up the sleeves. He jokes, "Preparing to enjoy my meal."

"By all means, get ready to chow down."

"Chow down. That is Western movie slang."

"It's pretty all-around American slang. Big portions and eat fast. Before we know it, we've surpassed our limits—so always travel with antacids." I realize we like to banter back and forth on our nations' differences. He's quick and funny and I enjoy it.

"Tums. Lots of different colors."

"Right."

"I suggest just slowing down."

"American's can't do that." I peer at him with a face full of faux astonishment.

He laughs. "Si. Americans are famous for their appetites." He orders a bottle of wine for us. "And also award shows. Americans like award shows." He teases, "When your movie opens and you are televised on the red carpet, you must give us a signal to show that you remember us."

"What should the signal be?"

"Perhaps pull your ear or pretend to brush a fly off your shoulder. And then, as an addition, you could wink." He winks at me; the side of his face crinkles with a smile.

"I am a terrible 'wink-er'." I tell him that when I try to wink—both eyes squint and whatever small movement there might be in my winking eye is unrecognizable. I show him and he shakes his head, feigning great sorrow for my inability and agrees that an alternative signal must be agreed upon.

"I could pretend to trip on my gown."

"And land face first on the carpet? No, not necessary."

"I agree. I do want to preserve my dignity." The waiter pours the Chianti that Matteo ordered. Delicious.

Our waiter suggests the specialties of the restaurant and we agree.

"You haven't mentioned your meeting." I unfold my napkin. "Did it go well?"

"I think progress was made." He straightens his fork and knife. "Perhaps your mother mentioned the problem that existed—in the 1966 flood—the one that still has reverberations today."

"What problem?"

"There is much good that happened because of those who came to help retrieve and restore artifacts. But, of course, there were also those who took advantage of the catastrophe. Looters. Opportunists who could not resist temptation. It is well-known, nonetheless. There is some evidence of an artifact—an important one—that might be now located. Not concrete, in this particular case, but rumors must be investigated. And I am a sleuth, tracking down clues."

"This is good news then."

"If it is true. Some artifacts, artwork or books were recovered, years later, when someone was incautious and put something in auction or on the black market. Si, treasures were found that way. Sometimes when there was a death in a family and old trunks and closets and secret caves were opened—a masterpiece was found. It had been hidden away and no one was able to enjoy it because then a thief would be revealed."

"I didn't know there was an on-going search. Fifty years later."

"It will go on indefinitely. Today was another clue that could lead somewhere. Perhaps I am one step closer. It is good I am patient."

I am impressed with his love for his city. "Florence is very important to you."

"It is my home."

Our salad and the polpo alla griglia arrive. The salad is tossed at the table with olive oil. The octopus is grilled and sublimely tender.

"Valentina told me that your family—and Bernadette's family—started in the wine and olive oil business generations ago. On properties next to each other."

"Generations of farmers. Gradually some sons turned merchants or professors or curators. Daughters married or chose a different path. It has to be that way in a family because it is soon evident a farm cannot support every person in the following generations. And everyone is not meant to be a farmer."

"Your grandfather joined the Uffizi."

"A path I follow. But the farms are still there. They are in a beautiful area only a few hours from Florence. Our cousins run them. We go to pick olives. Pick grapes. Pick flowers. Tomatoes. One of my cousins has built beehives. It is wonderful honey."

I toast him. "To your ancestors."

"The stories are told over and over. Much happy stories and some sorrow. Wars. Invasions. Survival. Love gone good, love gone bad. But what is not to be proud of?"

Our waiter arrives with a steaming hot copper bowl full of Rome's famous Cacio e Pepe, pasta tossed with pecorino romano cheese and freshly cracked pepper. The waiter divides the pasta, using wooden tongs to place half on a plate in front of Matteo and then placing the copper bowl in front of me.

"It's nice you and Bernadette have that history."

"Si. Absolutely." He sounds like a man who knows the woman in his life is special. I think Bernadette is lucky.

"Bernadette likes her work and she likes the travel. She loves Paris. Her mother wants her to stay home more. But Bernadette wants to not do that. She likes Florence and our countryside very much but she loves Paris."

"Is that something you two have to work out? Paris and Florence?"

"What do you mean?"

"You two—Valentina says you will get officially engaged some-time soon."

Matteo shakes his head, amused. "Valentina. She likes to have the world the way she sees it." He loosens his tie, explaining this allows for better enjoyment of pasta. He uses his fork to lift the bucatini strands and winds them around the tines. He doesn't meet my eyes, concentrates on his fork, "And now, I suppose—in your life at this time—you do not believe or trust in love."

He waits for an answer. Not really looking at me, but clearly waiting.

I take my time. My voice starts soft, but I try to add weight and assurance. I don't want to sound pitiful. "I have seen it—in different people. A special connection."

"Perhaps it will take some time to see possibilities again."

He eats. And nods his head, encouraging me to eat. "You must enjoy this so we can move onto the tiramisu. It is one of their specialties here."

"It will be too much."

"We are celebrating."

"My book?"

"And our first meal in Rome. That we have met and we are now eating our first meal in Rome. And Valentina loves tiramisu and we can toast her for teaching you Italian and inviting you to the opera."

"Let's not talk of dessert when this pasta is so incredible."

He enjoys that I appreciate everything Italian. "Valentina has insisted on delicacies for her gallery opening. She thinks if people like the food and wine, they will like her art more."

"Shall I bring Mildred? You met her the other night. After the piano concert, when we stopped for gelato. She is an artist too. Or is the opening gathering meant to be small?"

"Please, bring your friend. We want it to feel festive and crowd-ed. Italians like that and it is best for the gallery."

"I can ask my students if they would like to come if you are interested in more bodies."

"They are welcome. Please, encourage them."

"Valentina is lucky to have you as a brother."

"Remind her of that, will you?" He smiles as he finishes his pasta. "You have a brother, is that correct?"

"He's protective also."

"Good." He seems genuinely pleased to hear that. "You will go back to New York City? Not your home in Queens."

The waiter takes away our plate and bowl. I sigh, taste buds satiated. The room is packed, the music is classic, the food is exquisite. I think back; a week ago I could have chosen to lock the door of my apartment and dismissed the reality that life goes on with or without me. But how wonderful it is to feel its pulse and vitality. Not be ruled by events that hurt.

Event.

Is it now relegated to that? An event.

"I googled Queens. Because of you. Many famous people grew up in Queens. A lot of basketball players."

"Everyone famous who grew up there, moved away. Ended up living somewhere else. The house I grew up in has been sold two or three times since we lived there. Strangers live in 'my' house now." Images of growing up in Queens spring to mind. Sitting in the kitchen with my mother, watching her cook. My father and mother chuckling as they poured over the New York Times comics section every Sunday morning. My father working on his cars in the garage. My brother Rick mowing grass. Sitting on my chenille bedspread in my room, reading stories and writing stories and dreaming of being a grown-up and moving away to live an exciting life.

"I'll go back to Manhattan and—figure things out."

"Yes, I would imagine. And by the way. Your husband. I did not like him." Matteo signals the waiter to serve the tiramisu.

His statement is said matter-of-factly. No comment seems necessary. But I am surprised he has weighed in. And for some reason, I like that he has given his opinion.

The final highlight, tiramisu, is served. The mascarpone custard is sweet and smooth, the espresso adds a darker, bitter taste, the ladyfingers have soaked up the marsala wine and each bite melts in my mouth.

"My mother made this for me on my birthdays." I savor the tiramisu's lightness. "She would let me help her whip the cream and then I got to layer the savoiardi…"

"Ahh, you know the correct word."

"Si, she taught it to me. She said that when the Mud Angels were working, they would list their favorite Italian meals and imagine what it would be like to be eating them. Instead of the rare piece of stale bread or dried jerky."

"'Tiramisu' does mean 'pick me up'—or some just convert it to 'make me happy'."

I lick my lips appreciatively. "This does make me happy."

Matteo orders glasses of dessert wine for us. His voice is clear and soft, sure of himself. He weaves a tale of tiramisu's origins. "Some say, it was made first in northern Tuscany. For Grand Duke Cosimo de'Medici and it was called the duke's soup because the custard was very loose. Then someone—many think someone in a restaurant outside of Venice in a town called Treviso—decided to add mascarpone to the custard to make it more sturdy—and the espresso for the 'pick me up'. Now it could stand tall and alone. But there is another story that may or may not be true, but I like it. The bordellos of Venice and its regions, in efforts to attract customers, started to serve espresso after sex to its patrons—to combat the desire to nap. The espresso 'picked the men up' so they could go back to work to earn more money to come back and enjoy sex again. Other bordellos decided to follow suit, to compete. The most enterprising madam took it a step further and decided to put mascarpone, savoiardi, chocolate, together and serve it with the espresso for an extra pick me up. To make her bordello more special. And it did become so. And this is the tiramisu we love."

We finish the dessert. Smiling. It does make one happy. We head out into the cool night and head for the taxi stand.

I pull my shawl close.

"Your seminar is over in a few weeks." He opens the car door for me. "That is a very short time."

"Yes." I move across the seat of the taxi to make room for him.

He settles in and gives the driver the address of our hotel.

At the hotel, Pietro pours us glasses of Grappa di Brunello. I move to look at the artwork, fine pieces that look like they belong to the Futurism movement of the 1920s. Matteo and Pietro converse in Italian behind me, I don't try to make out the details of their conversation. The grappa stings my palate and it makes me feel light, loose and happy.

I hear Matteo's cell phone ping. He answers.

"It is Bernadette. Scusami." I turn to him, he shrugs. "I will take it outside. "

He steps out the front door.

I settle into a chair and Pietro puts a plate of biscotti and chocolates on the table next to me.

Matteo comes back in; the door shuts behind him. He looks distracted. "I will have to go to Paris on the last flight tonight. Bernadette—she is there and now I need to be there. You will be fine?"

"Of course." I feel a pang of disappointment. I remind myself that if Matteo had not had a meeting in Rome today, and if we had not happened to meet at the train station, that I would have been alone in Rome for the entire evening. I determine to consider myself lucky.

"Pietro will arrange for a taxi for you to the train station in the morning."

I thank him again. "E stato cosi gentile. Sono grata."

He smiles.

"Did I say that right? That you have been so kind. And that I am grateful."

"Valentina's tutelage has not been for nothing. I understood."

"I must tell her that you approve."

He is suddenly serious. "I do approve. Very much." He smiles, it's back to the light and bantering that we have so successfully mastered. "You are in the perfect spot. Casa Montani. You will sleep like an angel."

I climb the stairs to my room. Tell myself I have no right to wish we had another hour together to enjoy the late-night grappa. Why should I be disappointed because a knight in shining armor is off to his true damsel.

Chapter 21

I look at the address I scrawled in my notebook. 16 Via E. Poggi is a small street connected to Florence's Piazza della Indipenden-za—a tree-filled square elevated high enough to have kept the 1966 flood waters at bay. The piazza was designed in the late 1800s to commemorate those who fought for Italian unification—the Risorgimento. Crazy to think that between the fall of the Roman Empire, when people still wore togas, and the Italian unification in the 1860s, Italy was a patchwork of separate entities like the Kingdom of Naples, the Tuscan Grand Duchy, the Kingdom of Sardinia, the Papal States and the Kingdom of Two Sicilies. The Risorgimento movement took nearly fifty-five years to complete, but Italy was finally one country, ready for a new future. A marriage that has lasted. Children run in the piazza, groups of men smoke and talk, housewives chat with rolling shopping carts by their sides.

Angelica had sent me a text, telling me Domenico had talked to old Signor Velicchio's granddaughter. That she would be expecting me.

I reach a four-story centuries-old building, its soft pink paint is peeling, green shutters hang next to each window. The number 16 is carved into the stone next to a nearly hobbit-sized door raised off the street. Eight metal buzzers on a brass board next to the door. I look for Velicchio. Just then the stunted door opens and a teenager, maybe 13 or 14, ducking her head so as to not bump it on the mantle of the stubby door, steps out. She's got a leather backpack across her shoulder and wears tight capri pants. Ropes of beads adorn her neck and her high-top sneakers are covered in glitter. She has a sequin-covered cell phone to her ear, she talks animatedly, doesn't even glance my way. And then an older version of the teen steps out; the mother wears a rhinestone studded purple headband and sparkly drop earrings. Her lipstick is bright pink and flecked with glitter. I can see where her daughter gets her penchant for bling. I take the opportunity. "'Scusi, parli inglese?"

The mother-in-purple looks at me. "Si. Yes. I speak English. Directions you want?" She pulls on a pair of thin leather gloves, a deep purple that matches her headband.

"Grazie. I am hoping to find someone in the Velicchio home. Domenico Galli gave me this address."

She pats her hair; rhinestone bracelets peek out from under her gloves. "Si. I am a Velicchio. Maria Francesca Velicchio Sanna."

"Piacere di conoscerti. I am Lyn."

"Domenico told me about you. Dom and I, we were classmates. I had an interest in him, but he never gave me attention. But I still talk to him. Now I am divorced. Maybe I should have tried harder." She nods towards the pink building. "My Velicchio family live here in the 1960. Si. My father. My grandparents." She calls to her daughter. "Celestina! Aspettare, un minuto." She looks exasperated, shares her frustration. "She has boyfriend. Always talking on cell phone."

Maria Francesca waits for my next question.

"Domenico may have told you about my mother. She came to Firenze to help during the big flood in 1966—to help save art and books." I pull out my mother's journal. "I am hoping to find people who might have known her then. She passed away last year and I don't think I got all the details, things she wanted me to know about Florence. She drew this picture." I show her the sketch. "See, it says Poggi. She had a warm meal here. Cooked on a fire." Suddenly, emotions swell and I cover, quickly show her the group photo. "Domenico recognized Signor Velicchio."

"Ahh si, that is my grandfather when he was young."

"He was called Elvis?"

She rolls her eyes. "He and my grandmother loved to dance."

"He lives here still?"

"With me. Here. He is upstairs at this moment but he sleeps. He is ninety-two. His memory is not always good."

"I was hoping I could meet him. Domenico thought early afternoon…"

She points to her daughter who is now putting in ear buds and practicing dance moves. "And I forgot Dom talked to me about today. My daughter has appointment with dentist."

Disappointment surges. The teen, now deep into her music, spins with a grin on her face. I glimpse the pink plastic braces on her teeth. My mother used to take me to impatient Dr. Rosenthal on Bell Boulevard in Queens. He had no empathy, had no idea of my resentment of his bad breath and the pain he inflicted.

Maria Francesca interrupts. "If you are not in hurry, we will be back in hour. My grandfather should be awake then. We will see if he can talk to you."

I grab the opportunity. "I will be here. Grazie. Of course I will meet you here in an hour."

"Bene. Devo andare, I must go."

Maria Francesca slips her arm around Celestina's shoulder and they walk off. Quickly the teen manages to separate herself—wanting independence. We never appreciate our mothers when they are here.

———

I am back at the address on Via E. Poggi in forty-five minutes. I tell myself to be patient. At the top of the hour, mother and daughter turn onto the street. The girl suddenly sprints towards me, I wonder what's going on, but then I hear a bicycle behind me and realize she is waving at a tow-headed teenager who wears a neon-green nylon windbreaker and blue jeans. She hops onto the handlebars of his bike and they ride off.

Maria Francesca reaches me and sighs. "Boys and girls. Excitement and pain." She touches her sparkly earring as if to check it is still descending from her ear. "I called my grandfather. He will meet you now."

She unlocks the hobbit-sized door and I duck and fold my body to follow her over the stone lip into a vestibule. Mailboxes and bicycles. There is smell of simmering tomato sauce and garlic. "My parents live at the farm our family has. But Nonno likes it here. With me." We move up a stocky stairway to the courtyard; there are beds of flowers and stone benches. Statues of the Virgin Mary adorn the four corners. Maria Francesca's grandfather, Signor Velicchio, stooped and curved from scoliosis, moves through the doorway of his ground floor apartment to meet us.

"Nonno, I will help you."

"Va via! Va via." He barks, telling Maria Francesca he does not need her help.

Signor Velicchio looks like a scrubbed gnome; he wears a crisp white shirt, a purple and gold vest and yellow tie. His white hair is gelled close to his head. He nods to me. "You speak German. Maybe Swedish."

"English. A little Italian," I tell him.

"You don't look Swede."

"I'm American."

"You hunt for old news. Forgotten things. Good to keep past alive." He looks to his granddaughter, "Maria Francesca, offer grappa to our guest. I will have one too."

"Nonno, your doctor says no grappa."

"I don't want to live forever. Let me be and have grappa with a guest."

Maria Francesca emits a frustrated sigh, goes into the apartment.

He sits and grabs my hand, pulls me closer. "Si. Si. Angeli di fango. You and me. Together."

I am witnessing the confusion that Maria Francesca mentioned. I try to get him on track. "My mother was a Mud Angel—angelo di fango. I have a picture with you in it."

I show him the group photo. He points to himself. "That is me. I was in import-export with my father. I know French and German too. So I can talk to many."

"My mother. Her name was Jenny. There." I direct his gaze to the top row.

He leans back, doesn't focus on the photograph. "I was just married. My wife, Paola, was pregnant and did not want to stay home, she wanted to help. But I said no. Too dangerous."

I hand him the picture of my mother, holding a long, muddy, finely crafted silver candlestick above her head, a tired but triumphant smile on her face. "This is another picture of her."

He smooths his hair, studies my face. "You don't change."

"I am Lyn. Jenny's daughter. My mother may have come to this place. Do you remember? She wrote in her journal there was a dinner. Here. Maybe. Around a fire. On Poggi, this street. There were tomatoes in jars, like home-preserved tomatoes."

"Si. We built a fire." He waves his liver-spotted hand toward the center of the courtyard. "We dug a pit there. People bring the wood they could get, even old chairs and tables from garages. Italians don't throw things away—everything can be put to good use." He breathes in, his narrow chest expands. "Si. Si. My Paola had our first son. Here—in this home. She wanted to be in the farmhouse of her family but the roads were under water. No travel."

Maria Francesca comes out of the apartment carrying a tray. A bottle of grappa. A carafe of red wine. Three glasses. "Nonno, I brought wine too. Not everyone likes grappa."

"This angel likes grappa." He still has the picture of my mother in his hand. He looks at it.

I open the journal to show him my mother's drawing. "She drew this." I realize I can recognize the courtyard in her drawing. The tree, the corner statue of Mary with the Christ Child.

The old man nods. "My Paola was from a farm. She make use of everything." He shakes his head at Maria Francesca, frowns. "Now you go to the store. You don't pick tomatoes in the summer to put up in jars to eat in the winter."

"Nonno, I have a job." Maria Francesca's response is quick, I can tell they've had this discussion before. She turns to me. "He won't let me give away any of my grandmother's preservando le cose."

Signor Velicchio pats Maria Francesca's hand. Nods for more grappa.

She adds to his glass. Not much.

"Dancing. Love to dance. American. Rini dance that night. He never dance. He dance that night." He looks at the photo, turns to me. "What is your name?"

"My mother's name was Jenny."

He rests his elbows on his knees, giving support to his curved back. "I had a bed to come home to after I dig into the mud all day. Twenty hours sometimes. Paola and our baby inside her wait for me in the bed." He looks towards his apartment. "Just there. Cold night. Hot fire. I tell Paola she is too close to the fire. I yell at her maybe. She gives me a look."

Maria Francesca laughs. "Si, a bella Nonna look. You knew when she was not happy with you."

He starts to hum, his face darkens, can't find the words he wants to find. "Che notte. What a night. Music. 'Stop in the…'" His feet tap on the stone, he smiles at me. "You can dance. Sai ballare." He starts to hum again. "'Stop in the…'. Ahhhchhh." He is frustrated.

"'Stop in the Name of Love'." I ask him, "Is that the one?" I sing the words, *"Stop in the Name of Love, before you break my heart, think it oooo-ver…"*

He hums, moves his small, boney shoulders up and down. A broad smile creases his face. His hand grabs mine. "Ahhh, so bellisma. You dance. Rini gave me one dance. And also Enrico from Spain. He dance only one."

I try to imagine my mother, early twenties, singing and dancing with abandon, being free and beautiful. Men admiring her. Not the caregiver, the listener to my travails, the taskmaster, the teacher, the wife. An adventurer.

The muscles of Signor Velicchio's face lose tension, his eyes start to close.

"Signor Velicchio, I love that you danced with my mother."

His body twitches with an effort to focus. He gives his glass to Maria Francesca. "Must go."

I try to extend the time. "Signor Velicchio, do you know the names of others in this picture? People that might still be in Florence? Or—just anyone in the photo whose name you remember?"

He glances at the group shot. I know the watermarks and soft focus do not help. He shakes his head. "Remember Rini brought chips. Found in a grocery that still had a box high on a shelf. We thought we found gold." He chuckles. "Patata chips. Salt."

"Who is Rini?" I ask.

Signor Velicchio sighs, summons strength to stand.

Maria Francesca shrugs. "I don't know a Rini." Her pink lips descend into a grimace again. "I am sorry. I need to take him inside."

Signor Velicchio is suddenly angry, his voice rises in volume as he chastises Maria Francesca. She responds with Italian fervor, her hands waving in the air. They are speaking so fast I can only catch a word here and there. Finally, he waves her off, shakes his head. She turns to me. "He thinks I know a Rini. Sometimes he thinks I am my mother. Maybe she knew this Rini but I do not." She blows off the steam that has gathered inside her. "I will ask him more questions later." She gives me a business card. "I work at a lawyer clinic in the mornings. Near Piazza Repubblica. You come by to say hello."

I want to elongate my stay. See if any other tidbits of memory slip out. Show him other photographs. But I get up and put my hand out. "Grazie mille, Signor Velicchio. I am very happy to meet you. Would you mind if I took a picture of you and your granddaughter?"

He nods, tired. Maria Francesca stands next to him, she is a foot taller. She puts her arms around his hunched shoulders and he leans on her. I catch the moment on my cell phone. "Grazie. May I come back to see you again?"

"Si." He gives me back the photo of my mother and holds onto my hand. "We did something." He kisses my hand. "But remember. Paola knows I love her best."

Chapter 22

Rivenchy slips off her light leather jacket and admits, while in Venice over the break, she didn't do much actual writing. "But I let many ideas swirl around in my head. About Lavanna, working in the lingerie department. She loves the touch of things next to her body, touching fine materials with her fingers, wonderful leather shoes on her feet, to feel the strong hands of someone."

Vic agrees. "We know. She's got the sex thing going."

I smile. It's the day after meeting Signor Velicchio and a night of organizing my notes. Building a version of my mother, fifty years ago. Starting with a move from Kansas to New York, taking a chance on love.

Rivenchy continues, "But she is wondering if she now wants a someone—not an anyone. Lavanna's steps are not as slow as she walks by her favorite clubs—she does not go inside to stand next to strangers as she did before. She wonders if to remain the stranger is preferable—or if she desires something more?"

Beth Ann, in a mint green t-shirt dotted with sparkling beads around the neckline, leans forward. "I remember every word in your last reading. Lavanna and her silky undies. Made me go and buy some of the fancy ones in those stores by the Duomo."

"La Perla? Intimissimi?" Rivenchy asks.

"Oh yes." Beth Ann nods. "Unbelievably soft."

Rivenchy slips strands of hair behind her ears. "Good." She smiles. "Now let me tell you this funny thing happened when I went to Venice. I have been before, c'est vrai. I decided to stay away from the posh shops, to try to look at a different part of Venice through Lavanna's eyes. I walked to the Cannaregio district—down Calle della Malvasia. Tres bien, the cicchetti bars there, I ravage the small bites of food. I thought to ride in a gondola, so I looked for a spot. And there, at a dock, I see George."

"Really?" I ask.

Beth Ann giggles with glee. "Oh, how fun."

George is adjusting his Movado watchband; I can see he's enjoying the telling.

"George was there, deciding to engage the services of a gondolier. And he saw me and invited me to share a boat."

George snaps his watchband into place. "Fortuitous meeting. Just kind of fortuitous."

I wonder if it was. Just luck.

Rivenchy continues, "And then we saw Veec."

Beth Ann shouts in surprise. "What? That's like nearly impossible!"

Vic rubs his hands together, relishing the memory. "Yeah. We shared this gondola. Floated past those buildings that rise right out of the water. How'd they ever build 'em—that's what I wanna know. Did they have to swim down to the bottom of all that water to make sure everything was stuck in something solid or—who knows. We were going through these narrow canals—far away from that famous piazza place."

"San Marco." Rivenchy and George fill in the name.

"Right." Vic opens his bottle of water. "Saw a whole bunch of churches and then past that Doge's Palace and then to the place where they make gondolas."

"San Travoso." Rivenchy and George are in sync with Vic's itemization of their journey.

"Yeah. A boatyard right there—making gondolas." Vic takes a gulp of water. "Then I said I was springing for a topetta—one of those motor boats—not a fancy one for sure but got us somewhere. Not like snail travel with some fancy guy wearing a striped shirt using one oar."

Rivenchy winks at Beth Ann. "Some gondoliers are very sexy."

Beth Ann gives an exaggerated romance-starved sigh. They share a laugh.

Vic waves his notebook. "Yeah. That Murano island we went to—where they make glass. I took notes. I'm using that place in my story. I think Finn is gonna track down the fat nun there, it'll be where the hush-hush mysterious key to the Big Secret Organization's headquarters is hidden. In some glass ball or glass paperweight or something. I'll tell you about it later."

Beth Ann wants to know if everyone—except her—went to Venice for the weekend. She looks at me. "What about you, Lyn?"

The day and night in Rome floods back into my mind. I share my news. "I had a meeting at Cinecitta in Rome—at the film studio there. I met with a director who wants to adapt my latest book into a film."

Their excitement bubbles. They bandy congratulations and outrageous scenarios of interactions with Hollywood movie stars.

The real highlights of the trip I keep to myself.

Seeing Matteo at the train station.

The walk to the hotel, past the book stalls on Via della Terme di Dioclenziano.

Matteo's hand on my back as I walked away from Stan.

Casa Montani. The small hotel where I felt so snug and sheltered.

Matteo, in the reception area, waiting for me to join him for dinner, sipping his wine and reading a newspaper.

Beth Ann's question brings me back to the room. Her eyes are wide. "What did you do to celebrate?"

I tell them about the late-night dinner in the Trastevere section of Rome, "It's on the west bank of the Tiber River; in the Middle Ages artists and poets and the working poor lived there. Now there's lots of pricey shops and restaurants."

Beth Ann zeroes in on the area of most concern to her. "Oh, by yourself? Was that a lonely celebration? Just a little?"

I admit I was with a friend. And I tell her it was a perfect celebration.

Images of Matteo rolling up his cuffs to enjoy the Cacio e Pepe. Sharing the creamy tiramisu.

In the taxi back to the hotel, brushing shoulders.

Even the call from Bernadette to Matteo and his quick and unquestioning decision to fly to her in Paris. Making me believe that love is still possible.

"And when I got back here in Florence, I met an old man who may have danced with my mother in the 1960s. So, progress on my research too."

Beth Ann looks at me, her motherly face soft and kind. "You do look better. The brightness is back in your eyes."

Her kindness kindles the emotional fires that I thought I had squelched. I realize I'm still not at all steady. But I appreciate that disillusionment no longer clouds my eyes.

"Who's gonna read first?" Vic asks.

Rivenchy takes a delicate sip of her water, opens her notebook. "This is a petite part—about Lavanna and the gentleman salesman where she works." She reads:

Grayson follows Lavanna home. She does not want that. She wants him to exist only in the Rinescentre. In the store surrounded by new, nice, luxurious things. They have never had a conversation, no, not really. But now, as she leaves work and walks to her apartment he is steps behind her. She stops and faces him. Her first words to his eyes are: "Allez-vous en. Go away." And he does. Lavanna watches him go. She remembers seeing her father walk away. Down the street of Marseilles. The same stiff gait. She thought then it meant he was glad to forget her. But now, watching this new man and his rigid walking—she thinks she recognizes a hurt.

Rivenchy looks at us. "Maybe Lavanna is considering calling him back. That's what I am deciding."

I ask Rivenchy if she has a sense of what might happen if Lavanna did call him back. Rivenchy's shoulders rise and fall softly; her raised eyebrows reveal that she is thinking that the possibilities might be interesting.

Vic raises his hand, waves it. "I say take the power, baby."

"Veec." Rivenchy gives him a friendly glance. "Do not call me 'baby'. No woman likes to be called 'baby'."

"Nobody told me that before."

"Now you know." Rivenchy sniffs prettily.

I think of walking away from Stan. Walking away from our life in New York City, away from the apartment and the street I have called home. Walking away.

Charles reads:

Pynon, having given away all of his possessions, did wonder if he would regret leaving the trees and ponds and rocks and soft dig-able earth. The worms and seeds and insects and mice and berries he often ate. The bounty of the pond: frogs and water snakes and small fish. Pynon had only one special fox to say goodbye to; he padded to her den in the Maremma woods. He had dreams of burrowing with Bella, being the one she relied on. Bella greeted Pynon warmly and called him her favorite dreamer. He was conflicted then, by how she made him feel. But then he noticed a litter of small cubs sleeping behind her. A lean, protective fox, with a white patch on his chin, sat on his haunches nearby. Pynon felt his heart fall. He knew, in certainty, it was time to go.

He padded his way to the cave—the laboratory of Von Bron Fox. And there, Von Bron Fox and Pynon nodded to each other. Pynon entered the chamber.

There seems to be a thread in the first two readings. Change. Moving on.

Clearly, Charles has been thinking on this. "The star will be fantastical. A utopia-at-first-glance, then the underlying dangers will present themselves."

George wants to know if Pynon will become a warrior. "Does he shed his shyness to become a leader and preserve the utopia?"

Charles adjusts his glasses, rests his hands on his belly. "I suspect I'll be putting forth that there is no utopia. The way I see it—as long as there is free will and people have a burning desire to survive—there can be no utopia because everyone wants the world around them to suit them personally. On the timetable that suits them. Not everyone can get everything they want. When they want it."

George goes to the white board and writes his latest work in code, using the alphabet, mathematical symbols and numbers. Charles, using George's cheat sheet, decodes for all of us:

He can't lie anymore. Can't pretend. That
Thoughts and ideas evidenced in feelings
Are valid.

Charles looks up at George and asks, "Am I decoding all right?"

George nods. "Pretty much…" He continues to write and Charles unravels:

And though we can't calculate feelings on a scale of
One to ten
His feelings are off the chart and he cannot lie
Or hide another moment.

George holds up his hand to stop Charles. "I'll decode the rest." George, no longer hiding behind his code, reads from his notebook:

He approaches.
Her back is to him
For her focus is through the lens of the microscope.
He hands her a negotiation.
It is the question.
Do you think you could love me?
She turns to him. His eyes wide with the question.
Confusion or fear or relief it's been asked.

Beth Ann adds, "They are kind to each other. I like that."

George looks up at the ceiling. "He wants to feel her and for her to feel him."

I nod. "There are many people who are afraid of being honest about their feelings. Afraid a relationship could change too much if there's too much honesty."

"Oh, that's true." Beth Ann sighs.

During the break, I head down the stairs to the corner café for a late morning caffè americano. I wait at the counter, practicing my Italian with Benito, the barista. George enters and plucks a juice from the cooler and joins me. "I've lived in Florence for almost a year now. It was okay getting to know the city, the language. Now, I'm glad I joined a group. The thing is, I don't want it to end."

"Writers stay in touch. We have a common enemy and a common friend. Getting words on paper."

George nods, his eyes serious. "And it's up to us to decide how the story turns out."

I try to lighten the conversation, laugh. "You are so right. My mother used to say something like that."

"Well, just wanted to say, I'm glad I signed up for this."

I remind him the writers seminar is invited to a gallery opening at the end of the week. Before our last meeting. "Maybe we should go as a group."

George brightens. "I could organize that."

"It's all yours."

George hands Benito his two euros and heads out into the street. I see him join Beth Ann, Vic, Rivenchy and Charles in the sunlight in front of the Cathedral de Santa Croce, slip into his place in the group.

Chapter 23

Isit at the Biblioteca Nazionale and flip through my notes: The flood waters caused tanks containing naphthalene, a by-product of coal tar stored in heating oil tanks, to burst. My mother told me the naphthalene rose to the top of the waters and swirled in thin, shallow rivulets. I find a written reminder to myself that my mother told me she thought the oil smelled like mothballs; when she took our sweaters from the storage closet in the early autumn, she would always mention it.

I turn to another page of research. My mother's story of a Norwegian student who had been studying in Florence. He was scheduled to move out of his lower floor apartment in a historic but run-down building the morning of November 4 and take an early flight home to Oslo. He had planned to stay up all night, looking at a Florence lit with soft gas light and saying a long goodbye to the city. But the rain kept him inside in his cramped quarters. He drank a final bottle of Chianti alone and fell asleep and he woke up to the sound of river water gushing through his window. The water had already filled his room and the door was blocked, escape through the window impossible. The student had to scramble onto the top of a bookshelf and lay on it with only a foot above his face for close, fetid breathing room. Two days passed before the waters began to recede and the Florentine police, checking buildings, knocked on the window. The student reached his arms out to them as if they were his saviors. He was given a blanket, pieces of stale bread and eventually dry clothes. And according to my mother's telling, he didn't pursue the first available exit to Oslo, he joined the Mud Angels. No name. No way to find him. But a character to build in the story?

I feel the vibration of my phone. I wonder if it's a text from Verdine. Or Mildred trying to get in touch. I think for a moment of Matteo. I tell myself there is no reason he would be calling; I push that possibility out of my mind. Ridiculous. I pull the phone from my jacket pocket. I look at the source of the text.

Susie.

I delete it. Without reading it.

The sharp pain behind my eyes and the tightening of my neck returns. Every time I feel I can move on—for even a short period of time and get my mind back to my work—I am pulled back. I will myself to focus on my notes. I open my laptop and transfer my latest handwritten work into the computer. I will not allow Stan—or Susie—to take away my ability to attend on my work. They will get nothing else from me.

I turn to another page of the journal. This page feels thick. Haven't noticed that before. I realize it's two pages that have been taped together with double-sided scotch tape. I pry them apart, gently. Two 3x5 photos rest inside. One is a photo taken in the courtyard of the Uffizi. My mother stands, in knee high rubber boots and a shovel in one hand, in muck nearly up to her calf. She is flanked by other exhausted Mud Angels. Bone-tired but grinning. Their hair matted to their heads, their shirts and pants and jackets mud-covered. Their arms around each other's shoulders. My mother's handwriting on the back of the photo:

November 8, 1966. Gerta—Germany, Enrico—Spain, Jeanne—France (Paris), Monique—France (Lyons), me— USA, 'Naldo—Italy, Eva—Denmark.

I study their faces. The fatigue. The joy. The sense of camaraderie. Each face has a pureness of purpose etched in it. The tilt of my mother's head is so familiar, the wide smile. She leans on *'Naldo— Italy*; he is looking at her, the photo has caught him in mid-laugh. He has thick hair and it stands tall on his head, I imagine the water mixed with caked mud, is causing it to spike.

Another photo. A line of sleeping bags on a concrete floor. Pipes and machines in the background. A clothesline full of individual pages of ancient books hanging to dry. I look on the back, my mother's handwriting:

November 10, 1966. First dry night. Santa Maria Novella train station. Hanging pages of 12th c book. Eva—Denmark, Enrico—Spain, me—USA, 'Naldo—Italy.

Maybe it is the power of the unity of purpose. Could that a theme in my mother's story? Finding like-minded people who understand the importance of the task, the challenge of adventure. Proving art and its history is important. But there has to be more. The questions I wish I had asked. I think of all the time we had together, my mother and I—in the kitchen, in the car, waiting for the doctor, in the hospital room and all the questions I never asked.

An hour later.

I walk by Hotel Cascini and Lucia waves me in. She hands me an envelope. I know from the linen paper, the design on the envelope, the handwriting, that it is from Susie. Lucia met Susie last year when she visited me in Florence and now Lucia is excited as she lifts up a silver shopping bag. "Susie gave me this, look how top fashion it is." She lifts a yellow and orange beach poncho out of a bag. "Isn't it fantastico that Susie's business is doing molto bene?"

I hold the envelope in my hand. Lucia tells me that Susie hopes that I can meet her at Teatro dell 'Orio, a small tea and chocolate shop. That Susie will be there, waiting. She'll be in the back room.

My stomach feels as if it is tying into knots. I thank Lucia. My voice is low and tight and I go up to my apartment.

Another text. From Susie.

I turn the phone off.

I look at the envelope. I open it and take out the folded linen notecard. It is bright with vibrant green and blue stripes; I know it is from the Fabriano Boutique on Via del Corso. Always the best for Susie. She and I spent hours in the store, she appreciated the sophisticated graphics, the quality of paper, the delicacy of its weave.

I can't open the card. I don't want to read it. I don't want the bile to rise again and steal my presence of mind.

I put on my running clothes and shoes, quickly exit the apartment. I leave my phone behind. I need action. I move fast, down the street towards the San Niccolo tower. I toss the notecard into a trash bin. I charge onto the Viale dei Colli, then cut over to the centuries-old path that leads up the hill to Piazzale Michelangelo. I run; my adrenalin pounding. I pass tourists walking leisurely in the breezy late afternoon. I climb higher and higher and soon I overlook the Arno and the skyline of Florence. The Piazzale Michelangelo spreads out in front of me. I lean against the stone balustrade that frames the piazzale and catch my breath. See the massive bronze copy of Michelangelo's *David*, placed on its tall and wide pedestal. It dominates. Food trucks hug the perimeters. A few kiosks are set up to sell trinkets and t-shirts, dresses and hats.

I barely take it all in. It's the small events that abduct my thoughts; junior high school. October and the golden leaves in Queens' Kissena Park were falling. Susie and I were rollerblading. She took a bad tumble and the left side of her face was deeply scratched, cheek to chin, the skin torn. We hurried back to my house and my mother washed out the dirt and leaves. Susie skipped school for a week because she didn't want to be seen with the bruises. I told her she was too vain, that it was okay to show she wasn't Superwoman. She insisted that if she didn't like what was in the mirror, she knew no one else would either. She vowed never to rollerblade again.

I think of Susie visiting me at Sarah Lawrence. I was on scholarship there; she had opted to take classes at the Fashion Institute in New York City. She would take the hour and a half metro train to visit me, bringing bags of her latest designs. My roommates loved it, we'd slip on the dresses, shirts, skirts and hats and walk around campus, sure we looked amazing and irresistible. Guys playing pick-up soccer or sitting on the lawns smoking joints—those who didn't have dates for the evening—took notice. We'd have impromptu parties in my dorm room, danced with the guys, toasted each other with shots of vodka and, if the feelings were right, padded down the hallways with a chosen partner for private time in whatever empty room we could find.

I look at the Fiesole hills in the distance, my breath returning to normal. I wipe the sweat from my forehead and neck.

I remember the high school cafeteria. We sat at the same table every school day. Whoever got there first saved a place for the other. The memory of sitting in my family's kitchen at the end of double dates. We dissected the components of the best kiss. The best grope. The best X-rated fumbling techniques of seduction. Carrying thrift-store furniture down the Soho streets in Manhattan to Susie's loft—half living space, half studio. Shopping for prom. For bikini season. For my wedding dress.

The pink umbrella disappearing, just days ago, down a rain-filled street in Florence.

I close my eyes. Too much trust. I'm breathing hard again, rancor close to the surface. I wonder if there will ever be a time when I will not feel the duplicity so painfully.

The sun is low over the Ponte Vecchio. Darkness soon. I make my way down the wide low steps. I reach Piazza San Niccolo. It's full of locals and tourists, the atmosphere boisterous.

I stop for a "splash" of pinot grigio at Fuori Porta.

I order a salad. I don't eat it.

The sun slips out of the beautiful Florence sky. I stride back to my apartment in the nearing darkness, planning a hot shower and hoping it will clean off animus as well as sweat.

Susie steps out of the shadows near the door to my apartment building. She looks thinner. The sides of her mouth are drawn. We stare at each other for a long moment.

"Stan flew back yesterday. I couldn't go until I saw you." Her fingers dance on the strap of her purse. Her eyes try to hold mine but she blinks—too fast, too nervously.

"What do you want from me?" I am wary, but strangely calm, realizing my fury is providing me with a capacity for super control. I imagine baring my teeth and letting my eyes—red with the need for revenge—shoot deadly heat beams at her.

"I let it happen, Lyn. I crossed over the line and I knew it was wrong. Maybe I convinced myself if it was right for me it was right for everyone. I admit it, it was a moment that I didn't say no to but then it was like a snowball rolling down a big hill. I couldn't stop it and it just got bigger and bigger." Her words tumble out but I can tell she's been practicing her defense.

A Fiat honks, speeding down the narrow street, startling us. We step closer to the building because the sidewalk is so narrow. The car is followed by a motorcycle, the driver's long hair flies in the face of the woman riding behind him, she holds onto him tightly.

And then the street falls quiet again.

"We realize—Stan and I—that we didn't handle it right. Stan should have talked to you. Explained he wanted his freedom. And we should have waited. But we didn't. I'm sorry."

Did she expect an absolution?

"It was a drunken night; you were on your book tour. I dropped off the contracts—for my Beach Wear deal—Stan said he would look them over. I was just going to drop them off at your apartment. Stan had a couple other people there. We all had drinks. I was the last to leave…"

"Do you think I want to know the details?"

Susie grits her teeth, her voice strives for the logical, for some misguided rationalization to support her right to selfishness. "This is bigger than anything I have ever felt. And the consequences of not following my heart—I couldn't not follow my heart. That is death. Death."

"Even if it meant betraying our friendship."

"I couldn't think clearly. Maybe I thought you would see…"

"That you only pretended to really care about me?"

"I do care about you!" She shouts. Loudly. "I do care about you!" Pedestrians half a block away turn to look at us. "I do," she whimpers, her chin quivering.

"No. I can't accept that. Why deceive yourself, Susie? You'll just have to learn to live with your venal narcissism."

"You're being mean."

She is not going to turn this on me. I refuse to let her. My teeth grind against each other. I am now in protection mode, holding on to a deep need to cut off all feeling.

"Don't look at me like that, Lyn."

I expect my gaze looks completely empty because there is no connection to her.

Susie holds out her hands. "Lyn, I need your forgiveness. Sometimes I wake up in the middle of the night and I'm on the edge of a cliff. It's terrifying."

"I can't help you."

She wants to persuade me to see her side. "There were a lot of things Stan had to do—or that he made plans for—you didn't have time for them or just weren't that interested in some of them so I was like your stand-in. Stan and I did a lot of things together. I—just think—Stan and I are more the same. Have more in common."

"Do you want me to say 'have a good life'?"

Susie sticks her chin out. I've seen this look many times. I know it means she never intends to face the hard facts of her actions. What is right for her is right for the world. "Lyn. Isn't there anything I can do?"

"There's something I am trying very hard to do. Stop remembering you as my best friend."

I see that this hits her. Hard. I see it in her distraught face. How the cords in her neck flex. Her words come in glops, she chokes them out through wailing tears, upholding her justifications, "I didn't want to keep lying to you. I insisted we tell you. Just tell me what can I do."

"I want nothing more from you."

"Nothing?"

My response is unplanned but it's very honest. "I do feel sad about that."

Susie's skin is blotchy under her make-up. She glares at me, her eyes asking why I am not acting the way she envisioned, imagined; why won't I come to her rescue and absolve her?

Then I realize I'm crying too. That tears rush down my cheeks and I'm biting my lips. Hard. My throat aches. We stand across from each other—the canyon is impassable. We both gasp for breath through our sobs. Our hands spring to our faces in rushes to wipe the wetness from our chins and cheeks.

"Never?" Her voice is desperate.

Sadness. Shit. The emptiness grows.

"Bye," I say.

"Please."

"Bye."

I turn and walk away.

I just can't believe we end here.

Chapter 24

The next morning, I am submerged in dark dreams of walking on a cliff's edge. There is no path to walk and soft earth breaks under my feet. No end in sight, no real path, just pounding surf far below; worn sneakers on my feet cannot grip the dirt. Fast moving clouds are above and large. Heavy, testosterone-popping vehicles zoom on a road that is too close, the after-shocks of their passing join with bursts of burning air that scorch my skin. I am fully aware I am inside a dream and there is a strong interior skirmish to be released—but my brain pulls me deeper. I sink deeper into the Inferno; the never-ending hell. But then something stronger—my spirit—strains to secure release. The ground splits, my legs crumble and I hit the cliff's rocky edge, flat on my back and I body-toboggan over sharp rubble, accelerating to breakneck speed, I reach for the one small, anorexic crooked gray tree trunk that chokes out an existence in the rocks. My fingers enclose around its jagged bark, my shoulders are shocked by the sudden stop, feel nearly pulled from their sockets. I jerk awake. I'm sweating. I groan, realize the dream sums up the past week of my treacherous, nauseating, super-melodramatic journey. Vexed and frustrated with myself, and determining it is time to leave all weakness, self-pity and vulnerability behind, I head to the shower with hopes to rinse away the dream.

My hair is wet; I've wrapped my thick cotton robe close around me. I open the bedroom window to view the nearby rooftops. I see Frankie Firenze, the black cat with one white paw, staring back at me.

"Good morning, Frankie," I say.

His belly rests against the rounded red clay tiles. His eyes are hooded as if he is in the middle of a mid-morning snooze, but I sense the taut alertness of his muscles.

"I'm getting a late start today and maybe you are too. What kind of dreams does a cat have?"

He yawns, not interested in my question. His eyes tarry on a fat pigeon. Unaware of his presence, the bird struts across the roof, pecking at stray insects that make homes in the patches of moss that manage to thrive in the grooves of the tiles. Frankie's body compresses to maximize his power and then he bounds silently forward—and just when I am sure the pigeon will be his morning plaything—the bird, using its inbred survival faculties, shoots up, its heavy body lifted by ungraceful flaps of thin wings. Just in time it is out of Frankie's reach. Frankie lands soundlessly on cat paws and, undeterred, settles in again as predator in a half-snoozing disguise.

I move to the kitchen to make coffee. I know the early morning flight out of Florence is leaving in just a few moments. Susie will be on it. Putting distance between us. I feel the hardening of my heart, a key turning a lock on emotional access. A vow to just move on. Alone.

I see a large cream-colored envelope with *Benicio Becci Contemporary Gallery* scripted across its face that has been slipped under my door. I open it:

You are invited to the opening
of the exhibition of the works of Valentina Marcioni
19 h Venedri September 22
Piazza Carlo Goldoni, 4

A handwritten note on the bottom.

I look forward to sharing Valentina's night with you. If you
like to come early before the rush.
—Matteo

He must have dropped the invitation off at the hotel next door. Or had someone deliver it—if he is still in Paris with Bernadette. I feel a momentary disappointment that it wasn't a personal transfer. I realize how silly that is, that I would even expect a more individual touch. His friendship has already gone beyond courtesy. He has his own busy life, work and romance.

I settle on my balcony and sip my coffee, open my phone to look at the calendar. Valentina has canceled my Italian class so she can prepare for her show. The next few days include one-on-one conferences with the seminar writers, more research. My time in the city is growing short, the number of days decreasing at a rapid rate and I resent that I have fumbled on finding more threads that I could weave on the loom that is framing my mother's story. I want to be hard on myself, not give myself the excuse of the distraction of heartache. But it seeps in again; I count the few days before I head to the Florence airport. Much to face on the other side of the ocean—in New York City. The apartment, the dividing of a relationship. Different piles: the things Stan and I chose together. The things that came with each of us—from pre-wedding lives. My father's collection of books on vintage cars, my mother's framed antique etchings by Guido Reni, her framed print of a map of 17th century Florence, her own small paintings of snow on the trees in our backyard in Queens and of me on the tree swing—kicking hard to fly high into the sky.

Be methodical, I think. One day at a time. The actual division of stuff can be negotiated. On two salaries, the New York apartment is manageable. Neither of us could do it alone. My heart drops, I foresee a sale of the property I spent so much time trying to make a home. Another dissection of my life I had not expected to be up-ended.

A quick cold breeze and sound of approaching rain sends me to stand in the archway of my balcony door, out of reach of the sudden, cold, wet sprinkles. I watch pedestrians pop open umbrellas on the street below and bicyclists pedal faster, hoping to reach their destination before the dark, heavy clouds release their moisture in full downpour. I think of early November, 1966, the rains that never let up and deluged the city. I picture my mother, standing on the Uffizi's covered veranda looking up at the angry sky and perhaps wondering if it was time to search for a Noah's Ark that could promise the survival of humans along with the art of Florence. Is there a safety vessel out there? For emotional rescue?

I rinse my coffee cup and hurry to get dressed. I'm due to meet Charles for the first of the one-on-one conferences.

I see him waiting, reading at an outdoor table at the Caffe Rivoire in the Piazza della Signoria. I am aware of the closeness of the Uffizi Gallery; I remember Matteo's handwritten note on the bottom of the invitation. "If you like to come early before the rush." I wonder if he walks through the museum, passing by Botticelli's *Birth of Venus* or Titian's *Venus of Urbino* or Carvaggio's *Bacchus* every time he heads to his office. I envision him sitting at a desk, scrolling through clues that might help retrieve lost or stolen work—sifting through reports, through odd bits of information and getting closer to achieving the goals he shared with his father. Knowing him—and Valentina—gives me a sense of place here in Florence. Lightens my step.

I sit across from Charles; he looks up and closes his book. A ciocolata calda is front of him. He says, "One of the best hot chocolates in Florence."

I appreciate its thick, near-pudding creaminess. "Ahh yes, but I think, for me, a caffé americano."

Charles catches the waiter's eye and orders my coffee. He takes folded sheets of paper from the inside pocket of his jacket. "I have chosen the name of Pynon's star: Altro Mondo. I decided to stay with 'another world' but I will put it together so Vic will think it sounds more exotic: 'Altromondo'." He lays his five-page outline on the table and goes through it in detail. My coffee arrives and as I savor its bitter richness, I am swept into Pynon's journey that leads him to finally rise on his hind legs and beat his chest with his front paws and challenge those that would subjugate others and threaten their freedoms. Altromondo, in the final act of the story, is in danger of falling from the sky, burning through the atmosphere and exploding to nothingness—but Pynon digs deep to find bravery and commitment to save his new world.

I tease Charles. "You know Beth Ann will want to know if Pynon finds love."

He laughs. "And for Beth Ann, I will make sure he does. For love makes everything and everyone better. Mayhem and injustice are compelling, but love is enthralling. Even a stodgy Brit knows that."

I walk the mile along the Arno to meet Beth Ann and Jackson at Parco delle Cascine, it's in the neighborhood near the Opera House. She waves to me; she's got a nearly-neon green scarf wrapped around her neck for warmth and a green knit hat dotted with faux jewels on her head. We sit by the Narcisus fountain, the fount that tragic poet Percy Shelley used for inspiration when he wrote about a Greek who defied the gods in *Prometheus Unbound*.

"This is Jackson's favorite place—he likes to smell the fish in the Arno." Jackson sits on his haunches, his broad chest high, head thrown back to catch all the scents of the river. "All I smell is dirt, river water and the soap I used to give him a bath this morning. But not him. He gets the scent of the fish too. They are really superior to us, you know. Doggies."

I laugh. "In so many ways."

"Isn't this a great park? Lots of kids play here; parents bring them to the jungle gyms and I can hear them just squealing away with fun. Hearing the kids is best." She leans over to scoop a long stick into her hand. She tosses it. Jackson happily hobbles off on his three legs for the retrieval.

Beth Ann pats her heart. "See how he spoils me?" She tells me that she's found out that she likes writing stories about her travels with Jackson. "Maybe someone else will like them too. Like my sister. Maybe my kids one day."

A soft waft of air blows her blonde hair across her face. The few freckles she has across her nose have deepened in color, become more prominent, representations of all the time she's spent with Jackson in the Italian sun.

"Writing stories down makes me feel good. I think it's good for me just to see what comes out." Jackson lumbers back, he drops the stick at Beth Ann's feet. She scratches his ear and he settles in happily at her side.

I treat myself to a manicure and pedicure at Maniboo on Borgo Ognissanti to get ready for Valentina's opening; I choose bright scarlet polish to go with the red silk cardigan I plan to wear with the black dress I bought in Rome for the dinner in Trastevere, where Matteo raised his glass and murmured "Salute!" to commemorate my meeting at Cinecitta Studios. Where homeless sheltered after the war. I try not to think about selling the New York apartment. And then I wonder, what if Susie and Stan plan to take it over together? What if they plan to buy me out? They could have imagined that track already. Erase me more completely.

The sun is setting. I order a Negroni at Caffe Giacosa. The drink was named after Count Camille Negroni, a Florentine who liked his gin in the early 1900s. I decide to like my gin tonight. I call Mildred, ask her to join me to help stave off dark thoughts.

She arrives on her bicycle, her silver-gray hair brushed back off her face, her black turtleneck and dark jeans blend in with all the other fashionable Italian ladies in this ritzy neighborhood. We sit at an outside table and drink—and watch the shoppers in Cavalli and Cos.

"Look at all those men sitting, bored to their eyeballs while their wives or girlfriends or mistresses search for closet stuffers that will highlight their breasts, fit over their rumps, make their short legs look longer or make their long legs look less giraffe-y and never, never, under any circumstances, accentuate a bubbly belly." Mildred is on her second Negroni. "Relationships are torture."

"I agree." I am on my third Negroni.

"They test men's souls."

"Women's souls."

She chides me, "I meant 'men' in—as in all humans."

"I don't know if I can put 'men' in that species."

"You want them to be in the category of reptiles?"

"Better." I pick an ice cube out of my drink and put it into my mouth to melt. "Women are tortured more."

Mildred agrees, "We are more sensitive. We do feel. Unless a man has a very advanced feminine side, women do suffer more. That I can agree with."

"Thank you for agreeing." The ice cube is freezing my tongue and the pain feels good.

"I want you to feel better so I am agreeing." She orders two more Negronis. "We'll share."

"Good idea. You have one and I'll have one."

"That's the idea of sharing two." She eyes the olives in the bowl that has been put on our table. "That's a good color green."

"Mmmm." I take the orange slice from my drink. Chew on it.

"You should have told me you were in torment. You're a soldier. You soldier on."

"Why didn't you ever get married?" I ask her.

"I tried to tie the knot once. Well, a few times. But I could never see the future—down the road. Seeing wrinkles. Slower steps. Heartburn. Being okay with possible prostate problems. So I could never get to the 'I do' moment."

"Those aren't necess…necessa…that's a long word." The alcohol seems to have thickened my tongue. I can finally spit it out. "…necessarily things that happen." Our drinks arrive. We each, now, have two in front of us.

"But marriage is supposed to be for better or worse. No matter how crazy I was about one or two of them at the time. If I couldn't commit to the worse—if I couldn't do that, I couldn't waste anyone's long-term time. And lovers are fun. They come and go and when they go…it's like you start looking around the city like it's a candy store. Lots of juicy or sweet or tart…choices."

"You've had a lot of lovers?"

"Oh, yes." She stabs an olive with a long toothpick. "Variety is good. Different colors on the canvas. Only way to fly."

The next day. My brain is alcohol-sore.

I arrive at George's renovated, ultra-modern apartment near the Piazza Santa Trinita. His home is stark; white walls, the furniture gray and sleek. We move to the kitchen; I fashion my eyes into slits, trying to avoid the brightness of the white marble countertops and the shards of light that glint off the stainless-steel appliances. I sit in a leather-backed stool. He makes me an espresso. "This is a mini-Lucca A53 machine, the drip is decelerated to enhance the flavor extracted from the crushed beans—it uses a double-boiler strategy so the water is not boiled, it is heated with steam."

I lift the tiny white china cup and gulp the intense coffee, hoping it will clear the fuzz in my brain. I tell him it's ambrosial and biting. His face lights up, clearly this small success makes him happy. He slides open a teak-framed stainless-steel-fronted breadbox and lifts out a plate topped with cornettos and Italian cookies.

"In case you are hungry."

My stomach questions the wisdom of partaking. "George, you didn't have to…"

"Would you like jam?" He's like a child trying to please.

"I like jam." I mumble, now aware I will eat, just to make him happy.

He has three kinds: blueberry, blackberry and apricot, all arranged on a long Italian ceramic platter. The jams are in separate dishes with silver spoons standing like military in the thick fruit. He sets the platter on the counter and pulls a sheaf of typewritten pages from a drawer. He blurts out, "Maggie and Wallace have decided to spend a weekend in the New England countryside. I decoded it for you."

I nearly choke on my espresso. I look up to gauge his excitement. He looks ready to burst. His fingertips tap the marble counter awaiting my reaction. I need to keep my reactions focused on the writing. But I feel an inner glee he has decided to take his characters in this direction.

"That must have been fun to get down on paper. To imagine."

"It was not fun but when I finished, I did feel better." He ruffles his hair. "And, if all goes well, then they are going to talk about a small wedding and a long honeymoon." His face flushes and his lips crease into a soft smile.

I put the pages into my bag. "I definitely want to know the ins and outs of their decision."

He opens the refrigerator, again showing off his technology. "This is a Leibherr French model, the depth of the shelving units suits me, less wasted space. The temperatures automatically adjust in relation to the amount of foodstuffs filling the shelves." He takes out a bottle of champagne. "I got the evil eye at the wine store—but I bought French. Dom Ruinart Rose."

Hair of the dog. Maybe topping off my espresso with champagne will prove to be a hangover cure.

We toast to Maggie and Wallace and move out to his roof terrace. He looks out over the bridges of Florence and nods, pleased. "And I did organize everyone to meet here before your friend's gallery opening. I'll get Brunello and Prosecco so everyone will have a choice. And beer for Vic. Then we can walk to the gallery together."

"Eccellente, George." I toast him. "Molto bene."

Vic and I meet later in the day at the Santo Spirito tabaccheria where his character, Finn, walked past shelves of tobaccos and pipes to the back room and down a narrow staircase that led to the tunnel and secret room where his villain, Joseph Parn, considered torture. We walk out to the piazza and sit on the terrace of the popular restaurant, Borgo Antico. Vic orders a beer and I choose a Campari and soda. We have an unobstructed view of the plain, unadorned front of the Basilica di Santo Spirito. Vic points out the short, thin door on the eastern side of the church where the fat nun slipped into the first day Finn was following her. "You know Parn wants world domination. Lots of cartoon villains say they want that—but Parn is serious about real damage, all about control. It's all about power for him. His way or the highway." He hands me his notebook; typewritten pages are folded inside. "Here, my latest assignment. Giving you the notebook too in case you want to remind yourself of stuff."

More reading to do. I drop the notebook into my bag.

The waiter brings our drinks and a small bowl of potato chips. Vic grabs a handful and opens his mouth wide and drops them inside in bulk. He takes a long swallow of beer, sits back. "And I was thinking about what's really at stake for my hero, Finn. Besides feeling great if he can get revenge on a guy who took away his youth and stop a crazy maniacal tyrant from ruining the world. Maybe it's what we talked about in the seminar room—Finn needs to get a sense of who he might have been if he hadn't been indoctrinated to carry out Parn's plan. So how do you get to that, right? You can't just clean the slate. I mean, I was the typical jock in school—then I was a Marine, not cool for me to be artsy there. I didn't let anyone know who I really was until I took a chance and got some stories in some magazines. Finn has to get there. Let someone know who he really is."

His bluster has not decreased over the month, but I now recognize how it's tempered with a genuine desire to explore humanity. And to follow his bliss. I tell Vic, "It's another kind of adventure. More interior."

"I want it to be good. I mean, a fishmonger can write books, right? I can be bad ass, and still be like—be good?"

"Of course, Veec." Rivenchy has come up behind me. She settles into one of the cane chairs at our rickety table. Her elegance seems slightly out of place in this bohemian piazza. "I asked Veec if I could meet you here with him because I just want to give you this."

She hands me a La Rinescentre shopping bag; bright pink with its recognizable logo in white on its side panels.

"What is this?" I ask. I open the bag and take out a supple Tucci leather purse, copper in color, the perfect size for wallet and notebook. It has a long strap so it can be carried over the shoulder. "It is very beautiful. You didn't need to…."

"Inside it are the folded pages I spent yesterday and today writing. They are filled with all sex. And maybe it is better not to talk about it but that you read the story, at night, before you go into your dreams. I hope to inspire your dreams. That's another present to you." Her voice is light and teasing, her gaze is playful and open.

Vic shakes his head. "Give me a car chase any day."

She leans into him. "Excitement is excitement, Veec, we must all have our own personal ones."

Chapter 25

There is a crush of people in the gallery. I arrive with Mildred, she's wearing a long amber-colored dress with boots, orange bangles around her wrist and ear-to-shoulder orange-red hooped earrings. Her clear blue eyes immediately lock on Valentina's paintings. "Oh, these are marvelous. See you later." She grabs a brochure off a table and begins her exploration of the show.

A vibrant, excited buzz fills the large main gallery and its adjacent smaller rooms, each space accessible through brick archways and each filled with Valentina's colorful work. Red dots signaling sales are already next to several paintings. I see Matteo and Bernadette, they talk to a tall woman who must be Bernadette's mother because there is a similar hold of the head, the same long neck and sleek figure. Even the frown on the must-be-Bernadette's-mother's face matches her daughter's not-so-happy countenance. There's disagreement, a tension here. Bernadette looks up to Matteo as if she needs his support. He puts his arm around her back. I avert my eyes, wonder why I move out of that sightline so quickly. But I know it is partially envy. Their closeness. I search for Valentina, she is in the middle of well-wishers, wearing vintage Cavalli. I recognize it from her closet, the one that spilled over with designer dresses bought by the style-conscious Marcioni females throughout the decades. The dress is a shimmering Mediterranean turquoise, synched at the waist and softly draping to her knees. She wears outrageously neon-pink Pescer four-inch heels and red and pink checked bakelite earrings. Her unique pieces make her stand out—as the artist who is the point of the party. A pony-tailed man in a tight velvet jacket and black jeans and pointed, two-inch-heeled boots has managed to get her alone and I see him hand Valentina his card. I imagine he might own a gallery in another city—perhaps Milan or Rome—and is talking to her about showing her work there. She looks a bit flabbergasted and flattered.

"Lyn, let me introduce you to my wife." Charles is behind me. "I nabbed you a bubbly." I turn to see him holding an extra flute of Prosecco. A petite woman, dressed in a taupe suit and low-heeled comfortable shoes flanks his side. Their flutes are already half-empty.

"Freddy, this is my seminar leader. I've told you so much about her."

Freddy holds onto Charles' arm possessively and proudly. She tells me how much Charles enjoys the seminar and thinking about his fox. "He is crazy about foxes, you know. Did he tell you about Prince Philip wanting an autographed copy of Charles' book? I wanted him to use his real name, not that silly but lovable Richard Hindquarters, but my Charlie, he likes to stay hidden."

Charles accepts the tender of a canape from a passing waiter—a miniature arancini. He jokes. "I can't stay hidden too well, dear, because I can never deny myself a tasty morsel."

"That's all right, dear, you need your energy." Freddy fills me in, "I don't know if you recognize any faces here." She points them out. "The head of the city council talking to the manager of the Opera there, the Artistic Director of the Ballet has just joined them. The head of Tourism—over there in the white scarf, chewing on a carrot stick. And the mother of the painter of these marvelous pieces, Micheala Marcioni, just there in the jade green silk dress—the Chinese love that color. She is on many of the boards. The family of your Italian teacher is very connected."

I sip my Prosecco frizzante and study Signora Marcioni; I recognize her from the paintings in Valentina's apartment. Her dark hair is pulled back from her face into a severe bun and she wears large pearl earrings. Her angular face is strong despite her finely etched, delicate features. She is greeting the guests, acting the perfect mother-of-the-artist hostess. "The Marcioni family has been in Florence for generations, Valentina has told me. I guess I didn't think how deep their connections would be to the movers and shakers of the city."

A soft bell rings and a gallery assistant moves to one of Valentina's beach-scapes. She places a small round red sticker to the wall next to the painting. Freddy nods. "Look, another one sold. Good for her." She turns to me. "Who is that man who keeps looking over at you?"

"What man?"

"The tall handsome man with glasses—in the American sport jacket."

I spy Wyatt; he is across the room. He waves. "Yes. He is American. He's a new...acquaintance."

"Well, he has the eyes for you."

"Freddy, don't begin, dear." Charles tells me Freddy is obsessed with matchmaking. He tells her, "Lyn is married."

I take a gulp of my Italian bubbly; I don't want to get into the particulars of my marriage and its recent nose-dive.

Just then, Rivenchy moves through the gallery's open door and I notice many eyes move towards her. She is a work of art in herself, in a golden yellow dress, cream shawl and large turquoise stone necklace wrapped in layers around her neck. Vic, George and Beth Ann are only steps behind her. They are dressed for the occasion; the men in suits and Beth Ann in a full-ish floor-length pink skirt, green sequined tunic top. Charles raises his hand to gain their attention, they head our way. "They all met Freddy the other day, we all gathered at the Dante Museum, inspired by your appreciation of him."

Freddy leans into me and mutters, with good humor, under her breath. "It's a very singular collection of personalities, Lyn."

I smile, I couldn't agree with her more.

Vic lumbers over to us, his leather dress shoes less comfortable than his Nikes. "So this is pretty swanky."

Beth Ann nervously taps her sparkling hair accessory, it's in the shape of a butterfly. "And I think we fit in fine or am I just hoping that?"

I respond. "In my opinion, we blend in just fine."

Beth Ann eyes my black dress, red silk sweater and Manolo heels. "Maybe I should try black sometime."

Vic guffaws loudly. "That's a funeral color. You aren't near death now." A few people have turned around, including Signore Marcioni. All quickly peg 'a loud American'. Vic puffs his chest out, smooths the fine fabric lying against his gray polyester shirt. "Rivenchy picked out the tie."

Rivenchy eyes her choice. "Italian silk. Tres beau, non?" She gazes at Valentina's work. "The art of the ancients perhaps takes all the attention in Florence. Brava to the painters today."

George is at Rivenchy's side. He ventures, "May I get you a Prosecco?"

"Oui, George, merci."

"Same for me, George, I'll go all classy with the fizzy stuff," Vic adds.

"That's three Proseccos. In two hands. Not going to work for me, Vic."

Vic slaps him on the back, "Then let's both go and I'll get mine and Beth Ann's."

Vic and George move to the bar. Rivenchy notices a large canvas. "C'est irresistible. Shall we look, Beth Ann?"

Beth Ann follows Rivenchy. "Sure, explain it all to me. All I know is they sure are full of color."

Charles and Freddy amble towards the buffet table. I swallow more of the frizzante, it tastes crisp and its floral tones are fresh. I sip again and hold the liquid in my mouth for a moment to savor it. My eyes land on Matteo, he's now on the other side of the room. He notices me and raises his hand in greeting. Our connection is interrupted when an older, short gentleman taps him on the back, expecting attention. Matteo leans his head down, bending to hear whatever the man has to say.

I finish my first glass of Prosecco.

Wyatt joins me, he holds two flutes and presses me to take one. "Buonasera."

"Very good."

"I'm getting a few Italian words down. Your glass is empty. You have to be sipping steadily at these things or you look like a rube."

"Keep me from looking like a hick, please." I set my empty glass on a nearby table and begin on my second Prosecco. "These bubbles may go to my head."

"I'll watch out for you." He stands next to me, as if he is my guard. Protective.

"We met under strange circumstances, Wyatt, but you seem to be a nice guy."

"I am. We'll be friends in New York." He licks his lips, presses them tightly together, making a pronouncement.

"You're sure about that?"

"We have a history. Once you know something really significant about someone, there's a connection. And you either avoid each other or you let it be the first bond."

"You might know something about me but what do I know about you?"

"That I'm a nice guy."

"We'll see."

"Ahh, come on. Take a chance. Besides, it'll drive Stan crazy. I'll like that."

I am suddenly put off. "Don't use me for some little game you're playing at the law office."

"No, nothing like that. It'll just be an added bonus." He nods towards one of the smaller rooms off the main gallery. "I'll show you some of my favorites." We stroll through the arched opening to view a series of small works, variations on a serene courtyard where three women sit under the shade of a tree, all in different seasons. "I like these ladies."

I point to the summer scene. "Valentina's shown me this. It's her mother, aunt and grandmother. That's the garden in front of their home near Piazza Santa Trinita."

"Life looks idyllic."

"Not the constant American rush." I glance up at him, "When are you going home?"

"Tomorrow. Kind of hate to leave. Just getting a feel for the place." He looks over at Valentina. She is surrounded by a fresh group of first-nighters, talking animatedly with her hands. "She's got this in-your-face-honesty, doesn't she? Different than the women I know in New York."

Another soft bell rings.

Wyatt looks around, scanning the paintings on the wall. "Did you hear that? Another painting sold. Wonder which one. I better make up my mind. I'm determined to take one home with me."

"You're going to be an early Valentina Marcioni collector?"

"This trip's been a life-changer for me. Gave me some new perspectives. Gotta remember to not put twenty hours a day in at the office tied to my computer. More to life, right? I'll find you in a bit." He clicks my glass with his. "So really. You and me in New York. We'll be buds." He strides off.

I study the courtyard scenes. On the side wall, there's a rare collage; it's a small photo of Valentina and Matteo, pre-teenage years in shorts and t-shirts, they sit on the lip of their courtyard fountain, making faces for the camera. The photo is faded and bleached; Valentina has painted a wash over it, blending fun-filled reality with a brightly imagined Italian-jungle garden, a child's view of possibilities and mysteries to explore in her own front yard. Young Matteo looks all arms and legs, his hair flops over his face, nearly covering his eyes.

I hear Valentina's voice. "I feel like I'm going to throw up."

"It's looks like a very successful opening." We exchange kisses on both cheeks. "People are excited. And it's about your work."

"It's like putting all your babies up for adoption. You know they need good homes but you've gotten used to all their personalities and flaws. So, you want to keep them all."

"Not flaws, Valentina." I want to make the distinction. "Their particular elements."

"Some of these paintings were done years ago. I am a better painter now."

"They represent you at a specific time. That's got value too."

"I want to vomito. Do you say 'barfo'?"

"Barf. No 'o'."

"It's a good word."

"Try to enjoy yourself."

"How can I enjoy myself with everyone here, seeing into my soul? I feel naked and weak."

"You can fake confidence."

"With others. Yes. I will. Why not. But with you, my friend, I don't fake." Valentina's gaze drifts to the main gallery room. "Ahh, I see Wyatt. He is tall and looks so American, he is easy to spot. It is good you fell off my Vespa and introduced me to him." She leans into me. "Tonight I will try to spend special time with him because he is leaving tomorrow. I might cry for his leaving. I am not sure." She notices her mother making a beeline for us. "Ahh, here we go. My mama."

Signora Marcioni's visage is slightly reproachful, but she covers it with a social smile. "Valentina, hai salutato gli ospiti—have you talked to everyone?"

"Si, mama. I am getting to each person, I promise. Allow me to introduce. Lyn, this is my mama. Mama, this is my American friend."

She is an inch shorter than Valentina, but her slim presence is imposing. I catch the scent of her Bvlgari Omnia perfume, its hints of sandalwood, pepper and lotus blossom, its reputation for expense and refined taste.

"It is good for Valentina to have an American friend because I like her to be able to see the difference—to see the strength of the Italian tradition in relation to the young America that has little tradition. In comparison. You might agree—America has a long way to go."

I can see where Valentina got her straight forward, opinionated style. I don't know if she is criticizing me or just America in general. "We can learn a lot from Italy, I am sure."

"You are a woman traveling alone, si?"

Her quick change of conversation catches me by surprise. "I am here leading a writing seminar."

Valentina interjects, "She writes books that are sold in bookstores, Mama."

"You are married?"

"Mama, I told you about Lyn's terrible husband." Valentina with an apologetic shrug, looks to me and explains, "It just came out when I stopped in to see her new Gucci purse. We talk of many things, of nothings. Your story, it is something to share. So, I told her. And why not? It is what can happen in life. And speaking truth is good in life."

I wish I could sink in the floor and disappear.

"Oh, si. Yes, I have heard your story." Signora Marcioni's look is full of pity. And I sense criticism. "It is a world now where people— even wives and husbands—travel too much perhaps away from each other. Who knows. It is, sadly, how the world is now, hopping from place to place when home is perfect. So, it is a truth that people lose touch. Too many options, perhaps. But I am sorry for you. I tell Valentina that there are many men here, in our beautiful Florence that can make her a family and she can thrive here, with her art and teaching. Children. What does a mother of my age want but her children to be happy and to give her grandchildren?"

"Mama, tonight, no dreams of yours." Valentina looks around at the full gallery and takes a deep breath. "Tonight, it is about this."

"Si, bambina." She kisses Valentina on both cheeks, then holds her face in her hands for a long moment. "Tonight, we hear from Matteo and Bernadette. Do not forget. They want both families together."

"I know Mama. At dinner."

"Sono orgoglioso di mia figlia." She smiles at me. "I just told her am so proud of her."

I want to tell her that I understand some Italian but she turns to Valentina. "Matteo and Bernadette have big news. We'll hear at dinner. Be sure to not linger too much after the gallery show ends."

"Si, Mama."

Signora Marcioni bows her head elegantly in my direction. "Piacere di conoscerti—nice to meet you, American friend. Safe travels back to America."

Signore Marcioni and her expensive perfume are off to charm another guest.

"Wow. In America, we usually start with some 'small talk'. The weather. The news maybe. Warm things up before we get to know someone and slam their lifestyle."

"How can you get to know someone talking about the weather?"

"I'm just saying…"

Valentina's eyes search for Wyatt again. "My mother suspects I am having sex with Wyatt and she is worried. She wants her family to stay here, at her reach and hates the thought of Matteo or me being far from her. 'We must always stay Italian' she tells me. It is true, Wyatt and I enjoy very nice sex together. 'American style', he calls it." She grins, clearly recalling specific moments. "Very nice American style."

My curiosity is piqued. "What? You have to tell me the difference."

"Later."

Beth Ann hurries to us, motioning George and Vic to follow her. "Lyn, is this the artist?"

I introduce Valentina, "These are some of my seminar writers."

Vic puts his hand out to shake. "Great pictures. You can really make people look real. And the backgrounds all look like Florence too."

"That is the intention," Valentina says.

"Well, you got it done."

Beth Ann adds, "And you teach Italian. Lyn says she takes a class from you."

"Si, she is not an excellent student in Italian, but she is a very good American writer as you know. It is good she is working with all of you, at this time of heartache for her. I know you have kept her mind off the divorce she is going to be doing."

George, Vic and Beth Ann turn to me. Their faces register a blankness.

I am beginning to think Valentina is going to tell everyone about my crappy romantic history.

Beth Ann coos, "We didn't know."

Valentina continues, "Terrible betrayal. But she likes your stories, she has told me about some of them. And I am glad to meet you and if you want to take Italian, when you are here, let me know. I teach Italian because the solitary life of a painter can be too quiet. Who lives here in Florence?"

George raises his hand.

"You come study with me, perhaps."

"That might be a good idea," says George.

"It is a very good idea; I know these things."

George looks taken aback but drawn to her energy.

"You will enjoy Florence even more. So, be good to Lyn, she is very nice. And sad now, of course."

"Valentina." I want to strangle her. I try to keep the irritation out of my voice. "Stop. Please. I am fine."

Valentina looks at the writers as if she knows better. Then she excuses herself, "Very nice to make acquaintance but I must go, my Mama will think I am not acting proper. She insists I must talk to every person that is here." Valentina kisses my left cheek, then my right. She whispers into my ear. "I will make my way to Wyatt and give him my best look of passionate lust."

She marches off to be the center of attention. A trio of nuns stop her to toast to her work.

Beth Ann puts her hand on my arm, her eyes are teary. "I knew something was wrong. You didn't tell us you were unhappy."

"I'm over it." I finish my second Prosecco. I signal a passing waiter, exchange my empty glass for a full one.

"Oh, that never happens—getting over it," Beth Ann says with authority. "This can leave permanent damage."

"Not in my case." The semi-sparkling wine is making me a bit light-headed. I want to be left alone. Frustrated, I try not to show my rising pique.

Vic doesn't want to dwell in the conversation. "Well, love's a bitch I guess. But you seem okay to me so he must be the ass. Let's drink to him being the ass and not you."

I raise my glass. "Nicely suggested Vic. Here's to not talking about it. Moving on. Salute."

We toast and empty our glasses.

Beth Ann tells me they are headed to dinner and jazz at the club La Menagere. "Do you want to come with us?"

"You all gave me pages to read, remember. And I'm looking forward to doing that. For the rest of the night I will be in my apartment, on my couch, with your stories."

Vic nods. "Great. I'm really on a tear in mine. You'll get into it." Always confident.

Beth Ann squeezes my arm, still deep in her extraordinary facility for empathy. They head out of the gallery. I place my empty flute on a nearby table and feel a bubbly burp rise from my chest. I try to swallow it and concentrate on Valentina's series of portraits. One of her mother is formal, she sits in a chair, wearing a high-necked gown and lacy gloves on her hands. Signora Marcioni's eyes seem to look right at me, appraising me, reminding me of our differences—her position, history, Italian-ness.

"Buonasera, Liniana. You did not come early." Matteo is next to me, two flutes of the bubbly in hand.

I take the glass he puts forward and gulp another taste of the crisp effervescence. I feel the flush of it in my cheeks and a slight sway of my body in my four-inch heels. I will myself to steady. "Everyone else…must have…come early. I didn't think I was late." I wish I had eaten lunch.

"I was worried perhaps you could not find the place. Or that you became busy."

"I would not miss it." I wave my flute in Valentina's direction. "I am here for Valentina."

"For Valentina. Of course." He hesitates, looks at me closely. "Are you all right?"

"Happy to be here." I cover my mouth, hoping to mask another delicate burp. I am still in over-sensitive mode, sore from feeling pitied.

"I remember that dress. From Rome."

"How un-chic of me. Wearing the same dress twice." My sarcasm is very near the surface.

"No. Not when it is so very nice."

"You are too gallant."

"I'm trying to be."

A voice interrupts, calls to Matteo. It is soft, but somehow it carries past the moving guests and chatter. "Matteo, mio ragazzo preferito."

Matteo straightens and his smile takes on a sense of 'now it is time to pay attention to my duties'. "Please, Liniana, will you join me to meet my grandmother?"

He leads me to an elegant older woman who sits in an ornate wooden chair in the center of the gallery. She is next to an easel that holds Valentina's largest beach-scape. Guests gather near her, as if they are taking turns paying their respects. She holds her gnarled hands out towards Matteo. "Matteo, eccoti. Vieni da me. E questo un amica?"

Matteo bends to take her hand. "Ahh nonna. Yes, this is Lini-ana." He turns to me, very formal. "This is my grandmother, Signora Marcioni."

"I am the old Signora Marcioni. Very old." Her white hair is swept into a twist; she wears large diamond earrings and a bracelet of sapphires; her fingernails shine with soft white polish.

"Nonna, you are not too old, no troppo vecchio."

She brings his hands to her lips and kisses them. Puts her eyes on me.

I stammer. "Sono felice…" I forget how to finish the sentence and I have to resort to English. I damn the Prosecco. "I am happy to meet you."

"Ahhh. You are the one he talks of." She looks me up and down. "Many Americans carry the McDonald's and Burger King weight. You do not. Very fresh."

I am not sure her assessment is a compliment, but I mumble, "Grazie, Signora."

"I am told you are working very hard on your Italian language. Magnifico. It is good, an homage to your mother. Lei era un angelo di fango. Of the mud. Matteo tells me."

"Si. Yes. My mother came here and became a Mud Angel. She fell in love with Florence and always wanted me to spend time in the city. So, when I was asked to teach a writing seminar here—once a year—I agreed. Lo adoro. And si, I continue to work on my Ital-ian." I can feel beads of sweat burst from the skin of my forehead. I want to steady myself but there is nothing to hold onto. Matteo is standing a few feet away. Remote. The easy closeness of Rome has disappeared.

"One day the beautiful Italian language will just be there. I have no doubt, non ho dubbi." She smooths her hair. "You are writing her story?"

"I am working on it. I have done a lot of research…but I am still looking…for the particulars of her story."

"I lived through it. I am over 90 years old."

"I would never have guessed that old."

She nearly hoots with glee. "You are very kind. I helped at the hospital during the flood. My brother, Matteo's uncle, he worked at the place he loved, the Uffizi, but we lost him the year before the flood. Carlo took very ill and we lost him. I knew he would have worked tirelessly to help Firenze so I decided to work as if I were two people at the hospital where doctors tried to save him. I helped to move patients as the waters took over the bottom floors of the clinics. And moving medications. Blankets. I worked next to the Red Cross nurses. So many people needed help. The emergency electricity—it did not work. It was a bad time, but thrilling to be of use." She holds onto Matteo's hand again and says, "Mio ragazzo preferito." She glances at me, testing.

I rise to the challenge. "I understood. You called him your favorite boy."

"Ahh. Very good."

I look around, I want a waiter to pass by to take my flute of Prosecco. My hands are sweating; the glass feels slippery. I smooth my dress with one hand, hoping to dry my hand.

She tugs at Matteo. "You should take your friend Liniana to Signor Conti. He was finished with art school then, and he too did the hard work of an angel of the art and has lectured and written about it."

"He doesn't like to talk to people, nonna. He might bite my head off."

"Tell him it is a favor to me."

Matteo's voice sounds unsure but dutiful. "Buona idea, nonna." He glances at me, "If you would like, I would be happy to make the introduction to Signor Conti."

His grandmother taps Matteo on the arm. "You and Bernadette could ask. Arrange a meeting for Liniana with Signor Conti. It is something you and Bernadette can do together. Where is Bernadette?"

"She is showing Valentina's work to her friend from Paris."

"She spends too much time in Paris. Her mother is not happy with that." Signora Marcioni—the elder—turns to me. "Molto piacere di conoscerti, Liniana."

"Very nice to meet you too," I say.

She waves me towards her. I lean down, holding onto the arm of the chair for steadiness. She speaks low but clearly into my ear. "You like your Prosecco."

I swallow, hard. "Today, I forgot lunch."

"Italians know how to drink their wine. Many Americans do not."

"No disrespect, Signora Marcioni…"

"The elder."

"I just forgot to eat lunch."

"Have some bread. You will feel better." She pats my hand and pulls away, motioning for the other guests who wait to speak to her to come forward. "Now I must say hello to other guests."

Matteo and I move away and stand near a wall. I put my glass of Prosecco down on a table and lean back. A large burp gurgles. Moving my hand quickly to my mouth does not disguise it.

"Do you need anything?" He looks at me quizzically.

I hate that his look might be one of disappointment. I shrug, ask myself why I should care. "I liked your grandmother. She is very beautiful."

"Yes."

I see Bernadette. She is watching us. "Bernadette is trying to get your attention."

"Si?"

His eyes glance across the room. Bernadette stands with a good-looking man in a loose, gray, wool jacket. A scarf is draped around his neck. Red, metal-framed eyeglasses are hooked into his top jacket pocket. His coffee-colored hair is curly, like a mop on his head, the sides neatly barbered. A perfectly crisp blue shirt. Perfectly creased gabardine slacks. The energy that exudes from him is palpable and his attention is focused on Bernadette. Why not? Bernadette looks stunning, I am sure she has not drunk more than her limit of

Prosecco. Her short thick hair is straight and shiny, her lips perfectly colored a warm rusty-red. The angle at which she holds her head is generous, kind. She sends a smile towards Matteo. She excuses herself from the gray wool jacketed man and moves towards us.

Matteo puts his hand on my arm for a moment, leans into me. "We will talk later."

"Buonasera, Liniana." Bernadette's voice is soft, it is as if she is purring my name. I notice the wrinkle in the middle of her brow. "It is good to see you. May I ask if I can borrow Matteo for a moment?"

"He's all yours." Which, of course, he is.

They head off. I see the man in the gray wool suit quickly slip out the front door of the gallery.

I move to the buffet and slide three slices of unsalted bread on a plate, drizzle olive oil over them. The first bite is exquisite; I hope the second bite will start to soak up the alcohol. I look for a place to sit down, Mildred falls into step beside me. "That's Valentina's brother you were talking to. The handsome Italian I saw you with—eating gelato a week and some ago."

"Si."

"Whazzup?"

"Nothing. Why do you ask?"

"This whole place tonight—it's alive with a tornado of undercurrents. Don't you feel the tension?"

"I just feel like I need a big plate of pasta."

She points to a bald man in a finely tailored dark suit and yellow tie. "That man over there has asked me to dinner. Do you mind?"

"Go."

"He's very interesting."

"Go."

"Do you want to join us?"

"No."

"You don't mind?"

"Go."

She pats her hair, raises her arm; her bracelets jingle. "An opportunity around every corner." She kisses me on both cheeks and hurries to join her new acquaintance. They nearly sprint out of the gallery.

Another soft bell rings. I see Wyatt, standing proprietarily next to a small self-portrait of Valentina on her Vespa. He licks his lips as he watches the gallery assistant place a red sticker on the wall next to the painting. Valentina joins me, "I like to imagine it on his wall in New York City. You are responsible for this, Lyn, think of how we met when you fell off my Vespa, almost at his feet." Valentina moves to Wyatt. His arm goes around her shoulder and photographers take their picture. I can see Michaela Marcioni to the side, a watchful disapproval on her face.

The evening is winding down and people hurry off to make their dinner reservations. Charles and his wife wave, they're headed home.

Matteo is by my side. "I will try to arrange for you to meet Signor Conti tomorrow. With my grandmother's request, it will be okay."

"I don't want to add to your to-do list."

He looks frustrated. "I want to tell you what I think. We meet who we meet for a reason, si? I like to think there is an order to life, something that maybe we do not control, but things happen and it is up to us to take advantage of them."

I wonder why he is so intense. I pull back, try to joke. "Well then, yes, I'll take advantage of your connections."

"Good. I will text you. Thank you for coming to Valentina's first gallery show. Now I must attend a late-night supper with my family—and Bernadette's family." He looks distracted and I can see Bernadette at the gallery door, waiting for him. She is holding Matteo's grandmother's arm, steadying her. She seems anxious for Matteo to join her.

"I want the chance to talk to you," Matteo says. "But tonight, it is not a good time."

His agitation is so apparent. "Matteo. Is everything all right?"

"Yes. It has to be." He gives a tight smile. "I will contact you tomorrow."

He treads quickly to join Bernadette.

Chapter 26

The next morning is bright and clear.

I climb the steps to Parola for my Italian lesson. Valentina is in the classroom, her head in her hands. She doesn't look up.

"What's wrong?" I ask. "The opening was a huge success. Why do you look upset?"

"Because people make mistakes. And they don't even see them. They do not see that they are ruining everything. I see it. But no one wants to hear me tell them the truth."

"What mistake?"

"I wanted a marriage. But not like this."

"Oh." I thought of the phone call between Matteo and Bernadette in Rome. Matteo flying to see her. Matteo and Bernadette at the gallery opening. Her looking up at him, their closeness. Valentina's mother reminding Valentina of the gathering of the families. The engagement must now be official.

"Matteo refuses to stop her."

I am not following. "What do you mean—'Matteo refuses to stop her'."

"It is supposed to be Matteo and Bernadette."

"It's not?"

"Tutto e stupido."

"Who is getting married?"

"I told you, Bernadette."

"And Matteo."

"Why are you not listening to me? Matteo is not getting married."

"Who is Bernadette getting married to?"

"Some Frenchman." She spits it out. "French. How could she do that? French! She says she is going to live in Paris."

"She's marrying someone who lives in Paris?"

"Why do you repeat everything I say? Yes. Paris. I lose Bernadette. I lose someone who was supposed to be my sister-in-law. She now forces me to decide if I will like a Frenchman? How could she do this?"

"When did this happen?"

"Last night. After the opening. It was announced at the dinner for the families."

"Did Matteo know?"

"Si. He toasted them, said something about he is so happy his childhood friend has found great love. Stupido." Valentina shakes her head, looks up at the ceiling. "I know best. No one asks me."

"You and Bernadette are close, why didn't she tell you?"

"That's what I thought! Why does she not confide me in me? She told me her trips were all for business. But business and—this French person—turned out to be the same thing. It seems now. Her family is so sad. So sad. I am sad. Everyone is sad."

"But not Bernadette."

"No. She is so happy; she makes me sick."

"Matteo is sad?"

"Why wouldn't he be? But he refuses to fight. I want to punch him. And I was so mad, I was not kind to Wyatt and now he is gone.

We did have sex, but I was not totally happy so it was a good-bye that was not perfect."

"Sorry."

"I could make things perfect. All anyone has to do is ask me."

There is a knock on the door.

"Chi e la?" Valentina barks, her mood dark.

"Valentina, it is me, Matteo."

I straighten. Surprised, I feel my heart beat just a little faster. The feeling I had when I saw Matteo on the stairway unexpectedly, only weeks ago—before our first apertivo swells up again. I feel my cheeks redden.

He opens the door. Valentina growls, "It is the coward."

"Valentina, basta. The world is not yours to design." He turns to me, "Excuse me for the interruption. I knew, Liniana, you had a lesson today. I want to tell you I have contacted Signor Conti and he will meet you late morning. I will be happy to escort you to him. It is good that I stop for you here after your lesson?"

"Do you need to?"

"What do you mean?"

"You could tell me where I should meet with him. I can make my own way."

His eyes spark with anger; his jaw is tight. "I will be able to get you through security in a much more easy way. No inconvenience."

Perhaps he is dealing with Bernadette's news. Out of sorts. That's understandable.

"Then, si. Bene. Grazie."

Valentina insists I use a complete Italian sentence. "Do not make me look bad, Lyn. I am not happy today. Try to make me a little happy." She looks at me expectantly.

Matteo waits also. I search for the structure of the sentence, hope that I am making myself clear—that I do appreciate his time and that I do look forward to going with him to meet Signor Conti. "Si, Matteo. Grazie. Apprezzo il tuo tempo. Andra con te. Dopo la lezione. Per vedere il Signor Conti."

Valentina claps her hands together. "Meglio. Choppy, but okay. But you forget to call Matteo 'stupido'."

Matteo quickly moves to Valentina and puts his hands on her upper arms. She sneers again. He plants a kiss on her head. "Non preoccuparti, life will be fine. Now you are an artist of note, you just worry about yourself. Ti amo sorella."

Valentina grabs his hand and tells him she loves him too, but she wonders how he can break the hearts of all his family. That everyone knows Bernadette is perfect for him. That now Matteo should concentrate on taking down a Frenchman. Which should be easy.

Exasperation and weariness crosses his face. He glances at me. "Sorry, she is a bit crazy."

Valentina does not want him to apologize for her. "You are the one who is crazy, Matteo."

"I say basta, Valentina. Per favore." He turns to me, "I will be here, waiting for you. In an hour."

He quickly moves out the door. Closes it.

Valentina shakes her head. "I do not know what is wrong with him."

Chapter 27

An hour later, Matteo and I walk through a narrow, quiet street from the Parola Language School towards the Biblioteca Nazionale. No cafes here. No storefronts. The street is shaded, warm but not sun-filled. He seems serious and I wonder if he is thinking about Bernadette.

"Are you really all right?"

"Why not?"

"Bernadette's news."

"It is very good."

"For her."

"For everyone." He turns to me. "You do not know Bernadette well yet, but you must be happy for her."

I venture, "Do you think Valentina will come around and be all right with Bernadette's plans?"

"Si. My sister is dramatic and she thinks everything is about her. But last night, she sold many paintings and received two commissions. She will be too busy and happy with her painting to worry about me for too long."

"She worries?"

He smiles. "Italian women think that is their job."

He fills me in on the drama of last night—the meeting of the families and Bernadette's surprise announcement.

I am curious about his feelings. "Did everyone expect another announcement? One about you and Bernadette?"

"No one in our families ever took into account that Bernadette and I have known each other since children and, si—there is a kind of love there—but that we never talked seriously of marriage. My mother, she hoped. She loves Bernadette like another daughter. My grandmother was more realistic." He laughs. "She told me last night that no one waits so long to be married to someone if those two people are meant to be married."

"So, at least, you have someone who is not angry with you."

"My nonna is frustrated, maybe."

"Your grandmother?"

"She told me I was getting too old not to be serious about my future in love."

"Ouch."

"But I told her, there is nothing to be done. One must be patient."

I agree. "You can't hurry love—didn't the Supremes sing that way back when? And there was even a movie with that title too. In the late 1980s maybe—I saw it on television once. 'You can't hurry love'. It's a very important concept." I am chattering, being flip, I can't seem to stop talking. "Very important concept."

"Si. Questo e vero. True. Bernadette is an example. She met Philippe more than a year ago. She told me that she was feeling something for him. Unfortunately, she had to take into account that he is French."

I laugh. "You are terrible."

He puts his hand on my elbow. "He asked her to marry him. When you and I were in Rome. That is why I had to go to Paris that night and leave you. Bernadette wanted to talk, she knew it was be-

yond the time to tell her family. She knows, hopes, they will learn to love Philippe. It will work. Because he loves Bernadette." He points to the street below our feet. "Attento, the street is lowest here, and the stones are sometimes loose."

His touch is strong; I can feel the warmth of his fingers through my shirt. "I saw someone—at the gallery party last night, I thought he looked French."

Matteo laughs. "Ahh yes, it is easy to see a Frenchman in a room full of Italians. What is it about that?"

I feign seriousness. "It is the slight slouch, I think. Or maybe it is a look that says 'I am here but I could be somewhere else too, it does not matter because wherever I am, I make it the place to be.' Perhaps it's a very strong sense of their own important appeal."

Matteo's chuckle is low, surprised. He leans into me. "Are you saying they are superior to other men?"

I pretend to consider a very real possibility. "Perhaps I could publish an international ranking."

"And where would you put Italians?" He falls into the game.

"Top ten maybe. Very assured, very attentive." I tease, "They love their mothers. Their sisters. They want to be respectful and good and make everyone happy, even if actually being good isn't what they can accomplish—or want to accomplish—all the time."

"You have thought about Italian men like this?"

"No. I am just being silly."

"Liniana. I like to listen to you being silly—or not."

He stops. I pause beside him.

"And I want you to know that yes, my family hoped for Bernadette and me, maybe Bernadette over other women I have seen in the years since I have been seriously looking at women." His tone suddenly changes and he looks too serious.

I feel a sense of trepidation. I want to keep our conversation light. "Was that at age five or six or…?"

"Okay." I grin, teasing again. "I hope they weren't too devastated." I look ahead towards the Biblioteca as if to remind him that we do have a destination and that we are not there yet.

"Liniana. I want you to know this."

"Why?"

"Because I feel it is important."

I sense his eyes on my face. I am not returning his gaze and deliberately change the subject. "What time is Signor Conti expecting us?"

He checks his watch. "Ahh, yes. We do not want to be late."

We continue on, emerge into the sunlight on a wide street that opens up to a view of the Arno.

"Do you meet with your students today?"

"No. They have writing day."

"And you have only one week left of your seminar."

I am surprised that he is keeping track. "Yes."

"And then you will go to New York City."

The energy drops out of my step. "I should go back. Take care of things. Lots of things I should do."

He comprehends my angst. "I did not want to make you sad."

My feelings are bound in a thick fatty wrap of different emotions. Inside are layers of incredulity, resentment, disappointment and, most of all, a fury that rises and falls every day. A seething torment that I am unvalued, that I am so easy to set aside, easy to dispose of, that ultimately, that I am insignificant. I am furious that a treasured memory—standing in front of the church next to Stan, Susie at my side, my mother and father and brother in the front pew and friends filling the nave—is now a reminder to never trust. A reminder to avoid vulnerability. I try to explain, "It's more like a maddening apprehension. Wondering about all the things that I will have to do. How taking care of those things is going to bring up more feelings. And I am sick of feeling."

He stares. "You will because you will not die from this. I will leave the past behind. And we must decide—or at least hope—that the past will not scar us."

Aggravation rises. It's irrational but I suddenly I resent Matteo and his unasked-for platitudes, his presumption of a wisdom concerning my life. My voice is cold, "Please. No advice. You don't really know anything about me. You don't know the history of everything."

Matteo steps back as if I had pushed him. "No, I do not. I am sorry to speak in such a way to make you angry."

Rankled, I glare into the space over his shoulder. I know I am being unreasonable, but I can't help my frostiness. "I don't need Hallmark card bromides. I mean who really thinks that wordsmithing can make crap-filled relationship stuff go away. It's not words that change things."

"No, words cannot change things. It is time that changes things. We will not talk about it."

I regret my pique. But I don't apologize. I hold onto my gall like it's armor.

His voice is diffident, cool. "The reason I ask about your classes and your return to America—it is only because I want to spend time with you. As much as possible. I am hoping you will let me. But only if you would like."

Danger signals flare. My defenses gather to attack. Vexed, I move along, silent. I feel like a child who pouts, hates to be out of control and hates being pushed into a corner.

Matteo moves his hands as if to affirm that nothing that has been said is of any import. "I like the idea of sharing my Florence with you. Seeing it through those eyes. That is all, Liniana." He lightly teases as if to measure my resistance. "And, just as a bonus for me, it is a chance to look at your eyes that I like very much."

I want to hit him in the chest.

I realize that when I thought he was committed to Bernadette, I felt easy with him. He was spoken for and whatever attraction I

Gilli that sunny morning, the day after I arrived in Florence for this year's seminar. And the speedy rush of excitement when I saw him descending the steps of the Parola Language School as I arrived for my lesson with Valentina. How even my ears felt hot. And then, an hour later, his invitation to apertivo. Our first dinner—at Gino's restaurant. The piano concert. Gelato. The opera. Rome.

Memories I cannot now relish because they now stir intense feelings in my gut of advancing peril.

His smile seeks to break through my torment. "You look like a goose, seeing the hunter and not knowing where to fly."

"A goose? Is that some Italian saying?"

"A goose does not want to be shot. Taken. You look like you wonder if there is a place to fly for safety." He nods for me to start walking again, next to him. "Do not imagine I am asking more from you. We are friends."

We move forward. But I stay a step behind.

Scars. He had mentioned that scars can heal. I want to tell him I disagree. But I am worried I might cry. I want to tell him that I feel the raw wounds of a botched marriage and botched friendship etched deep into my being and that I am not convinced they will ever disappear.

"Liniana, we must not be late for Signor Conti." It's a gentle reminder, like he's removed himself from the uncomfortable conversation that has dominated our short trek.

Every bit of air, every particle of human chemistry between us feels cool. We take the steps up to the front door of the Biblioteca Nazionale.

"You are right." He sounds logical. "I do not know you well enough to give advice. I should not be so bold."

I want to make an attempt to make amends, I know I am being unfair. But my words are flat. "I don't want to be ungrateful."

He opens the heavy door for me, does not meet my eyes. "That is nothing to thank me for. It is what friends do. Right now, it is time for me to introduce you to Signor Conti."

Chapter 28

W e follow the tiny and severe librarian down the wide corridor. She wears an ankle length black skirt and a black headband and dark, heavy-framed glasses. Her incongruous canary yellow cardigan is our beacon as we head through a "Solo Personale della Biblioteca" door into the employee-only regions of the library. We pass open offices; I glance in and see workers intently typing on computers; many have small plants adorning their desks. Our footsteps sound on the stone floor as we continue to the end of the hallway.

Matteo speaks in a low voice. "Signor Conti is well known to be one who keeps to himself. He thinks only of work. He is tireless, conserving the art of Florence. He has never married. His life is here. In restoration."

The librarian stops before a large mahogany door. The sign

A voice booms from inside. "Entra!"

The librarian straightens her dark glasses and pushes the door open with her thin arms. Matteo and I enter a large office; the massive window on the far side reveals a view over the Arno and the San Niccolo tower. An older man, wearing a white lab coat, sits at a massive carved desk, his back to us. His thick shock of gray-white hair sticks up in many directions. The Persian carpet next to his desk is covered with a jumble of large, broken parts of ancient statuary. At least three marble arms. A foot with an ankle. An oversized hand that is broken in half, only two fingers remain. A part of a lower face; chin, mouth and jawline. The crown of a head. A small torso devoid of limbs and neck. I look around, shelves are filled with books and stacks of paper and more marble body parts that I expect were carved many centuries ago. Three computers stand side by side near the back of his desktop. All are now open to various sites.

He swivels around to us, but his eyes are still reading the work he holds in his hand. "Buongiorno, Matteo. Come sta la tua famiglia?"

I realize this is the man I have often noticed at the corner desk while I was in the reading room going through my research, working on the novel about my mother.

Matteo answers, "Bene. Grazie, Signor Conti."

Signor Conti has a long aquiline Roman nose—it has a conspicuous bridge and a slightly hooked shape at its end. The rest of his face is angular. He has narrow shoulders. His shirt, a bit wrinkled, is not quite tucked in. No tie. Yes, this is the man with the absent-minded professor-look about him.

Matteo continues, "I come to introduce my friend, Liniana. She is an American writer. Very accomplished. She is doing research on the Mud Angels."

Signor Conti nods in my direction, but his eyes do not leave the paper in his hand. I already sense that I am taking up too much of his precious time. "Si. Many people talk to me about gli angeli del

I look at Matteo. I am reminded he had to put family connections to use. Matteo does not meet my gaze. I have been a pain and peevish, so I understand his stand-offishness.

Signor Conti turns back to his desk, jots a note on a legal pad and carefully adds the paper he holds to the top of a tall stack of papers. "But prego—first, Matteo, I have one question for you. What about the agreement from our friend?" His question is deliberately oblique, an exchange that only he and Matteo understand. I suspect he is speaking in English to be polite to me.

Matteo's voice is guarded. "I believe I am making progress. I am expecting a call soon. Today perhaps. Soon, it is possible, I will have an answer for you."

"Bene." Signor Conti stands; he is over six feet tall. His thin shoulders are rounded, perhaps because of years bent over his desk. I am surprised at how energetically he moves. He goes to a file cabinet, pulls open a drawer, takes out a folder, filled with papers. He points his conversation towards me without actually looking at me. "I will give you some things. The facts are here and also some of my personal experiences from my memory that I have written down. From lectures I have done." He lifts out a group of documents. Some are copies of newspaper and magazines articles. "I have some things here translated into English. You do not read Italian?"

"Anything commuted into English would be appreciated. But I can read a little Italian…"

Matteo adds quickly, "And I will be available to help her translate."

I want to assert my professionalism and my voice sounds a bit more aggressive than I intend. "I am sure I can find a way to have all I need translated."

Matteo parries. "It is true, she will be fine without my help, also. Liniana is very resourceful and has experience."

I look to Matteo, is he offended? He looks at his watch. I know I have driven a wedge between us. But I am stubbornly resistant to do anything about it.

Signor Conti's back hunches as he hunts in the back of another file cabinet. He finally pulls out a crumpled article. "So, you want everything."

"I'll take whatever you have, grazie mille."

Signor Conti piles the papers on a long table. "History of previous floods. Water tables. Temperature charts. Reactions of international organizations like the Red Cross. Much information."

I don't tell him I have gathered information on many of these facts from other sources. That I am suddenly weary, thinking that this meeting may not bring new information about my mother's experience. "Fantasico, I look forward to reading. Everything."

Signor Conti overrides me, his voice professorial. "You must be thorough or what is the point?"

Matteo gives me a quick glance as if to confirm the assessment he shared with me of Signor Conti's single-mindedness. Then he shrugs apologetically. "I am sorry. I must go back to my office. I would like to stay but…"

Signor Conti interrupts. "We are waiting for answers, Matteo. The Uffizi is where you will be most useful, no?"

Matteo nods, he seems used to Signor Conti's brusque manner. "And Signor Conti, my grandmother would like to invite you for dinner to thank you for your time with our friend. A casual dinner, as she knows you like it."

"It must be her eggplant alla parmigiana."

"Si. What else would it be for you?"

"Bene. It must be a Tuesday. Tell her the first Tuesday of the next month. If it is possible for her."

Clearly, Signor Conti's life is very regimented.

Matteo touches my elbow. "Ciao. Good luck." There is no special warmth in his voice. We may as well be strangers. He moves out the door. "Grazie, Signore."

Signor Conti and I are alone. I am surprised that a shiver of nervousness runs through me. Determined to mine this interview, I quickly take my notebook from my bag, and my phone. "Do you mind if I record our conversation?"

He checks through the books on the shelf and acquiesces. "There might be something I say that will be good for your story. Who knows."

I activate the recording option on my phone.

Signor Conti flips through a large volume. "This book is about how no one knows the truth. Ever. Concerning the flood. It is about the investigation. Written by a journalist to explore if there were any fingers to be pointed for blame. But it is in Italian and about the levels of the dam, who opened the barriers when, who was notified and when. You can get much of this information from some of these pieces of paper I have already set aside for you. They will be in English." He puts the book back on the shelf.

"Grazie."

He adds another thick collection of papers to the pile. "Here are the big points. The dam broke, flood waters rushed into my Firenze. Streets are filled with water, debris—cars, trees, dogs, cats, birds, mud, sewage. People are stranded inside their homes or outside their homes. Firenze had to be saved. It was a very big disaster but the hearts of the Florentines did not stop beating for a moment. The mud. Thick. Everywhere. So much mud." He starts another stack of papers. "Everyone wanted rubber boots. I was lucky, I liked to fish and so already I had tall rubber boots."

I try to imagine a younger version of him, in high boots, pacing through Florence, his shoulder blades bent forward, his intense eyes taking in the catastrophe.

He goes to a shelf and chooses a thin academic journal. "This one is in English. Tells about how things were contaminated, how things rotted. Health was a worry. Worry about the cold. The flu. The typhoid. The mold and what it could hold. Great danger of bad health for many."

"Matteo's grandmother told me you were one of the first Mud Angels."

"I may have been among the first to be on site to volunteer. At first opportunity, I made my way to the Duomo, to see the extent. I cried when I saw the dark water licking at Ghiberti's Baptistry doors.

I stood and wept. I was not alone. So much destroyed—beyond help. Tears could not be held back. Historical records destroyed. Books—maybe 4 million books we realize later—damaged. Many from this library. In the lower floor. Here." He taps his leather shoe on the stone floor we stand on. "Pages from important books—the only existing copies because these were books before mass printing. Before Guttenberg press. Important books, handwritten and hand-painted; pages were found stuck to ceilings, to walls, to floors. Somethings were forever lost—things that were documented as part of the collections of the museums and libraries, that should have been found and were never found. Are they buried? Were they swept away? Were they taken? What Matteo continues to work on."

"You think many people took advantage—and stole things?"

He shuts his eyes and leans against the file cabinet for a moment. "Poverty. Greed. Desire. Who is the person who sees a chance to possess a work of genius for all his own—or for profit—and does not resist? We can understand the desire. But then we must examine ourselves. Stealing beauty that belongs to all people? I cannot abide the thought." He walks to another shelf, ruffles through a stack of papers, looking for something particular. "Matteo's father organized a group for investigation of this and Matteo took on his father's mission." He sighs, troubled. "There will always be questions. But I hope for answers in two ways. That I am wrong and no one has done such terrible crimes and indeed the art is beneath the surface somewhere, buried in a riverbed for someone in the future to find. My other hope is that if a piece of magnificence was stolen that it will be retrieved in my lifetime so that I can be the one to put it back on display for everyone to experience."

Signor Conti walks back to his desk. "But—to gli angeli del fango—and our name. Our purpose was to find, to dig, to retrieve and hand things off to those with knowledge of restoration. We worked all hours and our numbers kept multiplying—locals, foreigners, strangers, no one knew how many of them found their way to Firenze but they came. That is why we became known under the name 'Angels'—because so many just seemed to appear—sent by God.

And because we dug in the Mud, of course." He waves at a shelf of books. "There have been others that have written on this. I do not know how you will tell the story in a different way."

He's hit on my problem. I know I want to build the story of my mother and her personal experience of the flood. About her love for art. About the important time she ventured, alone, into adventure. But I have notebooks full of false starts, paragraphs inspired by her stories of working by candlelight, soaking hardened bread in wine so that it would be edible, holding her hands over a brazier to warm them, the stench of polluted water, feeling cold rain, the excitement of doing something that would have lasting consequences. But the facts and memories have not coalesced, I feel the need for a more personal, emotional core.

He puts all the papers into one pile and hands it to me. "This will give you much detail. You go through them and come back if you have specific questions. Matteo can arrange."

A clear dismissal. I am startled. I feel a deep, stabbing disappointment that this meeting will be so short. "May I show you some photographs?"

"I have seen many. Maybe later, have Matteo call me after you read everything."

Signor Conti sits back down and swivels in his chair, his back to me again. He boots up one of the computers. I don't want to be too pushy, for him to regret doing the Marcioni family a favor.

I put his handouts in my bag. I turn off my phone's recording app. "Grazie," I say. "For your time."

His question is only polite. "Why is it that you—an American— want to write about the Mud Angels?"

"The story will be about my mother. She was one of the Angels."

"So many. German. Brits, Australians."

I slide my bag onto my shoulder. "She came from America." And then I notice the name plate nearly buried on his desk.

Rinaldo Conti.

The hair on the back of my neck prickles.

And almost at the same moment, I look up and see an aged black and white photo tacked to the wall next to his desk. It is the same image as the photo my mother had in the taped-together pages of her journal. The one she had written on the back:

November 8, 1966. Gerta—Germany, Enrico—Spain, Jeanne—France (Paris), Monique—France (Lyons), me— USA, 'Naldo—Italy, Eva—Denmark.

There, tacked to the corkboard next to his desk, is my mother's smiling face looking back at me. "That's my mother!"

He looks up to see where I am pointing. "Jenny?" He turns to me and finally looks straight at me. His deep brown eyes are suddenly laser-focused.

"Jenny Bennett. Si. My mother."

And now he is no longer curt. "You are Jenny's daughter." It is not a question. "You are a writer." He says it as if he knows the answer.

His concentrated attention is unnerving. "Yes. I write novels."

My eyes move back to the photo. There is his younger self, standing next to my mother. I recognize the angular face, the wild hair—dark brown and even longer then. It is still sinking in. "You knew my mother."

He rubs his large hands over his forehead. "Si. Jenny. I knew Jenny."

The way he says my mother's name strikes me. He elongates it so it sounds soft. As if it exists as a sound issued under candlelight. As if it is connected to a deep, meaningful and intimate memory.

Another sense of peril rears inside me.

First it was the danger presented by Matteo. His desire to know me. And now this. A man who says my mother's name with whispered longing.

"You have her eyes."

I have been told that so many times. The same blue-gray eyes.

"Jenny's eyes. Si. So much like her."

I am uneasy, nerve endings prick to attention.

"And now you are here, to find out everything you can, and you will write a story about Jenny." He gazes at me as if he is a thirsty man, drinking in remembrances.

I barge ahead, wanting to negate my growing intuition that underneath this coincidence, something is amiss. "She told me stories. I took notes, I recorded some of them. And near the end, she told me about an old suitcase, in our attic. She wanted to see what was inside one more time. Maybe to share more stories with me. I don't know. I found a journal inside the suitcase. Photos I had never seen before. One of them is the same one you have on your wall. You knew her, Signor Conti. Si?"

He turns to look at my mother's visage. For a moment, he looks lost in it. Then he stands, unfolds his height. He strides across the room to two high-backed leather chairs in front of a massive bookcase that is filled with broken statuary. He stands behind one of the chairs.

"Please. I would like you to call me Rinaldo."

I tell him I met Signor Velicchio. Who talked about his friend, Rini, who had dinner over a fire on Via Poggi in 1966 and danced with my mother.

"Si. That is me." He motions for me to sit in one of the chairs. "Prego."

I put my bag down, feel the strangeness of his undivided attention. I sit. He positions the other chair to face me. He sinks into it. A low table is between us.

He says, "What stopped you from writing this story before?"

I feel his judgment. This is clearly a man who does not put off work; he gets things done.

"Well, I didn't feel ready to write the story for a long time. Maybe I wanted to think I knew my craft just a bit better before I started. And then—well, I got married..." I stop, I do not want to put the focus here. I rush forward. "I had a place to make a home. My father died." I make an effort to keep my voice from wavering. "And then I was focused on another project. A novel that I finished. It will come out soon." I can't understand my nerves. "Maybe there will be a movie adaptation. It is a possibility."

"Ahhh." He nods, absolutely unimpressed. He wants to know about the Mud Angel book. He waits for me to continue.

I take a deep breath and tell myself to find some truth. "And, well, I am not sure why but it became very important for me to get to know Florence better, to understand my mother's connection to this city. So, when I was offered a month-long teaching job here three years ago—a writing seminar—I took it. Then I kept coming back. And I guess I realized, too, that I needed to have time to live— live with the things she left behind. The things she left behind." My eyes swiftly and unexpectedly well with tears. My throat tightens. Finally acknowledging aloud that it was difficult to open the box-es she'd left for me. Smelling the soap that she used. Seeing her handwriting on bits of paper. Letters. Some of Rick and my artwork from elementary school. Things she had kept. Baby teeth. Finding one earring tucked into a box, deducing she had lost the matching one but still could not part with whatever memory this single piece contained. Airline ticket to Florence. Never used. Finding out more about a mother that I thought I knew so well—through boxes—and a journal—full of mysteries that I could not solve.

I dip my head, surprised at the grief nestling in my gut. I wipe away a tear that falls to my cheek. I try to move back into interview-er mode. Force strength into my voice. "You were a student too? At the time of the flood?"

"No. I had finished at University in Pisa the year before. I was trying to be an artist. I had a small studio, behind the Santa Croce. On Via Pietro Thouar. Not far from here. I thought perhaps my tal-ent was painting. But then the flood—the angry waters took all my work, smashed it and collapsed it. There was nothing left. But I was taught then by the river, it revealed to me a better-for-me pur-pose—that I must dedicate my life to conserving the work of the art-ists of Firenze that came before me. Keep their work accessible for more generations—many generations. For centuries. For forever, if there is such a thing. This is work that is never-ending." His large eyes have folds of skin gathered beneath them. I wonder if he gets enough sleep.

"My mother loved art. Its history. Preservation. Conservation. Restoration." I hear how lame I sound.

"Si. Yes. We conferred about that."

"You conferred?"

"Si."

The aggravation rears again. I don't like the ownership he has about my mother's interests. He seems to know her in a way I do not.

"I would let her know of our advancements. New techniques of restoration. The most recent finds."

Now I wonder if my peevishness stems from guilt. That this was such a big interest of my mother's and I, for the most part, made our relationship solely about me. My teen problems. My dreams. My guilt of not getting to her journal in time. My pervasive irritation—wherever it is directed—at Matteo, at this man in front of me, at myself, at Stan, at Susie. It is accelerating. I twist my hands together tightly, a general rage at everything that seems unfair.

He rolls up the sleeve of his lab coat. "Your mother may have saved my life. Many bad things thrive in the dirty water." He shows me his arm. "I have a mark, still. One day I reached down into the flood waters because I saw something—how do you say—twinkling?"

"Glinting?" The first word I think of, my voice sounds hard.

"Shiny. Si. I was showing off perhaps to your mother. I said I hoped it was a silver crucifix by Cellini or Botticelli or Fra Angelico. But it was a can of soup, opened with sharp edges. I bled—blood—for many hours. Your mother found disinfectant from the Red Cross and changed my bandages."

Envy joins the vexation, multiplying my antagonism. I did not want to imagine my mother bending over this man's arm, tending to his wound. I thought of the scraped knee I got from tumbling off my first bicycle. How she babied me and cleaned my injured skin and made me a peanut butter and jelly sandwich. She was mine. She cared about me, our family. I never pictured her caring for others like that.

"I have to say, Signor Conti…"

"Rinaldo. Prego."

"That's all right, I…"

"Please. I feel better if you call me Rinaldo."

I try to smile but my lips feel rigid. "I have to say that it is strange to me that you know so much about my mother. And that you seem to feel close to her. And I didn't know about you."

"It was a time of great energy, great exhaustion. We worked in mud, we went to sleep for short hours with mud caked on us, no hot water, always hungry. How could anyone else understand it if they were not here?" His head tips to one side and he rolls his fingers through his thick hair. "We had a purpose. Your mother. Myself. All of us. To put the city back together and to save the masterpieces. We were at war. On a battlefield, you get to know people. Very quickly."

I had never thought of my mother's experience as a war against the elements. Against time. I had imagined the intensity of the task, but not the intensity of the relationships.

"I sent her things often. To her Queens College, to keep her up to date on the work we were doing here." He motions to his office. "Restauro."

Why do I not remember her sharing news of Florence at home? Did my father not show enough interest? Had I not listened? Did I not engage enough in her deepest interests?

He rests his head on his fingertips. I am aware of the hollows of his face below the cheekbone. I can feel he wants to share her, but I am possessive. So I am cruel. I tell him, "She always wanted to bring us here. Her family—to share Florence with us. Her family…" I trail off, provoked at myself for being so pointed. "It never happened because—well there was always something more important in our family."

"Of course." His agreement is soft, reasonable. "She had a life in America that she could not leave."

"She loved teaching. And we—as a family—we were busy. She was always there for us." I wonder why I feel the need to own her.

"Si. I know that."

I don't want him to 'know'. I want all knowledge of her to be mine.

Rinaldo's hands move to rest on the arms of his chair, the veins of his hands are pronounced. "I remember the moment I met Jenny. I was sinking into a despair, seeing this very building—where I work now, the Biblioteca Nazionale—with water above its low windows and doors. Jenny arrived when the waters started to subside." He takes his time. "It was November 8, the day the backhoes arrived from Perugia. From that moment she arrived, she picked up my courage. One of the heads of the Laboratario del Restauro—Umberto Baldini—sent us, a group of angels, downstairs. The stink of the garbage in the water. The wet smell. Mud clung to everything. Shelves had collapsed. Pages of precious books were soaked and torn. Some that had been painted with gold leaf were—I saw with sinking heart—ruined. The gold leaf had flaked off—specs floated in the water's top. My desolation ate at me. Your mother was behind me and she said to me, very clearly, she said all was not in ruin. It is all here, she said, and just needs our help to be put back together. She said we can save these things. How lucky for us, Rinaldo. I remember her voice, 'Isn't that lucky for us, 'Naldo? That we can help'."

His story reminds me of mother's ability to see life as a project. That renewal was possible. I imagine what she would say to me, now, at this point, as a chapter of my marriage and friendship ends. "Lyn. Blank pages are there to write on. The future has yet to be written. You must stay strong enough to write it."

Rinaldo is deep into his memory. "Your mother and I joined the line to pass the sick, wet books up to the higher floors of the Biblioteca to safety. Some of us stood in the water in our rubber boots, and others in the line that went up the staircase and to the upper floors. To another line that passed the books to the restoration team. They made the decisions about the best way to heal the treasures."

"Yes. She told me stories about scraping mud off the books." I sound like a petulant child, wanting to one-up another's experiences.

"Si. We sat side by side, Jenny and me, with surgical blades. We were very careful. Hours trying to pry pages from one another. We listened to American music on the transistor radio—the Beatles and the Supremes—we sang 'You Can't Hurry Love' and 'Red Rubber Ball' and 'Yellow Submarine.' Even the Monkees' music. You know your mother had a very nice singing voice."

Resentment again. I know my mother's singing voice was perfectly pitched and warm. I don't want him to know that. I bite my lip. I don't want to lash out.

Rinaldo continues, "Restoration experts decided it was best to take apart the books and clean the pages one by one. We had to release the glue of the bindings, take each book apart and hang pages, one by one, on clotheslines in the driest buildings we could find."

"There is a photo I have. Her sleeping in the train station, the drying pages above her head."

"Ahh. Si. Many of the books were large, over 1000 pages. We use the train station lower floor. The water did not reach there. And there was an old furnace. Some heat. But even so, the mold grew fast. We had to cross our fingers."

I wonder if he took the photo of my mother with her curls pressed against her cheeks. I don't want to imagine him taking the photo what showed her as so beautiful. "My mother could only stay for two months. She had to come home because she had planned her wedding."

He interrupts me. "Jenny. Si. She told me she was sad, she felt she was abandoning us. She wanted to see even just one book put back together but never got to witness the progress. Never the result." His eyelids close, as if a great weariness descends on him. "Some books—they took years." He sighs. "Everyone missed her. I missed her. No one could forget her spirit. Very hard to forget her."

He's right. People did not forget my mother. She taught at Queens College for thirty-two years and received emails and notes from former students every year. Many went on to work in important galleries and museums across the country and they would send articles and newspaper clippings. Even her home town in Kansas remembered her. Every summer we all piled into one of my father's recently restored cars and drove back to the Midwest to visit her parents. Her roots. Every year she was invited to give a community talk at the high school auditorium on art history and how past decades and centuries of art could inform our lives. The auditorium was full, standing room only. We would go to the event and listen to her talk. My father would lean over to me and say, "Your mother is so smart. And she's pretty too." Later, my mother would put me to bed in the attic room of my grandparents' home. I would look out a small circular window to the Kansas fields. I remember her, every year, telling me the same thing—at age 7, age 8, age 9, age 10—that she wanted me to remember when I was a grown up with a family of my own that a child—no matter what age—should visit her parents at least once a year. That a person should honor their roots. The importance of family and being there for each other.

Rinaldo's voice brings me out of my memory. "People wanted to be close to her. Jenny. Your mother. She never was discouraged. You have inherited her spirit also, perhaps?"

I am suddenly tired. "I don't know. She always told me I was the inside of her head and my brother was her outside."

"Si, you have a brother. Older."

"Rick. Yes. How can you know all this?"

He gets up quickly, moves to his desk. He settles into his chair, pulls open the bottom drawer. He pulls out a very worn calfskin binder tied together with leather cords. I can see pages of handwritten pages and corners of photos bursting from it.

He opens the file. It has side pockets, filled with Christmas cards. I see my mother's handwriting on the envelopes.

A sudden sense of dislocation. She feels so present. I choke out the words, "What are those?"

His fingers flip through the Christmas card envelopes; they are heavy with Christmas stamps. Enough stamps to send envelopes overseas. The cards are in order—by year. "She wrote to me. Even sent pictures of you. And your brother."

He opens an envelope and pulls out photos. I see my mother's scrawl on the back.

1985. Lyn (age 4). Rick (age 7). Halloween.

The pictures look like migrants from a different era; they had been printed up at the local photo shop. Rick and I were in our costumes; I was a bee in black and yellow stripes and Rick was Superman. I held my mother's hand, but she was not wholly in the picture. Just her lower arm. My hand in her hand.

"There is one..." His fingers search through the envelopes. "Ahhh, here it is."

He lifts out an envelope. "This is from the year 2000. Here she wrote to me that you were at University and had decided to become a writer." He points to a sentence, "Here she writes that she expects success for you. That she was proud."

I take an involuntary sharp intake of breath. I can't stop the tears; my breath is getting shorter. I move to the window. Look out at the Arno. A long narrow scull skims the water; two rowers work in perfect coordination. I try to latch onto their rhythm to still the tornado building inside.

"And this one. The last one." He looks at it for a long time.

"That was her last Christmas card to you?" I move closer to see the postal stamp; it is dated the year she died. Three months after my wedding to Stan. On the stamp is an image of Luca della Robbia's Madonna and Child—a statue that she and I visited many times at the Metropolitan Museum in New York City.

"You knew her for only weeks." I feel this incredible urge to negate his place in her life.

"I understood, it was evident, she had to go home to America."

I remind him of what waited for her in Queens. "To get married to my father."

"Si. She had made that promise."

Had my mother wanted to stay? Had she done what she thought she 'should do'?

I want to own her totally. Own our family. "She was married at All Saints Church, five days before Christmas. I was married there too. December 20. I wore her wedding dress."

"She wrote that to me. That she was wanting so much for you to be happy."

My chin quivers. I breathe in more deeply.

He asks, "And are you?"

I drop my head; my hair covers my face. I hope he won't notice the tears spilling down my cheeks. But then my chest starts to heave and I can't stop the waves of emotion. I hate that I feel unprotected in front of this man who knows something of me. But nothing of me. I consider bolting, racing out of the room.

He gently asks, "Did I say something wrong? Do something wrong?"

"No. No." My words echo in my brain. And then I consider his question. And my answer. An understanding.

A weight lifts.

No, he did nothing wrong. That is absolutely true. He knew my mother and held her in high regard. How could that be wrong? I look at him; my resentment dissipates like clouds burned away by the sun. I am left just with sadness.

"My marriage is over." I sniff, thinking back to the day I decided to accept Stan's marriage proposal. "Maybe I tried to make a replica for myself, a sort of replica of my mother and father's life. I thought their life was perfect. I thought she was so happy."

He looks confused. "I think your mother was very happy. I could see that when I came to New York."

Shocked, I nearly shout the words. "You came to New York?"

"You were small. Maybe two or three. Your brother was five. Or six. I saved my money and came to New York to see your mother. Because I could not get her out of my mind. No one else ever. In my life." He gave a nearly inaudible sigh. "I am Italian. And yet it is still true. No woman ever made me feel the same way. So. I never marry. I thought about it, who does not want to have a wife? A family? When I went to New York it was for me to ask—if maybe. But when I saw her, I knew. She would not come back to Italy. It is when I realized…" He motions to his work around him. "This would be my passion, my life." His eyes close. "We walked through museums in New York together. Yes, I loved her."

The words I didn't want to hear. The ones that made me wonder about my mother's heart.

He continues, "But she was yours. She belonged to the family she promised."

"She told you she loved my father?"

He looks surprised that I needed confirmation. "She did not have to tell me. Si. He had her heart. And your brother. And you."

Tears pool in my eyes. "Love. What is it?"

He doesn't seem surprised at my question. "Perhaps no one can explain it. But when it is there, it is overpowering. But, you have to be daring. And take a chance on the pain that any emotion can bring. The good and the bad. You have to not be fearful."

"You sound like her."

"Jenny was not afraid. Whatever fears she met, she stood up and dug in and did not run."

My shoulders, that were nearly scrunched up to my ears, relax. I realize that I have come full circle. "I am glad you knew her. And loved her."

We look out at the Arno.

He smiles. "I have never told anyone this. You will maybe think I am crazy, but I am not. Sometimes, I walk in this building and I can see us, the Mud Angels, in lines, wet and cold and happy, passing treasures to each other up a line to their safety. Hoping that we are contributing to history. To the conservation of great beauty. Sometimes I can hear your mother's laughter. Her encouragement, 'do not despair, 'Naldo'. 'We can help, 'Naldo.' I know it is my imagination, but still, sometimes I like to imagine it. And she continues to encourage me every day."

We are silent. I watch the rowers on the Arno, the scull moving through the river so smoothly, barely causing a ripple.

"I am glad to have met you, Rinaldo."

He takes my hand and envelops it in both of his. "I know Jenny—your mother—wants, more than anything, for you to be happy."

I descend the steps of the Biblioteca. Clouds race across the sky. A dark grayness moves in and the cold wind kicks up. My hair whips across my face and stings my eyes.

Chapter 29

I sit on the edge of my bed and peel off my shirt. Let the cooling air push through the window and touch my bare skin. I slip off my boots. I pick up my cell phone. I want to call Matteo and—and what? I hesitate. How can I say that I am sorry I was an ass? That I felt scared, all of a sudden, when he said he wanted to spend time with me and I hadn't gotten used to knowing that Bernadette and he were not together. That a romance between them was Valentina's wish and not his. And would he be surprised to know that Rinaldo Conti danced with my mother? Loved my mother? My thoughts jumble, I can't organize them.

I hesitate.

And then I call. I hear his voice, in deep musical Italian: *Leave a message*. I click off, not wanting to stammer incoherently, saying something I don't mean. My thoughts and my intentions are too unclear.

I look out at the rooftops. I see Frankie Firenze, the cat, staring back at me. It's a silent conversation but I sense what he is thinking. "So, American lady. Talk about life-changing events. What are you going to do about it?" He licks his paw. Raises his chest to remind me of his strong self. He seems to say, "Where is your strength?"

I mutter, "I'm tough, Frankie. But I still have feelings."

I remember my mother, sitting next to me at the wedding dinner, holding tightly to my hand, her cheeks and neck thin and pale as tissue paper, but her eyes bright with hope for me. She leaned against me and whispered passionately, "Remember, Lyn. The more we have, the more we have to love."

I joked that she might have had too much wine, and was about to remind her that the actual saying is "The more we have, the more we have to lose." But seeing the flush on her face made me happy and I simply leaned over to kiss her cheek.

But she knew what I was thinking and she repeated her words, for me—and maybe they were also for her? She said, "Really, Lyn. The more we have, the more we have to love."

Rinaldo was handsome. My mother was beautiful. Rinaldo had been in a desperate state. My mother was kind, funny, she knew how to put one foot in front of another, see the tasks and take steps towards a goal. With grace and kind commitment. Of course he would fall in love with her.

I lean out the window. Frankie holds his spot. I tell him, "I just don't want to step on emotional land mines."

Frankie tucks his head to his bony shoulder, rubs his pointed ear against his fur. I imagine his thoughts: "Are you listening to yourself? A little volatility is necessary to shake things up. Things may settle just the way they should settle. Because you hurt now, do you give up on tomorrow?"

I remember once, my mother and I sat in the kitchen. I was trying to write a poem and I was in the middle of some teenage anguish. My mother was looking out the window, watching my father working on one of his cars. She was making him a tuna sandwich, putting it on a small plate next to a homemade chocolate chip cookie. She was humming, softly. I recall thinking her life was so plain and easy and my life was roiling because someone had looked at me wrong in the high school hallway and I didn't get a good grade on a paper and a skin eruption that I was sure made me look like a monster refused to stop growing on my face. Her humming was too satisfied, too cheerful. I'm sure I used my best obnoxious, jerky teen voice and asked her how she could be so tickled pink just making us all lunch when the world was so rotten. She looked over her shoulder at me, with interest. "Is your life rotten today, Lyn?" I told her life sucked big time, because people sucked and life was rotting and nothing was going to ever ever change. She left the window and sat next to me. "The one thing we can all count on in this world is that things do change. Today and tomorrow are two different days, Lyn." I argued, accused her of not understanding because her life was so set in stone. I mean, how could she be so joyful just being here in the kitchen in Queens making a tuna sandwich for dad? Didn't she want to fly off somewhere—take on the world? I pouted and groused. She said something that put me off. Too sexual for me at the time. She said that yes, she did care about making my dad happy because the moment she met him, a bell went off in her head and her whole body felt it. She said, "Lyn, my heart. When I met your father I could see you and Ricky—my children—the promise of you in his eyes." I am sure I rolled my eyes and I may have stomped out of the room.

I had not remembered that conversation. Until now. Her choice had been clear to her.

Frankie Firenze raises his chin so the harsh wind brushes against his entire face. He looks as if he is bathing in its power.

"You're so tough," I say aloud to him.

His gaze challenges me. "I don't give up. Why should you?"

Lucia knocks on door, calls out. "Lyn? I saw you come in. Why do you not have your phone on? Are you okay? Stai bene?"

I look at my phone. "Damn." I call out, "I'm sorry. I didn't realize the battery was low." I grab my robe and open the door. Lucia is in stripes today. Black and white striped dress, striped tights, her white vinyl boots. Her absolutely straight hair is shiny black, with a sparkly white stripe—skunk like—stretching from her forehead, past the crown of her head and glistening backwards. "Is that a wig?" I ask.

"Si. Magnifico, no?"

"It's very eye-catching."

Pleased, she waves off the compliment. "I am a walking piece of art. In Florence."

"Yes, you are."

"There is someone downstairs for you. He says his name is Matteo. And he says that it is urgent he speaks to you immediately."

I feel a fierce surge of excitement.

I look down at my robe, my bare feet. "Tell him one moment."

I open the building's door and step outside. The temperature has dropped. Gusting air rushes down the narrow street. My fresh shirt and quickly-pulled-on-jeans and loafers are definitely not fashion statements, but I didn't want to keep him waiting.

He is pacing on the slim sidewalk. He is on his phone. His dark blue jacket is open; his white business shirt is bright above his dark trousers. His hair splays in the wind. He seems agitated, as if every moment counts. He sees me and immediately disengages from his call. He hurries over to me.

"You called and did not leave a message," he says.

"I'm sorry." I shiver, cross my arms to try to hold onto warmth.

"I called you back. There was nothing."

"My phone's battery...sorry." I feel like I am apologizing in general—for my earlier behavior, for my phone, for making him feel compelled to check in on me.

He speaks quickly. "I am here because I must go to the country, not far from here. For a short meeting. I have come to ask you to come with me. You might enjoy the ride, the place we are going."

"You want to leave now?" I ask.

"Si, it is necessary."

"And you want me to come with you?"

He looks perturbed. As if he has made himself perfectly clear and my questions are unnecessarily dense and time-consuming. But he slows down, aware I may need a moment to catch up. "Si. If you are free, I would like you to accompany me to the country. While I have my meeting, my friend has arranged, if you would like, for his vineyard manager to take you on a tour. We could stop for a dinner, perhaps, on the way back. If you come, we have an hour and some minutes in the car. I have a driver waiting around the corner."

I laugh.

"What is it?" He looks impatient.

It hits me that his stated desire to spend time with me is something he is taking seriously. Even if it means fitting me in on his work's travel time. I am suddenly very happy.

"What is so funny?" He asks.

My mother's words spring back into my mind; 'Lyn, my heart, the future is waiting for you to write it.'

Matteo waits. I can feel the tension of his body. He needs an answer.

"I'll change. Get my bag. Three minutes? Is that good?"

"Perfetto."

Chapter 30

I've changed my oxford-cloth shirt for a casual Mariella tunic, my jeans for a skirt, my loafers for Ferragamo Vara pumps. I've put walking shoes and my Manolo heels into a bag, and a Saint Laurent satin blouse that zips up the back—just in case I need to look more upscale for dinner. I have a sweater over my shoulder and a raincoat over my arm. I am walking with Matteo around the corner.

"That was five minutes, not three." He puts his hand on my back. I pick up my pace to match his.

I dip my head to avoid the hard wind. "Matteo, thank you for inviting me."

There is a Mercedes sedan. A short and stocky driver stands waiting. He smokes a cigarette; his muscular arms and chest strain his black suit. Seeing us, he crushes the butt under his shoe and opens the back door. I slip in. Matteo quickly takes off his jacket and folds it as he moves around to the other side of the car and slides next to me. He drapes his jacket over the empty front passenger seat. The driver settles behind the wheel and, in a moment, we are on the road heading south towards the Chianti region.

Matteo turns to me—his long legs are bent and barely fit into the roomy back seat. "We are going to a castello outside of Greve. It belongs to a friend of the family's and I will have to conduct some business. Cristiano, my friend, has taken the reins of his family's wine business, he is fifth generation Italian winemaker." Matteo's cell phone pings. "Scusa." He reads the text as he apologizes. "This travel for me will not a holiday, I regret." He responds to the text and presses *send*.

I like seeing Matteo being quick and decisive—clear, cool and calm about his work dealings. I imagine him in an office in the Uffizi. Efficient. Dedicated.

Matteo continues, "But Cristian has one Scottish grandmother in his heritage and studied at University in Edinburgh—wearing a kilt he tells me. So he also has cellars where he makes whiskey. He is very good at what he does and we will have time to taste his wine—and whiskey. I think you will enjoy. I have in mind a very good place for dinner on the way back to Florence. If we are not too late. If you like."

"That sounds fine."

"I am surprised that I can be like a pushy American. Am I too pushy for arriving unannounced at your apartment and asking you to join me?"

"Pushy?" I laugh. "I know it is how we are perceived but that word, in America, is not usually used to describe a pleasant person or situation."

"Do you see me then, at this moment, as unpleasant?"

"No." More serious than I intend. I lighten my tone. "Adventures are good. The unexpected ones even better." I think of Frankie Firenze on the rooftop. He may give me a 'paws up' for this adventure. "I am the one who wants to apologize for earlier. I am not sure why I reacted so badly, but I think I suddenly got very nervous."

He teases, "It is because I was pushy. But it's only because your seminar is almost over."

His cell phone pings; another text. "Scusa, Liniana. I am sorry."

He reads the text; I can see it is a long one.

He composes his response and sends it. Turns to me again.

"Si. Molto buono." He puts his arm across the back of the leather seats. "So tell me. Was Signor Conti helpful?"

"He asked me to call him 'Rinaldo'."

Matteo's eyes widen. "How did that happen?"

I tell Matteo about discovering that Rinaldo and my mother worked together as Mud Angels. And how Rinaldo told me he loved my mother and how unsettling this news made me feel.

"Why would you be upset that someone loved your mother?"

"I was worried—what if she loved him back? What if she really wanted to stay in Florence and be with him, work with him, and all her life she regretted her choice to go back to America?"

"Do you think she did?"

"I know she loved my father."

"And you. And your brother."

"Rinaldo even came to New York to make sure. To convince her to be with him. But he made it clear. She chose us."

He smiles kindly. "Liniana, perhaps accept that your mother was loved by many men. If you look like your mother, I know she was beautiful."

A heady feeling surges through me. The compliment is indirect and casual, but it sneaks into me, and adds to my growing sense that adventure awaits. And I will not turn from it.

Matteo continues, "Feeling loved. That is nice for a woman. Even a man." He laughs, to relieve his earnest tone.

"It's the question of 'should'—a concept I struggle with sometimes. I wonder if my mother made the choice because she had already made a promise to my father—and her family had expectations and she felt she should not disappoint."

"Yes. There are always things like this that we do. Because we must live together. Trust each other. But the big choices, it is my opinion, they go beyond the 'should'. They have to go into the 'I want to'. They have to go into the 'I have to'. The 'I need to'. The big decisions. Like love. Marriage."

We are now in the countryside; I can see the rolling hills of Tuscany in the afternoon sun. I tell Matteo, "She told me once, when we were sitting in the kitchen, that when she met my father, she felt she saw 'her children in his eyes'."

"Ahhh."

I feel his eyes resting on me as I watch the countryside slip by. I break the moment. "So, other than that earthquake of new information, thanks to Rinaldo, I have a lot of articles and essays to read, lots more facts." It dawns on me in that moment. "Matteo…"

"Si?"

"I just realize. Because of Rinaldo—and you, because you introduced us—I think I have a way into my mother's story as a Mud Angel." I realize the truth of this in a deeply significant way and a swell of happiness envelops me. "I needed to be able to see her as a young woman. Not as my mother."

Matteo is silent, as if he wants to give me the time to enjoy the excitement of my realization. Of the investigation to come. Unearthing treasures buried in mud, unearthing unfamiliar sides of my mother, letting her be naïve and inexperienced and questioning and human and alive beyond the confines of how I had always seen her.

Finally, he says, "I am very glad it was a significant meeting."

His cell phone pings again. "Scusa. Scusa."

We arrive at Castello di Bianco an hour later. The Mercedes moves up the long drive lined with towering cedar trees. The main residence comes into view; its golden stone exterior and red-tiled roof are stately, but warm and inviting. Matteo tells me, "Parts of the estate were built in the 12th century. And then it was added onto—and onto and onto—over the centuries. Cristian spends much time in restoration and renovation."

Our sedan pulls up close to the front entrance and a man with ginger-red hair and a short beard, in pressed blue jeans and plaid windbreaker, rushes out the front door. Distressed, he motions for Matteo to get out quickly.

Matteo mutters, "What is going on?" He gets out of the car and Cristian hurries to him. I can hear them talk in low voices.

"Ahhh you are here. Finally. I expected you before."

"Mi dispiace, c'era molto traffico. What is wrong, Cristian?"

"Egli e qui ora."

Matteo's voice reveals his surprise. "Are you saying he is here? Now?"

"In the library. He arrived five minutes ago."

"No warning?"

"No. Nessun avviso. Bullocks."

Matteo takes in the news. He reaches into the car to retrieve his jacket, tells me quickly. "Something has happened. I will have to take care of it."

"That's fine. Don't worry about me."

He slips his jacket on quickly. The driver opens my door and I step out. Matteo hurries to my side and introduces me to Cristian.

Cristian is polite, but clearly agitated. "It is good of you to come. And you must feel welcome. I am sorry to not be your personal guide at this moment. I will ask the housekeeper—her name is Lourdes, she makes everything here perfect—to be your guide inside my home. She will take you to my vineyard manager for a tour of the estate if you find that to be something to enjoy."

I notice the middle-aged woman in a long dark sweater standing in the open doorway. Her sweater has *Castello di Bianco* written above the breast pocket.

Matteo turns to me. "Will you be all right, Liniana? I must go now. I think addressing what has happened in an expedient manner is very important."

"Si. I understand."

Matteo and Cristian hurry off. Lourdes smiles at me and asks, in slow English, if my travel was fine?

"Si. Grazie."

She continues, "I show you room where to sit. You may relax. And have vino. Carlina—direttore del vigneto—of the wine—will show you branches of the vino before all darkness comes. Primo. First. You may relax. Carlina come get you later."

The wind bites into my skin and I look up to see the dark clouds moving across the rising moon.

I feel the night's first drops of rain.

Chapter 31

Lourdes leads me through the impressive entryway to a hall where ancient tapestries warm the stone walls. Ahead are large double doors, they are open and reveal a library. Framed in the doorway is a small, nearly-bald, wizened man sitting in a wheelchair. His elderly form is parked near a window; oxygen tubes are hooked into his nose—the tank is strapped to the side of the wheelchair. The skin is tight on his head and face, brown age marks are prominent and there is a yellow-ness to his thin flesh that signals ill health. The muscles in his neck have given up, his chin nearly rests on his sunken chest. His tweed jacket is too big for him, the collar of his white shirt too wide for his shrunken neck. A handkerchief is clamped in one hand. A male nurse, in green scrubs and a cardigan sweater, stands to the side. The old man must be clued into his surroundings for as soon as our footsteps on the stone floor can be heard, he strains to raise his head. His rheumy eyes, red-rimmed, want to see who approaches. When he realizes we are not the ones he is waiting for, his head falls again to his chest. He looks beaten. As if his life does not make him proud.

Lourdes starts up a short flight of stairs. I follow and we are soon walking down another hallway that leads to a sitting room that overlooks the vineyard.

"Magnifico." Through the window, I can see that the rain continues to fall.

"Rain. This is no good for you and plans with direttore of vino."

"I am happy to just look out. Vigneto e bello."

She nods, agrees that the vista of rolling hills, lush with soon-to-be-harvested grapevines is stunningly beautiful. A representation of decades of care and bounty.

Lourdes sets a glass of wine on a table next to me and excuses herself.

I settle into a comfortable armchair and watch the rain increase in power. It beats against the window. I feel content to watch the storm and try to imagine what kind of business the old man in the wheelchair might have with Matteo.

Lourdes steps back into the room, carrying a tray of figs and cheeses. A young man, maybe twenty years old, also wearing a Castello di Bianco sweater, arrives to light the cut wood that rests in the large stone fireplace. He looks like he has been in the vineyards all day, his hands are thickly dusted with earth. Lourdes fills my nearly-empty glass, turns on the lamps that exude a warm glow into the room. She asks if I would like anything and as I am about to tell her that I have an amazing feeling—a feeling that I am in the right place at the right time—exactly where I need to be, Matteo and Cristian enter the room.

Matteo takes the chair next to me. I can tell he's working to hold onto his normal calm. I have not seen him like this. I lean in, I want to allay his unease. "Don't worry about me, I am fine."

"Si. That is good. But I have to tell you. Things have happened I did not anticipate. I will not be going back to Florence tonight. The driver will take you back, if you wish, or Cristian has another idea."

Cristian quickly pours two glasses of wine and offers one to Matteo. "Si, my idea. You are welcome to stay here in my home. I will tell the housekeeper to make up a room for you and a room for Matteo. He has stayed here before and he will tell you it is very comfortable. And I will arrange a dinner for you. It would be something very good for you to stay overnight here, si? It is raining, it is now getting late."

Matteo's fingers rub the face of his wristwatch. I feel he is trying to take care of things. His work. Which, at this moment, is very pressing. And to care for me at the same time. I ask him, "What would be better for you?"

His eyes hold mine. "I am sure you would be very comfortable here. If you do not have reason to be in Florence until tomorrow, this would be very nice. I do not know how long I will be working, and I am sorry about that, but to have you still here, when I am finished with my work, would be very nice for me."

I don't hesitate. "I can stay."

Matteo's face lights up. "Bene." He tells Cristian I have a bag in the car and please, could it be brought in and taken to the room that will be arranged for me? Cristian nods to Lourdes and she moves off to make arrangements.

I raise my wine glass in salute to Cristian. "Sei molto gentile, very kind."

Cristian nods, finishes his wine. "And now, Matteo. Let us take care of what we must. We go back now?"

"Yes. Si." Matteo's hand rests on mine for a moment.

Then they hurry out.

I wonder again about the old man in the wheelchair and how his eyes—that I had seen for just a moment—were saturated with unhappiness. At his ill health? At the weakness of his body? At a life unfulfilled? I think of sitting at my mother's bedside, she was aware that her body was now failing her at a rapid rate. She had lost her ability to speak long before and now, simply sitting up was difficult and even swallowing was a chore. She noticed my concern. One day she pointed to her pad of paper and pencil and I retrieved them for her. The task she gave herself was laborious, her weak hand shook. Finally, the words were transferred and I pulled my chair closer to her bed. She closed her eyes to sleep. I read what she had written.

I am clear happy peace.

I hear footsteps behind me. It is Lourdes moving into the sitting room. "Scusa, you would see your room Cristiano asked me to very good prepare?"

I smile because I think of Valentina and how, as a teacher, she would take Lourdes to task for proper placement of subject and verb. But the effort Lourdes takes to make herself clear to a foreigner and a surprise guest—makes me feel welcome.

I thank her. "Bene, Lourdes. Grazie mille."

A half hour later I am soaking in lavender-scented water in a large bathtub, surrounded by lit candles. There is a window that allows me to look out into the night. The storm obscures the outlines of the hills in the distance.

My mind drifts back to sharing gelato with Matteo after the piano concert at St. Mark's English Church. Sitting in the small piazza, being part of the convivial community, feeling incredibly comfortable surrounded by Florentines enjoying a warm night, the street musicians, glasses of wine or cups of gelato. Matteo, clearly in his element, sharing the city that he loves. Mildred happening by, sharing her artwork. How easy it was.

And the night, walking home, through Florence's narrow streets after the opera. Matteo—in his tuxedo jacket—standing in front of my apartment door, Valentina triumphantly announcing that she and Matteo and Wyatt are now my friends, that I must not worry about a divorce from a husband who betrays my trust. Matteo's face. Surprise. Anger. How I quickly slipped into my apartment building and closed the door and sat on the bottom step of the stairway, feeling pulled down by a malevolent force of gravity. I had put my head into my hands and sobbed. That night seems so recent and—at the same time—very much in the past.

And Rome. Matteo shepherding me past Stan. Shopping for a new dress. Shoes. Sitting across from him at dinner, enjoying the bustling restaurant, hearing the clank of copper bowls as they were filled with steaming pastas, smelling the herbs and oils and sweets.

The walk towards the Biblioteca Nazionale to meet Rinaldo. My anger at Matteo for making me even think about opening myself up. Being vulnerable again.

And seeing, through Rinaldo, how loving someone, even unrequited, can add to one's life.

I am dressed in my St. Laurent satin blouse and Manolo heels, sipping wine when Lourdes knocks and lets me know dinner is prepared. I pick up my thin cashmere shawl and drape it around my shoulders.

A table set for one. I feel as if I am a lonely princess in a vast castle, spoiled and pampered. The white bone-china plate gleams. The silverware is heavy. There is a small wooden plank topped with thin slices of prosciutto and salami. A small bowl of cured black olives next to it. A crystal pitcher filled with water and a decanter filled with deep red wine. It is 'breathing.'

The rain pounding outside.

"Would you like company for dinner?"

I look up. Matteo stands in the doorway. He leans against its frame, his eyes tired, the lines of his face drawn as if his belief in goodness has been tested and found wanting.

"Si," I say. "If you have the time."

"I do. And I am hungry."

Lourdes arrives with another place setting. She moves out of the room. I confide, "This is too formal for me. It's wonderful but how can I ever go back to waiting in line for my ready-made sandwich and coffee in a take-away cup?"

Matteo smiles. "Cristian is wanting to impress. Yes, he must do these kinds of things when the buyers of wine come through, they want to be treated special. But when I am here alone with him—we eat in the kitchen and slice our own prosciutto."

"Will he be joining us?"

"He is taking care of his uncle. Do not worry, he will expect a favor in return. Probably insist I provide a special Uffizi tour to a girlfriend or two of his." Matteo helps himself to a slice of salami. "Ahh, Barolo salami. Bene."

A roll of deep thunder and a flash of lightning. The view out the large window that overlooks the vineyard is illuminated momentarily.

Matteo shakes his head. "The storm is not good for the grapes this late in the season. More worries for Cristian."

"Can you talk about what is happening? I saw an old man in a wheelchair in the library. Is he Cristian's uncle?"

"Si. We spent the last hours in negotiation with him."

"Negotiation?"

"Cristian's uncle worked at the Uffizi for a short time. My father knew him well."

"What is there to negotiate?"

He leans his arms on the table. "You know my role at the museum. To retrieve lost work. Some of it from the flood of 1966."

"Yes." I wait for more.

"I cannot tell specific details; it would not be ethical."

"He doesn't look healthy."

"He is ninety-seven years old. And has been unhappy for the last many decades."

"Unhappy because of what he experienced?"

"Because of his actions. Of what he absconded."

"He took something?"

"He was tempted and fell short. True tragedy is always self-inflicted. I think so. Anyway. He is asking not to go to jail. He is asking to keep his reputation and for news of the retrieval not be in the papers. He wants to return a very special piece that has been missing for fifty years. To try to erase his mistake."

"Is that possible?"

"The lawyers and the museum board will get involved. After authentication and legal matters are taken care of—perhaps you will read of an important treasure recovered and now on display at the Uffizi."

I have an image of myself, in New York City, buying my morning New York Times at the corner newsstand, sitting at my neighborhood diner (wherever that might be) and reading the story. Not being in Florence for the unveiling of the found piece. Emptiness fills me.

Matteo stretches his legs out, there is stubble on his chin and jaw. He unbuttons his jacket. "He kept the work under lock and key. Deep in a cellar. Too ashamed to look at it. Having no enjoyment. Too afraid to face his weak moment. He could never hang it. Never sell it. It was too risky. I have been working towards this moment for years."

"Ahhh." I toast him with my wine glass. "The patience of Florentines. Americans try to muscle things a bit more, get things done at a faster pace. To your patience."

"Sometimes not so patient." He looks at me.

After dinner, the castello is noiseless, everyone must be retired for the evening. We climb the winding stone stairs; they are so worn that it's easy to understand why our footsteps are so quiet. Iron sconces hang on the stone walls, radiate soft and golden light. Tapestries showing scenes of fields and olive trees and workers harvesting grapes flow down the wall from the floor above, adding another buffer to any hard sounds.

Matteo is a full step behind me. I look down and see his black leather shoe gently land on a step. I glance back at him, he is looking carefully at a sconce, as if to measure its effectiveness.

He says, "It's just the right amount of light, do you not think? For the night, I mean. Sort of a reminder that the day is over."

"Yes. Beautiful."

"Tomorrow will be a complicated day at the museum." He is already thinking of the next day. I realize the lovely dinner and conversation about families, art, Rinaldo, his grandmother's heartache when Matteo's great-uncle—her brother—succumbed to cancer and how Signora Marcioni the elder and Signora Marcioni, the daughter-in-law, put aside differences to keep the family together are far from his mind.

We reach the landing. The rain pounds on the stained glass window. The hallway leading to the guest rooms, with its thick honey-colored walls trimmed top and bottom in grey stone, stretches to the right of us. We head in that direction, passing family portraits and oils depicting the Tuscan countryside.

The door to my room is ajar. A slit of soft lamplight spills into the hallway.

"You may be very tired," he says.

"Well, it's a lovely room and sleeping here will be very nice for me, I'm sure."

He puts his hand on the door, stretching his long fingers against the heavy wood, the watch on his wrist catches the light. He has reached from behind me, our bodies do not touch but I am aware of his closeness.

The solid oak door swings open to the large room—its dressing table, mirrors and chairs shine with old world beauty. The heavy soft green drapes have been drawn, the storm outside is hushed. The thick velvet bedspread has been turned down. Logs are burning low in the fireplace. Two bedside candlestick lamps with rose-colored shades lend a blush to the room.

"Yes, I can see it is pretty. You will be comfortable here?"

"Si. Bella sala." I move to the dressing table, drop my shawl on the chair.

I turn to Matteo. His eyes are on the fireplace. He is only a few feet away. If I reach out my hand I could touch him. I reach for my earrings, slip them off my ears, place them on the dressing table. I see a luxurious robe draped over the edge of the bed. "Cristian thinks of everything. Look, even a robe." I pass within an inch of him. My nostrils pick up his aftershave. His morning shave is long past, his cheeks would be rough against mine.

"Si. Cristian thinks of everything."

I move back to the dressing table, stand in front of the mirror and reach behind my neck to unclasp my necklace. I can't release it readily and Matteo's hands cover mine.

"I will help."

His fingertips brush my neck, they are cool. He undoes my necklace and moves to the dressing table to place it next to my earrings. He turns to me, blocking my image in the mirror. Studies my face, my lips, my hair. Finally, my eyes.

"I am hoping there might be more jewelry I could help you with?"

I smile, hear the teasing, soft curiosity in his voice.

I lift my arm to show off my thin silver bracelets. The ones my mother handed down to me. He reaches out, my wrist feels small in his hands. He pulls me closer; his eyes dedicated to my lower arm as if separating me from my bracelets is a major task that he must analyze and then construct a languid, methodical plan to ensure accomplishment. Unhurriedly, he slips off the silver circles. His eyes are questioning, they travel over my arms, my neck.

I hold up my hand. My wedding ring is in my kitchen drawer in Florence. But I have my mother's garnet and diamond band on my index finger. "I never take this off," I say. "It was my mother's."

"I wouldn't want you to do anything against your true nature."

There is a decanter of golden liquor and two crystal glasses. He pours two glasses, "A taste of Cristian's Scottish heritage?"

He hands me a glass.

The expanse of his chest is close. His belt buckle glints, reflecting the flames of the fireplace. I see part of my image in the mirror. And notice his image and mine, together. The side of his face.

"What do you see?" He asks.

I want to bring levity to the moment. I don't want to feel too much. I take a sip of the scotch. It stings my lips and tongue and slides warmly down my throat. I tell him his Roman nose makes me think he could be a descendant of the man who got in a romantic mess with Cleopatra. "You have the same nose as the statue of Marc

Anthony that's in the Uffizi's Hall of Inscriptions. And you might have his jawline too. No one has told you this before?"

He laughs. His strong hands touch my chin. "As far as I know, we are not related. And I'm not thinking of statues right now. I like that you are right here, in flesh and blood, that you are very real." He sips his drink, holds up his glass to look at the richness of the color. "Do you like this?"

"Very nice."

"The scotch?" He wants to be specific.

"Yes."

"And also the fact that we are here, in a warm room with a storm outside?"

"Yes."

"I like it very much too." He sips his scotch; he is in no hurry.

The bedroom is large but, it seems to me, we fill it at the moment. Everything around us is out of focus, fuzzy.

"There's more metal resting against my skin. Perhaps you can help me take it away?"

He looks interested; quizzical.

I turn to show the zipper on the back of my St. Laurent shirt. I wait. He treads closer. One of his hands moves my hair to the side, strokes it onto my shoulder. The other finds the tab of the slider. It is a silent pull, the teeth of the zipper part, the cool air of the room touches my skin. The shirt opens, slips off one shoulder and hangs loose on my body. His hands smooth over my upper back, the shirt falls to the floor. His fingers are around my middle. He pulls me to him. A trigger of excitement ignites. I lean against his chest, feel the outlines of his jacket, the coolness of his shirt. He turns me so we face each other. His lips descend onto mine. We kiss and then it is a kiss that does not end. My fingers dig into his shoulder, the thickness of his jacket a barrier. He carries me to the chaise, sets me down, leaning close to me, his mouth insistent in taking possession of my neck, my clavicle, the flesh that leads to my breasts. He moves away and I groan with disappointment. His fingers glide over the jersey of my slacks, down my legs, the curve of my thighs and calves; the touch feels electric. He pulls off my leather heels. He wrenches off his jacket and his shirt. He unzips the side closure of my slacks and pulls them off, letting them drop to the fine silk rug. The coolness of the night, the anticipation, the beauty of him sends shivers through me. The mirror on the dressing table glints in the soft light, the crystal decanter of scotch and our glasses sparkle, the storm adds to the volume of our quickening breaths. My heart beats hard, I am afraid for a moment that my desire will choke me. The need to have him closer consumes me, but I wait as he looks down at me.

His kisses are deep and slow. My arms wrap his bare shoulders, I am aware of his long muscles. His biceps as his arms engulf me. His lean, sturdy chest.

"Do I need to leave and look for my room?" He asks, his voice low, his question exhaled, hot on my neck.

"Don't even think about it."

Chapter 32

I am sleeping. Matteo's lips brush my cheek. My head is supported by lavender-scented pillows. I remember where I am. The night before. A shiver of contentment and then anticipation fills me. I slowly open my eyes, "What time is it?"

"It is very early."

He opens the drapes enough for me to see the early morning. The low sun is covered by dark clouds and the rain insists on pounding the earth. He walks across the room, I see he is tucking his shirt into his pants, fastening his belt.

"I will be traveling with Cristian and his uncle, we must arrive at the council room at the Uffizi in two hours. The board will be waiting for us—to hear what has been proposed last night. I must go in the car with them; I do not want Cristian's uncle to change his mind."

"Of course. You are leaving right now?"

"I'm sorry."

"I'll get ready." I move to slip out from beneath the comforter.

He puts a hand on my bare shoulder. "Please. It will be better to not have you in the same car. This needs to be kept a very private matter—for the uncle, for Florence."

"Oh. That makes sense." The sensitivity of the situation dawns on me as my mind shakes off sleep. I recall details of last night. Desire for repetition fills me. I want him stretched out beside me, I want to curl into him, touch him and have him touch me. Clearly, we are not on the same page for he sits on a chair to slip on his shoes.

"I have arranged a car to take you back to Florence. Anytime you like."

"That's good. I have to meet my students in the afternoon."

"The housekeeper knows to check in with you. Regarding timing. There will be breakfast. If you would like it in here…"

This all seems too businesslike. Too many logistics. Talk of schedules. I can see he is distracted. "I will be fine."

"It is raining still. You must keep warm. Dry."

"All right."

"Mi dispiace. I must go." He pulls on his suit jacket. He grabs his watch from the top of the bureau, slides it onto his wrist, snaps the links into place.

I want him to give a nod to last night's connection. Our bodies moving in tandem, our skins hot, wet, the sound of our hammering heartbeats. My fingers on his sinewy back, slipping down to the narrows of his ribs, his legs. His hands on my breasts, his lips on my nipples, his tongue exploring the center path from ribcage to my pelvis, my legs locking him to me. The memory of his hands lifting my hips, his hair falling over his face, his serious eyes fastening on mine, his firm mouth, his kisses.

Matteo pulls a tie from the pocket of his suit jacket.

"I will call you later, Liniana."

He looks so very Italian. So handsome. So very unattainable. I am stunned by my word choice. Unattainable.

I go into protective mode. "Sure. I'll be busy. Last days in Florence. The writers. You know."

His eyes bolt to mine, they are sharp. He looks put out, as if I am not falling in line. "Last night I will not forget," he says.

I joke because I cannot read him and his reserve unsettles me. "Well, I enjoyed it too. Sex during a storm. All that added electricity. It was pretty great."

He is startled at my flippancy. "So, for you, a storm is an aphrodisiac."

"Storms and scotch." I don't let up, I push. "Lightning. Thunder. Amazing punctuations to tantalizing titillations."

"Then how perfect the sky's gyrations could pair with scotch."

"Lucky for me."

"And fortunate for me to be here at the right time for a woman who responds in such a way."

I raise my eyebrows, keeping my tone light. "The scene was set for sex."

"Sex. Si." He turns from me and checks his image in the mirror.

I see that he has shaven. I long to trace his smooth jaw with my fingers.

His eyes land on my reflection in the mirror. "American women enjoy sex."

"All women. Well, that's a generalization, but I suggest it is a very high percentage when it is consensual, when partners say yes and mean it. Across all continents." I pull my hair up, stretch my bare arms above my head. "And I have heard men do too."

"From personal experience, I agree. The question is, when is it more than sex?"

"More than a romp in the country?"

"Romp? What is that word?"

"A roll in the hay, a bedroom rodeo, a jumping of bones, an exploration of the strange." I blabber, something in me determined to minimize the night.

"Strange?"

"We don't really know each other and we're not used to each other. In bed."

"No. That is true."

"So there would be the 'strange' element. Between us. Adds to the excitement."

"I don't know when to take you seriously."

"Matteo, I am a big girl. I enjoyed last night. That is all I am saying."

He seems irritated, looks at his watch again. "I would like to talk to you about this, because I have wondered what it would be like to kiss you and to hold you since we first had apertivo."

"What?" I choke this out softly, I am taken aback by his statement.

Cristian knocks on the door, calls from the hallway. "Matteo? We are ready."

Matteo looks at me.

Knowing that I am heading down a path that lets us both off the hook, I grin. "It's a common curiosity. For men and for women to wonder about each other. And now you know. What it is like to kiss me."

"Si. I do."

"So you can go now, take care of what is most important."

He walks back towards me. He leans down, his face is close. His dark eyes look into mine for a moment. And then they close and his lips seek mine. It's like a fire is lit in my belly. I want to throw my arms around him and beg him to stay.

But I don't.

He pulls away and expertly fixes his tie. Pats it flat to his abdomen. He fastens the center button of his jacket. "Common curiosity. That is how you explain it. So then I say, thank you for sex in a storm and exploring of the strange."

Cristian knocks again. "Matteo?"

He leans down for a quick buss on the cheek. Does not linger. He moves out, telling Cristian that he is ready and he knows they must leave. Now.

I collapse into the lavender-scented pillow. Study the fresco on the ceiling; the cherubs and garlands of flowers and smiling, naked goddesses. They look happy as they frolic.

I cannot join in their joy. I am unhappy with my chatter. The unwillingness to be real and let defenses crumble. Disturbed, I turn my head to the window. The rain continues and I know once I leave this warm and cozy room where life was perfect for one night and step outside, the wind will be cold.

Chapter 33

W e all stare at the delectable torta della nonna in the middle of the largest table on the terrace of the Caffe Gilli. Its crust is golden, the powdered sugar rests on its top like a sprinkling of a season's first snow. A plate piled with fine chocolates and fruit jellies is next to it. Sparkling Prosecco fills our glasses. The carousel, a short distance from us, is turning, its horses carrying tourists and locals—young and old—in an un-ending circle. It is the writing seminar's last meeting, the storm that began three days ago and raged over Florence without relief is finally lifted. The sun is pushing through the gray sky and soon we will be shedding our scarves and jackets to bask in a welcome warmth.

I raise my glass and toast the writers. "To a wonderful month of writing."

Beth Ann, wearing a pink satin baseball jacket, stands and raises her glass even higher. "Let's pretend it's the first day all over again. And we can start from where we are now and see where we can get."

She takes a doggie treat from her pocket and leans down to Jackson, who lolls happily at her feet. "Wouldn't that be a good idea?" He barks in a quick, guttural agreement and gums the treat off her hand.

Vic stops a waiter and orders, "Birra, per favore." Proudly, he announces, "See, I picked up some Italian."

Rivenchy shakes her head, "Cake, chocolate, jellies and beer. The combination, Veec—I don't know."

"Yeah yeah. The fizzy stuff looks good on you, not me. I'll toast you all with beer. So you remember me just as I am."

We all choose a sweet. Mine is a gelantina di frutta, a finely sculptured chewy jelly in the shape of a miniature green pear, complete with an earthy stem made of chocolate. It is rolled in sharp sweet sugar shards that melt on the tongue and allow the intense fruit flavor to dance on the taste buds.

Charles savors his cherry jelly. "My wife would like to extend a dinner invitation to anyone returning to Florence anytime soon. Freddy told me to tell you she likes you all. But she doesn't want to be saccharine so she would remind you she also likes karaoke and me."

I raise my glass once again, "To Pynon, Lavanna, Jackson, Finn and the fat nun, Maggie and Wallace—may they live long in our minds."

We clink glasses and share good wishes, "Cin cin!"

Beth Ann looks at the carousel and sighs. "I loved it when the fair came to town. I fell in love with a pink horse with a blue shaggy mane and big white rhinestones stuck to her forehead. I always thought if she was running away at night, they would be like headlights and show her a path."

George nods. "There's a carousel on the National Waterfront in D.C.—about an hour from Baltimore. I'd go there with my family. I'd ride the dragon seahorse with the swirly pointed tail and the 3-D iridescent scales. Think I thought I was Odysseus riding it, about to take on a Cyclops."

Vic looks at the carousel. "We called 'em merry-go-rounds. I'd pick a stallion. Real John Wayne. The one who's leading."

"But Veec," Rivenchy says. "On the carousel, the animals go in a circle."

"Yeah, but who's leading the circle?"

We laugh and I tell them about this particular carousel. "It's antique—more than a hundred years old. It's been taken care of by its owners, the Picci family, for the last five generations." I point to the top frame of the merry-go-round. "Those panels are painted scenes of Pisa, Venice, Bologna and Rome and inside when you are riding the horses, you can see painted panels of elegant Italian ladies— along with angels and Roman goddesses. Designed to capture your imagination."

Beth Ann notices the sculpted cherubs on the roof. "They're so cute. Their eyes are looking up to heaven, I guess."

I add, "And at night, when the carousel is spinning, lights illuminate the piazza. It's magical, it's beguiling, it's romantic."

Rivenchy nods. "And right across from La Rinescentre, Lavanna's favorite store."

I wonder at my intense affection for the carousel. "You can be any age, and when you are on it, you feel you're wrapped in a warm cloak of fantasy and transported to a world of absolute pleasure. Worries and sadness put aside."

I remember three days ago, I slipped into the car Matteo had arranged for me to complete my circular journey from the Tuscan countryside back to Florence. I had unpacked my bag, hung the St. Laurent shirt in my closet, set the Manolo heels on the shoe rack. I closed the closet door and still haven't opened it. I've chosen jeans and jersey shirts from my dresser, worn the loafers I had kicked under the coffee table in the living room and a jacket from the hook by the door. I didn't want to dwell on memories of Cristian's villa. And, as the days passed and there was no word from Matteo, I took this as a signal that this was a wise decision.

The music begins and the carousel goes round and round.

The waiter delivers our slices of torta della nonna, perfectly arranged with a fresh dusting of powdered sugar on each piece.

Beth Ann takes an appreciative bite. "Mmmm. I like this 'grand-mother's cake'. So creamy and lemony. And the pine nuts. Just crunchy." She turns to Rivenchy. "Do you think Lavanna will be happy and give the handsome man a chance?"

Rivenchy shrugs and raises her eyebrows suggestively. "Maybe. Depending on how good he is."

Beth Ann giggles.

Rivenchy is more thoughtful. "Or how good she allows him to be."

I am struck by her comment. The two-way street. I think of Matteo and our playfulness, our teasing touches, our drawing out of intimate pleasures, our testing of each other's appetites.

Rivenchy wants to share the last page of her story. She reads:

Lavanna wondered if she should open the door. She could leave it open so he wouldn't even need to knock. Oui, but that would give him the power. As long as the door was closed, she held the power. Yes or no. She looks out the window of her top-floor apartment—she has always liked to be as far removed as possible—and see the lights of the people living below. Those with homes and families. Those alone. Should she stay apart? She looks at the clock on the wall. He will be here in a few moments. She considers, should the door be open or shut?

I hear, over and over, the word 'should'. I think of Matteo's words in the car on the way to the country. "The big choices, it is my opinion, go beyond the 'should'. They have to go into the 'I want to'. Into the 'I have to'. The 'I need to'."

Beth Ann is wailing. "Lavanna has to leave the door wide open."

Vic swallows a small beer burp. "I can see she's kind of on a cusp."

Rivenchy leans over to George. "What do you think I should do, George?"

"Maggie and Wallace opened a door and it is okay."

Charles stands. "Scusi, I think I should personally choose the next plate of sweets." He corrects himself, grinning. "Well, that's not true. Not 'should'. I 'want' more sweets so I will get some. I follow my 'want', not my 'should'." He heads into the café to the candy counter.

Beth Ann targets me. "Your new novel, Lyn, did you make progress?"

"I think so. For a long time, there was a thick stone wall blocking me from it. Kind of like a wall protecting a fortress. I couldn't find the gate that led inside to the story. But a few days ago, I did find that gate."

"How?" Beth Ann brushes powdered sugar off her jacket, takes another bite of the cream-filled cake.

"I met a man."

Beth Ann nearly shrieks and a spray of sugar bursts from her lips. "Oh?!"

"A man who was in love with my mother."

Vic grimaces. "That could be problematical."

I laugh. "Meeting him helped me re-think my mother's story. Her whole life, really."

Beth Ann wants to be clear. "So it is a love story of someone else."

I nod. "Si. Not my love story. No, it is not my love story."

Charles arrives back at the table; he carries a transparent gift bag of sweets and six tickets. "I got tickets for the carousel. Who is ready for the ride?"

I choose the Palomino, she is in graceful mid-stride and looks straight ahead. Her mane is cream-colored and falls to the side, leaving her bright eyes with a clear view. Charles settles into a king's carriage with its roof shaped like the shell of Botticelli's *Venus on Half-Shell*. George swings onto a chestnut-colored horse and Beth Ann chooses a white horse with a turquoise saddle. Rivenchy stands next to her, holding onto a pole, gazing at all the shops and cafes that surround the piazza. Vic takes the horse just ahead of us all—it is a rearing stallion with black eyes and legs lifted high into the air.

The lively, ancient folk music of Tuscany begins, teases us. Anticipation grows. Then the carousel starts slowly turning—and gains in speed. I feel a fantastical pleasure kicking in. The lights, the colors, the smiles and wonder of all of us on the carousel delivers the promised temporary release of all worries.

Chapter 34

I zip up my suitcase. Sit on it to squish the contents together one more time.

Lucia is there, in a knock-off 1960s Gucci ruffled mini-dress. Her face is sad. "You are gone and I am not wearing my big sparkling ring yet from the boyfriend who is so slow."

"It's not your birthday yet."

"Two more weeks."

"Email me updates."

"I know it will happen. Then soon I will be married and happy."

She believes in her dream. I will not spoil it for her. "There are a few things in the refrigerator and on the kitchen counter. See if you want anything."

Lucia heads to the kitchen. "I'll take only the frutta, not your favorite cookies that will make me fat."

Mildred enters the room, my hairbrush in hand. "You forgot this in the bathroom." She's been doing the 'idiot check' around the apartment, to make sure I haven't left anything that I will be asking her to ship to the States.

"Thanks, Mildred." I unzip a corner of my suitcase and force the hairbrush into a corner.

She settles on the bed next to my passport, my chosen paperback for reading on the plane and my cell phone that has my boarding pass on it. I pick up the phone and check it again. No missed calls. No missed texts. It's like I've dropped off the face of the earth except for these two people who are fussing over me and my departure details.

Mildred crosses her legs, her red, short, funky Zanotti boot is bright against her dark jeans. "Next year? I'll look at the calendar and we'll pick some dates? You'll be an even bigger draw next year. Book being turned into a movie."

"If that all happens. Don't count my chickens before they are hatched."

"Expect the best, Lyn. Why not?"

"If you temper your hopes, you lessen the disappointment."

"That's a crock. Tempering anything is just cowardice. Disappointment will always suck and we know it can crash the spirit but if you don't expect the best—you cheat yourself out of happy moments. Maybe even happy days or weeks. Hope the best. For yourself. For me too."

"Are you still seeing the let's-go-to-dinner guy from Valentina's gallery opening?"

"He's left town for business. We had a nice few days, and I expect he will get in touch when he gets back." Her blue eyes crinkle at their edges and her look at me is pointed. "See how my hopes make me happy?"

The taxi waits at the front door of the building. Lucia carries a plastic sack filled with my un-consumed oranges and apples. She gives me a quick kiss and rushes back to the hotel to answer phones and man the reception desk. "Remember, Italy is always the fashion place. Everything happens here before America. Tornare al piu presto—come back soon, Lyn."

The driver puts my suitcase in the trunk, I keep my computer bag and purse with me. Mildred kisses both of my cheeks and tells me to have a safe flight. "And kick that asshole Stan in the nethers for me even as you realize he is not worth one more thought in any of your brain cells." She swings her bag over her shoulder and waves. She is heading towards the Ponte Vecchio, back to the illustration work that waits for her attention.

The taxi driver gets behind the wheel of the car. I look around one more time, across the street is the entrance to the massive Parco Bardini and its unobtrusive plaque and glass doors that hide the entrance to the peaceful, stately gardens. I look down the narrowing streets that lead to the San Niccolo Tower. I experience a sad pang to be leaving the soft grays and muted browns of the centuries-old buildings, buildings made of the stones carved from Tuscan hillsides.

I reach to open the taxi door.

"Aspetta! Wait!"

I see Valentina rushing up. She pulls me into a tight hug, her chin nestles into my neck and she nearly yells into my ear.

"You are my treasured friend and you must not be gone for long. I miss you already—mi mancherai tantissimo."

"Valentina. Amica mia. Thank you for coming to say goodbye."

"I will visit America soon and you and Wyatt will be my guides. Practice your Italian."

"I will. I promise."

"When is your plane?"

"An hour and a half."

"Go now. What are you waiting for?"

"You're the one holding me up."

"Then arriverdici my Lyn who I will miss."

"Say goodbye to Matteo." I don't know why these words bring up a sudden emotion. I sniff, covering my urge to cry.

"Ahh, I have not seen him. Something happening at work, I don't know. But I will remember to give him your thought."

I smile, don't want to show my disappointment. "Okay. Well, arrivederci."

We exchange cheek kisses. Valentina opens her arms and shouts, "I know you are so sad to leave beautiful Florence."

I slip into the taxi. "Grazie mille, Valentina. Ciao."

The taxi driver heads over the Ponte Alle Grazie. I can see the Biblioteca Nazionale and I think of Rinaldo's desk, overlooking the Arno and his generosity and his memories of my mother.

I can see the river is high, the waters are churning from the recent rains.

The taxi turns left, taking the Lungarno delle Grazie west towards the Museo Galileo and the Uffizi and the airport. I am next to the wall that protects the city from the waters of the Arno. Whizzing past it, I think of the pages resting on my computer, the opening pages of my mother's story, the saga of her experience as a Mud Angel. Her search for treasures in muck and mud—finding new parts of herself. I know working on her story every day for the next months will keep a part of me in Florence.

Tourists are lined up to enter the Uffizi. Its grand, gray-blue stone edifice designed by Vasari in the 16th century. I imagine the centuries of its wall spaces and corners filling with some of the greatest Italian art. If I do not think of the person who dedicates his life to preserving that legacy, I can concentrate on the awe I have felt seeing the Botticelli paintings, the altar pieces by Giotto, the paintings by Caravaggio and Titian, Michelangelo and Raphael; the gift of standing close enough to see the emotional, masterful brushstrokes of the artists.

The airport is crowded. The noise level is high, there is a mix of languages. French. German. Chinese. English. Danish. Italian. People arriving, people leaving. The café is packed, travelers buy cornettos, paninis and coffees. Backpackers exchange news of adventures, families corral children. Serious shoppers, surely calculating excess baggage charges, pull large suitcases filled with finds from Prada, Furla, Ferragamo, Pucci and Scervino past the escalator to make use of the small elevator to reach the second level check-in counters.

I check the departure board. My flight is on time.

But I delay heading to the escalator to access check-in. I know once I ascend, my departure from Florence will feel totally certain. I want to drift in these moments before I start the trip to New York. To everything I don't want to face.

I go into the small bookstore and look at the shelves. So many Florentine trinkets. Snow globes featuring the Duomo or the Basilica di Santa Croce or the Piazza Signoria. Polyester scarves imprinted with city maps. Cookbooks featuring chef Fabio Picchi's recipes, his Santa Claus-like face smiling back at me.

I think of my early morning goodbye to Frankie Firenze. He padded across the nearby roof and sat watching me as I opened the window to breathe in the fresh air. He looked satiated today. I gazed around, trying in vain to locate a pigeon or two. "You look fat and happy today, Frankie," I called to him. He calmly rubbed his ear against his shoulder as if to say, "And why should I not be? I do what I want and everything I need is here." I blew him a kiss. He yawned.

I buy a ballpoint pen; it is silver and covered with dozens of tiny purple Florentine fleurs-de-lis.

It is time to ascend the escalator.

I am at the counter. The very serious airline representative looks at me closely. At my ticket. At my passport. At my face. To check if it is really me. I know it is not the same me that arrived a month ago. But it is my face. I bend to lift my underweight bag onto the scale. I am now checked in and the airline representative, putting my bag on the conveyor belt that transports it towards the plane, reminds me to use the ticket on my phone to board. I see my bag slide away to start its journey to New York.

"Scusa." It is Matteo and he is at my side. "Could I hold this for you while we go someplace to talk?" His hand meets mine as he reaches for my computer bag. I let go of it, stunned. "Please, let us go this way." He puts his hand gently on my back and guides me towards a check-in area in the next room. No one is there, no travelers, no airline personnel. The scheduled flights announced on the boards above the counters do not leave for hours.

"Matteo, what is it?"

"I was caught in traffic."

"It's nice of you to come to say good-bye."

"I am not here just to be nice. Please I need to say this. I want to discuss with you what we did not discuss at Cristian's."

"I didn't know we left anything un-discussed."

"I know this is not a good time for you. That you are sad and you have been hurt and so you are angry and it is no time for a person to ask you to consider anything to do with your heart. I know you do not want to be serious."

I see beads of sweat on his forehead, see his chest rise and fall as if he has been running. "You were dealing with Cristian's uncle and we were in the country for you to be able to do your work. Nothing to discuss, I totally understand."

"See what you do?"

"What?"

"You do not listen. You push everything away that could be of more importance."

"I don't mean to. But your work is important."

"Of course it is. But other things too. Please try to listen carefully and allow what I am saying to sink in before you sidestep it."

"I don't sidestep."

"You are doing it again."

I feel the precipice. The ledge I stand on. The question of whether a safety net is in place looms. Matteo puts my computer bag on the floor, wedges it between his ankles. Being this close to him brings back the ache to stretch out beside him, rest in his arms and anticipate his mouth on mine, his fingers threading through my hair, rolling onto his body and wanting to fuse in perpetual connection.

His hands move to my face, I feel his warmth on my jaw and cheekbones, my skin blushing. He continues, "You make jokes to keep me away. Or maybe they are not jokes. Maybe you do not want me to come closer. Ever. I do not know and it makes me crazy. I have to say, I am not used to feeling this."

He looks confused and vulnerable. I want to comfort him even as a realization dawns on me. I blurt out, "You are used to girls fawning all over you."

"See! You joke. You think I am a lothario. A Casanova. A seducer."

I say softly, avoiding his eyes. "You are a very good lover."

This stops him. He suddenly kisses me. It lasts a long time and then he whispers in my ear. "What I want from you is the chance to be near you and to find you. And yes, you are right, we do not know each other for years or even months. We are strange to each other, but I think of you when there is even no reason and when I have many other things to think about. I want to gain your trust. I want to risk because all the minutes between our night together and this moment, I have been fighting against a great desire to barge into your apartment, into your seminar room, into your life and ask you if you could see a possibility that you—once you consider love as a possibility again—could see that it could be with you and me."

There is an incredible giddiness that erupts inside me and I swallow a gasp that achingly wants to break out of my chest. I blink away the tears that threaten.

He steps back. "Are you going to say anything?"

I finally find breath. "I am experiencing a great thrill just listening to your words."

"Really?"

"Si."

He has hold of my arms. "And with no storm in the sky? No scotch? You feel this thrill?"

I cringe, thinking of how I denigrated our night together at Cristian's villa. "You were so ready to leave. So fast. I didn't want you to think I was needy."

"I want you to need me."

My knees weaken and I lean against him, my chest on his, my eyes looking up at his handsome face. "Shit."

He strokes my hair. "This is surprising for me too. But I have a very persistent idea that I cannot get out of my head. I don't think it is crazy."

"What idea do you have?"

"I think it is better if you stay. Here. In Florence. You will feel the memory of your mother here, where she was a Mud Angel. It will be better for your book. Why imagine her adventure so many miles away? Imagine it here. The Arno, you will see it rise in the winter season with the rain and the snow melting into it from the mountains, you will see our breath in front of us as we walk. Signor Conti tells me to tell you, he would very much like to talk to you more, it would give him great pleasure. There is much he can show you."

"This is your persistent idea?"

"It gives you time. It gives us time. If, between us, it is no more than a romp or bedroom rodeo that you want, that is even okay for now. I can live with it because I will use that time where I make love to you over and over as an opportunity to change your mind. Because I want it to be more."

I think of my rolling bag sliding into the darkness behind the airline counter on the conveyor belt—on its way to New York City. I don't want to follow it there.

There it is. Beyond the 'I should'. To the 'I want'.

"Liniana, consider. What will do you do if you go back to America now?"

"I'll work on my book, arrange my life to move on from the past. And I'll think of Florence."

"And what would you do if you stay here?"

"I'll work on my book, arrange to move on from the past, think of Florence." It seems clear to me. "And write the next page of my life."

"Si. Is one option more appealing?"

I lift my face to be kissed again. "One choice does stand out."

"Stay, Liniana. Now. If you like."

I like his idea.

I like it very much.

About the Author

Jule Selbo has written plays, films and televisions series, in addition to books on screenwriting and film history. Piazza Carousel in her first novel. Jule lives in Portland, Maine and Pasadena, California. For more information visit https://www.juleselbo.com and follow her on Twitter at twitter.com/Jule Selbo.